WHEN
SKYLARKS
FALL

a Joe Box mystery

WHEN SKYLARKS FALL

a Joe Box mystery

by
John Robinson

RIVEROAK®
Good News in Fiction

COOK COMMUNICATIONS MINISTRIES
Colorado Springs, Colorado • Paris, Ontario
KINGSWAY COMMUNICATIONS LTD
Eastbourne, England

RiverOak® is an imprint of
Cook Communications Ministries, Colorado Springs, CO 80918
Cook Communications, Paris, Ontario
Kingsway Communications, Eastbourne, England

WHEN SKYLARKS FALL

This story is a work of fiction. All characters and events are the product of the
author's imagination. Any resemblance to any person, living or dead, is coinci-
dental.

First Printing, 2005
Printed in the United States of America

        1 2 3 4 5 6 7 8 9 10 Printing/Year 09 08 07 06 05

Cover Design and Illustration: Jeffrey P. Barnes

Aqualung lyrics by Ian Anderson. © 1971. Released by Capitol Records.

            Library of Congress Cataloging-in-Publication Data

Robinson, John Laurence.
  When skylarks fall : a Joe Box mystery / by John Robinson.
      p. cm.
  ISBN 1-58919-054-8
  1. Private investigators--Fiction. I. Title.
  PS3618.O328W47 2005
  813'.6--dc22
                                          2005015499

I owe them one

To my wife, Barb, as always,
All my love.
All my life.

And

To the Fire Choir at SRC,
When I grew weary of the task, thanks for holding up my hands.

And

To my brother, Michael Scott Robinson:
May 3, 1957–July 15, 2002.
Earth's loss, Heaven's gain.
Rock on, bro.

"The music business is a cruel and shallow money trench—
a long plastic hallway where thieves and pimps run free
and good men die like dogs.
There's also a negative side ..."

Hunter S. Thompson

"You snatch your rattling last breath
with deep-sea diver sounds,
and the flowers bloom like madness in the spring."

Jethro Tull, *Aqualung*

1

*D*eath by drowning is never like it's pictured in the movies. On the screen it's mostly a matter of keeping the actor's makeup straight as they struggle and gasp. What the camera fails to capture is what I was experiencing right now: panic, confusion, and mindless pain.

The old saw about feeling your heart hammering against your ribs is true. I know mine was, as I hopelessly tried to find a way off this boat. I was trapped below deck in the dark, in a sinking cabin cruiser. All around me the pitch-black room bulged with water, side to side, top to bottom. The cabin's roof forced itself hard against my skull, and except for what was in my lungs, the air in here was gone for good. Outside, the howling, crazy monsoon that had doomed the craft—and me—raged blindly on. Frenzied now, I frantically began seeking an exit, any exit, out of here.

That's when I felt a light tap on my leg. I reached down, but it was only the hand of the other man in the water next to me. What he wanted, I wasn't sure, but he couldn't have been much help.

Him being dead and all.

Somehow I kept from screaming in animal fear and desperation. Unless I could find a way out of this floating coffin, and right now, I'd be joining him in short order.

I started swimming hard and fast away from the corpse, through the dense blackness toward what had to be the only opening left down here, the hatchway I'd come down.

My lungs blazed with the heat of excessive CO_2 buildup, and if I could have seen anything, I would have bet that my vision was darkening around the edges. My mouth wanted to open wide to pull in something, anything. It was all I could do to not let it.

I knew the seconds I had left were ticking inexorably down to zero, and part of me almost laughed in gallows humor. On my last case, I'd very nearly been burned alive. Now it appeared I was going down to a watery grave, for reasons that still eluded me.

Well, that's not quite right. How I got into this mess bears telling ...

♦ ◊ ♦

Somebody once said that blind dates are only for those in the very peak of mental health. How is the person you're meeting going to look, sound, smell? Are they going to be a witty conversationalist, or as dumb as a post? Will they know who Andrew Wyeth is, or play Skittles with the escargot shells? I'm past blind dates now that I'm approaching the fifth decade of my life, but meeting a new client carries much of the same baggage.

I gazed across my desk at Tom Parker ... Colonel Tom Parker, as he was calling himself. Yes, I was aware of who the real Colonel Parker was (Elvis Presley's manager, in case you didn't know), and this guy wasn't him.

He also wasn't my client—yet—but that didn't lessen the man's zeal. Two minutes earlier he'd snagged me at my door as I was leaving the office on my way to salvage a little last-minute Christmas shopping. Since then Parker had been pitching me nonstop that I was "tailor-made" to solve his problem, which he'd yet to let me in on.

All he'd done was yammer that I came highly recommended; who'd done the recommending I was hoping he'd get to eventually.

But it didn't look like that was going to happen anytime soon. I held up my hand to stop him. "Mr. Parker, I—"

"It's Colonel Parker, son," he grinned. "Remember?"

He was refusing to look me in the eye while we spoke. Besides being creepy, I've never liked that. It always strikes me that the person is trying to hide something.

But there was another reason not to like him. Ever since Parker had accosted me, he'd been speaking in some weird, Georgia-cornpone accent that was as brassy as anything I'd ever heard. In truth, he sounded a lot like the guy that played Boss Hogg on the *Dukes of Hazzard* TV show. Looked like him too, only taller, fleshier, and with more hair. And like that actor, Parker also wore a white linen suit, which to me was complete overkill. It was December 22nd in Cincinnati, Ohio, for crying out loud.

"Whatever," I sighed. "I just wish you'd called ahead for an appointment."

"Couldn't wait for it. Miss Clark's only gonna be in town for a coupla days."

I frowned. "Who?"

"Kitty Clark!" Parker boomed. "Who you think I'm talkin' about?"

9

"That's what I'm trying to determine."

Now it was his turn to scowl. "You *have* heard of Kitty Clark, ain'tcha, son? Country Music Hall of Fame inductee? Wrote *Release My Lonely Heart And Let It Fly*? Sang duets with both Little Jimmie Dickens *and* Porter Wagoner?" He shook his head. "Maybe you ain't the man for the job after all."

"Maybe not," I allowed. "You're telling me you're somehow connected with Kitty Clark?"

"Connected?" Parker snorted the word. "Well, I should say! I'm her manager!"

I shook my head, leaning back in my creaky, old, cracked black leather desk chair. "Come on. First you tell me you have the same name as Elvis Presley's manager, and now you're saying you work for Kitty Clark." I smiled at him. "Did my buddy Nick Castle put you up to this? Even for him it's pretty lame."

Parker looked affronted. "It's for real, son. I'm neither jokin' nor jestin'. I know my name's the same as the other Tom Parker, but Tom Parker's who I am, and I really do run Kitty Clark's business affairs."

"And you're a colonel."

"Well, honorary." His reply was sheepish. "I'm a Kentucky Colonel. Got me a paper from back when Bert Combs was governor. Figured it couldn't hurt."

Great. Another fake colonel. My fifteenth summer I'd clerked in a paint and hardware store in my hometown, and one of the things I'd learned to do there was custom picture framing. That also happened to be the summer the state's governor (not Bert Combs that year) decided to give out Kentucky Colonel certificates in case lots. I must have framed more than thirty of them in our town alone. Ever since, that title has meant little to me.

I glanced at my watch, then back up at my guest. "Sir?" My tone was even. "Why are you here?"

Parker must have sensed my patience was wearing thin as he dropped his blustery veneer. "Miss Clark is scared. Somebody's been doin' some weird things, and she needs a bodyguard. I've heard tell you've done that a time or two."

"A time or two" didn't quite cover it. Back in my early twenties, shortly after my wife's death, I'd gone into a twelve-year alcoholic slide. During that time, to keep me in Scotch, I'd done some body-guarding stints, along with other things I'm less proud of. But that was more than twenty-five years ago, and I told Parker as much.

"Don't matter a lick, son," he said. "Miss Clark gave me direct orders she wants you, and that about covers it."

"Mr. Parker,"—I couldn't force myself to call him colonel, and it didn't look like he was going to press it—"there are a dozen other PIs in Cincinnati, most of them younger than me, and in better shape. Besides, you never said how she knows who I am. My name isn't exactly famous."

Parker gave me a look. "After the way you stopped that killer in that tower this past November? Heckfire, it was all over the news. You're bein' too modest."

"Maybe. So you're saying Kitty Clark asked for me personally?"

"By name. Her exact words were, 'Tom, this craziness has gotta stop, and I know the man for it, a local private investigator. Joe Box is who he is, and I want him.'" Parker shrugged. "And it's like I said. What Miss Clark wants, she most usually gets."

I gave him a lazy grin. "But what if I'm not for sale?"

"Huh?" That seemed to throw him. "You mean you ain't for hire? But—"

"I didn't say I wasn't for hire. I'm just not for sale."

"You're talkin' in riddles, son."

I leaned forward, folding my hands on my desk. "Here's the long and the short of it. Less than a month ago, I got shot in the upper shoulder while working a particularly rough case. I'm still not a hundred percent over that. Plus, one of the reasons I got into this line all those years ago was so I could pick and choose who I work with. Bottom line, I try to limit my jobs to folks that I think I can get along with. I've only ever seen Miss Clark on TV, and you, Mr. Parker, I don't know at all." I spread my hands with another smile. "You see how this works?"

"Not really."

"Let me make it plainer, then." I again settled back in my chair. "Sell me."

"What?"

"You told me your employer has a problem, one that only I can fix. Now that may or may not be true. But the thing is, it's only three days until Christmas, and outside my door there's a winter wonderland calling. I just don't feel like working this close to the holidays. So unless you can convince me I need to climb back in the saddle right now, I'm going to wish you a good day, and a merry Christmas, sir." I was still smiling. "And don't let the door hit you on the way out." Did I mention I didn't like this guy?

Parker swallowed. "Well dang … seein's how I can't hardly go back to Miss Clark empty-handed …" He fidgeted, then said, "I reckon I'd better explain the whole thing."

I just continued looking at him.

"See, here's the deal," he said. "Miss Clark's in town to get ready for a concert she's puttin' on at the Aronoff Center Wednesday night—"

"That's Christmas Eve," I broke in. "How many people are going to want to come downtown for a concert then?"

Parker's nervousness vanished in the light of my apparent stupidity about his boss. "She's Kitty Clark," he said, as if that explained it all, adding smugly, "They'll come."

Maybe so, but an entertainer of her stature didn't exactly get by singing torch songs standing next to a piano. There would be lighting guys for her show, scenery guys, sound guys, roadies … as I'd said, I'd seen her on TV plenty of times, and the logistics of her performances were staggering. To assemble a crew like that, persuading them all to leave hearth and home on the one night a year people wanted to be with their families would call for some deep pockets indeed.

But for the last thirty years, Kitty Clark had been rumored to be one of the richest women in America, and *the* richest in country music, so if anybody could pull off a holiday extravaganza, I guess it would be her.

"Fair enough," I said, "but where do I come into this?"

Parker gave me a sly look as he reached inside his coat. For one dry-mouthed, irrational moment I thought he was going for a gun—why, I have no idea; I guess I was still jumpy from the case that had nearly killed me this past Thanksgiving—but he only extracted a thin eel-skin wallet. From it he pulled a piece of paper and slid it across the desk toward me.

"That there's a check," he said. "Unsigned for now, but that could change. It's for a thousand bucks, drawn from Miss Clark's own personal account, and made payable to you." He paused. "For one hour of your time."

I didn't touch it, didn't even look at it. "That's a lot of money. Not even a top PI gets that much. Just who is it I'm supposed to kill?"

"Kill?" Parker yelled, his eyebrows heading north.

"Relax, I was making a joke. But the question stands. What warrants you giving me a check of that size?"

"It's like I said. You're to spend one hour with Kitty Clark, lettin' her give you all the particulars of what's got a bug up her back. Do all that and the money's yours. Even if you decide you don't wanna take the case, you still walk out her door a thousand bucks to the good."

"Pretty generous," I admitted.

"Heck-o-pete, son," Parker snorted, "there's people that'd *pay* a thousand bucks for an hour of Miss Clark's undivided attention. And it's like you said before …" He squinted one eye. "It's gettin' on to Christmas. Bet that money'd come in real handy right about now."

He warmed to the idea, leering at me. "Yeah, a big ol' good-lookin' hunk like you probably has a woman somewhere you'd like to spend some of it on." His chuckle was nasty. "Cash can sure grease the skids with the ladies. Right?"

Parker was a pig, no doubt. But he probably wasn't aware—I didn't think—that I'd lost almost everything in the world I owned, including my car, when my apartment house had exploded and burned last month. Pig or no, that thousand was looking awfully inviting. With a sigh, I pulled the check over. It appeared real, and I looked back up at him. "Okay, let me get this straight. I meet with your employer. Hear her out. And even if I don't take the case, this is mine?"

"That's the plain and simple truth, son," he grinned. "Deal?"

I waited a moment, and then nodded, uneasy with the feeling that what I'd just tacitly agreed to was going to turn out to be anything but simple. Folding the check once and slipping it into my shirt pocket, I stood and walked over to my coatrack,

Parker right on my heels.

As I pulled my London Fog off it I asked him, "So where am I meeting her?"

"Top floor of the Ohio Hilton," Parker smiled. "Penthouse." He pulled the door open. "Miss Clark does love life's finer things."

We both walked into the hall, then I turned and made sure the lock was engaged before we started down the stairs to the ground floor. As we went, I mused. A thousand dollars was a lot of money, true enough.

But as an all-too-familiar niggling began working on my spinal column, my bad feeling started blooming into a sick certainty that this would-be colonel had just bought my services far too cheaply.

2

*T*he snow bit hard at our backs as we exited my building, and I pulled my coat tighter around me.

"I hope you drove," I said. "My car's barely big enough for me. Two guys our size cramming inside, it'll put it down flat on its shocks."

I was referring to what I was wheeling around town these days, a sad and battered old Yugo. But seeing as how I'd gotten the thing for free from a dealer at my church, I really couldn't complain. Well, I mean I could, but it wouldn't make any difference.

The mustard-yellow little beast was a replacement for my dearly departed 1968 Junebug-jade, street-legal Cougar, which I'd affectionately called the Green Goddess. As I said before, though, last month she'd been lost in the same fire that had claimed my apartment building, so a free Yugo was what I was driving. But hopefully, not for much longer.

"Drove?" Parker barked a laugh. "Not hardly." He pointed. "I came over in that."

I looked, and wasn't too surprised at what greeted me. A limousine. I've noticed them gliding around town plenty of times, especially around the holidays, but I always have to keep myself from staring. Hillbilly to the core.

This one parked next to the curb was a honey, the muted color of old pewter and not much bigger than the Exxon Valdez. The Hispanic-looking driver, seemingly oblivious to the cold, was decked out in a crisp gray *Sunset Boulevard*-style chauffeur's livery, complete with knee-high black boots and a snappy peaked cap. He touched his finger to it as Parker and I approached.

"Gentlemen," the man smiled, opening the back door for us. We climbed inside onto tan leather seats as soft as butter. He gave a quick glance to make sure we were settled before shutting the door and getting into the front, looking at us in his rearview mirror. "Where to, Mr. Parker?"

"Back to the Hilton."

"Yessir." The driver put the car in gear and we pulled away so quietly that Parker felt compelled to lean close to me before saying the next.

"That's Tranquilo," he muttered, cocking a thumb towards the front seat. "Boy's from Mexico." He curled a lip in distaste before going on, "I don't much like beaners, but anymore that's about all that'll take limo-drivin' jobs."

I saw Tranquilo's eyes flick to the mirror. His face was a mask. I came near to telling him to pull over and let me out, leaving Parker to his bigoted mutterings, but that thousand was looming large in my mind, so I didn't.

But to show him that all gringos weren't xenophobic jerks, I leaned forward, resting my arms on the seatback. "Where in Mexico are you from, Tranquilo? By the way, my name's Joe Box."

He paused a moment, then said, "A little village called San Vincente, near Juarez." Tranquilo's accent was very soft, as if he'd spent a lot of time trying to rid himself of it.

"Hey, Juarez, I've been there," I smiled. "There's a little place near the fountain called La Cabeza de Oro. Serves the best fajitas I've ever eaten."

"Sure, La Cabeza," Tranquilo nodded with a small smile of his own. "I dined there as a boy. But it's been many years." He glanced back at me in his mirror. "When were you there last, Mr. Box?"

"After the war. Vietnam. I was there to look up a pal I'd served with, a fellow by the name of Rafe Martinez. Do you know the Martinez family?"

Tranquilo shook his head. "It is a common name. But in Juarez? I'm sorry, no."

"I hate to cut in on this gabfest," Parker broke in, "but can't you go any faster, driver?" He looked at me and shook his head, as if to say, *see what I have to put up with*?

"Holiday traffic, sir," the other man replied shortly, kid-gloved hands working the wheel. "I am doing my best."

"Well, your best ain't gonna be good enough if you cause us to be late to our appointment with Miss Clark," Parker growled.

The driver's mask was back, as firmly in place as before. "Yessir." We passed the rest of the way in silence.

Ten minutes later we arrived at the Hilton, pulling up under the long, covered breezeway. Parker's attention was drawn to a doorman scurrying over to us, and I waited until he'd gotten out before leaning back over the seat.

"Don't let the guy get you down, Tranquilo," I said. "Blowhards like him you scrape off your shoe."

He grinned back. "No problem, Mr. Box. I have met worse."

I was about to say something else when Parker leaned back into the car. "Are you comin' or what? We don't wanna keep Miss Clark waitin'."

I patted Tranquilo on the shoulder, then sighed as I climbed out. Let's not keep her waiting, heavens no. Her highness might get a case of the vapors.

Parker and I crossed the breezeway and from there on into the richly appointed lobby, which was decked out with the obligatory plush carpet, imported ferns, and brass geegaws all such places must feel they're required by law to employ.

The room was packed with rail-thin, skinny-hipped, old-monied guests both arriving and departing, and I was suddenly gripped with the wild desire to hop onto one of those shiny luggage carriers the bellhops were using and ride the thing from one side to the other, giving out a rebel yell. That'd wake 'em up. But I didn't.

We stopped at the marble-topped front desk, where Parker picked up the hotel phone. He punched in some numbers and waited.

A moment later he said, "Miss Clark? We're here. On our way up now. Yes ma'am." He hung up and turned to me. "Let's go."

We started moving across the lobby, went past the elevators, and stopped at a small blank wood-grained door.

"We'll take the private car up," Parker said, pulling out a key and inserting it into the door lock.

A private elevator to the penthouse. Why wasn't I surprised? The door slid silently open and the two of us strolled inside. As we entered, I noticed the car was small and claustrophobic, paneled in dark walnut and lit, what there was of it, with small yellowish recessed bulbs.

The door slid just as silently closed and we began rising. Parker went mute, staring straight ahead. A lot of people hate talking on elevators; I guess he was one.

Somewhere between the nineteenth and twentieth floors I started getting a whiff of faint gaminess. I knew it wasn't me, so I surreptitiously leaned an inch closer to my host and sniffed. Caramba. The man definitely needed to upgrade his deodorant, maybe try switching from *Eau de Swamp Rat* to a national brand. It occurred to me this would be one heck of a time for a stall-out.

But we didn't, and it was with a sense of relief in more ways than one when the bell finally dinged and the door opened onto the twenty-fifth floor. Penthouse. All out for sundries, notions, and high-toned country music stars.

We exited the car and began walking down a long, indigo-blue, deep-pile-carpeted hallway, flanked on either side by dark burled paneling hung with ocher-hued paintings of French peasants, all lit by low light in deep sconces. The only door I could see was a large walnut one at the end of the hall. I guess the effect the hotel was going for was elegance, but to me the sensation wasn't unlike sliding down the gullet of some great creature prepared to swallow me whole and digest me at his leisure.

Finally we reached the door, and Parker stretched out his fist, rapping it smartly.

We waited.

A second later it was opened by a thin woman of about my age and height, her short hair unnaturally black, framing a face that was at once too wide at the forehead and too narrow at the chin. The effect was magnified by her tiny nose, with whose pores the woman's makeup was fighting a losing battle. The only thing stopping the term "ferret face" from applying to her were her eyes. Behind her black horn-rimmed glasses they were large and luminescent brown, holding shrewd intelligence, but absolutely no humor.

Then I heard a voice from behind her. "Don't just stand there, Maria. Let 'em in."

I knew that voice. Who didn't? It had burst onto the national scene over forty years ago on the original Grand Ole Opry, which is still broadcast live on WSM out of Nashville. The song was "Goodbye, Mountain Home," the date was April 6, 1958, and the singer was Kitty Clark. I'd just turned five years old, and the thing I remember most about that night were the achingly pure tones of Kitty's singing as she accompanied herself on the mandolin, ably backed up by Bill "Tiny" Wyler on the pedal steel guitar. Her music came to us from the graceful wooden cathedral arch of our Philco radio's speaker, augmented by the soft sobs of my granny as my dad muttered in wonderment, "Ma, *listen* to her ..."

Kitty could do that to you. No matter what she sang, her voice was suffused with struggle, loss, heartbreak, and pain, all redeemed by an undercurrent of fierce hope. Hers was a country voice, and to country people like us, it was ours. With those few words Kitty had just spoken, she'd rocketed me back to my rustic Eastern Kentucky home, and I knew then why this poor little ragamuffin mountain girl had gotten so rich and gone so far.

Kitty Clark was our troubadour.

Maria stepped aside, allowing me to see the owner of that voice. A few steps further in, there the living legend stood ... and I hoped I hid my shock.

As I'd told Parker, I'd occasionally seen Kitty on TV, but the last time was back in the nineties. Viewing her now, I realized the technical guys must have had their work cut out for them. She'd rarely been shown in close-ups; when she was, the lighting on her was luminous and the focus slightly gauzy.

And, I saw, for good reason.

Kitty had always been small and fine-featured, but the brown-eyed, jewel-encrusted, shrunken old woman standing before me, plastered with heavy makeup and crowned with a platinum blond bouffant wig, bore little resemblance to the superstar whose face had graced top-selling country music album covers for over four decades.

"Well, come on in, gents." Kitty's voice was too bright by half, as she held out a small, claw-like hand to me. "I won't bite. Ol' Tom here can vouch for that."

I realized I must have been standing there like a dolt, so I did as she said and came on inside, Parker following.

The hotel's heavy-handed motif was continued in here, Louis the Fourteenth or Fifteenth, whatever. The effect was marred by soft music coming from the Bose system sitting on the credenza in the corner. I knew the song it was playing. Kitty Clark and Conway Twitty, doing *I'm About To Go Out of My Mind*, RCA, 1967. Maria softly shut the door behind us.

Taking notice of her frailty and feeling clumsy, I took hold of Kitty's hand as gently as I could. It felt dry and cool, like sticks wrapped in kid leather. But I doubted sticks had ever worn a Marquis-shaped diamond like the one on her ring finger.

She noticed me staring, and smiled as we disengaged hands.

"Ain't that thing grand?" She held her hand palm down, gazing at the ring. "One of my suitors gave it to me years ago. A sheik or some such. I can't rightly remember now. But he had good taste. Don't you think?"

Kitty then dropped her hand and looked up at me, still smiling.

"Joe Box ..." She murmured my name slowly, drawing it out, showing small, white, even teeth as she did. "We meet at last, as they say ..." The look Kitty was giving me was as odd a one as I've ever experienced. It was ... the only word that works is *ravenous*.

I barely managed to suppress a shudder, and not because of the cold outside; the temperature in the room had to have been nearly eighty. As I said before, I already wasn't feeling that great today, and it didn't help things any that the gunshot wound I'd suffered to the shoulder this past fall picked that exact moment to begin pounding like artillery.

But something worse than a bum shoulder was afflicting me. It now seemed very wrong for me to be here, the worst mistake of my life, as if just by being in this room I was about to open a Pandora's box of misery only God himself could shut. I shuddered now in earnest.

What was happening here?

My breathing began growing labored as the dark, close walls of the tomblike hotel seemed to press in. Add to that the hulking presence of Parker, the ferret-like Maria, and the grotesque Kitty Clark, and this whole affair was starting to have a surreal feel, like a French art film. All we lacked was a sad-faced mime juggling imaginary balls.

And like a wave crashing in, I suddenly wanted this hour to be over. I wanted to be away from these people, to be back in my apartment with my cat, to grab my thousand bucks and get in the wind.

3

ou all right?" Parker was staring hard at me. "You want a glass of water or somethin'?"

I doubted his concern ran deep. His solicitude was more to ingratiate himself with his boss than to express any fears he might have had for my well-being. But I decided I wouldn't give him the satisfaction of knowing how weird I felt.

"It'll pass," was all I said, willing myself to calm down. Thankfully my panic was already fading. It had been nearly a month since I'd been shot, and my six-week checkup with the doctor was coming up soon. It looked like I was going to need it.

"Whatever," Parker shrugged, his task of getting me here obviously done. "I'll leave y'all to it, then. Feel free to have Tranquilo take you back when you're done, Box." He looked at the other woman, Kitty's factotum. "Come on with me into the study, Maria."

They both crossed the room, and into another. Maria shut the door behind them, but not before turning and giving me a hard look of her own. What was *her* problem?

Before I could ponder that further, Kitty spoke up.

"I should've let Maria get you a drink before she left," she said. "But I reckon I can still fix as good a one as her."

Walking over to the liquor cart against the wall, Kitty picked up a square cut-glass decanter containing an amber liquid. I saw it was less than half full.

"I figure you for a bourbon man," she said, "so how's about we have some of this Kentucky sippin' whiskey?"

Bourbon? Regardless of my roots, that wasn't even close. Back when I was a hopeless alcoholic, my poison of choice was Scotch. But since becoming a Christian last August, the hardest thing I was quaffing these days was Vernor's ginger ale.

"No, ma'am. Thank you anyway."

"Your choice." Kitty's tone was airy. "But you won't mind me havin' just a teensy one, would you?"

I shrugged; why would she possibly need my approval for that?

Smiling, Kitty pulled the crystal stopper out of the decanter and poured at least three fingers into a squat, heavy-bottomed glass. That was a "teensy" one? I hated to think what she considered a big one.

She gave a mock salute with the glass. "Your health, Joe." With that she tipped the thing up to her mouth and downed half of it in one gulp.

Pulling it away, her lopsided grin let me know it wasn't her first drink of the day. I also had the feeling it wouldn't be the last, because now I was seeing something else. What Kitty couldn't hide behind that loopy grin was buried deep, beyond the glaze of her eyes. And having been down that road myself many times, I knew it wasn't a happy buzz.

It was hard-core desperation.

Holding the remnants of her drink, and still going for drunk-brave, Kitty plopped down on an overstuffed and decidedly uncomfortable-looking divan.

"If you ain't gonna drink with me, then you park yourself right here, Joe Box, and let me tell you about why I asked you to stop by." She patted the seat next to her.

"I'll stand, if it's all the same."

Her smile slipped a bit. "It's not all the same. Like I told you before, I won't bite."

That, I wasn't so sure about.

"Does it really matter whether I sit or stand, Miss Clark?"

"It does." Her answer was flat. "You're too tall. It makes my neck stiff looking up at you." She pointed at me. "Do like I'm askin' and don't sass your elders. People like us were taught better."

"People like us?"

"Southerners."

"How did you know I'm Southern? After all the years of living up here, I thought my accent had disappeared forever."

Kitty's smile was back. "Aw, we butter beans can *always* tell. Don't tell me you can't. The acorn don't fall far from the tree, as they say." She again patted the seat, keeping a firm grip on her drink with the other hand as she batted her eyes. "Please?"

Oh, why not? The sooner I heard her out, the sooner I could get my money and leave. I was due at my lady friend Angela's house later tonight, where she'd promised me an "early Christmas surprise." I'd have a surprise of my own when I showed her Kitty's check.

I sat down next to her. "Okay, Miss Clark. Let's hear it."

She took another pull of whiskey. "Well ..."

And with that Kitty's brassy demeanor suddenly vanished. Like a stage performer in a Greek play, she'd exchanged her happy face for a tragic one. Was the transformation real, or an act?

"I guess you might say there's been some ... weird things going on around me," was all she said.

I cocked my head. "How so?"

Haltingly, as if she was unsure now, she began relating her story.

♦ ◊ ♦

Kitty's problem started three weeks ago, she said, when the fan letter had arrived at her house just outside of Nashville. She told me, in a rather embarrassed way, that receiving a fan letter at all was getting to be a rarity these days. Enough so she'd left standing orders with Maria not to bother opening any such items. She'd do that herself.

What Kitty found inside the envelope was sweet. Odd, but sweet.

The writer said he was her biggest fan, from years back. To prove it, he related how Tiny Wyler, who'd played pedal-steel guitar for Kitty for her opening on the Grand Ole Opry, was in fact the backup for her regular man, Lester "Doc" Miller, who'd had the flu that night.

True, as far as it went, but Kitty couldn't fathom why her fan had picked such a strange item to impress her. Or why he'd felt the need to do so.

Then, two days later, the second letter came.

Like the first, it bore no return address. On a hunch, Kitty said she pulled the other one out to compare them. To her untrained eye, they looked like they'd been typed on different machines. The content seemed more of the same, obscure trivia about her life.

But there was a difference. It ended with a weird P.S.: **There's more where this came from. I know it all.**

Swallowing hard, Kitty shook her head. She'd known from decades in show business that crazy people came with the territory. They were part of the life, like studio costs and union dues. Even country music wasn't immune.

But then, exactly two days after that, what arrived wasn't a letter this time. It was a huge bouquet of flowers.

Maria carried them in from the foyer, to Kitty's delight.

"Roses and honeysuckle!" she laughed. "My favorites!" And they were, too. Kitty had never known anyone else who loved that combination. "Who sent 'em, Maria?"

She handed her a sealed envelope. "This was in the box with them, Miss Clark."

Eagerly Kitty tore open the envelope. But what was typed on the plain white card inside completely wiped the smile off her face.

She told me it was more personal bits about herself, items that somebody really had to dig for. Unsettling, true enough, but it was the note's conclusion that had really grabbed her. **Convinced yet, Kitty? You will be.**

"Maria!" Kitty snapped, trying to keep the fear out of her voice as she stopped her secretary in her tracks with her hand. "Who delivered these? What else was in that box?"

"A local florist brought them," the other woman replied. "Nothing else." She frowned. "Is there a problem, ma'am?"

"No." Kitty shook her head, hoping Maria wouldn't read the obvious lie in her face. "No problem. Go on, now."

Still frowning, the secretary nodded. "Yes, ma'am." She left the room.

Listening to Maria's steps padding down the long hallway, Kitty told me she'd groaned, her nails gouging her palms.

♦ ◊ ♦

"And that's how it was." The old woman turned anguished eyes my way. "Lord help me, Joe, I just don't know what to make of all this."

"Did you check with the florist shop, to see who'd ordered them?"

"Maria said she'd do it. When she got down there she said the old man who runs it told her some kid had come in that morning with the card and the money."

"Did they get a description?"

"Naw, the man said it was some skinny redheaded kid he'd never seen before." Kitty's tone was desolate. "The boy said somebody'd given him twenty bucks to place the order." She shook her head. "What could ... what should I ..." She looked away, her words trailing.

I thought there was going to be more, but it seemed that was it. Now it was my turn to do some brow-furrowing of my own.

"Maybe I'm missing something, Miss Clark, but it seems to me there's really no mystery here. You already know what this has to be, you said it before. A fan that really likes you. A fairly harmless one, I think. Granted, the guy's gone further with his adoration than you're accustomed to, but it's also like you said, that goes along with being rich and famous. Right?"

I'd said that last bit with a sneer that surprised me; what possible business of mine was it how much money or fame Kitty Clark enjoyed? But she seemed not to have caught it as she perked up.

"You really think so? That might be all it is? Just a nut or somethin'?"

Part of the hope in her eyes was alcoholically induced, true, but the rest seemed an almost childlike trust. In me? Surely not. I was having enough trouble learning the ropes of my new faith while keeping myself on the straight and narrow.

"But about him knowin' all about me …" she said.

I shook my head. "Nothing's private any more, especially with the Internet."

The light in her eyes dimmed a bit. "You'd be surprised the secrets some folks are holdin'," she said. "Internet or no."

"Well, that may be, but now that you've told me, what do you want me to do?"

"Nothin', I reckon. *If* you're really sure he's harmless."

"I'd bet money on it." I cleared my throat. "Speaking of which …"

Kitty unsteadily got to her feet. "Oh, yeah. Parker promised you I'd sign that check, I think."

She wobbled over to the cherry wood credenza with the Bose on it and pulled open a drawer, extracting a silver Mont Blanc pen. Holding out her hand for the check, she looked up at me. "That's what he told you, right?"

"Yes." I reached in my shirt pocket and handed it over.

Kitty regarded me for a moment, I suppose seeing if I'd relent and tell her to make it for a smaller amount. When it was evident I was prepared to wait her out, she barked a short laugh and proceeded to write.

"There y'are," she said a moment later. "Even though you didn't stay the hour." She flapped the check a little as she held it out. "But you might not wanna cash this. Tom tells me my autograph is worth quite a bit these days."

I took it, folding it once before taking out my wallet and slipping it inside. "I'll take my chances, Miss Clark."

Kitty laughed again. "You're hard-nosed, all right, just like I'd heard. But still and all, I'd kinda wondered …" Whatever else she was going to say was negated with a small shake of her head, and she gave a sad smile. "You have yourself a merry Christmas, Joe."

"This'll help, thanks. You do the same." I'd only taken a couple of steps when I turned to her again. "You know, ma'am, you paid me a lot of money to hear you out." I looked hard at her. "Was it worth it?"

Kitty nodded, still giving me that melancholy smile. "It was. I enjoyed our visit. More than you'll ever know."

Again I started walking away. I was almost to the door when she sang out, "Could I ask you a favor?"

I turned.

The hunger in Kitty's eyes and voice was back, stronger now. "If you ever come to Nashville, will you call on me sometime, Joe Box?"

Surprised at the offer, I returned the smile, trying hard to see the real person behind the paint. "If you have any more trouble, Miss Clark, I'm your man."

With that I walked out of that stifling room, away from the lonely old woman with the fake shiny wig and more cash than sense.

Legends die hard.

4

I pulled the Yugo up in front of Angela's, and it shuddered once before I shut it off. It was doing more of that lately. But I really shouldn't have been surprised. On my last case, I'd practically torn the guts out of the little car in my haste to save my lady friend from the killer who later that same night would shoot me. The thing simply wasn't meant to take the pounding I'd given it. Now it was letting me know it was time to either service it or consign it to the junk heap.

I got out of the car and locked it, then trotted up the flagstone steps to the house's front porch. My breath blew foggy plumes into the Christmas-scented night as I went, my mood lightening with each step.

Angela's dwelling is a vintage, well-kept, two-story dark-red brick Cape Cod backing onto old-growth woods. As I took in the house's tall pines bearing limbs laden with snow, and smiled at its chimney sending sweet hickory smoke up into the star-studded sky, it struck me that only somebody like Norman Rockwell could have done this scene justice. Kitty Clark and her weird entourage were already beginning to fade.

I knocked once, and a second later the door flew open. I was greeted by a woman whose beauty still makes me catch my breath.

"Joe!" Angela Swain grinned, grabbing my hand. "It's about time. Get in here and hang up your coat. We've been waiting for you."

I'd barely done as she said before she began pulling me bodily down the hall, giggling like a schoolgirl. I noticed she'd done something new with her raven hair since yesterday, something that made her incredible violet eyes glow even more richly. Top that with the light jasmine perfume wafting from her hands, and I began grinning myself.

"We? Who else is here?"

"You'll see," she laughed as we barreled into her den. "Surprise!"

I stared, astonished, at the tall, ramrod-straight, grinning gray-haired man standing over by the fireplace, then ran across the room and grabbed him in a bear hug.

"Sarge!" I smiled, still compressing him. "What the heck are you doing here?"

My old retired mentor from my Cincinnati police department days, Sergeant Tim Mulrooney—"Sarge" to us rookies—shot back his reply with a wheeze.

"Right now, getting squeezed to death. How about some of that for Helen?"

I let him go and turned to his wife of fifty-plus years, enfolding her in a much milder embrace.

"Man, it's good to see you both," I said as I released her. I turned to Angela. "This was the surprise, huh?"

"I knew you'd like it," she grinned. "We've been planning this for a couple of weeks."

"Tim and I had been hoping to come up here from Naples for Christmas ever since last summer," the older woman said. "Living in Florida has its perks, but a warm Christmas isn't one of them."

"It just ain't the same without snow and cold weather," Sarge agreed. "So in June we decided this year we were gonna head on up. Now when we go over to Jack and Sharon's house in Westwood to see the grandkids, Helen can watch 'em actually wearing the sweaters she made."

I smiled at the mention of Sarge's son and his family, though my heart wasn't in it. Jack Mulrooney is a detective on the CPD vice squad, and has always despised the closeness between his dad and me.

That fact was driven home in a major way on the case this past Thanksgiving where Jack's path and mine crossed so explosively. But if he's ever willing to bury the hatchet, so am I ... in his head. (Sorry, Lord.) Sarge and Helen know of the ill will their son and I have toward each other, but choose not to mention it. Neither do I.

"Well, everyone get comfortable," Angela said. She pointed to a navy blue love seat with two contrasting wingback chairs grouped in a semicircle before the cozily burning Rookwood fireplace. Soft Christmas music drifted from the stereo—*A Celtic Christmas,* by Eden's Bridge, one of my favorites—and in the corner her small balsam tree we'd decorated last week glowed cheerfully, the brightly wrapped presents underneath completing the scene.

"There's eggnog and hot cider on the coffee table for those that want them," Angela went on, "and Joe, I put out a whole plate of those Pepperidge Farm cookies you love."

"Orange Milano or Milano Mint?" I asked, hope rising.

"Both," she grinned. "Am I good or what?"

I gave her a wet, theatrical kiss on the cheek, giving her my best Jackie Gleason/Ralph Kramden. "Baby, you're the *greatest!*"

We all laughed as we sat down.

Sarge and Helen had taken the love seat. He snagged two of the cookies before ladling himself a cup of nog.

"So, you're surprised to see us, huh?" he asked.

"That's an understatement." I poured some cider for myself and put a cinnamon stick in it. "I know we've talked on the phone off and on since then, but Sarge, the last time we actually saw each other here in Cincinnati was back in August."

"The day my Tim led you to Christ," Helen smiled. "When my old Mick came home, he got off the plane beaming like the Buccaneers had just won the Super Bowl. He didn't even have to say a word. From his expression, it was obvious."

"Yeah, I figured it was just a matter of time until you came to your senses, Joe," Sarge said. "There were just too many prayers going up for you, boy, for too many years."

I started to reply, but was interrupted by Angela's phone ringing back in the kitchen. With an apologetic frown she excused herself and went to answer it. I heard her say hello. There was a pause, and then she shut the door from the kitchen to the den, muffling whatever else she was saying. Before I could think any more on it, Helen spoke up.

"What case are you working on now, Joe?" She took a dainty sip of cider.

"Kind of a strange one." I was wiggling my fingers over the cookies, trying to decide which one to devour first. With this choice, it was always hard.

Sarge laughed. "Do you get any other kind?"

"Yeah, smart guy, I do," I said, looking up and scowling at him. "Only last week I was hired to locate a straying husband."

"Probably kidnapped by the Russian Mafia," Sarge stage-whispered in Helen's ear, and she snorted a laugh behind her hand.

I shook my head. "Hardly. It was just the usual. I tailed the guy for a couple of days, and found out he was fooling around with his secretary." My decision made, I pulled a cookie off the plate and bit it before going on, "Of course, the secretary *did* turn out to be a man ..."

"Told ya it was a strange one," Sarge said to his wife, and she laughed again.

"I wonder what's holding up Ange?" I said, half-turning toward the door.

"Her legs," Sarge answered, and Helen shot a playful poke at his ribs. He went on with a grin, "Worried she's keeping secrets from ya, boy?"

I swallowed my bite of cookie. "She hasn't yet. But there's always—"

My words were cut off as Angela bustled through the door, her face flushed.

"Sorry about that, all." Her voice was a bit too bright, a bit too loud. "Salesmen." She forced a laugh, as if that explained it, then she sat back down. As she began ladling some creamy nog into her cup, her hand trembled the tiniest bit, making the metal utensil rattle a tinny tattoo against the bowl's rim. Placing the cup to her mouth, she proceeded to guzzle half its contents.

I frowned. Angela was acting the same with her innocent Christmas drink as I had with booze back when I was still a drinking man. Whatever had put that unnatural sheen in her eyes wasn't a salesman.

Not unless Lucifer had taken up pitching burial insurance.

"What kind of a person makes a sales call three days before Christmas?" I asked.

Sarge answered for her. "A desperate one."

I glanced at him. He was looking as hard at Angela as I was.

"All right," I said, again looking at her. "Who was that, really?"

"What are you, my keeper?" Angela's reply was just this side of a snap. "I told you already. A salesman." She picked up the plate of cookies, again trying to lighten her words. "How's everybody doing with these? Want more?"

Gently I pushed her hand holding the plate back down on the table. "Forget the snacks, hon. Are you all right?"

"Of course. Why wouldn't I be?" She shrugged, forcing another laugh. "I guess I just don't like talking with salesmen."

I glanced over at my old mentor and his wife. From their expressions, they weren't buying this any more than I was.

"I don't like talking to 'em either," Sarge said. "What was he trying to unload on you, Angela?"

She paused, and then said, "Siding. Aluminum siding." Another beat. "I think." Grabbing a cookie off the plate, she began nibbling at it with single-minded determination.

This was beyond weird. Lying is simply foreign to Angela's nature. That's the reason she's so awful at it.

"And you told him your house is brick, and he hung up, right?" I said.

She nodded, still nibbling.

"Good," I said. "I guess he'll go bother somebody else." Her only reply was a slight shudder.

Before I could say anything more, Helen beat me to it. "This cider is wonderful, dear. Tim and I haven't had hot cider in years. In Florida we simply don't drink it."

Angela turned a grateful gaze the older woman's way, obviously glad the conversation had taken a new turn. "To me, it just isn't Christmas without it."

Helen sipped at hers again. "Do I detect a bit of nutmeg in here?"

"Allspice." Angela smiled slightly. "Just a pinch."

Sarge jumped to his feet. "This is getting too sissified for an old Marine Corps rifleman like me." He looked down at me. "Joe, I know how much you like cars. Let's go outside and I'll show you what they gave us at the airport. Pretty snazzy."

The unspoken communication between us was unmistakable. Back when were riding in a squad car together as partners on the Cincinnati police force, each one knowing the other's nonverbal signals had helped save our lives on more than one occasion.

But I kept my reply light. "Sounds good." I stood as well, turning to the women. "We'll be right back. Don't eat all the cookies."

"Go on, the both of you," Helen chuckled, shooing us away with her hand. "Leave Angela and me to our girl talk."

Sarge and I grabbed our coats out of the hall closet before heading out onto the porch and down the steps. Neither of us spoke until we were standing by the Mulrooney's rental, which I absently noted was a silver Caddy DeVille.

"Man, oh man." Sarge was clearly as baffled as I was with Angela's behavior. "What was all that about in there?"

"I don't have a clue, but I don't like it," I said. "Not a bit."

"It's obviously got something to do with that phone call."

I glared at him. "You think? I'd give a month's pay to know who it was that got her so rattled. And as shaky as my finances are right now, that's saying a lot."

"If anybody can get Angela to open up, it's Helen," Sarge said. "Lots of times I wish we would have had her in the squad car with us as we grilled some perp. That woman could get a wooden Indian to tell you his life story."

"Right now I'd settle for getting to the bottom of this."

My friend didn't answer for a second. When he did, his words were said slowly. "Listen, Joe. I gotta say something here, and I don't want you to take it the wrong way, 'cause it's gonna sound bad." Sarge rubbed his nose. "I don't mean to pry, knowing how fond you two seem to be about each other, but ..." He shook his head. "Oh, nuts, I'll just say it. How well do you really know Angela?"

"What? What's *that* supposed to mean? Where do you get off—?"

"Now don't get riled." He held up placating hands. "I'm not trying to start anything. You know I like her. Helen and I both do. It's just that ..." He trailed off, tightening his lips.

I leaned a little toward him, dry heat flooding my face, my voice flat. "Just what?"

Sarge's reply was oblique. "You've always been more than a friend, Joe. More like a son. More of a son than ..." He shook his head again and started over. "Helen and me, we just don't want you to get hurt."

"You mean get hurt like when I lost Linda and Joe Junior in that wreck?" That came out nastier than I'd meant.

I softened my tone before saying, "Sarge, there's not a day goes by that I don't think of my wife and baby son lying there under the sod down at Spring Grove cemetery. A couple of times I came close to eating a bullet and joining them. Especially around the holidays. This Christmas Eve would have been our twenty-fifth anniversary. You should remember, you were our best man that night."

He nodded.

I went on, "All that saved me from offing myself was the hope that what I'd heard the preachers say back when I was a kid was true. That someday I'd see my family again. But that hope didn't become a reality for me until last August, when you led me to the Lord. You were my lifeline, Sarge. But in her own way, so was Angela. She ... how do I say it?" I looked away, then back at him. "She helped me *feel* again. Do you know what I mean?"

"I know." He nodded again. "And I'm not denying she helped bring you out of that pit you were in. All I'm saying is you went through a whirlwind romance with Linda. You barely knew the girl. It was, what, five months from when you two met until you got married? You've had even less time now with Angela, and I'm picking up the same vibes."

"And I think you're out of line." I was trying to keep the molten anger out of my voice before I said words that couldn't be called back. "So how about dropping it?"

Sarge must have realized how close he'd come to trashing our friendship, as he just shrugged and said, "You're right. I'm a meddling jerk. Consider it dropped."

There was an uncomfortable, embarrassed pause from the both of us.

Then I said, "What did we come out here for in the first place?" At that point, I'd genuinely forgotten.

"Angela's phone call."

"Right ..." With a will, I got my mind off of Sarge's comments about her, focusing instead on what had gotten her so upset. "Do you think Helen will have any luck?"

"Maybe. Angela is scared, and that's a fact. But if anyone can get your woman to open up, it's mine."

I looked back up at the house. "I wonder how long it'll take?"

"As long as it takes," Sarge said. "Helen's good, but slow. Let's get in the car so we can stay warm. I'm freezing my ears off just standing here."

He unlocked the Caddy, and we both climbed inside. He fired it up, the motor turning over at the first try. The hum of the DeVille's engine was soft enough to make a kitten's purr sound like a hard-core smoker in the last throes of emphysema.

Sarge flipped the dash control to MAX.HEAT, and seconds later waves of gentle warmth started flowing across my legs. I smiled. Some car, all right. This was the second time today I'd been inside a luxury ride. As I stared out the passenger window at my poor little beat-to-death Yugo squatting tiredly by the curb, my embarrassment sprang up afresh. Compared to the Caddy, my car looked even more shabby and forlorn.

My old friend and I sat that way for the next fifteen minutes, making small talk as he showed me all the DeVille's goodies. The thing I liked best was the heated leather seat. One of those caressing my posterior would make Cincinnati winter stakeouts a pleasure. Almost.

Finally the car's last toggle had been flipped and switch thrown.

"I guess that's all," Sarge said. "It could be there's a button here to make this thing climb up on its back tires and sing 'Yes, We Have No Bananas,' but I wouldn't have a clue where it is."

"I'm sold. Have the floor manager write it up. Tell him I want mine in red. Candy apple. I hope the payments are small."

"Twenty dollars and change a month," Sarge replied. "For the next eighty years." He looked up at the house as he shut the car off. "Helen and Angela have got to be done yakking by now.

Let's get in there and see what's what."

Our argument behind us, we climbed back out of the Caddy and mounted the steps to Angela's porch. We walked right in; knocking first seemed a bit silly at this stage.

We found the two women huddled close on the love seat, Helen patting Angela's hand. I couldn't be sure, but I think Angela had been crying. The tipoff might have been the tissue crumpled in her fist, or maybe the redness of her eyes. Either way, I was pretty sure I'd caught her weeping.

What a detective I am. No wonder I command the big bucks.

Angela nervously glanced at me before looking back into the fireplace. She silently stared at the flames for a moment, as if to auger their meaning. Then she drew a breath and said, "Joe, I need to tell you something." She was trembling like she'd spent the day in the freezer.

Sarge gave Helen a meaningful look. "Maybe we ought to give these two some privacy."

Angela looked up and touched his arm. "No, stay. Please. This isn't going to be easy." A smile flickered briefly. "I need all the help I can get."

"Sure." He shrugged, sitting down in one of the wingbacks.

I remained standing.

Staring once again into the fire, Angela's smile faded as she began to talk. But what she said next didn't seem to have any bearing on the situation.

"People change for lots of reasons, Joe. Sometimes they change because they want to. Or need to. But I changed because I had to. You see, I'm not who you think I am ..." Still staring, her words held sad wonder. "I thought this was all behind me. I really did." Turning away from the fire, her eyes were brimming. "Helen, how do I do this?"

42

The older woman put her arm around Angela's shoulder, giving it a gentle squeeze. "Just tell him, dear." Her tone was kind. "If anyone can understand, it's this man."

Angela went silent. Then she looked over at me. This must have been my day for strange gazes, because the one I was getting was an unsettling mix of shame and defiance. Then she pulled in another shuddering breath, and I had the feeling she'd made her decision with it, whatever it was.

"Joe ..." she started.

And what she said next made my world implode.

"I used to be a prostitute."

5

*F*or an endless moment, coherent thought and plain language deserted me. I went as mute as a fish, my insides as cold as deep space.

"What?" I said then in disbelief.

This had to be a joke. A sick one. Any minute now we'd all laugh. But Angela didn't do sick jokes. She didn't even like Monty Python. From her wretched expression, I knew she was telling the truth.

Unbidden, incredulous words fell from my mouth before I could stop them. "You mean you were a *whore*?"

Blind, insensate rage roared up inside me. Once again another woman, in a seemingly endless line of them since my wife's death, had played me for a fool. It was all I could do to keep from turning around and ripping her front door off and storming out of Angela's house, her life.

Sarge took a step my way. "Joe—" But Helen went and stood next to him, giving him a this-is-none-of-your-business warning look.

Tears flowed silently down Angela's face. "You can't imagine the shame I've ..." She swallowed. "You hate me now, don't you?"

From the corner of my eye I saw the other two taking this all in, but neither one was saying a word, letting the drama play out. Somewhere in the middle of all this mess I found myself dully surprised at Angela opening herself like this, but inspiring trust is what Sarge and Helen do best. Call it a gift.

I knew I'd hurt her with my outburst, and tentatively I reached down and touched her hand. The room was reeling, my voice ringing strange in my own ears.

"I don't hate you, Ange," I said. "It's just ..." I tried it again. "What do you mean, you were a prostitute?" Maybe she'd meant something else. Maybe—

"I mean I took money for sex. Plain enough?" Her inflection was even, but from the tightness in her throat I knew the cost to her was high. In the currency of the heart, she was gambling our future on this revelation.

"When?" The word felt like it had been wrenched from my chest with pliers.

"Thirty years ago," she said. "Back in the early seventies. On Easter Sunday in 1980, the day I became a Christian, I stopped."

I struggled with it, the loss and betrayal about to kill me. Angela? A whore?

"Why didn't you tell me this before?" I said. "We said we'd never keep secrets. Why tell me *now?*" Then I knew. "This has to do with that phone call, doesn't it?"

She gazed back into the fire. Another moment passed before she said, "His name is Mitch Cullen. He was my pimp." She looked straight at me then. "And my husband."

Once more the universe kicked me solidly in the guts. *"Husband?* You were married?" That sounded stupid as I said it, even to me.

"Yes," Angela said. "But like everything else with Mitch, it was a mistake."

I didn't answer, not trusting myself to speak. It was all too much.

Again I reached down to her, needing her touch, trying to understand. She recoiled from me. But not before I felt the heat from her skin burning like fever on my fingertips.

Sarge and Helen still hadn't said a word.

My tongue felt thick, rubbery, incapable of understandable speech. Somehow I managed to rasp the next: "Ange, are you sure you want to tell me this?"

She nodded in misery.

I straightened, readying myself for whatever. "All right, say it." I went on pointedly, "But know this. Once you start, there'll be no place to stop. Not until you've said it all."

"I never wanted any of this to come out," Angela choked. "Ever. I never wanted to hurt you ..." Her voice had again grown small.

Angela Swain isn't only a seasoned Christian, she's also a successful Cincinnati businesswoman, known far and wide as one of the country's most sought-after architects. But right now, at this moment, all that meant less than nothing. To me she sounded like a lost child, and I ached for her pain.

For mine, too, I guess. But she'd come this far, and I knew the core of strength that guided her daily wouldn't permit her to leave this unfinished, not now.

"You were right about that phone call," she said, nodding. "It was Mitch."

"Really." Steel came into my voice. "And he wanted what, exactly?"

"For me to meet him sometime soon. At his apartment."

"At his— You're not going, are you?

She shrugged. "Maybe."

"What?"

"He said he still loves me. Funny, huh?"

Angela's slight smile carried more hurt than any human had a right to bear. She shook her head. "But his brand of love was never enough to keep him ... from making me ..." She buried her face in her hands, lost in shame, and the moment seemed to hang.

Pulling her hands away, she drew in a shuddering breath.

"I was a child, Joe. A mixed-up, silly hippie girl with no education and no prospects. Wandering. And Mitch was ... Mitch." She stared at a place past me. "He was everything I wanted in a man. Or thought I wanted. Handsome. Smooth. Assured. He promised me the world."

She swallowed hard, now vacantly looking down at the parquet floor. "He said I'd only have to ... be with men ... until his art started to sell."

"Art?" I said. "What kind of art?"

"He's a sculptor," Angela replied. "Avant-garde." She shrugged. "Or he was. I have no idea what he's doing now." She paused for a moment before going on, "But ... but one of the things he'd always say to me, especially when I was having doubts that what he was making me do for money was right, was that someday the two of us would be able to suck life dry, and throw away the rind."

She hung her head. "And like the stupid kid I was, I bought it. All of his lines. All of his ... lies." Her voice trailed.

"So now he wants back into your life, after all these years?"
That made no sense, and I wasn't shy about telling her so. "That's
nuts, Ange."

Her eyes flashed, with some of the old Angela showing
through. "Let me tell you about 'nuts'. The night I came to the
Lord, Mitch went wild. Crazy. He went even crazier when I told
him I wasn't going to … do what I'd been doing anymore." Her
voice thickened. "He screamed at me. Terrible things. Horrible
things. He said that until his work started to get noticed by the
big buyers, the money I was bringing in was all we had to see us
through, and that I was ruining things for us. For him."

"Wait a minute. Hold on here." I was starting to get an even
worse picture of her ex now. "You mean he didn't work outside
at *all*? You mean you *supported* this … this …" Words failed me,
and I felt my fists tightening by themselves. Never a good sign.

"I told you I was stupid. But I got over it." Angela was looking slightly better now. Carrying this around all these years had
to have been hard beyond imagining.

"Mitch told me that by quitting I was wrecking his career
before it got started," she went on. "Not only his career. His life.
He said there 'was no way he was going to live with a Jesus freak,'
as he put it. He said he'd see me in hell first. His eyes …" She
blinked. "The madness in them was almost palpable. So before he
could throw me out, I saved him the trouble. I left first."

She paused again. "But not before he gave me this."

Reaching around the back of her head with her right hand,
Angela flattened and pulled the hair away from her crown with
her fingers. I squinted my eyes to see. Sarge and Helen, who still
hadn't said anything, leaned forward, but I doubted they could
make out what I could: a jagged scar puckering Angela's scalp.

Covered as it was by her long hair, it was no wonder I'd

never seen it. In the flickering firelight I could see the thing stretched maybe four inches in length, maybe more, going up from right to left at a forty-five degree angle.

"As I walked out the door that night, Mitch bellowed something vile and then hit me in the back of the head." Angela let her hair fall back in place. "I found out later he'd used the fireplace poker. There was a blinding white light, and pain, and then … nothing at all. I don't know how long I was out. When I came to, he was gone."

Helen broke her silence. "Did you get to a hospital?"

"Clinic," Angela replied. "A free clinic. There was one just down the street. They stitched and bandaged me, and said I was lucky to be alive. But I know now it was the hand of God that saved me."

"But the clinic did report it to the cops, right?" Sarge asked. "Got this jerk's actions down on paper?"

"No. I lied." She shrugged again, this time in embarrassment. "I told them I fell."

"Huh?" Sarge's eyebrows climbed in disbelief.

Now it was my turn to scowl. I'd finally acquired a worthy target for my rage: the man who'd started all this. Mitch Cullen.

"Ange, *that* was stupid," I said. "This guy could have killed you. He would have been guilty of at least manslaughter. Maybe even aggravated murder."

Sarge nodded in agreement, his expression grim. I'll bet he was thinking bad thoughts about this sadistic yahoo. I'll bet mine were worse.

"I just … couldn't make myself bring charges," she said. "I guess I felt sorry for him. All that anger. All that pain. And without the Lord in his life, no way to deal with it."

In our church, we don't believe in saints, at least not the kind you pray to. But Angela Swain is as close to one as I'm likely to see. She actually pitied the guy. And I was more convinced than ever I'd never really be good at this Christian stuff because, after having seen that scar, I didn't want Mitch Cullen saved.

I wanted his head on a pike.

"That still doesn't answer the question of what he's after," I said.

"He told me tonight he's been in Spain since 1990," Angela replied. "Then last year he said he came back to the States to visit the art communities in Portland and Austin, to pick up new ideas and techniques. Now he's moved back here, to open his own gallery."

"So he wants you to come over to his place to what, talk over the fun times you both had?" My laugh was harsh. "Man, that's great. I can hear old Mitch now. 'Say, Ange, like my work? By the way, I'm glad your head went back to its original shape.'"

Helen shot me a sharp look. I ignored it.

"I don't know what he wants," Angela said. "Or even if I'm going. But part of me is wondering if I'm supposed to, to witness to him again. He *is* my ex-husband, after all."

"I like the 'ex' part," I said darkly. "I like that a lot."

She hung her head again. "I'd finally had enough. I insisted on a divorce. Being afraid of the charges I might bring, he agreed. Then before I knew it he'd left the country. I thought he was gone for good."

"Until tonight," I said.

She nodded. "Yes. Until tonight." Once more she stared at the floor, again growing pensive. I had the feeling that paying a penny for her thoughts would only buy nightmares.

A couple of beats passed, then I said, "So where's Mitch keeping himself these days? I'd like to meet him."

Sarge narrowed his eyes. "What are you planning, boy, murder? Or just mayhem?"

"Who me?" My smile was innocuous. "I'm not planning anything at all. I'd just like to go over and say hey to the guy. You know, be a good neighbor. Maybe bring him a plant." By my bland expression, I could have given choirboys lessons in innocence.

It didn't fool my friend even a little bit, and he shook his head.

"Bullpuckey. I've seen that smarmy grin on your puss before. Every time it meant a carload of cracked bones, broken furniture, and scattered teeth. Not yours. Somebody else's."

"You must be referring to another Joe Box," I said. "I've reformed."

Sarge's glare deepened. "Yeah? Reformed like in the way you handled that punk shakedown artist?"

He was referring to an incident the previous month at my new apartment building, where a young jerk had been running a protection racket on the mostly elderly residents there. Although I'm not elderly, I *was* new, and the guy had tried his scheme on me.

Just once.

"The way Angela tells it, you mopped the hallway with him," Sarge went on. "He was out for hours."

"That's right. It was terrible." She was smiling now in spite of herself. "I never knew a human nose could be flattened so completely."

Now it was my turn to shrug. "I've always said a fellow picks up the oddest tricks in wartime. All I did was show the guy the error of his ways, explaining to him why it was wrong to try to extort money from old folks. As Huck Finn put it, the next day the dude lit out for the territories."

Sarge's laugh was coarse. "Could be he's still going. So long, screwy. See ya in Saint Louie."

We all were laughing now, the tension in the room easing by degrees. It seemed a revelation was dawning on me. God was beginning to hammer through my thick country skull the realization that nobody on this besotted planet of ours gets to the nearly five-decade point in life without some kind of baggage tacked on ... Angela included.

I should know. If you factored in my experiencing the disappearance of my mom when I was a baby, crushing poverty, later beatings from a drunken father, Vietnam, the death of my wife and unborn son on our first wedding anniversary, and my own alcoholism, my baggage was far worse.

But last August I had come to Christ, and along with that new start I'd gotten a clean slate. So Angela had a history. So what? Was it any worse than mine?

No, I had to admit, it wasn't.

As tough as it was for me to accept, I was beginning to realize that her past, like mine, had been left at the foot of the cross.

And there they would stay, forever I hoped.

But I couldn't have known, even as I laughed with my friends that bright chilly evening, that outside the house, far past the new-cut diamonds of sparkling Christmas snow, something foul was waiting.

For me.

Because the thing is, as much as we might want it to, as we might even desperately hope for it to, sometimes the past doesn't stay buried. I didn't know it then, but my life was about to take a hard left turn. A devil from the dark years, one I hadn't even known existed, had put me down for a visit.

And before he was done, his claws would tear out my heart.

6

*C*hristmas came and went, and Angela made no more mention of Mitch Cullen. But he was never far from my thoughts. Someday I knew we'd meet, knew it as sure as I knew my name, and when we did I'd have an accounting of all he'd done to her. I hoped I was more mature in my faith when that day arrived.

I was a bit surprised not to have heard any more from Kitty Clark. I wasn't sure she'd believed me that day when I told her that her faceless tormentor was probably just an overzealous fan; I'd barely believed it myself. But my assurances seemed to have worked, and I sincerely hoped she'd found peace.

But that peace didn't last.

The time was the middle of the last week of January when she next contacted me. Sarge and Helen had stayed in town until right after New Year's Day, and the four of us had rung in the holiday much the same way the whole world does, I suppose, with plenty of hope for the future, tempered by the harsh reality of the times. As the old men used to say back in the hills where I grew up, *pray, boy, but keep your powder dry.*

Kitty's phone call had come in around ten that evening, as I was in the middle of opening a can of cat treats for my room-mate, Noodles. Yes, thankfully, he's a cat.

Some people might take issue with that statement, because of his otherworldly appearance. Too bad for them; they're missing out on one terrific cat. Noodles has only one ear, and fully a third of his little body is wrinkled red scar tissue. Years ago, when he was a stray tabby kitten, I'd barely saved him from being burned alive by a pair of sadistic drunks. Because of his rough start, I only let people I trust come near him.

After all of our time together, I no longer see his scars.

Also, after our long residency at our place in Cincinnati, the Agnes Apartments, Noodles and I are finally getting used to our new flat here in Hamilton, a small burg north of the city. This is also where, incidentally, our church is located. Mine and Angela's that is. Not Noodles'.

While the new dwelling doesn't hold the classic old-world charm of the Agnes, it *is* less prone to blowing up. I hope. That's what Dempsey Miller, the owner of the Hamilton Arms, and head maintenance guy at church, keeps assuring me.

He says the furnace is new—well, newer anyway—and tells me it's checked regularly by the Hamilton fire department. Which I don't doubt is true. Still, those assurances don't keep me from going down into the basement every now and then and listening for any ominous ticking sounds coming from the thing. Just have your building explode one time with you in it, like I did, and you'd do the same.

I dumped the cat treats into what I was using as Noodles' dish, an official brown and white Cap'n Crunch bowl I'd sent off for back when we moved in. (He's also a cereal fan, any cereal, as long as it's sweet.) One of the treats stubbornly clung to the inside bottom of the can, and I reached a finger inside, trying to dislodge it. Normally I wouldn't have fed him anything at this hour; felines are as prone to obesity as humans.

But last November I thought I'd lost him in the detonation that had consumed the Agnes, and since his miraculous reappearance, every day with him I take as a gift. So if, as a late-night snack, my cat begs for his favorite Kitten Kuddle treats—which to him must taste like ambrosia, but to me smells like a fish-gut-encrusted Boston wharf at the end of a really hot August day—well then, Lord bless him, and eat hearty, my lad.

I sat the bowl on the floor and Noodles happily dove his head in, the chomping and crunching noises coming from his mouth making it sound like he was masticating gravel.

I sighed contentedly. All told, the day had been pretty good. It had started at eight that morning, when a courier service I'd done some work for in the past called up to hire me to ride shotgun in an unmarked truck that would be carrying bearer bonds from a high rise office complex to a bank over on Erie Avenue.

They said they'd gone such a low-profile route for the very reason it *was* low-profile; it's amazing the places you can hide stuff in when you do it in plain sight. Most people would be stunned at what might be laying snug in the trunk of the nondescript minivan or bass-thumping lowrider sharing the road next to them.

Although the contents of the vehicle were ripe for the picking for some rotten miscreant, it turned out the job itself had been pretty much a cakewalk. The driver, a large-framed, reedy-voiced, retired over-the-road trucker named Ed Whately, and I had done this a couple of times before, and we knew the ropes.

After arming ourselves with a pair of modified-choke

Remington 870 twelve-gauge shotguns—complete with checkered grips and recoil pads—before climbing in, as well as packing along our personal sidearms, Ed and I felt we were up for whatever challenge any bad guys who might amble our way would bring.

But the crooks must have all been sleeping in this morning. After my spending the entire ride listening to Ed bragging on his grandkids, we delivered the briefcase to the bank without a hitch.

After arriving back at the office building at ten, the courier service paid us each five hundred dollars in cash … which made me wonder exactly how much those bonds Ed and I had been hauling around had been worth. If they ever have me do it again, I plan to bring along something with a little more authority than my .38. Maybe a rocket launcher.

I spent the rest of the day at my office down in Mount Healthy, catching up on paperwork and lining up future business. Then I'd stopped at the grocery store on the way home, picking up some coffee and Frosted Flakes, along with some other odds and ends. After calling Angela and seeing how her day had gone, I topped off the evening with a truly fine supper, consisting of a can of cheap, off-brand chili with nachos on the side, washed down with two draft-style bottles of root beer. Properly satiated, I'd settled in for the night.

The ten o'clock news was just coming on, and the hellish sounds of today's latest round of mayhem were almost drowned out by the noise of Noodles' pleasurable smacking as he continued his personal search-and-destroy campaign. It was then that the phone rang. The crumbs from Noodles' snack were still stuck to my finger, so I wiped my hands with a paper towel, tossing it in the sink and pointing down at him as I walked across the kitchen.

"Not so fast with that. You're going to give yourself indigestion." I should talk.

As usual, he ignored me as he continued to fill his jaws. I maintain you've never been ignored until you've been ignored by a cat. They do it so effortlessly, and so well. I picked up the phone and said hello.

That's when Kitty Clark and her incessant problem roared large back into my life.

"Joe?" The voice was tremulous, and at first I didn't recognize it.

"That's right," I said, frowning. "Who's this?"

"Kitty … Kitty Clark." I heard her pull in another shaky breath. "It's started again."

She'd almost choked on the "again," and I leaned against the wall with a sigh.

"Well, my goodness, Miss Clark, as I live and breathe. Long time no hear. You know, I thought we'd discussed all this at Christmas. Feel free to correct me if I'm wrong."

"You ain't wrong. It …" She made an odd sound. "It didn't help."

Had she been drinking again? I made a mental note to have my home phone number changed to an unlisted one; these were just the kinds of interruptions I didn't like.

"Can you call me tomorrow?" I said. "At my office? We'll talk about it then. I'm in for the night."

"So am I." I heard the unmistakable chink of a bottle against a glass. I was right. She was drinking. There was a muffled sound of a gulp before she went on, "I need to talk now."

"Well, I don't," I said, firmly, but not unkindly. After all, she'd once been a client, albeit briefly.

"Please, I don't know where else to turn."

Holding the phone in my left hand, I sighed again and pulled over a kitchen chair with my right, sitting down in it heavily. As I did, Noodles looked up at me in alarm, his mouth so full of food it made him look like he was about to whistle for a taxi.

"Nothing," I said to him. "Just a client. Go back to your eating." I didn't have to tell him twice; he thrust his head back down and resumed his single-minded crunching.

"Have you got company?" Trepidation filled Kitty's voice. "Lordie, Joe, I didn't mean—"

"It's all right, it's just a—never mind, it's fine."

I leaned back and crossed my legs. Best to hear her out, calm her down, and get her off the line. In my bathroom an old-fashioned claw-foot tub waited, with a new Dean Koontz novel propped on the floor beside it. Both were calling to me loudly.

"This really can't wait until morning, huh?" I said.

"Joe, I'm so scared. The cards and letters have started back up again. Worse than ever. Personal stuff. Way too personal. And on top of that, now I'm gettin' phone calls."

I leaned forward in the chair. Noodles had padded off to the living room, where I knew he'd plop himself in front of the TV, waiting for me to come in. He's so predictable. "What kind of caller?" I asked. "Male or female?"

"I can't tell," Kitty moaned. "The voice on the other end is always so muffled and awful. They breathe or chuckle and then they hang up. But sometimes they don't even do that. Just drop the phone as soon as I say hello."

The solution to this seemed obvious. "Then don't answer your phone. Have somebody else do it. Don't you have like a butler or something that could do that for you?"

"Yeah, Maria, my secretary," she said. "Or old Blake. Feller's been with me for years. But that idea's no good, 'cause the calls mainly come at night." Her tone turned unaccountably sharp. "Anyway, what am I supposed to do, wake Blake up each time it rings?"

"If the money's right, I would," I said with a shrug. "But I'm not you, and I'm not him."

I rolled my head, trying to excise the tight knot in my neck.

"What I'd do," I went on, "if you're looking for my advice, is change my phone number. Yours is probably already unlisted, right?" Like the one I was planning to get for myself, first thing in the morning.

"Yeah."

"Well, it looks to me like the number got compromised. It happens that way sometimes. You inadvertently give it to the wrong person, and then you start getting flooded with unwanted calls. I know it's a pain to do it, but just change it again. It's simple, and that'll stop the calls right away."

"But I've done that, Joe." The shaking in the old woman's voice was unmistakable. "I done changed the thing three times in the past two weeks. It don't stop 'em for even a day."

Three times in the past two weeks? And that hadn't done the trick? I had to admit that was strange.

"Yesterday Tom even had me activate my caller ID so's I could tell where they were comin' from," Kitty went on. "When he checked the numbers he called the phone company. He said they told him they were comin' from different public pay phones."

In the other room, Noodles, aggravated at my inattention, howled for me. Normally I'd already be in my chair before the TV, and he would have hopped up on my lap, where I'd rub his belly until either he or I fell asleep.

This call I'd taken from Kitty had messed up his routine, and now he was letting me know he wasn't happy about it. If I didn't get off the line and get in there with him in the next few minutes, he'd get a serious kink in his tail over it and snub me for the next twenty-four hours. Cats.

"Well, then there's only one thing left to do," I told Kitty. "The phone company knows how to deal with harassment. Call them with this, then the Nashville cops. I'm sure with all the country music stars like you living around the area, the Metro police already have a plan in place to handle this very thing."

"I'll call the phone people, all right, but I'm not goin' to the cops with this."

I sighed. "Good night, are we back to that again? Just what is it with you and the police? Are you a secret felon? A leather fetishist? Are you hiding a shady past?"

I couldn't be sure, but the sound Kitty made on the other end sounded like a gasp. Maybe she'd just taken another slug of bourbon.

"Please, can't you help me?" she said then.

"You may think I can leap over tall buildings with a single bound," I replied, "but that's not entirely true. I have trouble jumping over my cat when he gets between my feet." She didn't laugh, and I went on, "Seriously, Kitty, what can one man like me do for you that an entire city of cops can't?"

"You can keep my name outta the papers. And that's worth a lot."

There, she'd finally said the magic phrase. My trip to the store earlier had taken nearly thirty dollars of the five hundred I'd earned this morning. Add in some bills to be paid in a few days, gas for the Yugo (which admittedly wasn't much), and a past-due credit card statement, and it was obvious my cash wouldn't last the week. Bottom line, I was strapped, and I had a hot prospect on the other end of the line who was begging for my help.

"Okay," I sighed, feeling as venal as Caligula. "When, and how much?"

"Right now, and five thousand bucks," Kitty answered without a second's hesitation. "I'll wire the cash to your bank, and have your plane ticket waitin' at the Delta counter in the mornin'."

"Hold on thar," I said, unconsciously mimicking her, and sounding uncannily like Quick Draw McGraw as I did. "I really don't need to fly to Nashville, Kitty. Not yet, anyway. Let me poke around up here for a bit first. I can always come down there if the situation warrants."

"Sounds real fine." The fact I'd taken her case seemed to have set some steel back in her speech. She was putting a lot of stock in my abilities. I sincerely hoped it wasn't misplaced. "How's the money for ya?" she went on. "Five grand enough?"

"Probably more than enough. I've got a buddy that's a computer whiz, and I'll call him first thing tomorrow morning. Between the two of us we should be able to knock this off fairly quickly. I'll refund the difference of what I don't use." Chivalrous cuss, wasn't I? This "Christian walk" business might yet prove to be expensive.

But she surprised me. "You'll do no such thing. Cash is one thing I got plenty of. That five grand is yours, and more if you need it."

Steady, Joe. Be strong.

"No," I gulped, "I think five thousand will be plenty. Really."

"You're the expert. Give me the name of your bank."

I did, and we hung up. A song was in my head. *Back in the saddle, again ...*

7

Rankin Quintus Blaine, Quint to his friends, is a giant of a man, both in size—he's nearly six and a half feet tall and four hundred pounds—and intellectual capacity. What he doesn't know about computers, and the hacking of same, isn't worth worrying about.

Quint and I met several years ago when we were called to testify for the state against a company accused of dumping industrial sludge into the Mill Creek. My part related to eyewitness testimony I'd seen during a particularly brutal week of winter stakeout work, while Quint was deposed regarding falsified EPA statements he'd recovered from the company's supposedly tamperproof database. Several times since then I've had to call on his expertise when I've hit a bad patch in a case, most recently in that nightmare from this past August.

But for all his computer savvy, that isn't how he makes his living, opulent though it is. What he does to put food on the counter, or, in his case, lark's tongues in aspic on his genuine Louis the Sixteenth *table d'hote*, I've yet to discover.

I know that his house—a sprawling, castle-like thing nestled in the environs of Indian Hill, Cincinnati's richest neighborhood—was left to him by his late sister. What she did for money is also a mystery. All Quint ever vouchsafed to me was that he holds clear title to the house, the land, various artworks and furnishings, a gold Bentley, a vintage Packard, and a Rolls-Royce Silver Shadow, with the resulting taxes he pays every January high enough to run a European duchy for a year.

Maybe with all that wealth, he doesn't *have* to work.

Another thing that shouldn't work is our friendship, but somehow it does. We're opposites in nearly every way. I like to invest an hour every morning duking it out with a heavy bag at the Y, while Quint gives new meaning to the term sedentary. He prefers rich, unpronounceable food; nachos and root beer suit me fine. I've never seen him clothed in anything but pricey duds, while I tend to wear what I tossed on the chair the night before.

And if that's not enough, I'm a struggling Christian, and Quint is Jewish … some might even say super-Jewish. Only recently I found out he's descended from a Russian rabbi who, a hundred years ago, was a personal friend of Tsar Nicholas the First. The rabbi just managed to escape the pogroms that later toppled that royal family. (Quint told me his ancestral surname was Baline, but an overstressed clerk at Ellis Island screwed up the paperwork.)

The only things we've found we really have in common are our affinity for classic films, and early jazz. That, and our love of a good puzzle, like this one with Kitty.

Quint must have heard me pulling up—no surprise there, I still hadn't replaced the muffler that had fallen off during my last case—and came out onto his circular drive to greet me, a grin bisecting the broad, black-bearded face above his charcoal-gray cable-knit sweater.

"What in heaven's name are you driving, Joseph?" he asked as I got out, his hazel eyes twinkling. (He always calls me Joseph for the sole reason he knows how much I hate it.)

"Yeah, I guess you hadn't seen this little number yet," I replied as I kicked the door shut.

"A Yugo." My friend's grin grew wider as he gave the car the once-over. "Amazing. Exactly how much grease do you have to smear on to wedge yourself inside?"

"Don't *you* start," I scowled as I pocketed the keys. "Angela still thinks watching me trying to get in and out of this heap is the funniest thing since the hogs ate grandma."

As we started walking back up toward his mansion's massive oak front door, Quint said, "I knew from our phone calls you'd lost your Cougar in the explosion that destroyed your apartment house." He cocked his thumb over his shoulder as we went. "But how in the world did you end up with *that?*"

"I'll thank you not to sneer, Mr. Blaine. It was a gift from a car dealer at my church. At the time, I couldn't be choosy. I still can't."

"Ah, yes, your church," he murmured, pushing the door wide. I entered ahead of him, and he went on, "I'm still trying to picture you ever voluntarily going inside a church. Unless it was for your funeral. And then it wouldn't be voluntary, now would it?"

"Pal, the more you natter on, the more you worry me," I said. "We need to have a talk about my faith. Real soon. When you're ready to drop your snotty attitude and listen."

"Don't hold your breath, Joseph. Your lungs aren't that strong."

I didn't deign to answer. We came into his living room, but

that mundane term doesn't really convey the scale of the area. Calling the expanse before us a "living room" is like calling the *Queen Mary* "a fair-sized boat." Although I'd been in here dozens of times before, the room's sheer vastness and opulence still takes my breath away. I wasn't about to let Quint know it, though.

I noticed a massive painting above the fieldstone fireplace. "That looks new."

Quint walked over to where a silver ice bucket perched atop a cherry wood highboy. From the container he pulled a frosted bottle of Stolichnaya vodka, his poison of choice. If my friend has any failings at all, it's his weakness for ice-cold Stoly, which he buys in case lots.

He poured three fingers into a tall tumbler, and held it out to me in offering. I shook my head, as he must have known I would. Even before I swore off liquor, I never drank vodka, chilled or no. It always reminded me of paint thinner ... and yes, I *have* tasted that.

"It's a Rembrandt." Quint pointed at it with his glass. "From his later period."

"Yours?"

"I wish. It's on loan from the Cincinnati Art Museum while they finish the new wing." He took a long pull on the vodka, smacking his lips before going on, "I know a fellow who knows a fellow, you might say."

I whistled. "I hope you have good insurance."

He laughed. "Yes. A bit." He set his glass down on a crystal coaster atop the highboy and turned to me. "Now. As to why you're here."

"You know how much both of us are into music. Especially female singers."

"Yes indeed." Quint nodded and then said, "Which reminds me, before you leave, I'd like you to partake of my latest acquisition." His voice lowered conspiratorially. "One of Sarah's."

"Sarah Vaughn?"

"What other Sarah would I mean?"

"How would I know, Quint? For all I know, you could have meant Sara Lee."

He scowled. "Don't be obtuse, Joseph. I discovered it through a source of mine in Europe. An extremely rare 78 done in Paris when Miss Vaughn couldn't have been more than twenty or so."

Quint owns one of the largest caches of 78 vinyl jazz records in the world. He kissed his fingertips. "Simply exquisite. And the recording itself is nearly pristine. Nary a scratch."

"I'll bet that set you back a tidy sum."

"The best things always do," he averred. "But you were saying…?"

I motioned to some wingback brown leather Morris chairs. "Could we sit down?"

"Where are my manners? Of course." Quint settled his bulk into the nearest one, and I took the one directly across. The rich meaty scent of the leather wafting up made the thing smell good enough to eat.

I leaned forward. "How familiar are you with country music?"

He curled a lip. "Familiar enough that I can't stand most of it. A bit of bluegrass now and then is all right, I suppose—Bill Monroe, Ralph Stanley, Flatt and Scruggs. And on occasion I enjoy some old Woody Guthrie, although that would be classified as folk. But most country music, at least to my ears, sounds like someone boiling cats."

I winced, remembering Noodles, how I'd almost lost him months earlier. I shook it off and plowed on. "Familiar enough to have ever heard of a singer named Kitty Clark?"

Quint's face brightened. "Ahh, Kitty Clark. That's different."

"Then you've heard of her."

"I should say I have."

"Tell me about it."

He reached up and deftly picked his glass of Stoly up off the highboy, taking another delicate sip before settling back in his chair.

"I shall," he said. "And it's a tale worth hearing, as I discovered Miss Clark's talents quite by accident."

He curled a finger on his chin. "Let's see, this must have been, my goodness, nearly twenty years ago. I was due in Brussels, to meet with my consortium there, but my flight had been grounded by bad weather at JFK. My pilot was livid about the delay, as I recall.

"As we sat in the airport bar, waiting for the runways to reopen while I nursed a Stoly—which wasn't nearly cold enough, by the way—I heard the most marvelous singing coming from the television. I nudged a patron at the next table, asking who that person on the screen was. He looked at me like I was an idiot, and said everybody knew who she was. I rather brusquely told him I didn't, else why would I have asked? His surly reply was she was a famous country-music star, and that her name was Kitty Clark."

Twenty years ago. "I remember that night. That was her big Christmas special on ABC."

"Christmas." Quint nodded. "Yes, that was the time of year, as I recall." His smile was sly. "Although I tend to think of the season in terms of Hanukkah."

"So you liked her singing?"

"Liked it? It made me weep." He shook his head. "Not the song, of course. That was some maudlin, backcountry trash—not one she'd written, I later found out. But her *voice*. It was like … words fail me."

Quint's eyes shone with the memory as his throat closed with emotion. "Joseph, it was simply one of the sweetest things I'd ever heard. And as I wept, I wept not only over that voice, but for the fact it was wasted in such a tawdry genre."

He slowly closed one eye. "Jazz. *That* would have done Kitty Clark justice. Not that …" he waved his hand. "… hillbilly clap-trap."

I didn't point out to my friend he was in danger of stepping all over my heritage, so I merely said, "Is that why you didn't ever buy any of her albums?"

Quint gazed at me a moment, an odd expression on his face, then carefully he set his glass down on the floor beside him. "Wait here. I want to show you something."

He left the room, leaving me to ponder Rembrandt's painting above the fireplace, and the fop ensconced therein. The fop glared down at me in return, obviously embarrassed at having been captured for posterity wearing such silly clothes.

A few minutes later Quint returned, bearing a squarish box. He set it at my feet, and took his chair again as he picked up his drink. "That's from my vault. Look inside it."

I frowned, then opened the box and peered in.

Inside nestled ten LPs, and I lifted the top one out with a smile. I knew it well: *Skylark*, by Kitty Clark, RCA, 1960. It was her first album to have gone gold, selling over a million copies worldwide, and whose title song won Kitty her first Grammy award. On it her vocals were ably set off by Floyd Cramer's piano stylings, Chet Atkins' smooth guitar work, Boots Randolph's wailing saxophone, and by other top musicians from Nashville's famed Printer's Alley.

I went through the rest of them, lifting each record out one by one. All Kitty's.

I looked up. "Detective that I am, I noticed that, oddly enough, none of these appear to be jazz, Mister I-Only-Like-Jazz."

"I never said I only like jazz, Joseph," Quint retorted. "It's just that, given a choice, I'd rather listen to jazz than listen to anything else."

I picked up *Skylark*. "Then why own this?"

"I told you, Kitty's voice is unique. I'd imagine she could pull random names from the telephone directory, turning them into an improvisational ditty, and it would still be riveting. By the way, I once heard Ella Fitzgerald do that in London, on a bet. Fascinating."

I slowly flapped the album at him, grinning, not saying a word.

He sighed, exasperated.

"So, yes. I own some of Kitty Clark's music. So shoot me." He reached over and gently took *Skylark* from my grasp. "And I'll thank *you* to treat this with respect. It happens to be number one of the very first pressing. Virginal, with the liner notes personally autographed by the singer. Worth quite a bit of *gelt*."

"I'd imagine so." I leaned back. "How much do you know of her background?"

"Why all the questions, Joseph? Are you ghosting her autobiography?"

I've known the man long enough to know he could be

counted on to be circumspect about my cases, so my answer was honest.

"No, but I did meet her when she was in town for her show this past Christmas." Quint looked surprised, and I went on, "Actually, it was a couple of days prior to her show. Kitty had sent her handler, a really oily guy named Tom Parker, around to my office—"

"Tom Parker?" he broke in. "As in Elvis Presley's manager?"

I cocked my head. "Now how on God's green earth do you know who Elvis Presley's manager was?"

Quint sniffed. "I'm a musical snob, Joseph, not a musical illiterate."

I let that slide. "The upshot of his visit was, Parker told me some weirdness was going on, Kitty was in fear of her life, and she wanted to hire me to do something about it."

My friend smiled. "My. That sounds ... melodramatic."

"It had all the trappings," I agreed. "When I got to her hotel I'd found Kitty had surrounded herself with enough odd characters for the next Addams Family special."

"So did you? Do something about it, I mean?"

"I'm not sure. I did take her fee to hear her out."

He brightened. "Her fee? How much?"

"A gentleman never tells, Quint," I admonished. "You ought to know that."

He pursed his lips and nodded. "Yes. I do. My apologies."

"Anyway, I heard her out, and when she finally wound down, I said it sounded to me like an overzealous fan, and told her she should just ignore it."

"It has the vulgar semblance of a publicity stunt," my friend sniffed again. "And that saddens me. Someone like Kitty Clark shouldn't have to resort to cheap theatrics."

"Normally, I'd agree. On the drive over to see her that day, I thought, here's a famous singer who realizes she's on an unstoppable downward slide to her golden years. So she sets out to create a make-believe boogeyman to inject some much-needed life, and hopefully press, into her career."

Quint was staring at me, and I shook my head.

"The problem is, once I was there with Kitty and talking with her, she seemed anxious to avoid publicity. She just wanted it over."

"I wonder." Quint pulled gently on his lower lip. "Surely you're not going to tell me this was anything other than a cry for attention."

"Like I said, at first, I thought it was just that." I paused. "Now I'm looking at it differently."

"How do you mean?"

"A gut feeling."

He narrowed his eyes. "You're rarely wrong with those, Joseph. Say on."

I did. For the next few minutes I filled him in on my meeting with Kitty Clark, and how scared she'd apparently been of her secret admirer.

"Telling it that way, it sounds like she had a legitimate concern," Quint admitted. "Granted, any twelve-year-old with access to the Internet could have found the information that had Miss Clark so agitated. But it's unsettling to think anyone would actually use such facts, and go to such lengths, to cause the poor woman distress." He went on with a scowl. "And to what possible end? A few laughs?"

"Fun's where you find it," I said, shrugging. "So they say. I guess the rich get their fair share of annoyance."

"I don't," Quint said. "But then I tend to keep a rather low profile."

Living in this place? I thought, but kept that to myself.

"At any rate, you said the letters ceased coming," he continued, "and to that I say good riddance. So in sum this appears to be nothing more than the prank of a sick mind. Perhaps her tormentor has moved on to greener pastures. One can only hope."

"Hope dies hard, Quint."

Once more he squinted. "Have I ever told you how much I hate it when you get that tone? Every time you do, I picture storm clouds gathering."

"Kitty called me last night," I said. "It's started back up."

My friend frowned. "More letters and gifts?"

"And now phone calls," I said. "At all hours. Weird ones. When Kitty answers, all she gets is either muffled laughter, or nothing at all, then whoever it is hangs up. But what makes it really disturbing is that she told me she's changed her number, which was already unlisted, to another one three times in the past two weeks."

Quint slapped his hands on his massive thighs. "Well then. I'd say it's high time she dismissed you and involved the police." He spread his hands. "No disrespect intended, of course."

"None taken. I recommended that very thing. She refused."

"What?"

"She said she still wants me to handle it," I said. "Handle it how, I'm not sure."

"Be that as it may, Joseph. You're still honor-bound to call them, even if she won't. It seems to me Miss Clark's need for safety trumps her desire for privacy."

"So do I, but let's say I call the cops. And tell them what? As of right now, this person, whoever he or she is, hasn't really threatened her. So what do I say? Someone is sending her fan mail? Or flowers? For famous people, that comes with the territory."

"Harassing phone calls don't. She should involve the authorities on that alone."

"Parker convinced her to activate her caller ID. When the phone company checked them, they said they were coming from different public phones."

"Then she ought to register her complaint with the phone company."

"I'm ahead of you. I told her that too. She didn't like it, but she agreed. How much good it'll do, I haven't a clue."

"And while all this transpires, this mystery person remains a mystery."

"Yep." My smile was brittle. "That's where you come in."

Quint drummed his fingers on the arm of his chair. "Ah. So *that's* why you're here. Once more you need my help to solve a puzzle." He grinned. "How utterly delicious."

"You guessed it. Are you game?"

"You need to ask?" He moved his hand, as if reading a banner. "A damsel in distress, starring Kitty Clark." His grin grew wider. "You know, I believe I'm going to like this."

A word of explanation is called for here. My old friend wasn't being callous at Kitty's trouble. That's not his nature. It's just that when it comes to a chance of helping me with my cases, he tends to get … excited.

"Is your system fired up?" I asked, standing.

The computer room at Quint's house is filled with enough high-tech gadgets to outfit a moon base. So he tells me. He's never let me see it. When the time comes for him to do whatever magic he does in there, it's only after he makes sure the door is firmly closed behind him, like an ancient Druid priest entering into his sanctuary. He says it's for security purposes, but at times I've wondered if he really has a supercomputer in there, or if he simply dons a black robe and casts runes … not that I approve of such things, you understand.

I didn't have time to ponder it as he stood as well and said, "It's always fired up. Let's go."

Without waiting to see if I was coming, Quint quickly headed for a side door, me following in his wake. The door opened into a long hall, which we paced down briskly. The hall ended at a metal portal sporting a nine-digit keypad where its knob should have been.

Hiding the door from me with his bulk, Quint rapped out a sixteen-number code almost faster than my ears could follow. There was a soft buzz, and he placed his right palm on a polished area directly above the pad. I heard a click, and he soundlessly pushed the door open. As he did, I got the same quick glimpse of the room's interior I always got, that of a dark expanse intermittently lit by a greenish glow—computer screens, I guess.

Then he was in and closing the door behind him.

I knew I might be in for a long wait, and having been through this drill before, I warily regarded the only piece of furniture in the hall: a spindly, evil-looking chair that was new when Thomas Jefferson was still sharpening the nib on his quill pen. This item and I were old adversaries, and with supreme caution I eased myself into it. I knew back cramps would surely follow if I dared spend more than an hour at a time in the beast. Surprisingly, I'd only been in it half that when the door swung wide and Quint emerged, a pensive expression clouding his features.

I got to my feet. "You've looked happier."

"Not unhappy, Joseph. Simply a bit … unsettled."

I stared at him, the question unspoken.

"Let's return to the living room," he said. "I could stand a drink."

We began walking back down the hall, and again Quint grew oddly quiet. I glanced at him as we went. "As Wilbur said to Mr. Ed, why the long face?"

There was another beat before the other man answered. When he did, it seemed to come from left field. "It shouldn't be surprising when we discover our heroes have feet of clay, yet it always is. And that discovery shouldn't sting us like fire, but invariably it does."

"A little cryptic today, are we?"

He pursed his lips and again shut up. We kept walking that way until we were back in his living room and seated in our respective chairs, me with an expectant look, Quint with a fresh Stoly in his hand. The grandfather clock in the far corner ticked away, waiting.

When finally my friend spoke, he came at the subject from an oblique angle. "Have you ever pondered on exactly how Kitty Clark got her start, Joseph?"

"Not really, no. Why? Is it important?"

He motioned with his drink. "Consider the question before you answer too quickly. Miss Clark had to come from *somewhere*, didn't she? I mean, she didn't spring whole onto the earth, like Juno from the forehead of Zeus."

I shrugged. "It never seemed like that big a deal. I guess every famous person was once nonfamous, every superstar learned his craft as a spear-carrier. Even Kitty Clark."

Quint nodded. "Indeed."

I found myself growing irritated. "Where are we going with this? You found out where Kitty hails from? So what?"

"No, I didn't get that far. I didn't need to." He shook his massive head. "Nor did I wish to. Not after I discovered who it was that funded the beginnings of her career."

He again went maddeningly quiet, now staring at a place on the wall next to the Rembrandt painting. The guy on it looked as anxious as me to hear the rest.

"Well?" I finally exploded.

Another moment passed. When Quint swung his gaze back to me, his was answer flat. "The Mafia."

The word hung in the air between us like a stink. Now to Quint, joking is as alien as table manners had been to Genghis Khan, so I waited for a punch line that never came.

A few more seconds strolled by before I replied with a disbelieving grin, "The *Mafia?*"

He raised an eyebrow. "Just so. Is it that hard to comprehend?"

"Yeah, it is," I said. "If I ever thought about the Mafia being the money men behind singers, I'd picture them as handling Las Vegas lounge acts. You know, crooners. Brassy women with cigarette holders and low-cut dresses, men with oily pompadours and sleepy eyes. Like that. Why would they even think about country music?"

Quint's reply was arch. "Simple. Money." He tented his fingers. "I'll bet you've also never considered how much raw revenue country music generates in any given year."

"I'll bet you're about to tell me."

He lifted his shoulders in a helpless shrug. "That's just it. I don't know. No one knows, exactly. But I researched it once, and what I found was staggering. CDs, sheet music, radio shows, theme parks, television, fashion, games, movies … the list of country music products is endless. More than rap, more than pop, much more than classical or jazz, very nearly on par with rock."

"Not too bad for an art form that got its start with guys playing banjos and jugs."

Quint frowned. "Laugh, kookaburra. But you won't laugh this off: I discovered the name of the thug who fronted the money to launch Miss Clark's admittedly stellar career."

That shut me up. "Who?"

A sour look crossed his face. "Does the name Tony Scarpetti ring a bell?"

"Scarpetti ..." I scratched my head. "Yeah, a local boss. Wasn't he investigated a few years ago for trying to rig construction bids on Section 8 housing in the West End?"

"That was merely window dressing. In this area of the country alone, Scarpetti owns controlling interest in several racetracks, nightclubs, meatpacking and produce warehouses, restaurants, what have you. He's also heavily involved in the dock workers' and printers' unions, and in 1998 just barely beat a RICO indictment for interstate cigarette trafficking."

"So what you're saying is this Scarpetti guy is a bad egg."

"Rotten, Joseph. And extremely dangerous, or so I've heard. Due to his age—and some say due to the eruption of recently dormant syphilis—his mental faculties apparently have begun deteriorating. They say the man's mood swings are noteworthy."

"'They'? Who are 'they'?" Before Quint could answer, my grin was back. "You know, this is great stuff. Has anybody besides me ever said that you are a by-gum treasure trove of information? How is it you always know so much? About so much?"

He spread his manicured hands. "Look around. What else do I have to do with my time?"

"So you're saying this nutcase mobster Scarpetti was Kitty Clark's patron."

"In her early years, yes," my friend said, nodding. "Scarpetti also has a son, Vinny, who may figure into the mix as well. Beyond that, the information grows sketchy. You'll need someone closer to Scarpetti's organization to find out more."

"And where would I find such a person?" I held up a hand. "Wait, don't tell me. You know a fellow who knows a fellow."

Quint pulled a pen and small notebook from the pocket of his suit, flipping the book open as he began to write. "My contact's name is Frank Buchessi …"

Idly I noticed the instrument he was using was a Mont Blanc, just like Kitty's. The rich and their pens.

He tore the paper out and handed it to me. "You'll find him across the river in Newport, working as a janitor at a rather dissolute club called Secrets. It's on Monmouth." Quint reached over and tapped the paper with the pen. "The address for the club is there as well."

I folded the paper once before putting it away. "How do you know this Buchessi guy?"

Quint's smile was slight. "It's quite a story. One I'll be happy to tell you another time. Or perhaps he will; you'll find him a rather talkative gent. Suffice it to say I 'helped him out of a jam once,' as Frank would put it. He also said if he could ever return the favor, just to say the word. I've never had occasion to take him up on his offer. Until now."

Using the pen, my friend pointed at my pocket containing the note.

"There's also the name of another club that came up in my search," he said, "one Scarpetti also has interest in. Something called The Wasted Effort."

His lips twisted in a wry grin. "With a name like that, it has to be a quality establishment. I'll leave it to you to discover its importance. If any. Give me a little time to set up the meeting. While it's true Frank has no problem keeping a confidence, his hours can be erratic. Plus, he's a rather odd duck. I'll have to convince him you can be trusted."

That sounded like a cue. We both stood and I held out my hand. "Once again, you've amazed me."

He grasped my hand in return. "Sometimes I amaze myself."

As we began heading toward his door, I said, "All you need is a good woman to make an honest man of you, Quint, and you'd have the world by the tail."

His smile in return was mocking. And, it seemed to me, a bit sad.

"A good woman," he sighed. "You don't know how much I wish you were still a drinking man, Joseph, because there's another story I've yet to tell you. One about a woman. Unfortunately, it can only be told between good friends at a late hour, with many drinks between them."

He paused, and then went on, "But, since neither of us appear to be getting any younger, and you've given up demon rum, perhaps I'll tell it to you soon, drinks or no."

We stopped, and I placed my hand on my friend's massive shoulder.

"I'll hold you to that. And the next time we get together it'll be pleasure, not business, I promise." I lowered my voice. "It just so happens I have in my possession a recently acquired copy of *Metropolis*. Uncut and fully restored."

"Fritz Lang's 1929 silent masterpiece," Quint breathed. "Uncut, you said?"

I nodded.

His tone turned even more hopeful. "Orchestrated?"

"The powerhouse boys. Berlin Philharmonic."

"You bring the movie," he said. "I'll supply the lobster."

"Deal," I grinned as we finished walking outside and over to my car. I pulled out my keys and opened its door. Then shoehorning myself inside, I put it in gear and drove away.

8

As good as his word, Quint called an hour later at my office to tell me he'd cleared the decks for me with Buchessi. He also told me that he'd set the appointment up for 2 p.m.

"But a word of caution is needed, Joseph," he said. "Frank loves to reminisce. He's quite liable to bury whatever information he has in sheer verbiage."

I assured Quint I was a past master at culling wheat from chaff—I *am* a farmer's son, after all—and told him once again I appreciated his help.

"Just end this torment for Miss Clark," he said before hanging up. "I don't want a solitary thing affecting her ability to move me to tears. Do that and we're even."

Before heading out I checked with my bank; sure enough, Kitty's money had arrived intact. Yowza.

After a light lunch at my old friend Mr. Sapperstein's deli in Northside, I got back in the Yugo and began making my way down I-75. Once on the Brent Spence Bridge I crossed it into Covington, then from there I passed over Route 8 into Newport.

I know there are several ways of getting into Newport from Cincinnati; I just happened to like this one.

When I got to Monmouth Street, I hung a left, heading back toward the river, passing the town's famous clubs and bars lining the way. Once again I was struck by how tawdry and cheap they appeared in the cold light of day. What made it even stranger was I knew these places were only shadows of what they'd been a few years ago, when the city, in a desperate bid to reclaim some semblance of civic pride, had begun morphing them from full-nudity strip joints into rather silly go-go bars.

I pulled right up in front of the entrance to Secrets, not surprised to find a parking spot there at this hour of the day.

Getting out, I gave the place the once-over, trying hard not to curl my lip at the frantic salaciousness of the joint's gaudy sign hanging out over the sidewalk. It didn't help the place's appearance any that the sign was bracketed by sleazy posters of heavily made-up women, their come-hither looks as fake as their body parts.

One poster in particular stopped me, not because of the beauty of the female on it, but by the sheer dull vacuity in her eyes. I could tell at a glance that, whatever else was going to happen in this person's life, she was long past caring.

I shook my head. And I used to be enticed by this stuff? Caramba. Top that by the fact the entire place was enhanced by blown bulbs and peeling paint, and the total effect was one of life-crushing despair.

Pushing the sticky, filthy glass door open with my palm, I went in.

I hadn't gotten three steps inside the lobby, fetid with the stench of week-old food coming from the greasy spoon next door, when I felt a hard tap on my shoulder. I turned.

What greeted me was Alley Oop's cousin. I'm not kidding. The man was maybe thirty and buzz-cut, built like a barrel, with close-set piggy eyes and funky breath that put me in mind of rotten bacon.

"Bar's not open yet, pal," the caveman rumbled. The air wafting from his mouth nearly made my hair fall out.

"Just as well," I said. "Even when I drank, I wouldn't drink here."

That must have caused Oop's brain wiring to arc. He blinked. "Whattya want, then?"

I needed to get away from that stink. Either that or show this guy Mr. Sapperstein's pastrami that I'd had for lunch.

"I'm here to see somebody," I said. "Frank Buchessi."

Oop blinked again. "That old rummy? What for?"

"Enquiring minds want to know." I smiled and edged away from him.

Oop frowned. "Huh?"

I pointed toward a door off to the side. "Through there?"

"Nah, that's a prop room," he wheezed. "Lights and feather boas and junk like that." He cocked a meaty thumb at the door next to it. "That's it. Through there, down the steps."

"Thanks. Your job as a poster child for public education is secure."

Oop was still puzzling that one out as I exited the way he'd shown, finding myself negotiating my way down ill-lighted and rickety stairs. But I made it without incident, and at the bottom found myself before a door bearing, in yellow stick-on letters, the word "janitor."

I knocked on it, the old, nearly petrified wood rough on my knuckles. A second later I heard a chain slide back, and the door creaked open.

I was greeted by an old man with a sweet-potato nose and bright red hair, but whose large frame was bent, as if he'd recently lost a lot of weight.

"You must be Box," he said by way of greeting. "My name's Frank. Frank Buchessi. Friends call me Bucky. Quint told me on the phone you was coming." The hand the old man held out was pale and liver-spotted, but as we shook I was surprised at his grip. It was firm and steady, not at all what I'd expected.

He must have noticed my smile, and returned it as we released hands. "Come in. Excuse the mess, as they say."

The room was small and dank, with dusty spider webs gracing the ceiling corners, and was permeated by an ammonia smell—the cleaning kind, not the other kind. Buchessi seated himself behind an ancient wooden desk. I chose to remain standing.

"About that grip," he said with pride. "Pretty strong for an old guy, huh? Surprised?"

"Not really. Where I come from, I grew up with farmers who could still hand-milk a dozen cows a day when they were well up into their eighties."

"I squeeze a rubber ball." Buchessi reached into his middle desk drawer, pulling out a dingy red one, almost black with dirt from use. "A pool player named Dunk Smallwood give me this back in 1934, when I was six. Dunk worked a hall down close to the lake on Chicago's South Side, and said it kept his hands strong."

Buchessi began compressing the ball. "Dunk liked me. He paid me a dime each time I ran and brought him a bucket of beer from the bar around the corner. The guy drank like a fish, so I never lacked for money. In those days a dime bought a lot for a kid." The old man shrugged. "What am I saying? Back then

I knew grown guys who'd fight somebody for a dime. Hard times."

"So they tell me." I was glad Quint's report of this man's gabbiness appeared to be right. I also idly wondered if Buchessi had known Al Capone. No, probably not at six.

He put the ball away and leaned back in his chair, throwing one elbow over its back. "Where ya from, Box?"

"Right now, across the river. But I was born in Toad Lick, down in Clay County."

He nodded. "Yeah, I figured ya for some kinda stump-jumper."

Remembering Kitty Clark's crack about my accent, I said, "You mean from my manner of speech?"

"Nah, just a feel. Something I'm pretty good at, and I'm seldom wrong. Plus, you gave it away with that thing you said about growing up with farmers."

So I did. "How did you get all the way from Chicago to here, Bucky?"

He held up a finger. "I told ya, only my friends call me that. And you ain't one. Yet."

"My mistake."

"S'all right," he shrugged. "You're still a young guy." Nearly fifty was young? "People today, they got no respect," he went on, ignoring my question. "Old days, ya call somebody by a too-familiar name, before he says it's okay, ya might end up clipped. Even here in Newport. I seen it happen."

Now we were getting to it. "Sounds like you know a lot about the area."

His reply was cryptic. "I know lots about lots of things."

"Mind if I sit?"

Buchessi motioned to the chair on my side of the desk. "It's a free country. For a little while longer, anyway."

I pulled a nearby rusty metal folding chair over to me and eased myself down in it, hoping it would hold. It did.

"Thanks." I pulled out my little spiral notebook and Bic pen, uncapping it. "Is it okay with you if I take a few notes?"

Buchessi flapped a dismissive hand. "Quint said you was good people. Why not?"

"Okay. Let's start with The Wasted Effort. Know much about it?"

The old man smiled. "I knew it from back in the forties, when it was a real fancy, snazzy casino called The Lucky Hit," he said. "Lotsa famous people did shows there. Dinah Shore, Jimmy Durante, Al Martino, the Ink Spots … back then coloreds could sing in places that wouldn't let 'em eat there. Weird, huh? Even Sinatra was there one night. Let me hold his coat while he ran the tables. Paid me a hundred bucks, too. Nice guy."

Buchessi leaned forward. "Lotta people think the place was called The Lucky Hit because the specialty there was blackjack. But the real reason was, Scarpetti got the cash to build it in a sweetheart deal from some New York people for him whacking one of their competitors. I always heard those boys were fair." He nodded. "That sure proved it, at least to me."

I was writing as he spoke. "You're talking about Tony Scarpetti, right?"

"That's the one. He's got lotsa names. Some of the old neighborhood *paisans* call him Tony the Cook, or Tony C, because as a young guy he worked as a short-order cook in a diner in Clifton. That was before he started slapping leather as a runner for some of the numbers guys on Mohawk Avenue."

Buchessi leaned in and squinted. "That was also where he got the nickname Tony the Cutter. People say it was because

Tony's old man was a butcher, but the real reason is that he loved knife work. Close-in jobs." The old man winked. "You know what I mean."

That I did. As a kid I'd known of a clan of moonshiners called the MacElroys, who lived way back in the hollers of Clay County. The old man, Lem, was regarded as a fellow good with a blade, and his sons, one of whom died in Vietnam the year before I went, weren't slouches either. That, along with their canny shooting skills, kept the revenuers away, for the most part. Those that didn't take the hint were never seen again.

Frank Buchessi wasn't the only one in the room who'd grown up around unsavory characters.

"So Tony built The Lucky Hit as a casino in the forties," I said. "How long before it changed to what it is now?"

Buchessi scratched his chin. "Lessee. As far as strip joints, Newport was wide open right up until the late eighties, but by the mid-fifties the Feds was coming down hard on the casinos here. The city government was as corrupt as ever, and Uncle Sam was trying to rein in the wilder places. Tony heard The Lucky Hit was on the IRS list for closure, so he beat 'em to it and changed it to a strip club and called it The Wasted Effort. He named it that because not only was it his way of thumbing his nose at the Feds, he made it a rule that any dancer there only *stayed* a dancer, and never rented herself out for other things. And it worked."

The old man shook his head in amazement.

"Brother, did it. Those kinda places was all the rage back then, 'specially with the UC college kids and businessmen on expense accounts. Tony'd never admit it to anybody, least of all me, but I think he made more money with it as a club than he ever did as a gambling joint."

"I guess that's not true any longer, though."

Buchessi nodded.

"Ya got that right. The city government got reformed a few years back, and since then it's been death for Newport's strip business. Now they just wear little bikinis and such. Nudity and good times are out, Newport-On-The-Levee, family restaurants, the Aquarium is in. It's almost like the whole town got religion or something."

"Tony's been feeling the crunch?"

"Here? Sure," Buchessi said. "But Tony never was one to put all his eggs in one basket. He's got interests in Vegas, Reno, Tahoe … even in offshore banking, I heard. He'll always land on his feet, if his punk son doesn't trip him up first."

I checked my notes. "That would be Vinny?"

Again Buchessi held up a warning finger. "Never call him that to his face. Not unless you're tired of living. He likes to be called Vincent. Nobody calls him Vinny. Not twice."

"Hates it, huh?"

"Like poison." The old man's voice had gone flat. "See, one of Tony's other gang monikers is Mad Tony, but the 'Mad' part should go to Vinny … Vincent." Buchessi shook his head. "Here I warn you about it and now *I'm* saying it wrong. Bad habit to get into."

"So the kid's a loose cannon?"

"Kid? He's forty if he's a day. But yeah, Vincent's a different breed of cat from his old man." Buchessi shrugged. "Now Tony, if he needed to whack somebody, it's only 'cause they deserved it. He's rough, yeah, but it's a classy kinda rough, the old-world way. The rituals, the respect, the honor. To Tony, they still mean something. But with Vincent, all his class and good talk and education is all a … ah, what do ya call it, like a skin …"

"Veneer?"

"That's the word. Peel it away, and underneath you'll find as nasty a piece of psycho nutcase as you'd ever see in your worst dreams. Lemme give ya a for instance."

The other man clasped his hands on the desk, warming to the story.

"Two years ago, Tony had a slight heart attack. Nothing big, but enough so he knew it was time to start grooming Vincent to someday take the reins. So Tony gave him a job. Seems there was a little Puerto Rican guy running a meth lab out in Brown County, where Tony owns some horses. Now Tony can't stand drugs of any kind, and he *hates* Puerto Ricans, so he tells Vincent, take care of the guy. Do it clean, but do it now. It was like a test, see. And Vincent passed it, but the *way* he passed it … brother."

Buchessi shuddered.

"Vincent and two of his crew catch the guy on Vine Street late one night. They hustle him into their car and speed off. Three days later some hunters up near Chillicothe find the Puerto Rican kid's body in the woods. He'd been beat nearly to death, but that ain't the worst."

Buchessi's eyes grew huge.

"After Vincent and his boys trashed the guy, they crucified him upside down on a big tree, naked. Ain't that awful? *Then* they built a fire under him out of his own clothes, while he was still alive, the coroner said. Vincent said that was how Roman soldiers dealt with their enemies. 'Course the guy was dead by the time the hunters found him. Sick, huh?"

"Really sick."

Buchessi went on, "Now with Tony's health on the skids for real, he's given Vincent and his boys even more power. He sees the end coming. One of these days, and I got the feeling it won't be long now, Tony's gonna hand it all over."

"How's his mind these days? I heard it wasn't good."

The old man shrugged. "Who, Tony? He has his good days and bad. Like all of us."

It was time to broach the subject. "Did he ever say anything about bankrolling Kitty Clark's career?"

"Kitty Clark? The singer? What's she got to do with it?"

"She's the reason I'm here today," I said. "And if Quint told you I was an all-right guy, he told *me* you could keep your mouth shut. Especially with this. Was he wrong?"

"No, he ain't wrong," Buchessi said. "I owe Quint a lot, so if he wants me to keep mum about you being here today, I will. I'm an old guy, what do I care?"

"Thanks. But back to the question. Did Tony ever mention financing her?"

"Not in so many words," Buchessi allowed, "but it was common knowledge among the crew. Tony always had his eye out for talent. Singers, dancers, comedians, it didn't matter. Usually the ones he fronted money for tanked, but with Kitty, he hit pay dirt."

Now we were getting to it. "How did that come about?"

Again the other man scratched his chin. "This was, lessee, the early fifties, fifty-four or five, thereabouts," he said. "And it's kinda weird how it happened. See, Tony had a sister, dead a long time now, Teresa her name was, who trolled area churches for new talent."

I frowned. "Churches?"

"Yeah, churches. You might not believe it, but some of the best talent comes from churches. Sam Cooke, Aretha Franklin … somebody said even Little Richard got his start singing in a church."

"But those were African-American singers," I said. "Kitty Clark is anything but."

Buchessi grew animated.

"That's the whole point. See, one night Teresa's in this black church way over in Avondale, 'cause she heard they got this young white girl there with a voice that could tear your heart out. The night Teresa went, sure enough the girl had the whole place in tears, wailing, jabbering, swaying ... wild."

He nodded at me. "You guessed it, it was Kitty. Anyway, when the service was over, Teresa found her at the back, packing up her guitar. They talked a while—Teresa was real good at drawing people out—and Kitty admitted she was on the run from a bad marriage. She also said she needed a break, like now. Teresa took her home, cooked her a nice meal, then hooked her up with her brother Tony. The rest was history, as they say."

A bad marriage. I'd need to check into that. No telling what a ticked-off ex might do to cause his former spouse pain.

"Tony booked Kitty at The Lucky Hit?" I asked.

"Not at first. He had a club called Spike's, over in Bellevue, gone for years now, that he used for tryout acts. After two weeks there, with Kitty playing to a packed house every night, he moved her to the Hit. That's where the daily papers finally took note. A coupla big write-ups and she was on her way."

"Quint told me Tony bankrolled her first album."

Buchessi nodded again.

"Yeah, it was on the old King label over in Cincy. Payola was big in radio then, before the scandals ended it, and Tony greased a few country station disk jockey palms to play some cuts off it. He didn't have to do it long, though, because the listeners ate it up. Kitty was singing every night at the Hit, and that's where a talent scout caught her act. A month later she got an offer from

RCA Victor and was off to the races. She never looked back."

I was still writing. "How far did Tony stay in?"

"At first? All the way. What the record companies didn't pay for, he did. Clothes, trips, jewelry, limos, you name it."

"When did it stop?"

"A few years after Kitty did that first Grand Ole Opry gig. By then she was sitting pretty, and bought out Tony's interest."

"He didn't balk at that?" Somehow the idea of a thug like Tony the Cutter walking away from a cash generator like Kitty Clark didn't make sense.

"It goes back to that honor thing," Buchessi said. "Tony felt he'd had a hand in starting her career. He'd made his pile, and now he was releasing her to the world."

"I bet Vincent wouldn't have let her go so easily."

The other man barked a laugh. "I bet you're right." Then he cocked his head. "Y'know, I been square with you, Box. Now return the favor. What's all this about? You being here today, I mean?"

I smiled and didn't answer.

His smile in return was slight. "I get it. You ain't telling. Code of the West."

"Something like that."

"Well, here's a news flash for you, pally." Buchessi's intonation had again gone flat. "If you're even thinking about messing with Tony or Vincent's interests, or any of their crew, your 'code' won't be enough to cover the flower bill for your funeral."

I grinned. "It's good to have friends like that. I have a few of those myself."

"I'm telling you straight, Box. These guys don't play. Whatever you're involved in, if it means mixing it up with the Scarpettis, you're dog food. Truth."

"They sound like awfully dangerous characters, all right," I agreed.

"This ain't funny. You want another story? Show ya how cold Tony can *really* get?"

Buchessi settled back in his seat. "This happened, I dunno, six or seven years back, when Tony was healthier. Seems he had interest in a club down in New Orleans called Scully's. It was in the French Quarter. Nice place, clean, the girls weren't skanks, the customers drank like the liquor was free, everybody was happy. Everybody but Tony. See, Tony's accountant had found out the club manager was cooking the books. Not much, little bits here and there, but over a year the joint came up nearly sixty grand short. Now you'd think the answer about what the guy had pulled would have been easy. Whack him, spread the word, walk away. But no."

Buchessi shook his head.

"Word was Tony had a heart for the guy, the guy had done him a solid sometime in the past. So Tony tells his boys, scare him. Rough him up, take him out in the Gulf, make like you're gonna drown him, I don't care, all I want is my money back." Buchessi shrugged. "Shoulda been simple. But it wasn't. It went completely wrong."

He leaned forward.

"Coupla Tony's crew, Johnny Piccolo and another soldier, go down there, snatch the guy—Walter was his name—as he's walking out of a hillbilly restaurant eating a po'boy shrimp sandwich. They throw him in the trunk of their car and haul him out to some rattletrap dock in the marshes, where they proceed to beat the liverwurst out of him for a day and a half. When that's done they toss him in a rented boat, some little open-top thing, whataya call it ..."

"A skiff?"

"That's it. They take the boat maybe three miles out, where the Gulf goes from that nasty brown—you seen it, right?—to where it gets real dark blue. Musta been five miles deep. Walter's feet are chained together, and they got a steel cable locked around his wrists. He's shaking like a leaf the whole ride out, he's sure he's gonna end up as fish food. But remember, this was all just to rattle him, get him to spill where he stowed the sixty grand.

"As a final touch Johnny says, 'This is the spot', and kills the engine. Then he grins and reaches under the boat's seat and lugs out a fifty-pound mushroom anchor attached to a big rusty chain."

The old man's voice tightened.

"By this time Walter's wet himself; he knows what's about to happen. Johnny clips the other end of the chain to the cable between the guy's wrists, then he lifts the anchor up and balances it on the edge of the boat.

"'Last chance, Walter,' he says. 'Tell us where the money is or we go back a guy short.' And with that, the stupid guy freaks."

Buchessi's expression was one of wonder.

"He jumps up, eyes as big as saucers, and begins screaming for his mother. It's wild. The boat's rocking, Johnny and the other soldier are yelling at Walter, telling him to sit his skinny butt down, for crying out loud, and then *bam*, before you can spit, the anchor slips off its perch and hits the water, pulling the chain and Walter with it overboard like a stooge in a magic show."

Buchessi spread his hands.

"Gone. Just like that. Not even a bubble floats up."

The old man reached in his desk and pulled out his rubber ball and again started squeezing it rhythmically.

"That night Johnny and the other soldier get drunk as monkeys, 'cause they know the next day they're gonna have to make that long flight back here to give the news to Tony, tell him Walter's dead and the money is gone for good. They'd messed up big-time, and they knew Tony had greased guys for less. But it had to be done. Running was out, 'cause they also knew if they ran, Tony would send other soldiers after *them*, and they'd end up like Walter. Or worse. So in the morning, sick and scared and quivering, they get on the plane and come home. But you know what Tony did when they told him?"

Buchessi shook his head in amazement.

"He *laughed*. He laughed and said forget the money, he just wished he'd been there to catch the look on the guy's face as he went over. That it sounded really comical." The old man pointed. "*That's* the kinda guy Tony the Cutter is."

There was a pause, then I said, "I'm thinking something here, Mr. Buchessi. I'm thinking you seem to know an awful lot about Tony Scarpetti and his ways." I smiled. "Why exactly is that?"

He didn't reply, and something clicked. "Hold on. That day in the boat." I looked at him differently now. "You were there, weren't you? That's how you know." My smile grew. "You were Johnny Piccolo's partner."

The other man's reply was as flat as the gray paint on his walls. "What if I was?"

"I answered my own question," I said. "You're one of Tony's crew."

"Was." Buchessi pointed a gnarled finger at me. "I'm retired."

So he said. Like most of us, what I know about organized crime is only what I've seen in the movies, but I'm pretty sure a major tenet of membership in the mob is that once you're in, you're in for life. Retirement comes only with pallbearers.

"You'd know more about that than me, Mr. Buchessi. What I don't understand is why you're so forthcoming today. I know you and Quint go back a ways, but does that friendship buy immunity from Tony Scarpetti's wrath?"

The ex-mobster laid the ball down and folded his hands on the desk, his look as intense as I've ever seen on a man.

Then he said, "You ever heard the saying, 'made guy'?"

A moment passed before I answered. "It's a Mafia term, right?"

He narrowed his eyes. "We never call it Mafia. Never. That name was thought up by the press, years ago. We prefer 'Cosa Nostra.' It means, 'our thing.'"

"I did hear that once, now that you mention it. See if I'm right on this. My understanding of a made guy—and like I said, Mr. Buchessi, correct me if I'm wrong—is he's a soldier who's done something so superior for his boss, his *capo*, something so outstanding, he's basically bulletproof. Other families can't touch him without starting a war. That about it?"

"Pretty close," Buchessi allowed. "Ever see the movie *Goodfellas*?"

"It was a while back."

"Remember the Joe Pesci character? The ceremony? The one where he was supposed to get made?" The other man nodded. "That's what I'm talking about."

I didn't bother reminding him that Joe Pesci's character had thought he was going to be made that day, but ended up taking a .38 slug behind his ear instead. But that led to an obvious question.

"All right, I'll grant you, you're a made guy." I motioned around with my hand. "So how in the Sam Scratch did you end up here?"

"That was Vincent's doing." Buchessi's expression darkened. "Being made keeps ya protected from other families, all right. But it don't protect ya from the boss's son when he decides you're getting too old, and ya can't cut it no more."

I frowned. "Tony didn't intervene? I know blood's thick, but that seems weird."

"Some days Tony don't remember me," the old man said. "What am I saying, some days he don't even remember himself. Most a' the time I just consider myself lucky that Vincent stuck me here with this crummy job, instead of having me whacked."

"So tell me, Mr. Buchessi," I said. "What superior thing did you do to get made?"

His voice dropped to a rumble. "That, you'll never find out. If you ain't family, it ain't important. Just know that I am. Otherwise, we wouldn't be talking."

"Why *are* we talking?"

His reply was as even as glass. "Because nothing matters anymore."

I shook my head. "You'll have to unpack that for me."

"It's simple." Buchessi bent forward, hands clasped. "For all our differences, Tony and me, we got something in common. The most common thing there is." He smiled. "The end. For us both."

"I don't understand."

"It's like this ..." Buchessi's smile grew into a grin. "Every day Tony's mind goes away a little bit more, and inside my gut I got an inoperable tumor the size of a casaba melon."

Well sir. That explained his wasted body, and also why he was so garrulous. Facing one's own mortality can loosen your tongue. I'd seen that for myself from my time in combat.

"So death holds no terror for you, huh?" I asked.

"Nope. The worst that could happen to me already has. In less than four months I'll be dead, and Tony as good as. Our secrets will die with us. If I can just manage to keep clear of that crazy fool Vincent until then, I'll be home free."

"Home, maybe," I said, "but where?"

Buchessi squinted one eye. "What's that supposed to mean? You cracking wise?"

"No. It's just that, if it was me, and I knew I had only four more months to live, I'd be making arrangements as to where I'd be spending my time on the other side."

"What other side?" Buchessi scowled. "There *ain't* no other side." He curled his lip. "You sound just like my sister. She's a nun. Carmelite. Always ragging me about my immortal soul. Going on and on about how much she don't want to see me rotting in hell."

"Sounds like she loves you a lot."

"What do you know about it, Box?" the old man snarled. "That's just it. You don't know spit about it. This life here is hell enough, and I seen enough of it to last me forever." He folded his arms. "Quint or no Quint, I've had my fill of you. Beat it."

I stood. "Not a problem, I got what I needed. Thanks for your time, Mr. Buchessi."

"Don't mention it," he muttered, looking away.

I walked over to the door. Then putting my hand on its rusty knob, I turned. "Less than a hundred and twenty days to breathe isn't a long time, Bucky."

I didn't much care whether Buchessi liked my using his nickname or not. I hoped my bluntness about his illness would cause him to pay attention to what I was going to say next. It must have, because now he was staring straight at me, the color gone from his face.

"Live them well," I said, returning his gaze. "And the best way to do that is to live them for eternity." I pointed at him. "Find a Bible. Read it. And call your sister. Now."

Buchessi's mouth dropped open. I took that as my cue and left.

9

The next step in this thing was to ask Quint about checking into Kitty's records about her ex-husband. Also I wanted to ask him to see what he could do about getting me an audience with Tony Scarpetti.

Not that I was really looking forward to that, you understand. Who would? But Scarpetti was the following link, a link that would bear some inspection. I figured to call my friend as soon as I got back to my office.

Wheeling the Yugo into the parking lot at the building where I work, I found I was breathing hard. I suppose I was unconsciously trying to ease the hot knot of tension in my stomach over the prospect of actually getting to meet a real Mafia don. Too much time spent watching episodes of *The Untouchables* as a kid, I guess. I parked and got out, locking the car door, then walked into the entrance of the place.

Now when a person hears the words "office building," naturally they assume an edifice designed for that purpose. Not mine.

The place where I work is really a rehabbed old four-unit

dingy red brick apartment house dating back to before the Eisenhower era. The layout is fairly standard for the time, two steps up onto a small covered concrete apron, through a door to an inside common landing, and then more stairs going up to the second floor.

The ground level contains the first two businesses. On the right is a small custom printing shop, signs, cards, flyers, what have you, and called, not surprisingly, Pronto Printing. On the left is a place I spend way too much time in, Whizzer Jokes and Novelty. Whether the occasion calls for joy buzzers, string poppers, snakes in a can, or the odd whoopee cushion, Whizzer is the place, and the owner, Toni Maroni—I swear, that really is her name—is your connection.

The second floor holds the Allenby Insurance Agency, and my place. If the Allenby name rings a distant bell, it's probably because you've heard of the owner, Reggie Allenby. Ten years ago Reggie was a starting fullback for the Cincinnati Bengals, but a late hit by a monster defensive end in the last five seconds of the season opener that year destroyed his left knee, and ended his career. Today, after more than eleven surgeries, Reggie gets around all right, but he's never since watched another game, high school, college, or pro.

I pulled the outside door shut behind me against the January chill, stomping the gray snow off my shoes as I removed my gloves. I'd just put my foot on the first tread of the stairs going up, when I was stopped by the sound of my name.

"Mistah Box!"

I knew that voice, and smiling, I turned. It was none other than my friend, and the owner of Pronto, Mr. Yee/Lee. Before I go on, a word of explanation about this guy, and his unusual name, is called for.

Mr. Yee/Lee is a smallish Chinese man of uncertain age, who happens to be, in order, a lightning-fast ukulele player, five-card-stud poker maven, and unabashed hard-core Communist.

In addition to that, he's also one of the finest print craftsmen I've ever encountered.

But that's not his most striking characteristic.

Mr. Yee/Lee possesses the worst harelip, with its attendant speech problems, I've yet seen. For his own reasons, he's never tried to have it corrected, instead using his affliction as a source of immense amusement. He seems to enjoy watching people trying to make sense of his speech.

Which brings me back to his name. Some days he'll call himself Lee, but when I do that, he changes it and says no, it's Yee. Okay, Yee, I'll say. No, he replies. It's Lee. And so on. Once, he switched back and forth between his monikers no less than thirty-two times in the same day. I counted. And each time he did, it was with merry devilment in his eye.

"Mistah Box!" he said again, lightly touching my arm. "Your new cards are ready."

Actually what he said, I can't faithfully reproduce phonetically, but I've known him long enough to get the general drift. What he was referring to was a new order of business cards I'd placed.

My old ones, in my opinion, were just that, old and staid, with black flat lettering on plain white card stock. Since last August I've been trying to get across to Mr. Yee/Lee what it is exactly I'm looking for. I picture something exotic, but not overly so, reflecting a good mix of solid business feel, along with a touch of danger. That's a lot to ask of a small rectangular piece of cardboard, but Mr. Yee/Lee feels he's up to the challenge.

Unfortunately, what he keeps coming up with ranges from

the ridiculous to the surrealistic, with the occasional side trip into something approximating what I'm after. Today proved no different. He held one out between an ink-stained thumb and forefinger.

"I have worked hard on this one, Mistah Box," he said with pride. "This one I am sure you will like."

I took it from him. As usual, the structural competency was without question. The stock contained a rich linen content, and the raised lettering felt good under my thumb. But it was the color of the paper and ink that threw me, yellow and green, respectively. It looked like something off a Saturday morning cartoon. Scooby Doo's calling card.

I handed it back. "I don't think so, Mr. Yee."

"Lee," he replied. "What appears to be the matter with it? You have said you wish something eye-catching." He held it an inch away from the tip of my nose. "Does this not catch your eye, Mistah Box?"

"That's not the point, Mr. Lee—"

"Yee," he broke in.

"Whatever. I don't want to be known as Joe Box, Clown PI." I gently pushed his hand away from my face with a smile. "But I have to say, I do admire the creativity. At least you're on the right track with it." I patted his shoulder. "Keep going, Mr. Yee."

I turned away and started mounting the stairs again. I'd just reached the turn when he called out, belatedly, "The name is Lee!" Chuckling, I took the last few risers up to the landing, and put my key in my door. Twisting the knob, I went in.

My office is anything but spacious, and it took only five steps to reach my battered oak desk I'd picked up—with help—at a yard sale a while back. The thing is probably sixty years old if it's a day, made in a time when craftsmen took pride in their handiwork.

And they hadn't skimped on this rascal. The wood they'd chosen had been aged well, to a deep, buttery-rich brown. It's an inch and a half thick all over, and contains a fine, close grain. The resultant object, while not overly large, weighs as much as a Buick. If I ever move from here, the desk comes with me ... somehow. Maybe I'll get Quint to help.

Speaking of which, it was time to call him. I sat down in my squeaky office chair behind the desk and dialed the number. It rang twice before he picked up. Unlike Kitty Clark, Quint answers his own phone ... his one nod of unity with the common man.

"The Blaine residence," he intoned. What a class act. You or I would just say hello, or he might have just grunted, "Quint's," like it was a bar. But the way he answers fits him.

"Quint? It's me."

"Joseph!" I heard my friend's smile clearly over the connection. "How did it go with Frank?"

"Pretty well. It turns out the guy knows almost as much as you do about where the bodies are buried. But you were right about him being a motor mouth."

"If anything, I probably understated it just a tad. But you got what you needed?"

"Almost. I have another couple of favors to ask."

Quint sighed. "Why am I not surprised? What is it this time? A seat on the space shuttle? An audience with the Queen?"

"Not the Queen," I said. "King, maybe. First, though, I'd like for you to check to see what you can dig up on Kitty's ex-husband. His name, occupation, where he's living, whatever. And then I need for you to set up a meeting for me with Tony Scarpetti."

The phone in my hand went silent for so long I thought it

was dead. Then Quint said, "I trust that last part is a joke. Albeit a poor one."

"Frank confirmed what you'd found out. Scarpetti was Kitty's patron, back in her early days. I'm thinking he might have a line on who might be doing this to her."

"And I'm sure Frank also confirmed the fact that Scarpetti is as dangerous as a rabid dog," Quint interjected. "Worse. At least a rabid dog isn't *trying* to be a killer."

"I really don't have a choice," I said. "He's the next link in what's getting to be an increasingly greasy chain. If he doesn't know who's doing this, maybe he can point me to someone who does."

"The one thing Scarpetti might point you to is an early grave, Joseph," Quint countered. "Please. I must dissuade you from this."

"Can't." My answer was flat. "This is where the trail leads. I have to follow."

My friend sighed again, and it sounded huge and sad over the wires. "Once, again, dear boy, you're insisting on being a buckaroo. It'll prove to be your undoing one day."

"Maybe," I said. Then I grinned. "But not today."

Quint muttered some words I won't bother repeating, then he said, "All right. I'll see what I can do. Should I call you back at your office?"

"Yeah, here's as good a place as any. Until you do your magic getting me a face-to-face with Scarpetti, I'm dead in the water."

"I wouldn't use the words 'Scarpetti' and 'dead' in the same sentence." Quint's tone was somber. "For too many people, that has proved to be just the case."

♦ ◊ ♦

As good as gold, he called me back half an hour later.

"It's done, Joseph," he said by way of greeting. "To start off with, the situation regarding Miss Clark's ex came to a screeching stop before I ever really even began. It seems someone was paid a tidy sum of money to seal her records behind a firewall bigger than any I've yet encountered. Prior to 1956, she simply ceases to exist."

A "tidy sum" to Quint must be a jaw-droppingly huge amount of cash.

"And you can't breach it?" I frowned. "I've never known you to say that."

"As I said, someone spent a lot of money on this. Only one nongovernmental source with that much gelt comes immediately to mind."

I sighed. "Which brings us back to the Mafia again, and Tony Scarpetti."

"I've set up the meeting for five o'clock tonight at the Leaning Tower," Quint said, and he went on, "Against my better judgment, you understand."

The Leaning Tower is an upscale pizza place over in Hyde Park. The pies there aren't any better than what you might find at the corner mom-and-pop pizzeria, but since a small cheese one at the Leaning Tower goes for ten-fifty, you convince yourself they are.

"Why there?" I asked, then I said, "Don't tell me, Scarpetti owns it."

"Not only owns it, it's where the don does most of his business."

"I thought the bent-nose boys tended to operate out of seedy dives along the river. Hyde Park seems a bit out of character."

"You've watched too many old gangster films," Quint said.

"It's a new millennium now. So they tell me. Chalk the move up to Scarpetti's son, Vincent."

"Vincent," I said thoughtfully. "Will he be there too?"

"Who knows?" my friend croaked. "Joseph, are you *sure* I can't talk you out of this?"

"Ah, Quint, it's all rock and roll anyway," I said, with more bluster than I felt. "I'll be fine."

We hung up and I checked the clock. Four p.m. Just enough time for me to put on a clean shirt and call Angela. On second thought, I'd better call her first. Doubtless I was more rusty at this courting business than I thought, and could have been mistaken, but last night when we'd talked on the phone it seemed to me she sounded a bit … off.

Once again I picked the thing up and punched in her cell phone number. At this time of day, work-hound that she is, I knew she would still be on-site.

Angela's firm had won the bid to do the rehab work on RiverTower, a large, twenty-million-dollar apartment and office complex going up on Second Street. It was an edifice she'd taken serious pride in initially designing, but it had been nearly burned to the ground last November by the killer who'd hoped to take Angela and me with it. With the hours she was spending helping to get the complex finally ready for tenancy, I think its rebirth carried a type of healing for her.

Her phone rang three times. Four. Five. She had caller ID, so she obviously knew it was me. What was going on? I almost disconnected then, thinking I'd misdialed, when at last she picked up. But she didn't say anything.

"Hello, Ange?" I finally ventured.

"Joe." Her reply was guarded. "What do you want?"

"I just wanted to say hi, darlin'."

To me, she sounded really weird. Or really ticked. I tried injecting an airy tone into my voice. "That's what people do when they like each other, right? Just call up to say hi? I'm just calling up to say hi." I paused, and then said, "Hi."

Another stretch of phone hiss slid by, then she said, "I'm kind of busy here."

"Why the cold shoulder, babe?" I was going for the Mister Jolly routine again. "Are you stressed out? Uptight? Are you in need of my patented, world-famous back rub?" Again she said nothing, and suddenly I knew what was bothering her. And my fake good humor fled like snow in August. "He called you again, didn't he? Mitch Cullen."

"Yes," she said finally. "Last night, as a matter of fact. Right before you did."

"Really. How about that." As I settled back in my chair, it squeaked like the hinges on an iron maiden. "Why didn't you say anything about it when we were talking?"

"So now I have to tell you every conversation I have? That'll grow old."

"Not every one, no," I countered. "Not even half. Just the ones with him."

Her answer was as flat as roadkill. "Odd. I thought I made it clear you're not my keeper, Joe. It seems to me I said that to you only last month."

"Yeah, last month you made a lot of things clear, didn't you?" Again there was dead silence, and I feared I'd crossed the line. "Sorry. That was uncalled for."

"It's all right," she sighed after a moment. "You can probably tell this business with Mitch has me all upset. Again."

"Well, yeah, no shock there, I'd guess it would." I shook my head in consternation, even though she couldn't see it. "For

Pete's sake, Ange, why talk to the guy at all? Hasn't he hurt you enough?" Then something occurred to me, and it wasn't good. "Wait a minute. You're not still thinking of trying to share your faith with him, are you?"

"Maybe." She turned defiant. "So what if I do? Are you saying he doesn't deserve a second chance? Some people are just hell-bound, and Mitch Cullen is one of them?"

"I'm not saying anything of the kind, and you know it." I rubbed the bridge of my nose. It felt like a tiny man was tucked in far back behind my eyes, busily working away with a pickaxe. "So how did you leave it with him?" I already knew the answer to that.

"Mitch told me there's something he needs to discuss with me. It could be this is the opening I've been praying for." Another beat came and went, then she said, "He asked me to meet him tomorrow. At his place." Another pause. "I've decided I'm going to go."

"We," I said simply.

"What?"

"If you're planning on meeting Cullen, I'm going with you."

I heard her pull in a breath as she started to burn off a reply, but I broke in.

"Think about it, hon. It just makes good sense, for your safety if nothing else. What's that scripture you keep quoting me? 'One puts a thousand to flight, two puts ten thousand'? Something like that."

She had no comeback for that. I must have been getting through, so I decided to put the finishing touch on it.

"Plus, don't forget," I said. "You're a single Christian woman, good-looking as all get out, meeting a single man at his apartment. Call me old-fashioned, but there's a little matter of decorum, as well as your image, to consider. Just think of me as your—" my lips turned up in a smile at the irony of it—"your chaperone."

There was another long stretch of nothing at all, then she said, "Good-looking, huh?"

"Pretty as a speckled pup."

"And that's a good thing?" Her tone now was rueful. "Brother. A chaperone, at my age. Can you believe it?" She sighed again. "All right, you win. I'll tell Mitch we're both coming."

"Good," I said. "I'm sure that'll flat out make his day."

10

---

*T*he rest of the afternoon I spent doing PI paperwork-type things. I realized I was checking my Felix the Cat clock on my wall every ten minutes. His eyes were going side to side with every tick, and his normally goofy smile now seemed mocking and cheesy.

As it got closer to four-thirty, I found my hands growing damp. I knew from experience Angela and her prayer partners at church sent up a special word for me daily, but it was probably a good idea for me to do one of my own. A meeting like the one I was headed for doesn't come along every day.

Finally, it was time. That thought put me in mind of one of those scenes in an old prison picture, the one where the chaplain with the sorrowful eyes comes to escort the condemned man to the gas chamber. "Come on, Rocko," the priest says to him. "It's time."

I shook that off with a shudder. Thinking like that could do me no good at all.

Enough. It really was time to get after it, as poor old dead

Sergeant Nickerson, my platoon leader in Vietnam, was fond of saying. I pulled my coat off the rack and left my office, pulling the door tightly shut behind me.

It made the most final sound as it did.

I took the steps down to the small foyer that led outside, and at the front door I met Toni Maroni, who was also leaving. It looked like she was closing up shop early.

"You too, huh?" she said, turning and locking her door before going on, "Slow day. I plan to draw a warm bath and whip up a mug of sweet cocoa when I get home." She turned back to me, regarding me critically. "Now there's a man with a lot on his mind."

Toni is my age, but her age and countenance fit her profession. She stands about five-foot-nothing on tiny feet, with hennaed, frizzy hair over a scrunched-in face, giving her the mien of one of Tolkein's Middle Earth creatures come to life. But Toni's one of the most giving souls I've ever run across, and I knew her remark carried genuine concern.

"Have you ever had to do something you knew you had to do, but dreaded doing all the same?" I asked.

"Yeah, like when I told my third husband to hit the bricks. That man had the prettiest black hair…. I'd sometimes spend hours, just looking at it." She narrowed her eyes. "Of course, when I found out another woman had been running her hands through it, suddenly it didn't look so good. But we were talking about you. What's up, anyway?"

I knew I couldn't tell Toni any of this, client privilege and all that, so I said nothing.

She nodded. "A case, huh? 'Nuff said. One of these days I'll learn not to ask. But here's a little something I'll bet won't violate your rules." She reached into her jeans pocket and pulled a small object out, putting it in my hand. "Take a look at this, mister hotshot private eye, and tell me what you think."

I peered down at the thing. It was a small, brown, oval-shaped, carved something. More than anything else, it looked like a monkey grabbing his tail. And for some off-the-wall reason, its inherent silliness made me grin. "What the heck is it?"

"What's it look like?"

"I don't know." I looked back up at her. "A little piece of wood?"

"Funny. It's a carved peach pit. A monkey, as a matter of fact. Now you know."

Never let it be said Joe Box doesn't know his monkeys.

She bent near it, poking at it with a stubby forefinger. "See his little ears and face? Cute, huh?"

"So what's—"

"I'm thinking about carrying 'em," Toni said. "Fella stopped by earlier today, a disabled navy vet. He said he carves 'em, bags at a time, and wondered if I could sell 'em. Man must eat a bargeful of peaches." Again she regarded me. "How much would you charge for one? If you were me?"

I looked at it closer. "I don't know.... From the loop in the tail, it might make a nice key ring thingy, for a kid." I straightened. "Maybe a dollar or so would be fair."

She nodded. "A buck each. That's about what I thought too. And the fella told me that getting me a steady supply of 'em shouldn't be too hard. He said he can make as many as I want. Says he doesn't have a whole lot to do with his day, but to carve peach pits into monkeys."

"How much are you planning to give him for them?"

Toni grinned sheepishly at that, and stared at the floor. A moment later she said, "Two dollars apiece."

I smiled. "Softie."

"Yeah, you should talk." But she didn't deny it as she looked back at me, her shy grin lighting up the entire foyer. It seemed that way to me, anyway.

"My first husband, Ned, was a navy man," she went on. "Not that that's any excuse, but I guess I just have a heart for swabbos down on their luck. And Ned sure was. A lot."

"Toni, you have a heart for anybody." I started to hand the monkey back. "I suppose you'll be wanting to sell this one tomorrow."

She shook her head. "Nah, you keep it, Joe. I already paid the fella for it. Anyway, I saw the way you acted when I put it in your hand. Could be I'm onto something. Maybe other people will feel the same, and I'll be able to sell a ton of 'em for old Mr. Sailor Boy."

It was all I could do not to pat her cheek as I left. As long as there are people like Toni Maroni fighting the good fight of common decency in this benighted old world, all the evil Scarpettis ever born can't win.

♦ ◊ ♦

My happy frame of mind faded quickly once I was back again behind the Yugo's wheel. Rush hour traffic in Cincinnati isn't a treat at the best of times, never mind having to fool with it when I knew what was waiting for me at the other end.

But I negotiated it well enough, and it was five o'clock straight up when I arrived at the Leaning Tower Restaurant on the upper side of Erie Avenue.

The place is huge, a smoked-glass and chrome edifice taking up nearly half the block, and from the line of people standing outside it in this weather, waiting for seats, there must have been a booming business in usury-rate pizza I'd missed in the news.

I didn't figure on joining the throng as I parked as close as I could to the front door. You know, in case I needed a quick get-away. Getting out of the Yugo, I stomped through the gray slush around back, crossing the loading apron as I came up to the employee's entrance.

The door was under an awning, up at the top of a half-dozen concrete steps. Upon reaching it I saw there wasn't a window in it, but rather a buzzer on the frame to the side. I gave the thing a shave-and-a-haircut tappity-tap, figuring if I acted jaunty enough, it might help calm the butterflies staging their convention in my gut.

So far, it wasn't working.

I waited, and a minute later the door opened. Instead of the white-garbed kitchen worker I'd expected, the greeter before me, put plainly, was a bank vault wearing a suit. I wish I could say I'm kidding. I'm not.

The man was seven feet tall, and half as wide, with long, ape-like arms ending in hands the size of telephone directories. He was also the proud owner of one of the oddest faces I've ever seen—and I've seen my share.

The guy's cheeks were rough and pebbled, like he shaved each day using a cheese grater, and his black hair was slicked back over a large skull sporting a tiny ear on each side, ears like you might find on a child. His eyes were a flat muddy brown, giving nothing away as they regarded me, but the weirdest thing about him was his forehead. It hung out over his eye sockets nearly an inch, a bony promontory as fissured and lumpy as a Klingon's. Maybe in the past somebody had worked this fellow over with a meat tenderizer, I don't know, but the net effect was as if God himself had slit the guy's forehead flesh open and stuffed the area behind it with road gravel, suturing it shut with tiny stitches you couldn't see. All he lacked was a green pallor and neck bolts.

"Yeah, whatta ya want?" My interrogator was obviously less than overjoyed at my presence. I still couldn't get over how solid and dense he appeared, like the stuff found in a neutron star. His body looked to have been constructed from old reinforced concrete blocks and spent lead shielding someone had stolen from an atomic power plant.

I managed to tear my eyes away from his cranium. "My name's Joe Box. Mr. Scarpetti is expecting me."

"Yeah?" The guard—and that had to be his job; the odds he was a moonlighting GQ model seemed remote—cocked a disbelieving eyebrow at me. "Got any ID?"

I grinned. "What, am I being carded?"

His return look wasn't nearly as cheery. "Show some ID, pal, or show me your back."

As tempting as it was to try it, this guy wasn't worth aggravating. Besides, he could probably break me in thirds and use my shinbone for a backscratcher. And if that wasn't enough, the velvety cream Armani suit draping his huge frame had been cut well, but still couldn't hide the telltale bulge tucked under his armpit. With his mass, I figured him for a .44 Magnum kind of man.

Add up his bulk, speech, and appearance, and the guard was almost a parody of a Mafia thug, straight out of Central Casting. It could have been that's all he in fact was, just intimidating window dressing.

But I wasn't fool enough to find out. I dug into my back pocket, pulling out my wallet and flipping it open to my license.

He took it from me, robotically scanning it with his eyes, top to bottom, side to side. His thorough examination made me wonder if he wasn't a real guard after all.

A moment later he handed it back with a nod. "You're him, all right."

Well, thank goodness for that. It seemed I was spared yet another identity crisis.

The guard pushed the door wide, so I could get through. And so he could follow me. "Come on. The boss is expecting you."

I squeezed past him, entering a kitchen like hell must have for its shift workers. The temperature in here was incredible, at least a hundred and ten degrees, moist degrees at that, but it didn't seem to be bothering the large, jabbering men throwing pizza dough into the air, turning them into spongy wheels as big as Chrysler hubcaps.

One side of the room was filled with ovens, the other side with walk-in industrial-size freezers. We passed between steam tables laden with pies already built. Above them hung sharp gleaming cutlery and steel stockpots clad with brass bottoms, ready for the next course.

Regardless of the heat, the smells in here were wonderful. Garlic, basil, oregano, tomato, provolone, and other things I couldn't place, but mouthwatering all the same. Just as I felt myself about to melt onto the floor in a puddle of marinara sauce, the guard and I reached the swinging doors leading into the dining room.

Going through, we narrowly missed colliding with a busboy scurrying in with a tray of dirty dishes. The guard spat something at him in Italian. The kid shrugged his apology but kept moving, yelling out more Italian to the dishwasher as he did. This place was busier than a flea circus.

The doors between the kitchen and the dining room had to

have been made of miracle material, because they'd barely shut behind us when the decibel level dropped 90 percent. Now, instead of cooking clatter, what filled the air were instead the muted strains of an opera, *Carmen,* by Bizet, if I wasn't mistaken. Quint's classiness was rubbing off on me.

The opera had just reached a point, one of many, I'm sure, where the coloratura soprano was headed for the stratosphere and then some, but the guard and I didn't pause to appreciate her efforts. We kept crossing the crowded dining room, the patrons oblivious to us.

At last we approached a large mahogany door set into the wall on the right side of the room, with a waiter standing next to it. By his nonchalant slouch, the employee gave the appearance of being the laziest one in existence. That's what I thought at first, until I looked again.

Until I saw his eyes.

While the other staff was bustling around, taking orders, bringing plates, swapping flatware, filling glasses, this guy just slowly surveyed the room, side to side, back and forth, exactly like the kitchen guard had done to my card when I'd handed it to him. And why not? The waiter was obviously a guard as well, although not nearly as big as my escort.

We reached the door and stopped, and King Kong tilted his head my way.

"This is the guy the boss has been waiting for," was all he said. A bit ominously, in my opinion.

With that I was effortlessly handed off, my erstwhile companion heading back toward the kitchen, maybe to grab some supper, maybe to rip out the busboy's spine. Probably to him either was a pleasant diversion.

The hard-faced "waiter" opened the door for me, giving me

a what-are-you-waiting-for, idiot, look. I gave him a look of my own to complete the set, and we went in, the door silently closing behind us. It seemed I wasn't going to get to hear how Carmen got out of her predicament after all.

I made to push past the guard when he stopped me with a stiff hand to my chest. "You didn't really think you were just gonna waltz in on Mr. Scarpetti like that, did you?" he said softly.

"What do you mean?" Although I knew.

"I mean, assume the position, butthead." He roughly turned me around so I was facing the hall wall.

As a former cop, I knew this drill—well—and I did as the guard said, spreading my hands and feet and leaning against the wall at a forty-five degree angle.

With a quick expertise doubtless born of years of practice, the guard began patting me down. This guy was good. Not only did he check the usual spots on me for a gun or knife, waistband and armpits, he even felt around my ankles, looking for the backup piece, like some cops, and most felons, like to keep on them.

I saved myself the effort of letting him know he needn't have bothered; I'd left my .38 at the office before I came over today. Suicidal, I'm not. Finally satisfied, he turned me back around to face him. "Okay," was all he said.

I smiled. "As one pro to another, that was well done. What's your name, anyway? I'll be sure to put in a good word for you when I see Mr. Scarpetti."

My attempt at humor fell as flat as the pizzas they served here, getting zero reaction from the flat-panned guard, not even a sneer. This guy really was pretty good.

He pointed. "This way."

I didn't have to be told twice. Like I'd done since I got here,

I was to go first. With my new companion two steps behind me, we began padding down a stark hallway that gave a new meaning to the term "nondescript."

The ceiling above us was off-white, the walls slate gray, and the blue carpet only a shade darker than either. Unlike the hallway at Kitty's hotel last Christmas, there were no recessed sconces here, no burled paneling, no French peasant paintings. Only monotony. Thankfully I didn't have to endure it very long, as we approached the twin to the door of the one we'd come in.

I thought the guard might have to give the thing a surreptitious coded knock—maybe two short, one long, three short—but he didn't. I really had seen too many old speakeasy movies. He simply reached around me, rapped on it twice, and waited.

A second later the door opened wide to reveal yet another man, but one the exact opposite of the kitchen guard.

This new guy was maybe five years younger than I was, and just as tall, but as thin as an excuse. He was movie star handsome, with hooded, emerald green eyes brimming with intelligence, although the moodiness in those eyes put me more in mind of Robert Mitchum than Sean Penn. The man possessed a rich, swarthy, olive-hued complexion, but there his Italian good looks ended. His razor-cut sandy hair above his aristocratic face he could have borrowed from an Irishman.

He lifted an eyebrow to the guard, the question unspoken.

My escort nodded. "He's clean."

The man turned his attention back to me, finally speaking. "Come in, Mr. Box. We've been expecting you."

I nearly swooned. His voice was a marvel, making me blink at its sheer beauty. Its tone was deep and smooth and mellifluous, like Ed O'Herlihy's on the old Kraft cheese TV commercials. If this guy ever flopped in the Mafia, he could always make it in talk radio.

I found myself smiling at him, even though I didn't want to—his voice was just that gorgeous—and followed him into the inner sanctum. The other man was left in the hall, presumably to take me back when I was done.

At least, I hoped I'd be leaving the same way I'd come in, on my own two feet. And I suppose that since I'd just been thoroughly frisked for weaponry, it didn't bother the new guy to lead the way inside.

Where the hallway had been austere, the room we were now entering was tastefully elegant. Quint would have felt right at home. The sea-green carpet was deep-pile cut, nicely setting off the mahogany paneling around it and the recessed lighting dotting the ceiling.

Back here, the restaurant sounds not thirty feet away simply ceased to exist. The soundproofing was excellent, nearly 100 hundred percent deadened. And that could have a downside. Anything could happen in this room, anything at all, and it wouldn't disturb the patrons scarfing their pies and quaffing their wine. I needed to keep that in mind.

The room's furnishings were as first-rate as its construction. I'm no connoisseur of such things, but the heavy black leather sofa against the wall, the solid-looking desk perched atop the Persian rug, and the deep, manly chairs scattered around all gave the appearance of a London smoking establishment. Oddly enough, there wasn't an ashtray around.

My guide pointed to one of the three dark club chairs arranged in a loose semicircle before the desk. The only objects I could see on it were a Tiffany lamp, what appeared to be a day planner, and a blotter with a heavy ink pen centered in the middle.

"Please, have a seat," the man intoned. "My father will be right out."

Father? Well sir. Then that would mean Mister Golden Throat here was none other than Vinny—excuse me, Vincent—Scarpetti, Tony's son ... and the more dangerous of the two, if Frank Buchessi could be believed. I needed to keep that in mind as well.

Lowering myself into the massive chair, I found it hard not to sigh with pleasure at the muted squeak of its rich skin. One of these would sure go dandy back in my own office. The chair, plus the rug. Well, they wouldn't really, but a man can dream.

Vinny, or Vincent, or whatever he wanted to call himself, chose to remain standing, taking up a position just behind me and to the right. I settled further back in the chair. If I was going to be in for a wait, I might as well get comfortable.

But I didn't have the chance to. Not thirty seconds later, a door on the left side of the room opened. Out of it rolled an old man in an electric wheelchair, his left hand zipping his trousers, while behind him a freshly flushed toilet gurgled merrily.

Although the man himself was wizened and gray, his black eyes were hawk-sharp, taking me in all at once. His thin lips mashed in a line as he gave me a curt nod. Unless I missed my guess, this was Scarpetti senior, alias Tony C, alias Tony the Cutter, alias Mad Tony, the *capo di tutti capo* of Cincinnati. The Mafia don.

My bowels clenched, and suddenly that toilet looked awfully necessary.

For me.

But I resisted the urge to dash in there, instead remaining

seated. For some reason it seemed important for me not to stand up in deference to him. Whether it was God's leading not to give respect, or my own cussedness, I don't know, but there I stayed.

If that upset the old man, he didn't let on. He just continued staring at me as he wheeled himself behind the desk. I stared back, not wanting to speak first. Childish, huh?

On reaching his destination, Tony Scarpetti leaned forward, folding his large, wrinkled hands in front of him on the blotter. As I regarded them, those hands seemed so ordinary. Hard to believe the knives they'd wielded, the guns they'd caressed, the windpipes they'd throttled.

Scarpetti cleared his throat, sounding for all the world like a pit bulldog growling. "You Box?" he said at last, as if he didn't know that already.

No, I'm J. Edgar Hoover. That's what I nearly said, but didn't. What I in fact said was, "Yep."

The old man nodded again, then looked past me at his son.

Vincent spoke up in pear-shaped tones. "He's clean, Pop. Lou checked him." Lou, I guess, was the man who'd frisked me.

Scarpetti cranked his head my way, his voice a rumble. "Frank tells me you got some questions." Buchessi, I took it he meant.

I made my reply just as flat. "That's right."

"Questions ..." Scarpetti's tone was contemplative as he lightly scratched his chin with a thick yellow thumbnail. "Sometimes, y'know, they're not entirely healthy things to have."

"I know that, Mr. Scarpetti." I knew where he was going with this, and figured to cut him off at the pass. "My questions have nothing to do with your business."

"Everything's my business," he replied cryptically. "And it's not 'Mr. Scarpetti.' You are here at my pleasure. You will address me as Don Scarpetti, or you will not address me at all." Behind me, Vincent snorted a suppressed laugh.

"All I'm here for is some background, sir. That's all."

The old man nodded. "On Kitty Clark. On where I stood with her, and her with me. Frank told me that too. Asking about the two of us is also not an entirely healthy idea."

I shifted in my chair. Suddenly it didn't seem as comfortable as it had a minute ago. "Anything you tell me stays in the strictest confidence, Mister ... I mean, Don Scarpetti." I figured I'd go ahead and humor the old gangster. The alternative if I didn't do so being something I really didn't want to consider. "In this room or out of it," I went on. "The last thing I want to do is to get on your bad side."

Scarpetti's rubbery, purple lips twisted up in a sardonic grin as he held his bent right index finger out at me. "*That,* I can believe." Behind me, Vincent sniggered again.

The older mobster sighed, settling back in the wheelchair's seat as he laced his fingers across his withered midsection. "I heard Kitty's been having trouble. That's the only reason I'm even listening to ya. What kind of trouble, that I ain't heard."

"How could you have possibly known that?" I blurted without thinking.

His chuckle sounded like somebody dragging a rusty bike chain across macadam. "Out of respect for the lady, and our past, you got three minutes. Go."

I hoped I could get it said in three minutes. The only auctioneer I'd ever known was my second cousin Horace, and he'd died of lockjaw. But I dove in anyway.

"I know you financed the start of Kitty's career," I said. "And in all likelihood you also paid a computer genius to seal off the records of the years before she came to you. But as interesting as that is, that's not what I'm here for." I moved my weight around on the chair once again. "Don Scarpetti, here's the long and the short of it. Kitty's hired me to investigate some threats that have been made against her."

He frowned, leaning forward. "Threats? What kind of threats?"

I shook my head. "I'm not sure. And that's just the problem. They're not real threats, nothing you could pin down. Just anonymous notes and letters, revealing parts of her life that only she knows. Well her, and maybe her ex-husband."

I took a chance, then, staring hard at him. "And maybe you."

Behind me, I heard Vincent softly hiss.

Scarpetti narrowed his eyes, his tone dark. "Y'know, time was, Box, a guy said to me what you just did, he'd be carried out of here feet first and bleeding. On his way to the hospital. Or the morgue. Time was." He smiled then. "Good thing for you I'm sick."

I'd noticed his face in fact carried an unhealthy reddish mottle, and I went for crazy-brave. "But you could still have it done, couldn't you?"

His smile grew. "Sure. It's easy. Lots of people owe me favors. Of different sizes. Many are in my debt. They would consider it an honor to pay one off, *capisce*? An honor to me."

Scarpetti rubbed his hands together, the sound dry as sand whispering across a crypt.

"I could buzz for Lou," he went on. "He'd do it, and like it. Or I could give you a session with Carmine. You met Carmine when he let you in the kitchen. A session with Carmine would be very interesting for you, Box. A time long remembered." A vein began throbbing in the old man's neck.

"Carmine is the big guy?" I said. "Little bitty ears? Cab-forward head?" Scarpetti nodded, and I said, "Yeah. We've met."

The mobster started to answer, but I cut him off, plowing ahead. "Don Scarpetti, it's like you said before, you're a man that can get things done. And that's what Kitty needs right about now. Somebody that can get to the bottom of this. Because the fact is she's scared spitless of this mystery person."

He didn't answer, and I went on, "I also know that you two have some kind of a history together, but that's not the reason I'm here tonight. I'm just thinking maybe you could use your influence to help her find out exactly who it is that's got her so upset."

Instead of replying, Scarpetti just stared at me, the vein now writhing like mad, his face gone completely blood red. I guessed my three minutes were up. I stared back at him.

His gaze continued, unbroken, and I shifted uncomfortably. We went like that a few more seconds, each looking at the other like a calf at a new gate.

What the devil—?

I've done a lot of fun things in my life, but this wasn't one of them. But no way I was going to break eye contact first, however long it took. I had my reputation to consider, after all. I've always been pretty good at these contests, even as a kid, driving my older cousin Ray crazy with it.

But after another ten seconds had passed, with neither of us saying anything, I found it wasn't as much fun as I remembered. Behind me, Vincent had grown deathly quiet.

I was just starting to think of how weird this whole thing was getting, when it got a whole lot weirder.

Suddenly Scarpetti went, *"Uhhhhh …"* really loudly, and his mouth flopped open. Then his eyes went completely out of focus. Threadlike, a long, thin tendril of brown saliva began stretching down out of the corner of his mouth, heading for the blotter.

And then the old man giggled like a schoolgirl.

I stood up in shock. "Lord have mercy," I muttered, only to feel the weight of Vincent's hand pressing me back down into my chair.

"It's all right, Mr. Box," he said. "It's nothing I haven't seen before."

He walked around to the side of the desk where his father sat, tittering away, running his thick fingers through the swirls of spit on the blotter in front of him. Vincent leaned in, putting his own fingers on the desk's edge and pressed something underneath it once.

Almost instantly the door I'd come in swung wide, revealing my good friend Lou. A nasty-looking SIG 9mm hand cannon filled his palm. His expression was grim. He took one glance at Scarpetti senior, then swung the gun at me.

"Put it away, Lou." Vincent's dulcet speech was utterly calm. "Pop's had another episode. Take him home. Leave the wheelchair. I'll spare him that indignity. When you arrive back at the mansion, call the doctor. You know the one I mean. Go out the side entrance."

Lou nodded once and crossed the room with purposeful steps. Reaching the old man, he tenderly lifted him from the wheelchair, sliding his arm around the mobster's back. Without even seeming to strain, Lou half-pulled, half-dragged the staggering Scarpetti to a door on the opposite side of the room. Pulling it open with his left hand, the old man still securely held, they both stepped through it and were gone.

Vincent walked over and shut the door. When he turned back to me, his voice was wintry. "Well. I suppose a word of explanation is called for."

"No need for that. Frank filled me in about your dad's condition."

Vincent's eyebrows rose. "Really? That's not like him. Frank's never told anyone else about it. I don't think so, anyway." The younger man frowned. "This is extremely disturbing. I'll need to speak with him about it. First thing tomorrow."

I hoped I hadn't just signed Buchessi's death warrant.

"He told me about himself, too, and his own illness," I rushed on. "I wouldn't be too hard on him, if I were you."

"But you aren't me, nor will you ever be in my position."

Unlike his voice, Vincent's smile wasn't a bit pretty, and he cupped his left elbow in his right hand, his left forefinger curled on his chin.

"You know, I've always fancied myself a fairly good judge of character, Mr. Box," he said. "Would you like me to give you a thumbnail view of how I read you?"

"Sure," I shrugged, wondering where we were going with this.

"You want mercy for Frank. I mete out justice. You go out of your way for others. Most of the time. And I decide what's best for me. Always." Vincent's lips pulled away from his teeth as he dropped his hands. "How am I doing so far? Did I peg you right, or didn't I?" I didn't answer, and he went on, "So which way will it go for our talkative, errant Frank?" The younger man now held out both hands, palms up. "Mercy, or justice?"

Vincent's chuckle sounded downright harsh to my ears. "Yin and yang will decide it, Mr. Box. Not you. Not me. But this." He gently bobbed each hand up and down. "Life's dichotomy will have its way, the delicate dance. Because, at the end of the game, we each call our own tune, no 'Lord's mercy' required."

I regarded him with what approached pity. "Do you really believe that?"

"With all my soul." Again he chuckled. "Assuming I have one."

No doubt about it, tomorrow would prove to be a hard day for Frank Buchessi. It's not like I'd forced him to be so gabby, though. Cold comfort, but it was all I had.

Sighing, Vincent sat down in the chair so lately vacated by his father, slowly rubbing his hands on its tubular arms. It was obvious—to me, at least—in his mind he was just counting the days until Tony had an "episode" he didn't come back from. The rights of succession.

Unconsciously striking his father's pose, Vincent clasped his hands, leaning in. When he did, he nearly put them down on the blotter, right in the puddle of Tony's drool glistening there. He only stopped himself at the last second. With a loud, disgusted oath Vincent violently swept the blotter to the floor. A few seconds passed, then he drew a breath and seemed to compose himself.

"Mr. Box," he said, now back in control. "Out of respect for my father's wish to share this information with you, and only that respect, I'll continue where he left off. Then you shall leave this establishment, and not come back. Ever."

Respect. There was that word again. What was it with these Mafia types, that they give each other the consideration they deny the rest of the world?

The younger mobster went on evenly, "And after you've left, on your journey home to whatever hovel you inhabit, I'll leave it to your probably too-vivid imagination as to what will happen should what we discuss here become public knowledge."

Unbidden, the picture of me crucified upside down to a tree came to mind.

And why not? Frank told me Vincent had already done it once before, to the Puerto Rican guy. He probably wasn't shy about doing it again, if the need arose.

My smile was as firm as I could make it. "Not a problem. Like you said, my imagination is way too active as it is."

He just nodded. "So where were we before our interruption?"

Vincent's tone was utterly calm as he placed his folded hands on the now-clean surface. This man could give sharks lessons in coldheartedness.

"Kitty Clark," was all I said.

"Her" He nodded again. The way he'd said that single word was packed with meaning. "My father has told me all about his dealings with that woman. Many times."

"Dealings?"

Vincent's voice was still uniform. "Dealings such as how once Kitty had been established as a bona fide star to the world, she repaid my father's generosity by disavowing him completely, not even deigning to send him so much as a card on his birthday." He shrugged. "Simply put, Mr. Box, that callous, gaudy shrew broke his heart. Sometimes I think he still grieves."

Had this guy really just used the word 'callous'? Unbelievable.

"That's not how I heard it," I said. "I heard it was an amicable parting."

I studiously avoided mentioning the fact it was Frank Buchessi who'd told me that. Maybe if I didn't say his name anymore, Vincent would forget whatever he'd planned for him tomorrow.

Yeah, and if pigs had saddles, they'd be thoroughbreds.

"Truth can be a ... slippery commodity." Vincent's beautifully haunting voice was still cold. "Many times—check that, most of the time—truth is only what we say it is."

I really didn't feel like getting into a philosophical discussion with the son of a Mafia chieftain, debating the differences between faith and nihilism, so I just let it slide.

"So do you have any idea who could be doing this to her?" I asked him.

"None at all." Vincent's smile was now arctic. "And I don't care. To my mind it's sweet revenge, but years too late."

Venom fairly dripped from his words. "During my boyhood years, it was always 'Kitty this,' and 'Kitty that' coming from my father, like he was a smitten teenager." The other man nodded. "And you're correct, Pop did call in some favors with a sympathetic judge to have Kitty's records sealed back in the fifties, even before the advent of computers. After their arrival, he continued to fund that sealing, through means that need not concern you. And although later she utterly rejected him, he never got over her. Even today, forty years on, he still speaks of her with fondness."

Like he doesn't speak about you, I thought. As galling as it was for me to admit it, I was beginning to think I had something in common with this man. I knew exactly what he was feeling.

With Vincent, it was his father's love affair with a woman he'd groomed for worldly success, to the exclusion of all else, resulting ultimately in the exclusion of his own son. With me, it was my father's love affair with booze, ending with that same exclusion. In our own way, Vincent and I had each been crippled because of those warped loves.

"If I knew who was doing this to that harridan," Vincent went on, "causing her so much pain and distress, I wouldn't consider stopping him. As a matter of fact, I'd cheer him on, and buy him a drink. Ten drinks. If that didn't do it, I'd buy him a whole distillery, with taps for the barrels."

"You really hate her, don't you?"

"Hate's another nebulous word, like truth," he said. "If you mean, do I hate her like I hate braised liver, then no. If you mean, do I hate her and wish her dead, then yes."

"Why not do it, then?" I couldn't believe I'd just said that. But surely I hadn't planted a thought that hadn't already been there. Unlike I'd done with poor Frank.

"I'm still my father's son," Vincent said. "And his feelings come first." He gazed meaningfully at the door Tony had been carted out of. "For the time being, anyway."

The unsaid conclusion of that being, Vincent Scarpetti would have Kitty taken care of in his own time, when he was in the position to do it with impunity. When Tony was finally dead. And there wasn't Thing One I could do to stop that day when it came.

I knew I'd done no good here at all, and I stood. "Thanks for your time. No need to get up. I can see my own way out."

Vincent's look of dismissal at me was calcimine as he tented his fingers. "As you wish. Be sure to give Kitty my best."

His smile was a grimace. "Tell her I'll see her soon."

11

*T*o say I didn't sleep well when I got home that night would be an understatement. The dreams I had were fierce. I found myself on a long black beach under a scalloped sky, alternately being chased by Tony Scarpetti, his son Vincent, Carmine the Human Goalpost, and another shadowy figure I feared more than all of them.

Once, for some odd reason, I found myself fleeing Kitty Clark, her pruny lips crinkled up as she stretched out her hands toward me. As she ran, she kept saying, "Give us a kiss, Joe, give us a kiss." Wow. And I couldn't even blame pepperoni pizza for this one; Noodles and I had split the last of the Frosted Flakes before we'd gone to bed.

The next morning found me cranky and on edge, as if some vandal had coated my mattress with sand. Even Noodles picked up on it, and kept his distance as I wolfed down three chocolate donuts and a half-pot of coffee before it was even six a.m. Between the sugar rush and the caffeine high, I was loaded for bear, in perfect form to meet Angela's abusive ex-husband. If the guy even looked at me crossways, I planned to feed him his left arm.

It was seven when I called her. "Hey, it's me. What time am I picking you up?"

"Noon, I suppose." Then she sighed. "You're really going through with this, huh? Sticking close to me."

"Like a tick on a beagle," I said. "We discussed this yesterday."

"Yes, and I'm still less than happy about it."

I didn't bother replying to that. Normally I go out of my way to avoid saying or doing anything that would cause Angela stress, but this time wasn't one of them.

"Pick me up at RiverTower," she said. "Main entrance." Then she hung up.

First Kitty Clark, then Vincent Scarpetti, and now Angela. Evidently this was my week to upset people. Next on my list would be Noodles. Not that he's a person, you understand, but the analogy holds.

I showered and dressed, then refilled his food and water bowls. Again. The way that cat goes through food, he must have a tapeworm in him the size of a garden hose. After that was done, it still wasn't yet eight o'clock. I'd done about all I felt like doing around the apartment, so I headed over to the office, to do more of the same there.

When I arrived, Toni was with a customer, Mr. Yee/Lee was cussing out his balky printing press in flawless, incomprehensible Mandarin, and Reggie Allenby was out on a sales call. That left nobody to talk to except the picture of my dead wife I keep on top of the file cabinet, and I didn't want to go there right then.

Seeing as how I was between cases, with time hanging heavy, I spent the next hour sitting in my office chair, doing my Steve McQueen routine from *The Great Escape*, the one where he bounced a baseball off the walls of the "cooler" the Nazi guards had kept him in. I used a scuffed-up tennis ball with the fuzz gone, caroming it off the far wall, the floor, and back to me, over and over.

I'd gotten up to eighty-one times without a miss when Mr. Yee/Lee pounded on his ceiling with a broom, screaming at me to cut it out, already. At least, that's what I assume he said; who could tell from up here?

Finally it was eleven thirty, and time to head to RiverTower.

Arriving at the fifteen-story-high complex, I found Angela already outside the construction fence, waiting. It appeared she'd thawed some as she gave me a peck on the cheek after climbing in the Yugo.

Well, boy howdy, things are looking up, I thought, as I put it in gear and we began heading back in toward town, and Cullen's. The address of his apartment was deep in the Over-the-Rhine section of Cincinnati. The weird name bears some explaining.

As the city's historians tell it, many years ago a wide canal ran down the middle of what's now Central Parkway. The neighborhood surrounding it then was populated by a large number of German immigrants who'd come to ply their trade on the killing floors of area stockyards, and it was they who'd dubbed the canal the "Rhine," after the large river in their native country.

And that's how the community came to be known as Over-the-Rhine.

A charming story, but there it ends. The canal is a hundred years and more gone, filled in and paved over, and most of the descendants of those stockyard workers live quiet, industrious lives in the white-bread suburbs of Western Hills or Covedale or Delhi.

The classy brownstones the thrifty Deutchlanders erected

have degenerated into crack houses or worse, and the whole blighted area is now known for its murder rates, prostitution, and gang warfare. On any given day or night, on any given street corner, more high-risk drug traffic is plied in Over-the-Rhine than either Jerry Rubin (a Cincinnati native, oddly enough) or Timothy Leary could have imagined in their best pharmaceutically-induced rhapsody.

And Mitch Cullen's apartment house was right in the middle of it.

"Apartment house" may be a bit of a misnomer. The building we were approaching did indeed contain apartments, but it should be noted the "house" part once carried the prefix "slaughter."

A few years back, in yet another frantic stab at reclaiming the area, an enterprising group of Swiss investors had converted the dowdy old Schloss sausage works into a trendy dwelling designed to command obscenely high rents from its yuppie tenants. When it was unveiled, the complex, now known as the Vine Street Galleria, had made the news, and I'm sure old Mitch felt quite smug in his new digs.

But the way I looked at it, the poetic justice of a violent evolutionary U-turn like Mitch Cullen residing in a rehabbed German meat-packing plant was almost too delicious for words. I don't think the irony was lost on Angela.

I know it wasn't on me.

We drove slowly, vainly trying to find an open slot. The looks we were getting from the few visible residents were as vacant as the burned-out buildings they lolled in front of. Parking was at a premium here; why, I don't know. It was obvious most of the vehicles lining the street hadn't been moved since heck was a pup, as my granny used to say.

"I still think you should have stayed home," I told Angela as we swerved, narrowly missing a pothole deep enough to hide Saddam Hussein.

"And I still say that would have been pointless," she retorted. "I'm the one Mitch wants to see. Remember, I'm the one who was married to him."

"I'm trying to forget that," I said. Then I added, "'Fess up, Ange. Did you bring me along today for my sparkling company, or for my bulldog-like protection?"

"I didn't 'bring you along' at all. You insisted on coming."

I grinned. "Yeah, I did, didn't I?"

We drove on a ways. In one of the recessed abandoned store doorways we passed, I saw a decrepit old wino drop his pants and squat down, right in open view. Thankfully Angela was looking out the other side of the car and missed that show. I shook my head.

"*Caramba.* What kind of a person would live here on purpose?"

Still staring, she murmured, "Any kind you'd care to name. Con men, alcoholics, transients, petty thieves, drug-crazed teenagers, the down and out, the hopeless, the insane … And prostitutes. Like that one there."

I followed her gaze.

What Angela was looking at was a heavily made-up woman tottering around on scuffed yellow platform shoes, clutching the tiniest black purse I'd ever seen. Her blondish wig, which to me looked the tragic aftermath of an explosion in a weasel factory, crowned a face as seamed as a dried apple.

The woman's age could have been anywhere between thirty and sixty, and she was dressed, if you could call it that, in a torn leather miniskirt topped by a dirty, too-tight green bodice. She started to grin drunkenly at our car as we passed, the grin only disappearing when she saw Angela sitting next to me.

Then we were past her.

Angela craned her head back toward the creature before resuming looking out the windshield, her expression unreadable.

"I think I know that woman," she said after a moment. "Or at least one like her. Women selling their bodies for money, or for a chemical high to escape their wretchedness." She paused, still gazing out the window, then said, "The kind of woman I once was." Pity glistened in her eyes as she met mine. "Good heavens, Joe, this is such an awful place. I got free, but not these people. They're still trapped in their misery. Whoever first said 'there, but for the grace of God, go I' spoke truer words than he knew."

I reached over and squeezed her hand. "We don't have to do this, you know."

"You don't." She swallowed. "But I have to." We drove on in silence.

Finally we spotted an opening in front of a series of sagging row houses, still a block back from Cullen's address. I figured it was as close as we'd likely get, especially with the weather beginning to turn sour, and with only minimal jockeying I squeezed our car in between a couple of wrecks. The one in front was a faded blue Toyota Camry of mid-80s vintage, swaybacked and satchel-fannied and sitting on tires as bald as Vin Diesel's head. The car in back of us was a dusty gold '65 Ford Mustang, always one of my favorites.

Shutting the Yugo off, we got out. I took a glance at the Ford and shook my head. While the paint job was okay, the ride would have been cherry if someone hadn't flamed out the entire interior in the dim past. All that was left now was melted plastic, burned leather, bare wires, and stench. Not for the first time was I glad we'd taken the Yugo. The little beast was in good company here. Anything vandals did to it would take me days to notice.

I pocketed the keys as we started walking. We didn't encounter any more winos or, thankfully for Angela's sake, any more hookers. A few lewd catcalls floated from the darkened doorways we crossed, along with drug offers and worse, and she gripped my hand tightly. I squeezed back in reassurance. A bit further on, and at last we were there.

As I said before, the opening of this building had made the local news, but the small television screen really hadn't done it justice. Somebody once said that watching a dying neighborhood going through a resurrection is a sight to gladden the heart. Maybe, but it's still a jarring experience to encounter an elegant structure like the Galleria fronting a dirty, trash-blown street, bracketed by dilapidated wrecks on its left and right as its sisters.

The new owners had removed the Schloss signs and sandblasted the brick exterior, leaving the high mullioned window frames in place. Instead of the original industrial pane, they now contained gold-colored, thermal-sealed glass. Topiaries in large copper urns stood on either side of the lustrous oak and beveled-glass front doors, and a jade-green awning with the building's name in script on the side jutted out over the sidewalk, a sidewalk that appeared new, but I noticed stopped exactly at the property's edge.

Underneath the awning stood a smiling blond six-foot-tall doorman, just like the kind you'd see in the movies, wearing clean white gloves and a uniform that wouldn't have looked out of place in the Turkish navy. His toothy smile dipped slightly as he held the door for Angela and me; I guess his radar told him we didn't belong in such a place, at least I didn't. But he was

well-trained, and his only comment as we entered was a murmured "good day, folks."

The inside of the place was about like I'd thought it would
be, but I cranked my head around anyway, staring like a rube. I
was struck by the similarity between this lobby and the Ohio
Hilton's. The polished-brass-and-imported-fern traveling salesman obviously had made a killing here too, with the end result
being both glossy interiors finished out about two degrees richer
than they had to be.

Angela and I strode over to the elevator bank and punched
the button on the first one we came to. We walked inside the
richly appointed car and the door slid closed. As we rose, I
leaned in toward the buffed brass control panel and bared my
teeth at my reflection, checking them for crud.

"Classy place your ex-hubby has," I said blandly.

Angela poked me in the side. "I expect you to be on your
best behavior here."

"Always," I smiled. "Anything for good old Mitch."

"I mean it, Joe," she said darkly. "This is for Mitch's sake. It
may be his last chance to get right with God."

"I know that, Ange. I aim to keep my trap shut. I'll only open
it if things threaten to turn interesting."

"I don't want them to 'turn interesting.' You're here to chaperone. Nothing more."

I made as if I was touching an invisible cap. "I live to serve,
ma'am."

She blew out a breath and shook her head. "You're incorri-
gible."

I grinned. "At the very least."

Finally we reached the sixth floor, the "Executive Suites"
level as the label on the control panel so tastefully put it, and the

doors silently opened. We walked out onto plush, tight-weaved, maroon Berber wall-to-wall carpet that must have cost fifty dollars a square foot.

As we began strolling down the butter-cream painted hallway, I noticed we were being accompanied by soft chamber music coming from somewhere. I looked up and around, frowning.

After a few more steps I stopped and leaned over a potted bushy plant, parting the stalks with my fingers.

"Joe!" Angela hissed, drawing up short. "What are you doing?"

"Looking to see where the devil that music is coming from." I was working my way down toward the mulch chips. "There has to be a hidden speaker in here somewhere."

She lightly slapped my shoulder. "Quit that! You act like you've never been anywhere nice before."

"I don't know," I said, straightening. "Your place is nice. Church is nice. Vietnam, now that wasn't nice. Neither was the shack I grew up in." I stared down the hall. "And I'm starting to get the feeling that, regardless of the swellness of this building, Mitch's apartment isn't going to be nice."

"What do you mean?"

"I don't know. Just a sense."

"That 'fey' thing again?"

"I don't know," I said again. "Maybe. What could he be involved in that would be stirring it up?" She didn't answer.

Once again we started walking, checking the numbers on the doors. Discounting the music wafting by, the hall was as silent as Grant's tomb.

Then we were there.

"Six twenty-one, right?" I asked.

Angela checked the piece of paper in her hand. "Yes."

"Odd it isn't six six six," I said as I rapped the door smartly with my knuckles.

We waited. A moment later the door noiselessly opened, and I got my first good look at Mitch Cullen. As I did, I reflected that in my various talks with Angela, with all her experiences with this man, I'd never before asked her what he looked like.

Maybe I wanted to see him for myself, to savor the prime moment of encountering the kind of scum who wouldn't think twice about the wrongness of bashing in a woman's head with a fireplace poker. Right about then my Southern-bred deference to the fairer sex threatened to rise up, and it was only with a will I managed to force it back down.

As the apartment door swung wide, I'm not really sure what it was exactly I expected. Whenever the term "artist" is bandied about, I think of milky esthetes with poor respiration and an aversion to direct sunlight.

Mitch Cullen wasn't like that in the slightest.

He was in his early fifties, darkly handsome, easily topping by an inch my own six-foot-three height, his longish brown-going-gray hair pulled tight into a ponytail. His barrel chest threatened to rip out of his stained denim work shirt, and as we sized each other up, I met eyes as flat and gray as burnished gunmetal.

He didn't speak or blink and neither did I, giving him back gaze for gaze. I suppose we'd be standing there still, like two kids squaring off in a schoolyard, if Angela hadn't spoken up.

"Mitch." She'd said his name coolly. "You're looking well."

Looking over at her, Cullen's face split into a smile, showing capped teeth as white and even as the crosses at Arlington.

"Hello, Blaze," he said. "Forget well. You look fabulous."

Blaze? The only name that came to mind was Blaise Pascal, the French philosopher. Unless … that was Angela's *street* name?

All by itself, my right hand began to ball into a fist.

She must have sensed that and she reached down and placed her hand over mine. It relaxed, and as our fingers inter-twined, I almost grinned. By that simple wordless action Angela had said, *I'm with him, Mitch, not you.*

Hah. Eat my dust, jerk.

"Mitch, I'd like you to meet Joe Box," she said. "Joe, Mitch Cullen."

Reluctantly I pulled my hand free and held it out.

"It's a pleasure," I said. Well, it wasn't really, but Granny always told me that's what polite people are supposed to say.

After a moment's hesitation, Cullen did the same, his hand closing around mine. As we started to shake, he tightened his grip more firmly than was necessary, his smile unchanged as he began compressing my bones.

Oh, yeah? I knew this game. I returned the constriction, squeezing just as hard.

Here's the thing. I'd grown up on a farm, the poor kind, and when I was older any milking that was to be done naturally fell to me. As a result, over the years I developed a bonegrinder that can bring most men to their knees, never mind a bozo like Mitch.

He felt the power bearing down and his eyes widened as his smile slipped a bit. But he was game, and tried to match it. I sim-ply increased the pressure.

You're the artist, dolt, not me, I thought, as we continued to shake. *And your hands are more important. Let's see what you've got.* We both continued to mash harder.

Sweat was now beading Cullen's upper lip, and a second

later as we broke contact, I was perversely pleased he'd let go first. *Winner and still champ, Joe Box.*

"Well, come on in, both of you." Cullen was trying for gruff brightness, like the contest he'd lost didn't count. But I saw him surreptitiously flexing his fingers as he tried to mask the pain just the same. "Take a look around."

We did, and it was all I could do not to whistle at the surroundings. Like the man himself, Cullen's place wasn't a thing like I'd thought it would be. Regardless of his tony address, I was somehow expecting a failed-artist's keep—a cramped, dark, dingy warren, redolent of rat droppings and candle wax.

Not hardly.

Before us spread a spacious, open expanse, all one big room, well-lit not only by the decorator floor lamps standing about but by huge skylights above. Taking up the far third of the room were massive benches covered in metallic scraps, and flanked by large, upright, painted cylinders. From my days as a youth working on hot rods, I recognized the things as acetylene and oxygen tanks. In between the benches squatted a heat-discolored metal monstrosity, at least six feet tall and just as wide, obviously Cullen's latest project.

He pointed to some Danish modern furniture to our left. "Have a seat."

Angela and I took the sofa, and within three seconds of my weight settling I knew I wouldn't be in it long. The thing might as well have had "back sprain special" stitched in needlepoint on the cushions. The Danes may be whizzes at pastries, but in my estimation their furniture skills lay somewhere to the east of the Goths.

"Wow, I love what you've done to the place," I said. Right. Regardless of the brightness of the room, the effect was totally ruined by small hideous statuary scattered around, and bloody paintings stuck to the walls, evidence, to me at least, of a twisted mind.

I found myself staring at a horrid framed something that for all the world looked like a rendering of a flayed pig, mouth open in mid-scream. Art, I guess. I noticed Angela was studiously avoiding looking at it.

Cullen frowned as he took a chair to the side. "You were in this building before they rehabbed it?"

I pulled my eyes away from the monstrosity. "No," I grinned, "I just love what you've done, that's all." Angela gave me a sharp kick on the ankle. "Although it pains me to say that," I added.

Cullen shook his head. "At the rents they get here, somebody better love it."

"So you're doing pretty well for yourself, huh?" I leaned back, lacing my fingers behind my head. Angela shot me a look.

I feigned innocence. "What? I just think it's great that Mitch is doing so well. You'd be surprised at what some folks have to do for money. It ought to be a crime." I smiled at him. "You'd agree with that, wouldn't you, Mitch?"

He cocked his head, his tone pensive. "You know, pal, you've been in my house less than a minute, and already I don't like you much."

I shrugged, still smiling. "Take a number. And I'm not your pal."

Cullen looked at Angela. "I'd really prefer he not be here, Blaze. There are a few things we need to discuss."

She scooted a millimeter closer to me. "Whatever you need to say can be said in front of Joe."

"Goody," I said. "I hate being excluded." My smile slipped a bit as I looked at the guy. "And don't call Angela 'Blaze' again.

145

Or you and I will have some things to discuss."

Cullen just laughed. "Odd. I don't believe I asked your permission."

Undoing my fingers, I started to fire off a reply, but Angela spoke first. "Please, the both of you, just stop."

We stared at each other a moment longer, then Cullen broke eye contact. He turned his attention back to Angela.

"I'm wondering why you agreed to my invitation in the first place," he said. "As I remember, the last thing you said in my presence was that you never wanted to see me or hear my voice again."

"You violated that last Christmas," Angela replied, "when you called me."

"I'm surprised you talked with me at all that night," Cullen admitted. "And even more surprised you so readily agreed to come here today."

He leaned forward, clasping his little-bitty-weak girly-man hands together. "May I ask why? I mean, I know what it is I want to ask *you*, but what is it you're after here? Another debate on religion?"

Undoing his hands, he cocked his thumb at that nasty thing on the wall.

"If you're still into that Jesus trip, you might as well know that over the past few years I've gotten rather far afield of whatever version of God you're into. So I imagine we're still worlds apart in our beliefs."

That explained the feeling I got in the hall.

"So what else could it be?" he went on. "Money? If it's alimony you're wanting, we're a couple of decades past that. Ask a judge."

"I don't want anything from you, Mitch," Angela said flatly.

"Least of all alimony."

"Well, good," he said, straightening. "Seeing as how you're not getting any."

I didn't care for Cullen's snotty tone, really did not, but I kept my yap shut. Angela seemed to be giving as good as she got. So far.

"What's your purpose in coming here, then?" he said.

Her reply was even. "To save your immortal soul."

Cullen laughed, a raucous sound. "I'll be a son of a gun. I was right the first time. More religious crapola. Here I'm all set to offer you a business proposal, and you want to talk to me about God." He shook his head, still chuckling. "Blaze, my love, you haven't changed a bit."

I held up my index finger. "That's one."

He looked at me. "What?"

"Nothing," I smiled, putting my hand back in my lap.

Before Cullen could reply, Angela beat him to it. "You're wrong, Mitch. I *have* changed. You may not believe it, but once was a time that if I'd been offered the chance of watching you die horribly, at the cost of my own life, I wouldn't have hesitated a second."

She regarded him with more pity than he deserved, in my opinion.

"But I've grown," she said. "Now I know you're in just as much torment as I was."

"Oh, please." His sigh was theatrical. "Save it for the choir."

"The choir doesn't need it," she replied. "You do."

"Be that as it may. Do you want to hear my proposition or not?"

She shrugged. "All right. But only with the proviso that when you're finished, I get one last turn."

Cullen nodded. "Agreed." He settled back in his seat. "What I'm offering you is the chance for you to really make your mark in this town." He motioned around with his hand. "As you've probably surmised by now, I've done well with my art over the years—"

It looked like he was gearing up for a speech, and I broke in on him. "I was wondering about that. For instance, that thing you're working on in the corner. What's it called again?"

Cullen looked at me as if I was wearing a sweat-stained John Deere cap, with a piece of hay between my teeth. His reply was arch. "'Confluence of Equality.' Like it?"

"It's different," I allowed. "But I was thinking. Seeing how it's six feet wide, how are you planning on a buyer ever getting it out of here to take home?"

"It's not meant to be sold," he answered with exaggerated patience. "It's meant to be therapy. I only work on it to relax, to free my muse. I designed it to be broken down and reassembled, as many times as I want." He shrugged. "You may not grasp the concept."

"Sure I do," I grinned. "Kind of like an Erector set for grown-ups."

Cullen's lip curl was better than Stallone's. "That's not the term I would choose."

"Whatever. But if I were you, I'd give it a different name."

"Really," he smiled. "I love a critic. So what would you call it?"

"'Big Rusty Iron Thing,'" I answered. "That gets me, Mitch—" I patted my chest with my fist—"right here. I mean it, man. It's guys like you that make me appreciate art."

Cullen shook his head at me in dismissal, not even deigning to comment as he again turned his attention to Angela.

"I've done a fair bit of traveling the past twenty years," he said, "but now I've come back here, to my roots. I'm finally ready to open up my own gallery, just off Fountain Square. I've timed it to coincide with the fountain's reopening. And I need someone with the drive and the vision to bring that gallery to life. The strength of vision to match mine."

His tone turned impassioned as he again leaned forward, staring hard at her. "You're right, you've grown. So have I, I think." Cullen smiled in what I'm sure he thought was a boyish way.

"You may not know this," he said, "but I've followed your career closely, ever since I heard you entered college to study architecture. And you've done well. No one can deny that. But now it's time to move to the next level. I believe you've got what it takes to make my vision a reality." He spread his hands. "Will you join me, Blaze?"

"That's two," I spoke up.

He turned to me. "What *are* you talking about?"

"Nothing," I smiled.

Cullen sighed, looking back at Angela. "I know it's a lot to ask," he said. "And I know how busy you are. I also know our beliefs don't mesh. But don't you see?" He clenched his fists. "That tension, our history, is exactly what will make this project fly. Because like it or not, you're the only one who truly understands what I'm trying to say through my work."

Angela didn't answer, and Cullen gritched around on his seat. "Look, I know in the past we've had our difficulties—"

I bent over in a coughing fit.

He glanced at me, then back at her. "Promise me this much. You'll think about it. Will you at least think about it?"

"I don't need to," Angela answered without hesitation. "The answer is no."

"What?" Poor guy, he almost sounded hurt. "But why?"

"Because God is saying no," she said.

Cullen frowned. "I don't understand."

"I know." Angela's smile was tender. "Mitch, what you thought was a passing fad all those years ago is my life now. Serving God is what I do. Serving him first in everything. That includes making business decisions. And who I make them with."

She reached over and gently touched Cullen's hand. "I only take jobs my heavenly Father gives me the green light to take. You can't believe how many headaches I've saved myself by listening to him, how many traps I've avoided. And unfortunately," she sighed, "I'm getting a real check in my spirit here. So I'm sorry, the answer has to be no."

Cullen was still staring hard at her. "I'll pay twice your fee. Three times. Name it."

Angela's laugh was tinged with sadness. "Mitch, Mitch, you really don't get it, do you? This isn't about money. It's never been about money. It's about obedience. You could offer me a hundred times my fee, and the answer would still be no." She again shook her head. "As I said, I really am sorry. But I can recommend—"

"Save it," Cullen snarled, jumping to his feet. "Just save it."

Angela straightened. "All right, fine. I've heard you out. Now it's my turn."

"You can save that, too," he snapped. "I wasn't interested in your God then, and I'm not interested now. Not when he's 'told' you that I'm not good enough for your business."

"That's not the question—" she started, but Cullen cut her off with a disgusted wave.

"You were right," he spat. "You've changed, yeah. For the

worse. What started as a religious aberration has deteriorated into an obsession. You're sick, but you don't see it."

"*I'm* sick?" Angela said in disbelief, but Cullen went on as if he hadn't heard her.

"I offer you a year's pay for two month's work, and you turn up your nose. Refusing me, the best thing you ever had in your life. And all because of that filth religion of yours." He shook his head. "It's intolerant bigots like you that are destroying the arts everywhere. It was a mistake asking you to come here. I know that now."

And the next words that fell out of Cullen's mouth were incredibly stupid, even for him.

"I really believe I should have hit you harder all those years ago, Blaze," he said. "You might have turned out differently."

"And that's three," I said as I stood up, and smashed my fist square into the middle of Cullen's completely unprepared face.

He went down like a felled oak, and Angela gaped at me.

But the guy was tough, I'll have to give him that, and with hot copper blood pouring from his split gums, he got to his feet. Rugged as he was, he was slow as molasses at Christmas as he swung a punch at my face that seemed to come from a different area code. I blocked it easily and threw my weight into my left, sinking it deep into his gut, and again he crashed to the floor. Angela grabbed my arm.

"No, Joe!" she pleaded. "No more!"

I looked at her a moment, then pointed at him where he lay. "Stay down, dimwit."

The devil must be growing some profoundly dumb followers these days, because I watched in wonder Cullen roll onto his hands and knees, preparing once more to get up.

Shaking my head, I was setting my feet to have another go

when I felt Angela's tug.

"Enough, Joe," she said. "Please."

Amazingly, I saw her eyes were filling with tears. For me? Or for him?

I sighed, and looked down at him. "You never deserved this woman, Cullen. If it were up to me, I'd beat you from now until suppertime. Consider this your lucky day. Think on it often."

Head hanging, blood dangling in thick strings from his mouth, he nodded.

I turned to Angela. "Are we done here?"

A single tear ran down her cheek as she stared at her former husband, who was still on his hands and knees. "God help him, we're done." We began walking away.

The door was almost before us when my spine started tingling.

I turned in disbelief to find Cullen had somehow gotten to his feet. Worse, he was clutching a large, nasty piece of angle iron in his meaty fist. Worst of all, he was swinging that piece of heat-seared metal at my head as if his life depended on it.

I ducked as Angela screamed, the object whizzing past.

Cullen tottered, off-balance. Before he could recover I stepped in and began raining blows on him, each word punctuated by a grunt. "I. Told. You. To. Stay. *Down.*"

That last bit was accompanied by my left fist crashing into his jaw, and with that Angela's ex crumpled to the floor for a final time like an imploded building.

Blood drops the size of pennies were welling up on my knuckles, my poor abused shoulder pounding hard enough to draw cold sweat from my forehead.

I turned to Angela. She was crying.

"Okay," I panted. "*Now* we're done."

12

W ell, that could have gone better." Saying that, I looked over at Angela, who sat frowning with her arms folded as she looked pointedly through the windshield. We were headed back to RiverTower, and she'd not uttered a word since we left Cullen's apartment. "Right?"

She didn't answer, and again I cut my eyes her way, splitting my attention between her and the traffic.

"Come on, Ange, what's your beef here? Should I have allowed old Mitchie-boy to get away with that last crack? Is that what you're saying?"

Her words were clipped. "I'm not saying anything."

"Yeah, tell me about it." Again she didn't answer, and once more I glanced at her. "You know, I don't do the silent treatment thing well. Never have. I need to know what you're thinking here."

"Really, Joe?" Uncrossing her arms, Angela looked straight at me. Though her eyes were still puffy from crying, they flashed a clear warning. "You *really* want to know what I'm thinking? How about what I'm feeling?"

"Okay, feeling then."

"You may not like the answer."

"Try me."

She resumed gazing out the windshield. "I'm feeling embarrassed."

I figured as much. "At me beating your ex-hubby into the floor? Or the fact that I enjoyed it?"

"At your childish lack of self-control." She snapped her head back toward me. "And you'd better believe it won't end here. I know how vindictive Mitch is. He'll go straight to the police with this, and make it look like this was all your fault. He's good at that." Looking down at them, I saw she was rubbing her hands together. That's what she does when she's really, *really* agitated. "Honestly, Joe, what came over you? You took things way beyond what was required."

"*I* took them? Ange, the jerk practically said he'd like another chance to bash your head in! What was I supposed to do, disregard it?"

"Words. That's all they were. Just words."

"Words sometimes start wars," I said darkly.

"And you sure started one with Mitch, didn't you?" she shot back. "A mature man would have walked. But not you. Never you."

"Mature." I barked a laugh. "That's one thing nobody has ever accused me of." I tried it again. "Ange, it boils down to this. Somebody should've settled that punk's hash a long time ago. Today was his day. It just so happened I was the one to draw short straw."

She resumed looking forward, not replying.

I clammed up too.

We drove on that way a bit.

Another mile passed by, and then I said, "Are we going to fight much longer?"

She gave me a long, amazed stare. "*What* did you say? Tell me you didn't say that."

"It's late, and I'm hungry. Fighting always makes me hungry. Back in Vietnam, lots of times after a battle was over, I was so famished I'd have eaten a cow's leg, if I could've found one. So if our fight is going to go long, I could use a sandwich. Maybe some nachos. I'm feeling rather faint."

"*Faint?*"

I nodded, trying to look gaunt. With my frame, that wasn't easy.

That got her. Angela turned away, but not before I caught her smile.

"Tuna," I said. "Crackers. A hardboiled egg. Anything." I sucked in my cheeks.

"I can't believe this," she muttered, slowly shaking her head. "The man is shameless." She looked back over at me. "Faint, huh?"

"That's the word." I said, nodding again. "Wasting away. See?" I held up a shaky hand.

"Yeah, I can tell you've grown really weak." She blew out an exasperated breath in pure consternation, and what she said next wasn't directed at me. "Father God, what kind of man have you gotten me hooked up with?"

"A knight born a thousand years too late," I answered at once, dropping the starvation routine. "Slaying dragons. Thrashing evil warlords. Rescuing my lady's honor." I grinned at her. "And there you sit, all snippy and thin-lipped, pretending you're mad about it. Tell the truth here, Ange. You're crazy about me, right?"

Her laugh was rueful. "Heaven help me. Yes. I am."

"Well, you see, that's good." I beat my fingers on the car's wheel in soft rhythm as we drove. "That's real good. It's great to admit it, isn't it? Honesty. That's the ticket."

She buried her face in her hands, laughing harder. "You rotter ..."

I grinned again. "It won't be so bad. Loving me, that is. I mean, think about it. Some women make quilts to relax, or throw pots. You get to help build a Christian."

"What a notion!" she gasped, pulling her hands away. I believe the magnitude of the challenge—me—was finally dawning on her. "I'm going to need all the help I can get."

"It'll be a full-time project," I agreed. "Clear your calendar."

I dropped Angela back at her work, more happy than I'd been in weeks. Maybe our storm had blown itself out, and from now on it would be clear sailing.

But as I began tooling back to my office, I was realist enough to acknowledge that probably wouldn't be the case. With the two of us coming from such diverse backgrounds, I knew it was only a matter of time until the next blowup, maybe worse. My lightheartedness was fading by the second. Brother. The J. Geils Band summed it up nicely. *Love Stinks.*

When I got there, oddly, there weren't any cops waiting. Mitch must have been planning something else for me. Something unique.

As I came in, the red light was blinking on my answering machine. Hot dog. A new client, maybe? Then I saw the caller's number revealed in the gadget's little window. Kitty Clark? Nuts. This woman was the rash on my feet, and I was fresh out of powder.

But I pushed the Play Message button on it anyway.

"Joe? Kitty. Call me as soon as you get this. Tell me what you found out." *Click.*

Not even a "have a good day," or "talk to you soon." But in light of what she was going through with this craziness, I decided to cut her some slack. I punched out her number and waited through only two rings, before it was picked up.

"The Clark residence," a carefully modulated and sexy female voice answered.

What the—? Who the heck was this? Then I remembered. This had to be Maria, Kitty's secretary, the little rat-faced woman who'd looked at me so oddly back in Kitty's hotel room at the Ohio Hilton.

"Kitty Clark, please," I said, in just the same way. My, weren't we a cultured bunch.

"May I ask who's calling?"

"Joe Box."

"One moment," Maria murmured, and the line instantly was filled with a song. One of Kitty's, of course. This one was an upbeat tune from her later period, a duet she'd done with Roy Clark (no relation), called *Flip That Card, You Rascal.* I remembered it mainly from Roy's insanely fast guitar-picking work done during the song's bridge. Lots of gangly hillbilly boys had worn bloody blisters on their fingers trying to copy it. To my knowledge, none of them ever came close.

The song was just entering that bridge when Kitty came on the line, ending it.

"Joe? What did you find out?"

"Fine, Kitty, and yourself?"

"Huh?"

"Missed a step, didn't you? You were supposed to say, 'hi,

Joe, how you doing?,' and I'd say, 'fine, yourself?,' and you'd say, 'oh, fair to middling.' Like that."

There was a pause, then she said suspiciously, "You been drinkin'?"

That made me laugh. "No, Kitty, not a drop. I'm just teasing with you, trying to get you to loosen up." I paused. "It's not working, is it?"

"I'm about as tense as a long-tailed cat in a room full of rockin' chairs," she said. "I hope you got some kind of news for me. I'm about to croak down here."

My attempt at humor had failed. She really was upset, and I wasn't helping.

"No. I'm sorry," I said. "My computer friend obtained quite a bit of background on some of your associates, and I ran a few of the leads he came up with. Unfortunately, I've struck out all my at-bats."

"Well, then, if you ain't doin' no good up there, I'd say it's time you came down here." Her tone brooked no comeback. "I told you that before, mind. Night before last."

I sighed. She was right, but I didn't have to like it. "Okay, I suppose you're right. How do you want to play it?"

"That Delta ticket I mentioned will be waitin'. The next flight out tomorrow mornin', whatever time it is. I'll call 'em, and you be on it. When you get to the Nashville airport, I'll already have Blake there, standin' fast to pick you up in the limo."

"Sounds okay," I said. "Who's Blake?"

"I mentioned him to you the other night. Old black feller, pretty white hair, sweet as can be. Been with me for years. My butler and chauffeur. He'll be holdin' a sign with your name on it at the terminal. I'll make the thing myself. You can't miss him."

Not unless the Joe Box Fan Club was there too, with signs of their own, and I lost him in the teeming throng of eager faces.

I knew when I was beaten. "I'll see you there," was all I said, and hung up.

Later on, much later, I would remember this conversation, and the shattering impact it would have on my life, and Kitty's. Looking back, I should have refunded every penny of her lousy five thousand dollars, done it right then with a smile and a thank you, Jesus.

If I'd done that, maybe we both still could have walked away whole.

13

*N*ine o'clock the next morning found my flight from Cincinnati touching down at the Nashville International Airport. On the flight down I'd been ruminating on where my altercation with Mitch Cullen would likely lead. The obvious answer was, no place good. With the way he'd carried on over the possibility Angela might have been there to hit him up for alimony, it was plain the boy was driven by greed. Once he'd had the chance to think on it, he might well end up preferring charges on me for assault. Which was true, I *had* hit him first. And with Angela as a witness, I knew he'd have no trouble making them stick. The best I could hope for was a sympathetic judge. What an unholy mess I'd gotten myself into.

The landing was a bit on the rough side, but once on the ground, and after fifteen minutes of driving around on the tarmac, we finally taxied up to the jetway. There we sat again until the bell dinged at last, letting us know it was time to deplane.

With a sigh of relief I pried my fingers free of the armrest. It's not what you're thinking. I like flying, I really do, even with the crowded flights and abysmal service that seems to be the industry standard these days. And it's not takeoffs and landings *per se* that tighten me up, either. My phobia is stranger than that. Ever since my service time in Vietnam, I've never been able to enjoy the act of either getting on or getting off an airplane.

The first time I got on one, at the other end of the trip I found I'd been transported to a different world, and not a good one. When the plane's door opened, my gooseberry green, nineteen-year-old senses had been instantly assaulted by the heat and stink and musky fear peculiar to that part of Southeast Asia in the early seventies. As soon as I smelled that odor, something visceral in my hindbrain stood up and said, *we need to leave. This is a bad place. A really bad place.*

And it was.

A year would pass before I next got off an airplane, this one depositing me back at LAX, my point of departure. But the Joe Box who stepped off that aircraft was a far different man than the Joe Box who had left a year earlier. During my time in-country I had killed men, and watched others kill men, in more ways than Dante could have dreamed of in his Ninth Circle of Hell. But here I was, whole and mobile, while many of my bros weren't.

And too many of my bros wouldn't be coming home at all.

The point I'm trying to make—and I'm making a real hash of it, I know—is that every time I enter or leave an airplane, I enter or leave Vietnam. Weird, but there it is. Anyway, that was then, and this was now ... and if there's a more convoluted phrase in the English language, I'd like to hear it.

Although I hadn't packed anything to place up in the overhead bin, I still had to wait patiently, or not so patiently in my case, while the other passengers retrieved their own gear. It has never failed to amaze me how one person can jam enough items in one of those tiny spaces to outfit a family of four in Botswana, but the lady in the seat just ahead of me had managed to do it. With lots of tugging and pulling and mighty grunts and oaths, she finally got her stuff free. When she did, the fifteen of us she had backed up behind her nearly to the rear restroom cheered. The things some folks will go through not to have to check their baggage.

Finally done, the rest of us trudged off the plane behind her. I was one of the last to leave, walking through the connecting tunnel leading from the fuselage into the terminal. As I got inside the place, and once again made my way past security, the throng I found myself facing was about as bad as I'd thought it would be. But they obviously weren't the Joe Box Fan Club, just the usual motley group of happy folks greeting the usual motley group of weary travelers you'll find at any airport in the world. I stopped in the middle of them, scanning the sea of faces for an older black man holding up a sign with my name on it. As Kitty had promised, he wasn't hard to spot. Twenty feet away I saw him.

Kitty's chauffeur-*cum*-butler, Blake, was a short, barrel-chested black gentleman of indeterminate age, with a shock of wool-white hair above a set of dark, merry eyes that were fairly bursting with good humor and intelligence. What really gave the game away was the small, rectangular white sign he held at chest level with my name inexpertly scrawled on it.

"Mister Box?" The man smiled as I approached him.

"That's me. And you have to be Blake."

"I am, suh, I am," the other man said, his broad Tennessee accent thick and good-sounding. At least to my ears. Still holding the sign with his right hand, Blake reached for my suitcase with his left, only noticing then I wasn't carrying one.

"Traveling light today, I see," he chuckled, lowering his hand. "Gotta like a man that travels light, yes indeed. I trust you had a nice flight."

Dropping the sign into a nearby waste can, Blake pointed toward a far door. "There's where we're headed, suh. Got the limo waiting. Polished her up real pretty today too, and waxed it twice. Give you a nice, smooth ride out to Miss Kitty's place. Follow me please, if you'll be so kind."

I fell into step beside him as we began heading the way he'd pointed, presumably toward the short-term parking area.

"Don't you need to see any ID?" I asked him, only partly in jest, as we walked. "How do you know I'm not just a guy cadging a free ride in a limo?"

Blake chuckled again.

"Not much chance of that, suh. Miss Kitty, she already told me what you looked like, the kind of man I was to expect." He gave me a sideways glance as we walked. "And we're all expecting a lot. I surely hope you're not the type to disappoint."

"Frequently, Blake," I said, with as much truth as I could muster. "Ask most of the people I know. All I can promise is just what I told Kitty. I'll do my best."

The other man pursed his lips and nodded, as if I'd spoken a universal verity.

"That's all a man can do, suh, is his best," he said. "At the end of the day, that's all any of us can do. And that's the Lord's honest truth."

What the heck, maybe I *had* said a universal verity.

Walking through the wide double doors, I was struck with how different the weather was from what Cincinnati was enduring this time of year. The air here was warm, almost balmy, and regardless of the burned jet fuel odor permeating it, it smelled like spring to me.

"What's the temperature today?" I asked, glancing up into a brilliant blue sky dotted with puffy white clouds. I'd wisely forgone wearing my overcoat on this trip.

"Seventy-four degrees, and partly sunny," Blake answered at once, as if he'd primed himself for this very question before he'd left home. "Unusually warm for us this time of year, even this far south of the Mason-Dixon. Supposed to get clear up to seventy-six, the weatherman was saying on the cable TV. Warm enough I might even get me a bit of fishing in this afternoon." He nodded. "Gonna be a mighty fine day, suh, mighty fine."

He'd get no argument from me on that. Owing to a freakish jet stream, when I'd left Cincinnati two hours earlier the temperature was eighteen, and the sky as gray as slate. Definitely no contest here.

Now we were approaching a silvery-colored stretch limousine parked next to the curb, clearly in a 'no parking' zone.

"Here we are," Blake sang out, pulling the keys from his pocket and giving something on the ring a push. The limo chirped twice in reply, and from the inside of it I heard the door locks pop up. A car alarm, naturally. Of course, any would-be thief planning to steal Kitty Clark's personal ride would have the devil's own time trying to fence it.

Blake opened the door to the plush passenger compartment. "Please get in, suh." I hesitated, and he frowned. "Is there a problem with the vehicle, Mister Box? Because if there is, I can call Miss Kitty at the house in Belle Meade right quick and—"

"No, no, that's not it," I assured him.

I wasn't really sure if I could put into words exactly what my deal was here. After all, this past Christmas I'd had no problem with riding in the back of a similar stretch limo with Tom Parker on our way to Kitty's hotel room at the Ohio Hilton. Our driver that day had been that long-suffering young Mexican guy, Tranquilo.

And I guess if you pinned me down, right there was the problem in a nutshell. That day I would have much rather sat up front next to Tranquilo, enjoying his company and hearing his stories, than have had to endure Parker's bad breath, B.O., and racial slurs.

But I hadn't done that, instead choosing to plant myself in the backseat like I was a bigger shot than I am ... which admittedly is pretty small. So although there was no way I could make up that slam to the young Mexican, I could darn well not do it again here. Symbolically lame, I know, but what the hey.

"I'd just like to sit up front with you, Blake, if you don't mind," was all I said.

He regarded me quizzically. Deep in his eyes I could read cautious openness balanced against too many years of bad experience. The openness won out, as I'd hoped.

"Not at all, not at all," he smiled again. "The ride up there is just as nice."

Blake climbed in the driver's side, me the passenger's, and we closed the doors. He started the car and put it in gear. Almost without a sound the big-engined beast glided away from the curb and merged like oil into the airport traffic.

The chauffeur/butler looked over at me as we went, a sly grin on his face. "What do you think of the ride, suh? Didn't I tell you it was smooth?"

"Like butter on a hot skillet," I agreed. "By the way, how did you avoid the airport cops hanging a parking ticket on this thing, seeing where you'd left it?"

The other man laughed lightly. "A ticket in this town? For

Miss Kitty Clark's own personal car? As they say, suh, that'll be the day."

"Yeah, but you still took a bit of a chance, it seems to me. I'll bet there are plenty of other limos around with this same color, especially in such a rich city."

Blake's sly look was back. "That's very true. But none other with a license plate that reads SKYLARK." He chuckled again, happily patting the steering wheel. "That song was sure a lucky one for that lady." He flipped down the sun visor, exposing a flat rack containing maybe a dozen or so CDs out of their cases and secured with elastic straps. "That's just some of her stuff, Mister Box. I can put one on if you'd like."

"No, I'll pass. I'd rather hear you talk." I lightly started scraping my bottom lip with my thumbnail. "Tell me, Blake, since you know her well. What kind of a woman is Kitty, anyway?"

He started to answer, but I held up that same hand, cutting him off. "And I don't mean the usual chamber of commerce line. I'd like the straight story. Man to man."

Blake's easy demeanor faded a bit, and he grew serious. "All right, I will, but where do I begin?"

For a dry-mouthed moment he took both hands off the wheel, flapping them helplessly for a second, before putting them back down where they belonged.

"There's so much," he said. "Do I start with how she took in a homeless raggedy black man she'd met at a charity benefit, while serving him soup she'd cooked herself? How she took pity on that man, and paid to have him sent to school to learn the honorable trade of butlering? How she then hired that same man to aid her as best he could?"

I cocked my head at him, saying nothing.

"How she gave that man the only real home he'd known

since he was twelve years old?" Blake continued. "Christmas presents, and cake on his birthday, and a sure enough weeklong vacation every year? I could go on, suh, but I perceive you're getting my drift."

"So you're saying Kitty Clark is bighearted?"

The old man's sunny grin was back. "Do fish jump in the spring? Does the robin feed its young? Yes, I'd say bighearted is the word, just about the perfect word."

"All right, let's agree she's an earth angel," I said, to myself as much as to him. "So if that's the case, who could be trying to send her right over the edge of sanity?"

Blake's cheery look had vanished to the point I doubted it had ever been there at all. "I don't rightly know, suh," he said. "But I would like five minutes alone with that gentleman in a room with a door that I could lock. Yes, I'd like that a *powerful* lot."

There really wasn't much that I could add to that, so we drove for a while, taking the "scenic route," as Blake called it. Part of that trip we spent negotiating our way through the modern glass-and-steel urban clutter of Nashville.

But clutter or no, I'll have to admit Nashville was one of the prettier towns I'd ever passed through. Some of the architecture in it was striking, including a life-size replica of the Parthenon in Athens, Greece, and a building whose top looked uncannily like a giant mock-up of Batman's cowl.

"What the heck is that thing?" I asked as we passed it.

"The BellSouth Building," Blake replied, and he laughed. "Kind of famous around heah. With those dual pointy towers way up on top, it puts a person in mind of Batman's head, doesn't it?"

"I'm thinking that very thing."

Blake gave it a last glance as we went by. "At six hundred and thirty-something feet for just his head, that'd make ol' Batman a real big crime fighter. I'd hate to see the Joker."

We both laughed then, and so passed another forty or so pleasant minutes as we seamlessly exchanged the modern Nashville skyline for the fastnesses of Belle Meade.

14

*T*he road Kitty's house was on was a narrow two-lane job, twisting and turning its way through copses of winter-bare black oaks and sycamores, and past tangled clusters of wild blackberry vines. I would imagine that springtime on this stretch would be noteworthy.

I turned to Blake. "How much farther is it?"

"Oh, I 'xpect a mile. Soon as we pass the entrance to the Danbury house, then it's one mile exactly further on." He looked over at me. "That's the Danbury of Danbury Mills fame, you understand."

I'd heard of Danbury Mills, knew it well, in fact. Noodles and I had enjoyed their breakfast cereals on more than one occasion. I almost made a remark about that, but Blake continued. "There it is, suh. The Danbury place."

I looked, but I couldn't see it. All I could make out was a pair of massive stone edifices as we went past, flanking a drive-way going off to the right. Between the monoliths loomed a gate that would have given an Abrams main battle tank a tense few minutes. But of the house itself, nothing. In fact, for the past fifteen minutes we'd been passing various brick and stone gates of differing sizes and thicknesses, but not a dwelling to be seen. That struck me as unusual, and I told Blake so. He simply laughed again.

"I take it you've never been to California, and seen where the movie stars live?"

"No. I mean, I've been to California a few times, but I've never taken any of the tours."

With one hand on the wheel, Blake motioned with the other to the general countryside. "Belle Meade puts me in mind of Topanga Canyon or Malibu, seeing how the homes are set well off the road. They're all hiding places for the rich and famous, I think."

"Really. So tell me, Blake." The gaze I was giving him was steady. "What secret is Kitty Clark hiding?"

He frowned. "Why, nothing. Miss Kitty, she just likes a place to get away from her fans and such, when life begins to burden her down."

Disbelief must have clouded my face, because his voice grew hard.

"Her life isn't all glamour and parties, Mister Box," Blake said. "I should know. I've seen that for myself. Sometimes ..." He licked his lips and shook his head. "Let that pass, suh. Truth is, I'm not so sure if I should be speaking in such a manner at all. There's just a way about you that I 'xpect causes most folks to naturally open up."

"Thanks for the compliment, but we're well past the time to be shading anything. I need all the help from you I can get, if Kitty means for me to end this harassment."

Several beats passed before Blake said, "All right, if you think it'll help. But it's bad." He paused again, then said, "Sometimes, especially these last few months, I've come into Miss Kitty's bedroom late of a night, and she'd be having the terrors something *fierce.*"

"Terrors? What do you mean?"

"Nightmares, suh." Blake didn't look so chipper now. "Terrible ones. Many's the time she'll be thrashing and moaning in her room something dreadful, calling out a name I can't rightly make out. When I come in, I'll find her sitting straight up in her bed, her hands stretched out like she's reaching for something she can't quite get hold of." He shuddered. "Or maybe it's something else. Something she's lost. Who can tell? But her fingers will be twitching and jumping and she'll be calling out that name, over and over again, all the time crying her heart out like a little baby child."

He turned troubled eyes my way. "In the morning, she doesn't remember a thing. Isn't that awful? All that pain, and she doesn't remember ..."

Just one more weird turn in a case that already had exceeded its quota. But all I said was, "Pretty awful, all right."

I didn't have the chance to pursue that. Like an actor getting ready to go out on stage, suddenly Blake brightened. "I've been yammering on, and heah we are already ..."

"Here" was a black strip of asphalt, going fifty feet back before encountering a large brick entrance straddling it. Across the driveway and between the brick structures brooded a large filigreed iron gate, with a matching brick guardhouse to its left.

As we pulled up, Blake was grinning like a kid. But he didn't fool me, even for a second. I knew this look from its opposite when I'd played high school football. He'd just put on his game face.

For Kitty.

An older gray-haired guard leaned out of his little window, which was right next to the limo driver's side door.

Blake nodded to him. "Got Mister Box with me today. Miss Kitty called for him, and heah he is."

The guard didn't even bother bending further down to see what I looked like. I guess if I'd been vetted by Blake, that was good enough for him. He simply pulled his head back inside, and a second later the gates swung wide.

I honestly didn't pay much attention to the drive up to the house. My mind was elsewhere, wondering where Kitty's nightmares figured into all this mess. If anywhere. The next thing I was aware of, Blake had parked the car and was pulling my door open.

"This is the place, suh," he smiled with quiet pride. "Miss Kitty's own house."

Getting out of the car and going inside the mansion, I felt it was only right to look around the place like a hick, to humor Blake if nothing else.

The house's overriding characteristic was that it seemed to be a dwelling for the rich lifted straight from the movies, chock-full of big chandeliers, *objets d'art*, curving polished staircases, and hallways you could bowl in. Check out any Dick Powell/Myrna Loy picture from the thirties and you've seen one just like it. But something about this place didn't feel that old.

Our steps echoing hollowly as we walked, I said to the other man, mainly to be polite, "Pretty fancy house Kitty has here. What's the age of it?"

Blake shook his head. "I can't say for sure. Not as old as you might think. I know Miss Kitty built it sometime back in the mid-sixties, so near on forty years, or close enough."

I thought so. That would have been about the time the tabloids would have started braying about how loaded she was. With money, that is, not liquor. That had come later.

Still moving through the house, I asked Blake, for curiosity's sake as much as anything else, "How many servants does Kitty have?"

"Myself and the maid, Veronica," he replied. "The guard's a temp. And that's all."

Now that surprised me. "No gardeners? No cook?"

Blake shook his head. "Remarkable, isn't it? No suh, Miss Kitty, she likes to do that herself. Every meal served here she cooks. And she's not bad by half. The only time that changes is when we have a large dinner party on the grounds, and that she has catered. Even then I imagine she'd rather be cooking than entertaining."

That fit in pretty well with her coming from Southern stock; country women tend to be like that. "Who cooks for you all when she's on the road?"

He grinned. "Why, that would be Mister Mulligan."

"Mulligan?" I frowned. "Who's he? I thought you just said there wasn't a full-time cook here."

Blake chuckled. "I meant Mister Mulligan stew. We in the house are left to our own devices when Miss Kitty isn't here. The job of cook then usually falls to me, as I'm a dab hand at hobo stew. Many years of practice at it, suh, don't you know."

We passed a large, immaculate window. "You said she gardens as well. I take it you mean flowers and such." I motioned to the huge lawn outside. "Not all that there."

"When the flowers are in bloom, yes suh," Blake said. "The yard, she contracts that out to a service. But if she could physically do it herself, why, I believe she would."

So it appeared the singer's entire permanent staff consisted of a butler, a maid, Parker, and Maria. Kitty's cheapness sure cut down on the on-site suspects.

Off the main hall we came to a room fitted with large white six-panel double doors, one of which was opened inward.

Blake swept his arm toward it. "This is the parlor, Mister Box. Miss Kitty is inside, waiting for you. I'll announce you, suh."

This was going to be a first. I'd never been "announced" before. Not unless you mean the times a bailiff would call my name when I was dragged into some podunk court or another on a drunk-and-disorderly. But that doesn't count.

"Miss Kitty?" Blake intoned, taking two steps into the room. "Mister Box is heah."

Her voice rang out from somewhere inside. "Fine, Blake. Send him in."

He turned to me. "Miss Kitty will see you now, suh."

The pageantry complete, I moved past him into the room, expecting to hear the blare of heralding trumpets. But all I got was Kitty Clark saying, "Well, Joe, it's about time."

It was at that, and I walked over to where she was sitting, in a large, comfortable-looking chair by a big bay window. Incredibly, she was in full stage regalia, makeup and all. Didn't this woman ever unwind? The chair's mate was across from it, and she pointed. "Park it there, Joe. This here's my bird-watchin' window. The view's right pretty."

So was the parlor. It reminded me of the sitting room at Quint's, right down to the huge fireplace on the far side with a painting over it. I did as she said, settling into the chair.

She motioned with her chin toward the window. "Be real quiet now, and take a look at that out there. Cardinals, two of 'em, a male and a female, havin' themselves a time."

Out on the vast expanse of brown lawn, a pair of redbirds were cavorting and chasing each other through the bare limbs of a black walnut tree. They were fast, almost like children with wings, and seemed as carefree as I knew Kitty wasn't.

"Look, look there," she said. "The male keeps flyin' under the female, kind of like he's protectin' her. Maybe from cats." She sighed at the sight. "Ain't they pretty? And ain't it a wonder how the male is the bright-colored one and the female is so dull?"

I smiled. "Kind of the opposite of people." I figured I'd let her ease into this as she willed. Five thousand dollars buys a lot of my patience.

"Opposite of *some* people," Kitty sniffed. "In my line a' work, I seen some men dress so fancy they'd make Liberace look like a ragpicker." She wrinkled her already wrinkled nose. "Good musicians, I guess, but kinda hard to take serious."

I just chuckled and didn't say anything.

Kitty sighed again and turned away from the window, now addressing me directly.

"Guess you're wonderin' why it is I had you come all the way down here."

"The thought crossed my mind, yes. More than once, as a matter of fact."

She shook her head. "I dunno, Joe. Maybe you're right. Maybe it was stupid. Could be you're right in thinkin' this whole thing was really a stupid idea. But I hope you're wrong. I just figured that, with you bein' down here, right where it's all happenin', maybe it'll jar somethin' loose in your head."

I did laugh then. "That's one way of putting it."

She scowled. "You know what I mean. I'm tryin' to say that maybe by just bein' in this house, it'll make you more aware, like."

In her stumbling way, I had to concede that Kitty might just have a point. A lot of times in an investigation, my physically being in the place where the crime or whatever had occurred will sometimes bring me a few chess-jumps closer to the solution.

And in light of that, there was one piece of evidence I needed, right away. "I'd like to see those letters you were sent. Are they handy?"

"I knew you'd be askin' that. I've got 'em right here." Kitty reached into a sewing basket down beside the chair, pulling a handful of envelopes out. "They's six of those awful things, all typed by somebody, and you'll find I've put 'em in the order they came to me."

She handed the stack over, and I placed it on my lap. Swiftly I began leafing through the envelopes, checking their postmarks.

"I know what you're lookin' for, and I already checked 'em," Kitty said. "They ain't two postmarks alike on any of 'em. They're each from a different city, each from a different state." She furrowed her brows. "How do you figure that, Joe?"

I was still fanning through them as she talked.

"There are a couple of ways," I began, and then I stopped, lifting one up. "Wait a minute. The date on this one is only a couple of weeks ago. Where are the ones you got from before that, at Christmas?"

Kitty didn't answer, but instead began staring down at her hands. Another moment passed before she said, "I ain't got 'em anymore. I ... I lost 'em."

"*Lost* them?" I said. "They're evidence, Kitty. Pretty important evidence, at that. Maybe you just misplaced them."

"No, they're gone. I'm sure of it."

"But—"

"They're gone, I'm tellin' you!" Kitty's eyes flashed in anger, as much at my persistence as at her carelessness. "You're just gonna have to make do with what you've got."

I regarded her for a second, and then I shrugged. "All right. You're the client." I opened the first letter and read it.

In bold caps it screamed **YOU'RE NOT AS SMART AS YOU THINK YOU ARE, KITTY. I KNOW IT ALL. EVERY DIRTY THING ABOUT YOU. AND MORE.**

I flipped it over, but the backside was blank. Holding the paper up to the light, I didn't see any watermark. It had the appearance of plain twenty-pound-weight bond, and the typeface on it was 12-point Times New Roman. Next to hydrocarbon molecules, what I was holding was the most common stuff in the universe.

Kitty was silent, but I could feel her hopeful eyes on me, as if she thought I could divine the identity of her tormentor just by touching what I held in my hand. Even Sherlock Holmes wasn't that good. I put the letter back in its envelope and bypassed the rest, figuring they'd only get worse, as I went for the last one.

I wasn't wrong. It was pretty bad. **THERE ARE GOO-GOO CLUSTERS UNDER YOUR BED, KITTY. DON'T EAT TOO MANY TONIGHT. THEY'LL JUST GIVE YOU NIGHTMARES. THAT'S MY JOB.**

"What in the world is a GooGoo Cluster?" I said.

"It's a kind of candy they make down here," Kitty replied. "Real messy and real good. Like a big wad of butterscotch and chocolate and marshmallows and peanuts all mashed together. I'm a fool for 'em."

I glanced down at the letter, then back up at her. "And you keep them under your bed?"

In spite of the inherent humor of it, her face was stricken

with dismay. "I do. In a box. And nobody knows that, Joe. *Nobody.*"

"Somebody does. Are you sure you didn't let it slip to someone? A friend?"

"No. It's a … a special treat for me. Some folks smoke or drink. I just like eatin' a GooGoo right before I go to bed." Kitty's voice grew clotted with fear. "Whoever knows that must have been in my bedroom." Her sound climbed in volume. "Maybe even when I was layin' there sleepin'! Maybe—"

She was working herself into a state. That would do neither of us any good, so I cut her off. "We don't know that, Kitty." I made one last stab at reason. "Are you *sure* it's not time to bring in the cops?" I held the letter up. "This could be serious stuff."

"No." She was still adamant. "No police. A thing like this gets out … land sakes! GooGoo Clusters! The press'd have a fun time with that! I'd be just some crazy old rich woman with a stash of candy under her bed, afraid of the boogeyman. No!" She stamped her foot and pointed her finger at me. "No, Joe, you're it. This is your show."

Right about then I regretted ever hearing the name of Kitty Clark, but I was stuck.

"All right," I sighed again. "Let's keep going."

Kitty seemed to relax some. "A minute ago you said there was a couple of ways to get those postmarks to be comin' from all those towns. Like what?"

"Well the first one is fairly simple," I said, getting back into the rhythm of it. "The most obvious thought is that this guy has enough funds that he can afford to fly to each of the cities these came from and mail each letter from there. That's not too practical, though. Even if you had the money, it's an utter waste of time. Or, it could be he has friends around that are willing to mail them for him. Again, unlikely." I tapped the letter with my index finger. "No, I think the most logical course would be to use a blind drop."

Kitty frowned. "Blind drop?"

I nodded. "Here's how it works. There are companies around who will, for a fee, remail a letter for you from anywhere in the USA. Usually they have branch offices in all the major cities, and what you do is to write your letter, seal it, address it, and stamp it. But instead of sticking it in the mail, you put the whole thing in a bigger envelope addressed to the blind drop company in say"—I looked at the postmark on the letter I was holding—"Lubbock, Texas. Somebody there opens it, takes your letter out, and drops it in a Lubbock mailbox. Simple, and untraceable. It's done all the time, and couldn't be easier." Again I held the letter up, flapping it gently. "I'll bet you ten bucks that's what we've got here."

Kitty was shaking her head. "Well, I'll be dogged. Pretty slick, this guy."

"Maybe not as slick as he'd like to think," I said. "He's bound to have slipped up somewhere. It's just a matter of finding out where. We'll get him."

I stood up, secure in the belief that even as I'd said those words, they were more akin to bravado than confidence. Truth is, I'd said it as much to build up my own hope as Kitty's.

I folded the letters in half and put them in my pocket. "If it's all right with you, I'd like to keep these. Maybe there's something about them I'm missing. I'd also to take a little stroll around the place, and see what's what."

She stood as well. "Sure, let me get Blake to help you."

"That kind of defeats the purpose, Kitty. I need to do this at my own pace, by myself. Do I have your permission?"

"You got my undivided blessin', if that'll help end this. This is the maid's day off, so all that's around here is Blake, Maria, and Tom. If any of 'em look at you cross-eyed, you tell 'em I said it's okay."

"Maria and Tom," I said. "Where would I find them?"

"Upstairs, in my office, probably. Maria's typin' up some of my correspondence, and Tom should be finalizin' the plans for my USO tour this summer."

That stopped me. "USO tour?" At her age? That had to be one of the sillier things I'd ever heard of. Most of the soldiers and sailors serving hadn't even been born when Kitty was in her heyday. The idea of a group of them willingly choosing to attend one of her concerts rather than one where, say, Brittany Spears was shaking her merchandise beggared the imagination. I looked closely at Kitty, trying to see if she was joking. She wasn't.

"Yeah, Tom's settin' it up," she said. "'Course, I know I'm gettin' a bit long in the tooth to go clear over to Iraq or Germany or such. Most of my shows are gonna be set pretty close to home. First one will be at Guantanamo Bay Naval Base in June."

Guantanamo? Now, that would be one for the books. But if Cuba could survive the depredations of Castro, I supposed they could weather a concert by Kitty Clark.

That suddenly conjured up a bizarre mental picture of old bristle-puss Fidel clapping and yee-hawing with the crowd, and I covered up my laugh with a cough.

"I'll check your office first, and say hi to Maria and Tom while I'm at it," I said. "Which way is it?"

"I'll show you."

Kitty walked back over to the parlor door, her narrow hips giving her a slight arthritic roll. She stepped into the hall where I joined her, and she pointed down it. "See that staircase? Go up it and take a right. First door on the left off the upstairs hall is the office. Come on back when you're done, tell me if they said anything helpful."

I began walking down the long, brightly painted, echoing hallway, noting as I went that it was decked out top to bottom with real marble statuary and oil paintings in gilded frames. From all earthly appearances, it seemed our little country gal had done all right for herself.

I started ascending the curving staircase at the end of that hallway, but stopped at the landing halfway up before I made the final turn. Something had halted me there, and I leaned in close.

It was a large canvas capturing Kitty's first concert at the Grand Ole Opry. Impossible to tell now when the painting had been done, but it showed her from a time back in the late fifties, when she was still a young woman, and her music brand-new. I knew I'd never seen this work, and for sure I hadn't been at that concert, being only five at the time, but there was something disturbingly familiar about it.

I shook my head in dismissal and mounted the last ten steps up to the second floor. As Kitty had told me, I took the left turn into her office, and as I did, I almost ran into Maria coming out.

"Mr. Box." Her tone was cool. She used one hand to push her black glasses more firmly against her little nub of a nose, the other mashing some papers against her bony chest. "I thought I heard your voice downstairs. It's quite distinctive. Tends to carry, you know."

"You say that like it's a bad thing," I grinned, figuring to goad her a little. "As a kid it sure stood me in good stead when it came time to call the hogs. Or my dad."

She grew more chilly still. "How may I be of service today?"

You might try warming up to room temperature, I nearly said, but my answer was a bit more civil than that.

"You can't, really. I'm just kind of nosing around here, getting the lay of the place."

Maria's smile now was downright wintry. "Really. Rather like a dog."

Granny always told me never to slug a woman, but the temptation was powerful. I smiled in return. "Even better. Like a bloodhound."

Before our sparring could degenerate further, another "distinctive" voiced boomed out from inside the office. "That you, Box?"

Ah, the dulcet tones of Tom Parker. I stepped past Maria and went on inside. "You guessed 'er, Chester," I said.

Parker was over by the filing cabinet on the room's far side, scribbling something on a legal pad.

I looked around the place in admiration. Now this was an office.

The area before me was large enough to serve as a living room—or two—complete with a cherry desk, credenza, three wooden filing cabinets, and other assorted office-type stuff on the right. On the left was a full sitting area, containing a leather-and-brass-button love seat and sofa, a large mahogany coffee table, and three black floor lamps. There was even a dorm-size refrigerator on the floor and a small microwave oven on a counter along the back wall. Five college boys, or three NFL full-backs, could have called this space home.

Parker noticed me rubbernecking around, and he placed the legal pad in the filing cabinet, shutting the drawer before turning to me. "Gettin' your fill of our little nest? What can I do you for?"

"Nothing much." I picked up and put down a paperweight

I'd found on Kitty's desk. It was a glass bird, hand blown to my eye. A skylark, of course. "I'm just seeing what's what."

Parker glanced at Maria, who'd come back into the room. Her responding look was just as weighty. I was getting the feeling those two didn't like me much. To say it was mutual would be an understatement.

"Is Kitty cool with you hangin' around her office like this?" Parker said.

"Oh yeah, Tom, cooler than cool." I smiled at them. "Say, I hope you two aren't looking at me cross-eyed. Are you?"

"Come again?" Maria frowned. Tom just appeared blank.

I shook my head. "Nothing. A joke."

Now Parker was the one scowling. "Yeah, well there ain't nothin' funny about what Kitty's had to put up with lately. It's makin' her become forgetful, and I'm havin' to take up a lot of her slack." His short, dry laugh sounded almost like a bark as he shook his head and fiddled with his pen. "I sure hope you're worth all the money she's payin' you, Box."

"You know, you're the second person today that's questioned my professional abilities," I said pointedly. "If y'all don't stop, you're going to give me a complex."

Parker opened his mouth to answer, but I held up a hand. "You guys just go on with whatever it was you were doing. I'll be out of here before you know it. Pretend you don't see me."

"That won't be a strain," Maria muttered as she seated herself at the desk and started busying herself with some papers on it. I don't think she'd meant for me to hear that crack. Or maybe she did, and just didn't care. It was obvious her lowly opinion of me remained unchanged, and mine of her. I doubted we'd be exchanging Christmas cards.

"So what are you folks working on?" I asked innocently.

Once more they swapped looks, and I grinned. "It's okay, really. I've been cleared at the highest levels."

After a moment Maria said, "If you must know, I'm paying some bills." The unsaid finish of that was, *not that it's any of your business.*

"And doing it very efficiently too, I'll bet." I looked over at Parker. "Tom, you?"

He shrugged. "Finalizin' Kitty's concert plans at Gitmo." I noticed he'd used the service diminutive for Guantanamo Bay. Former military, perhaps?

"Well, isn't that fine," I said. "Busy as beavers, the both of you. It's good to see real American industrialism on display."

"Are you about done in here or what?" Parker said in exasperation. "It's not like Maria and me don't have anything better to do with our day than to jaw with you."

She nodded once in agreement, her eyes hard behind the lenses of her horn-rims.

On the wall above the desk, a large framed photograph of a boat caught my eye. As I stepped over beside Maria's chair to get a closer look, she scowled. I ignored her.

The boat in the photo was a honey, more like a small yacht, with clean lines and a sleek, swept-back look. The landscape of the lake it was floating on looked familiar.

I turned away from it. "What's this?" I asked Parker.

He looked up from his work. "Kitty's boat. The *Skylark.*"

"Of course. What other name would she have called it?" I returned to the picture, giving it an appreciative gaze. A second later I felt Parker's presence next to me.

"That thing is sure one sweet piece of work," he said. "It's a Sea Ray Carver 440. A 2003 model." He began sounding off the craft's stats. "It's forty-four feet long, with a fifteen foot beam."

"That's the width, right?" I broke in, looking at him.

He stared at me. "You don't know much about boats, do you?"

"Not much," I agreed. "Now guns, that's a different story."

Ignoring me, Parker again faced the photo. "The engines are twin 420 horse diesel Cummins. With those power plants inside, that baby can flat get after it. And it's got the largest below-deck cabin you'll find on any craft of its size. Comfort and speed both. Pretty good combination."

"Are you selling them, Tom?" I grinned. "If so, write me up an order for one."

He snorted. "You wish. A boat like that retails for a cool half-million."

That drew a whistle from me. "Does Kitty let you drive it?"

"Yeah, smart guy, she does," he snarled. "Lots of times. More than her, even. Matter of fact, I'm goin' up there this weekend to get it ready for the season."

"Where is 'there'?"

"Lake Herrington, Kentucky. Right outside of Danville."

"That's why that shoreline looks familiar," I said. "I've fished that lake before."

"Not usin' anything like the *Skylark* you haven't," Parker smirked.

"No, not anything close," I admitted. "But then a johnboat doesn't use as much gas, either." I returned to the picture. "I can't say I care for the wrought-iron benches you've got bolted on the fantail, though. Although it proves Kitty has classic Southern bad taste."

Again he scowled. Much as I hated it, it was time to end their baiting.

"I guess I should mosey on," I said. "I'll leave the both of you to it. As I said, you two continue with your duties, and I'll just wander the house and grounds a bit."

Parker started to reply, but Maria jumped in. "Certainly, Mr. Box, feel free," she said. "And if you need any assistance from either of us, please don't hesitate to let us know." She looked at Parker, and then at me, now smiling at me broadly. And mockingly, in my opinion. "Tom and I are at your disposal."

That smile of hers was as genuine as an old-time Indian agent's. I hadn't heard such insincerity since Dick Nixon's I-am-not-a-crook speech.

I just returned it and nodded. "Thank you, Maria. I appreciate that."

Pleasantries completed, I took my leave of those exceedingly gracious folks and made my way back downstairs to the parlor.

Kitty was once again in her chair, watching the cardinals. She turned her head my way when she heard me come in. "Did you find Tom and Maria all right?"

"Oh, yeah. Charming as ever, those two. And no, they weren't much help."

"You don't like 'em much, do you?"

"What's not to like?" I smiled.

But she wasn't buying it, and her eyes grew narrow at my tone.

I shrugged. "You know, almost every day I check the Private Eye Secret Manual for its operating guidelines, and so far I haven't found anything that says I have to be pals with the people I deal with. All I have to do is find answers for them. Nothing more."

"Does that go for me, too?" Kitty's smile was tentative. "You like *me*, don't you, Joe?" She was staring at me in an odd, anxious way. For some reason, it seemed it was extremely important for her continued well-being for me to answer in the affirmative.

But I've never lied to a client. Never in over twenty years.

And I wasn't about to start now.

"No, I can't honestly say I like you much," I said evenly. "Should I?"

Kitty pulled in a shuddering breath as her smile vanished, and she teared up. That one obviously had hit home. It appeared to me she'd taken it a lot harder than was warranted.

But she rallied gamely, and tried to create a better one. "Well, why not?" She seemed to fairly glow with fake brightness. "What's not to like?"

"I really don't see the point of this, Kitty ..."

"Is it my house?" She stood and swept an arm around the room. "My money, my car, my stuff? What?" Her eyes were still fever-bright, her voice chipper as a chipmunk's, but her breathing was ragged. "Come on, Joe. I can't tell you how important it is for people to like me. What do I need to fix here? How can I get you to like me? How?"

This was pitiful. Beyond pitiful. A woman as rich and self-sufficient as Kitty Clark, lacking for not one material thing in this world, and all she could think about was changing herself to secure the approval of others. And of me. She was one hurtin' pup, as Granny used to say, and if ever there was a perfect time to share my faith, this was it.

But then, like a sneak thief, my old nemesis self-doubt crept in and tapped me on the shoulder, like it always, maddeningly does. I wavered, and that's all it took. The moment passed.

"There's nothing for you to fix, Kitty," I said. "It's just me having a fairly bad day. Don't worry about it."

She continued staring at me. Then she seemed to relax a bit, and nodded.

What a coward I was. Someday, without a doubt, I was going to be called on to explain my belief in Jesus to another person, possibly at a crisis point in life like Kitty was experiencing. I knew that day was coming as sure as anything.

And when it did, I hoped I wouldn't blow it then like I'd blown it just now.

"Well, off with you then," Kitty said. "Take your liberty in roamin' around the place. You already told Tom and Maria I said it was fine with me?"

"I told them, Kitty."

"Blake too. If you see Blake, tell him."

"Sure, Kitty. Blake too."

I turned and left the old woman then, still trapped like a fly in amber, still bound in her pain and her fear. My guilt hung like a weight of iron around my neck.

♦ ◊ ♦

I spent the rest of the afternoon just as I'd said, checking the house and grounds. I've done a bit of home security work from time to time, and from what I could see, the firm Kitty had hired here had done a bang-up job. The alarm system they'd installed was first-rate.

I know. I'd unknowingly tripped a hair-trigger motion sensor when I walked into the backyard where the cardinal show had occurred. I hadn't taken three steps onto the verge when a raucous hooting erupted from inside the house. It went on that way for a few moments, loud enough to wake the dead, the sound itself dying a second later.

Blake stuck his head out the upstairs window and yelled down at me. "Sorry Mister Box! I should have remembered to turn it off!"

I waved back at him. "Not a problem. Although we probably just got Kitty kicked out of the 'Keep Belle Meade Quiet' campaign."

He laughed and slid the window closed.

A half hour more of me strolling the landscape didn't turn up anything new, so I went back inside. For the next two hours I meticulously combed the house, from the attic to the basement, from the gourmet kitchen to the Art Deco bathrooms (all seven of them). Nada. Nothing. Zip.

Tired, still battling the galloping guilts, and as puzzled as ever, I went back into the parlor. Not surprisingly, Kitty wasn't there. It was two p.m., after all.

I found Blake out in the hall, holding a bucket with some rags in it by the handle.

"Cleaning something?" I said. Sharp, that's me.

He smiled. "I'm headed to the garage. Gonna give the limo another wash."

"Again?"

"Why, yes suh. I wash it every day, unless it's raining."

He began moving back down the hall, on his way to the garage I suppose, but I stopped him, touching his arm.

He turned. "Suh?"

"You or the maid haven't seen anything … out of the ordinary around here, have you?" I knew what his answer was probably going to be, but I had to ask.

"No, Mister Box. I believe I would have told you that, on our way out here from the airport today." His expression grew kind and his voice softened. "Growing frustrated, are you?"

"You could say that." I shook my head. "I really am better at this than it looks, Blake. I'm a competent investigator, appearances to the contrary."

"I know you are, Mister Box. Else Miss Kitty wouldn't have hired you."

I blew out a breath. "I feel like I'm failing her on all points.

It's like I'm missing something here, something big. It's right under my nose. I know it. I *sense* it."

"And your failure to find it is making you doubt yourself," he smiled.

I cocked my head. "You really are an extraordinary man, Blake."

"Thank you, suh." He made as if he were going to pat my shoulder, but stopped, and placed his hand back down at his side. "I've been watching you today. You're good. You are, suh. I was wrong to have doubted. You'll find it, whatever it is."

"I hope so. Have you seen Kitty?"

"Yes, suh. She's in the music room." Using the hand not holding the bucket, he pointed down the hall, opposite of where the staircase ascended. "Five doors down on the right. She goes in there sometimes to calm her spirit."

Like David and King Saul, I thought.

I did as Blake said and found Kitty in a large room filled with musical instruments. She was seated at a twelve-foot Steinway concert grand, slowly plinking out random notes with her index finger.

She'd heard me come in, and looked up, smiling at me tiredly. "So you found my hidin' place. This is where I come to make the world go away. Eddy Arnold sang that."

I took in the room. In addition to the piano, there was a full drum set, various guitars and banjos, even a violin laying in its case on a table. "Do you play all these?"

"To some extent or another," she said. "I'm best on this"—she nodded down at the piano—"and the guitar. That one over in the far corner is my favorite. Roy Acuff gave it to me near on to thirty years ago."

I bypassed that instrument as I walked over to another table, where I picked up a familiar object I'd spied. An autoharp. Remembering a little bit of how one was played, I pressed down the appropriate keys and strummed out a C chord. It sounded sweet.

"I've always liked these," I said, placing it back in its case. "It seems I remember my mother playing one, when I was real small."

I heard some papers fall, and I turned. Kitty was bent down sideways from her seat on the bench, picking up sheet music that had slid off its wooden stand above the keyboard.

"As much money as I spent on this piano, you'd think somebody could figure out a way to keep the music from fallin' off," she muttered. I went over to help gather it up, and she smiled faintly. "Thanks. I'm growin' old. It weren't the piano's fault, but mine. My poor old hands are gettin' a mite shaky."

I put the music back were it belonged, and she laid one of her hands on mine. "You didn't find nothin' here today, did you." It wasn't a question.

"No." The light seemed to go out of her eyes, and I went on, "But I'm not giving up, Kitty. Neither should you."

"I'm not." The breath the old woman drew was more of a shudder even as she tried to look brave. "You can do this, Joe. I know it. If anyone on earth can do this, it's you."

I hoped so. But I couldn't shake the feeling time was winding up for Kitty Clark. And that she'd hired completely the wrong man to handle her problem.

And her nightmare was only going to get worse.

15

Winter melted into spring, and I heard no more from Mitch Cullen. Which was disturbing in and of itself. A guy like Cullen wouldn't just accept the beating I'd given him and walk away a better man for it. No, whatever he was planning for me he'd address in his own time. All I could do was to try and be ready for it, whatever it was.

Strangely, I'd also heard nothing more from Kitty. I wasn't fool enough to think her tormentor had stopped his campaign; whoever was sick enough to put her through this wouldn't cease after just a taste. Like some nasty disease in remission, he'd simply gone underground, to fester and throb, undoubtedly to re-erupt in a more virulent form.

But even I'd miscalculated just how bad things would really get.

The time was a warm mid-April, after both Easter and income tax season had arrived. I could make a crack here about "life in the midst of death," but I won't.

The relationship between Angela and me was in a weird

spot, neither progressing nor regressing, but just kind of there. We'd gone out on a few dates, and of course I'd sat next to her at Easter services at our church, but for the most part she'd kept to herself, pleading work stress and long hours. Which I don't doubt was true.

Still, I was getting a bad sensation that she was beginning to seriously rethink where we stood. Worse, so was I. I was wondering if Cullen had contacted her again, and she was keeping that from me. That was dark territory in and of itself.

At its root, I guess I just couldn't get past the fact that Angela wasn't Linda, and never would be. I'd heard of widowers who never got over their love for their first wives; maybe I was one. If so, the situation between us would only grow more cold and distant.

It was with that cheery future weighing hard on me that Kitty's phone call came in that evening.

Another Saturday night had arrived, and I was in my easy chair, Noodles on my lap, both of us watching *The Searchers*. Periodically I'd feed him a piece of popcorn from the bowl on the table. He'd delicately lift it from my fingers with his teeth, all the while never taking his eyes from the screen. In all probability he was simply mesmerized by the moving shapes and colors, but who can really know the mind of a cat?

The movie had reached the climactic part where John Wayne and Jeffrey Hunter were entering their fourth year of their quest to find the missing Natalie Wood, and things looked bad for the boys. It was right at the part where they were inspecting some hostages the cavalry had rescued from the Apaches that the phone rang.

"Ah, nuts," I muttered, putting the tape on pause. For Christmas I'd bought myself one of those TV/VCR combo sets on sale, to replace the free old black-and-white job that Dempsey Miller had supplied with the apartment. The way the marketing of DVDs had taken off recently, VCRs were almost extinct, and I'd bought my set for practically nothing. The store manager had even offered to throw in a handful of free movies to close the deal, and I'd snatched every one of the Duke that he had.

I set the remote on the small knotty pine table next to my chair and stood, sending Noodles tumbling to the floor. Deep as I'd been into the film's plot, I'd honestly forgotten he was there. But I knew he wouldn't, as he gave me a look of incredulity that I'd had the nerve to do that. With a muttered snarl and switch of his ruined tail, he crawled under the sofa, undoubtedly to plan his revenge for a more suitable time.

The phone was on its third ring by the time I'd padded into the kitchen in my sock feet. Picking it up, I silently vowed my next purchase would be an answering machine. "Hello?"

"Joe? Joe, you gotta help me! Now! He's gone crazy! Are you there? *Joe?*"

What the devil …? I pulled the phone away from my ear, looking at it in disbelief. The harsh voice coming from the earpiece from that far away was tinny and garbled. But for all that, it sure sounded like … oh, no. It couldn't be.

I put it back up to my head. "Kitty? Is that you?"

"Who'd ya think?" she shrieked. "Patsy Cline?"

"Oh, for the love of—" I shook my head, scowling at her gall. "Do you have any idea what time it is?"

Kitty's timing, as always, was impeccable, and the sense of déjà vu I was getting was strong. This conversation was all too similar to the one from this past January, and look how well *that* had gone.

"I'm watching a movie with my cat," I went on. "One he's never seen. Whatever this is can keep until tomorrow."

That was about as civil as I planned to get with her. I started to hang up the phone, but her voice grew even more frantic.

"He's gone bats, I'm tellin' you, bats!" she shrilled.

Sighing, and with a creeping sense of inevitability, I put the phone once more back up to my ear. "Who's gone bats?"

"That's what I been tryin' to tell you, if you'll let me! Tom!"

"Parker?"

"Of course, Parker!" she hollered. "What other Tom would I be talkin' about? Tom Sawyer?"

The reply I almost gave her couldn't be said to a woman, so I said nothing at all.

"He's gone to steal my treasure!" she said. "I know it! And you gotta stop him!"

Treasure? This was a new twist. As in pirate treasure? Gold, silver, what? There wasn't a doubt in my mind now. Kitty Clark was 100 percent cracked.

I tried to keep my speech calm, as if I was soothing a spooked horse. "Kitty, I want you to take a breath, and start over."

Amazingly, I heard her do just that, pulling in a deep one before she said, "All right. Listen up. Here's what happened. You remember that Tom is my manager, right?"

"Yes," I said slowly, like I was talking to a mental patient. "I remember."

"Well, over the past few months I suppose I've said more to him than a body should. Sometimes when I've been drinkin', I run my mouth way yonder too much."

I knew what she meant. I'd done a lot of that myself the years I'd been on the bottle. To my everlasting embarrassment.

Kitty went on, "Somewhere along the line, I told Tom about the treasure I got hid in the safe aboard the *Skylark,* up on Lake Herrington."

"You have a safe on your cabin cruiser?" I replied stupidly. "Why?"

"My own reasons," she snapped. "Anyway, he knows all about it, and he's on his way up there to steal it."

I said nothing, and she plowed on, "See, these past coupla weeks Tom has begun questionin' or contradictin' every stinkin' thing I say, sayin' he knows best about whatever it is, makin' me look like a fool in front of the help. Tonight we got into it real bad, goin' round and round about the latest delay on the openin' of my theme park, over near Jackson. So finally I thought, 'the heck with this noise,' and I just up and fired him."

"Fired him? For real?"

"Yes, for real!"

"Kind of sudden, wasn't it?" I asked, considering how hard it would be to work for such an unhinged woman. To my mind, she'd done Parker a favor, and he didn't realize it yet. Or maybe he did, and had beaten feet for greener climes and saner employers.

"Naw, like I said, this has been comin' with Tom for a while," Kitty said. "And Maria ain't been no help at all. Tonight I finally had my fill of the boy, and I canned him."

Like the ham he is, I thought, and said, "So you think he's having his revenge on you by taking a trip clear up to Lake Herrington, which I've fished a *lot,* to steal a secret treasure you've hidden aboard your private yacht." That sounded incredibly corny, even as I said it. "Okay. Call the cops."

"I ain't gonna do that. Remember, I've always made it clear—"

"No cops, no press," I finished for her. "I remember, Kitty. You've never let me do otherwise." I rolled my head from side to side, to loosen my neck kinks. "What if I say no?"

"You won't," she said, her tone flat. "I already paid you five grand. You gonna stiff me?"

Wow, score one for the old lady.

"That was to solve whoever had been tormenting you," I reminded her. "This is a bit far afield of that."

"Yeah, and you ain't been doin' such a great job for me, have you, Joe?" she shot back. "Seems to me you owe me this."

For all her lack of verbal skills, Kitty Clark hadn't gotten to her station in life by not knowing what buttons to push on a man. But I tried one last time just the same. "Maybe Parker just went out for the evening. Grown men do that, you know."

"Don't talk to me like I'm a child!" she growled. "I know what's goin' on. I'm old, but I ain't deaf. When I fired him last night, Tom—he said all right, he was gonna steal my treasure instead. He's out to rip me off, Joe, to ruin me."

Ruin her? Discounting all her other wealth? That must be some treasure she had.

"You gonna help me or not?" she said.

Not, I almost said, but didn't.

"You win, Kitty," I sighed. "What do you want me to do?"

"That's better." I could almost picture her nodding. "Grab a paper, 'cause I'm about to give you some numbers you'll need to remember."

"Just a minute."

I set the phone down and went back into the living room, where I keep a pad and pen on my table beside the chair. As I reached for it, from beneath the sofa Noodles snarled and shot out a paw, catching the toe of my sock with his claw.

We tugged with each other for a moment before I yanked free. Hissing now, he pulled his paw back. Oh boy. Was I going to pay for this tomorrow with him.

Sitting back down at the kitchen table with the items in hand, I picked up the phone.

"Okay, Kitty, shoot."

"Write these down the way I tell 'em to you," she said. "Ready?" She then proceeded to read the numbers off slowly, and I did just as she said.

"Repeat 'em back to me," she ordered.

"Five, three, two, seven, eight, eight, two, seven, eight," I read off, and I set the pen down. "That right?"

"You got it."

"What exactly *have* I got? What do these numbers mean?"

Her tone again turned harsh. "You're the detective. Detect."

I looked down at them, marching across the paper. "Only one thing immediately comes to mind. They're the combination to the safe on your boat."

"Bingo," Kitty said. "Right on the nose, Joe. The original numbers were six, nine, seven, five, nine, five, two, seven, five. If you look at 'em on a phone dial, they spell out a word. MYSKY-LARK. I thought that up myself when I bought the safe, 'cause it helped me remember the combination. But then I decided to change it."

Actually MYSKYLARK was two words, but there was no sense in making Kitty more upset than she already was, so I just said, "Why did you do that?"

"Because I realized that what I know, Tom knows," she replied. "For a while now, I been gettin' an uneasy hunch about his thievin' ways, that maybe he was plannin' on skimmin' me bad some day. So a coupla weeks ago I had Blake drive me up to the lake in the limo and I changed the numbers on the safe to what I just gave you."

"Yeah? So what do *they* spell?"

"That ain't important."

"Then why give them to me at all? You've said that all you want me to do is to stop Tom from getting in your safe. Why do I need to know the combination?"

And for the first time since I'd picked up the phone, I sensed uncertainty in Kitty's voice.

"Just a ... feelin' I'm gettin'," she replied slowly. "A feelin' that maybe it's time somebody else besides me knows how to get at my treasure. In case they ever have a need to. I get those kind of feelin's every now and again."

So did I. I was getting a strong one here. And not a good one.

But I didn't let on as I picked up the pen once more. "When did Parker leave?"

"Not more'n a few minutes ago." Kitty began rushing her words. "If you leave right now you can catch him, Joe. Catch him and stop him. I know it."

"Where do you keep the *Skylark* berthed?"

"The big dock on Gwynn Island. Know it?"

"Yeah, I know it. Like I said, I've fished the lake before."

"Well, then go."

She hung up the phone with a bang.

I stared at the thing again before replacing it back on the wall, my thoughts dark. If I had that five thousand bucks right here in my hot little hand, and Kitty Clark standing before me, I gladly would have taken that wad of bills she'd given me and—

About then I felt a rubbing around my calves, and I looked down. Noodles. He was purring up at me apologetically as he head-bumped my legs.

"So, come to make up with me, have you?" I scolded. "Too little, too late, pal. I'll have you know these socks you wrecked were a Christmas gift to me from Mr. Sapperstein, the deli man. You remember him? The guy who lets me have his corned beef scraps for your supper? For free?" I shook my head. "Some gratitude, cat."

Noodles rolled over on his back, presenting his scarred belly for me to rub.

"Naow?" he pleaded.

That was about as close to "sorry" as I was going to get from him. I sighed and started stroking him with my foot, using the toe of the sock he'd mangled.

"You're something, you are," I said. He just purred louder, curling his paws against his body. I did that for a few more seconds, then I pushed him away and stood.

"A few-minutes-old lead." I looked down at him. "That's what Kitty said Parker has. Let's see if I can cut that."

♦ ◊ ♦

Ninety seconds later I'd changed into blue jeans, gym shoes, and a too-tight UC tee shirt, and now I was jammed behind the wheel of the Yugo, heading up the highway interchange toward I-75 south. At the last second back in my bedroom I'd picked up and then tossed down my jacket. For some reason, I'd felt it would only hinder my movements. Anyway, April up here was warmer than normal; I hoped it would be the same down in Kentucky, too.

As I sped down the blacktop, another thought occurred to me. With my left hand gripping the steering wheel, I used my right to punch out Quint's number on my cell phone.

He answered in two rings. "The Blaine residence."

"Quint? Joe. Listen, I need you to do me something."

"Of course, dear boy. You might not believe this, but I've been staring at my phone all evening, hoping you'd call."

"Funny. Get a pen and write these numbers down."

He must have picked up in my voice that now wasn't the time to joke around, because he merely said, "I have a pad and pen right here, Joseph. Give them to me."

By memory I said them, and he repeated them back.

"All right, now what?" he asked.

"Run them through that high-tech computer system of yours. Kitty Clark gave them to me tonight. Why, I'm still trying to fathom. I need for you to tell me if they spell anything."

"Spell anything? What do you mean?"

"I mean, if you looked at them on a telephone keypad, you'll see they have letters that go with them. Run the numbers I gave you that way and see if anything comes up."

He sounded dubious. "Very well. But I can tell from the ambient noise I'm hearing you're calling from that rattletrap you call an automobile. Are you in some sort of trouble?"

"No." Then I went on truthfully, "Not yet, anyway. Call me back as soon as you find out anything."

I knew the curiosity was killing Quint, but he simply said, "Running a numerical sequence this long may take a while. Stay close."

"I'll be right here, buddy."

As we rang off, I pressed the gas pedal down even further on the Yugo. I hoped she had enough spunk left in her cylinders to make the three-plus hour trip down to the lake.

And back, a part of me reminded the other. *You'd like to come back, wouldn't you?* Well yes, I admitted. I'd like that a lot.

♦ ◊ ♦

A bit later I crossed the Brent Spence Bridge into

Kentucky, and almost immediately the air in the car felt heavier, more dense. I cranked down the window. The humidity was more noticeable now.

Great. Ten bucks and a bowl of Skyline chili said we were about to get ourselves an April thunderstorm. This time of year the spring weather could turn unaccountably nasty, stormin' weather, as Granny used to call it, and many times it meant a hearty dose of wind, hail, and thunderous downpours.

Just the kind of weather to take a nice, calm, middle-of-the-night road trip down to a whitecap-whipped lake. *Kitty, I hope you know what you're asking me to do here.*

Ninety minutes after that I'd turned off I-75 at the Lexington ramp and found myself on the Bluegrass Parkway, heading toward Highway 27, and the Danville exit. The rain had started up in earnest an hour ago and now had grown as bad as I'd feared.

The Yugo's wipers were keeping up with the deluge, but barely. The seventy-five-mile-per-hour speed I was maintaining didn't help. If the downpour started hammering any harder, I'd be forced to pull off and wait it out, and Parker would win the race by default.

And that, as my gunnery instructor in the army used to say, was an unacceptable outcome.

A half an hour earlier, my cell phone had rung. It was Kitty. I really didn't have time for her, and what she'd said to me made no sense, as garbled as the transmission was. Just a few words about something being real this time, then nothing.

On either side of the highway, huge boulders, freshly wrenched from their cliffs, had tumbled down from the ridges the military construction engineers had cut across and blasted through. Some of those rocks were nearly as big as my car. I tried to shut out the picture of one landing across the road in front of me. The Yugo would lose, without a doubt.

It was as the rain was reaching a crescendo that my cell phone rang again. I thumbed the call button. For her sake, it'd better not be Kitty again.

"Yeah," I barked.

"Joseph? Quint here. My goodness, what's that howling I hear?"

"Rain. A freaking monsoon. What have you got?"

"As I'd feared, running the sequence took longer than I thought. But remember, I said it might."

"Yeah, yeah," I said impatiently. "Get to it, would you? I'm a little busy here."

If Quint was upset at my brusqueness, he didn't let on. "A string of that length will, through its sheer volume of combinations, result in a few recognizable words. But one word in particular fairly jumped off the screen at me. It was a name. It—"

Thunder crashed right then, as loud as an artillery burst, effectively scrambling what my friend said. A few seconds later it had rumbled away far enough that I could speak again.

"Repeat that, Quint. You broke up. What did you say?"

More static ground its way through, sounding like burning, crackling cellophane, then I heard him say, "—name. A name you've told me only a select handful of people—" I was only getting snatches now. Then I heard, "—spell out your name, Joseph. *Your middle name.* Are you lis—?"

More static, worse, but the next came through, as clear as a bell.

"They spell out JEBSTUART," Quint said.

Then the thunder roared again, and the connection died.

16

The driving rain was making visibility nearly impossible, but that didn't make me ease up on the gas any as I negotiated the twisting roads leading down to the dock at Gwynn Island. Kitty had said that Parker didn't have more than a short lead, and if I could just keep the Yugo from flipping over on these bends, I could still cut that lead in half.

A bright flash of lightning and booming thunder erupted. Right at that moment, not twenty feet ahead, an ash tree as thick as a phone pole toppled across my half of the road. With a gasp I whipped around the thing and then was past it, almost before the event registered in my brainpan. Man, that was close. Not for the first time, the thought occurred to me that, as pretty as heaven sounded, I really didn't want this to be the night I went.

The road grade began to lessen, and I knew I was in the home stretch now.

Three more turns through the blinding rain, the trees above whipping their branches, and I was there, the pavement finally widening and flattening into the parking area where fishermen backed their boat trailers into the lake. But no fishing was going to be done this evening. The rain now was coming in sideways, the wind howling like a lost soul.

As I got out of the Yugo, the car door was nearly torn from my fingers. Instantly I was soaked to the skin. Not a fit night out for man nor beast, as W. C. Fields so memorably put it.

I had no idea a night could be so black, or so wet, or so miserable. As I splashed across the darkened parking lot, I didn't see Parker's Lexus, but that didn't mean anything. He could be parked on the other side of the bait shop. That's where I would have been.

Cautiously striding onto the rain-slicked dock, I noticed, off to my left, the lights were out in the shop, no surprise. If the owner, Dale Vosser, had any sense, he'd be inside his house up on the hill, drinking something warm and cuddling with his wife.

Right then the lightning double-flashed, followed by a thunderclap that rattled my fillings. In that brief glimpse I saw the dock itself was nearly deserted of boats, most of the owners having wisely gotten them off the lake earlier. The two remaining vessels, an aluminum johnboat and a fairly nice Bass Tracker, were being mercilessly battered against the pilings. I doubted either would be recognizable as watercraft by dawn.

But those two doomed boats were all that the lightning had revealed. Where was Kitty's cruiser? I would be massively ticked if it turned out I'd made the decision to embark on this harrowing drive, in this frog-strangling weather, based on Kitty's bad intel.

Then I remembered something. Last fall, when I was down here to do some late-season largemouth bass jigging, Dale had told me he was planning on adding an extension to the dock, putting it around the far side of the bait shop, where the water was deeper. He said he thought the extension would attract a richer clientele, with larger boats. In Kitty Clark, at least, he'd achieved his goal. So the *Skylark* had to be here. But where—

My question was answered as, above the nearly ceaseless thunder, I heard another sound: the low, throaty, unmistakable roar of big marine motors turning over. There was only one person I knew of nuts enough to be taking a boat out in this impenetrable deluge.

Parker.

I'd come too far to lose him now, and I began running along the side of the shop toward the new extension, my feet making wet, hollow, slopping sounds on the wood as I flew. I hoped I would know where the turn was in all this blackness. It wouldn't do to skitter off the edge and go over the side.

In ten more strides I was there, but too late. I'd miscalculated my arrival by seconds. Through the hammering rain I could just make out the running lights of the *Skylark*, ten feet out from the dock and pulling away, Parker at the wheel on the upper deck, throttling up.

What I did next has to rank in at least the upper ten of the world's dumbest stunts. Don't ask me why, but instead of turning back toward my car, figuring to get him another day, I suddenly increased my speed, now running full tilt to the dock's edge. *This is insane*, a part of me told the other part, but by then it was too late. I'd launched myself out over the dark, crazed waters toward the rear of the cruiser.

I very nearly didn't make it, and it would have served me right if I hadn't. But God must watch over fools and private eyes—and I was both—because even as my hands closed over the back railing, I saw Parker push the throttle up. The motors' rumble grew to a bone-rattling roar. I almost slid off then, and desperately tightened my grip.

Well, wasn't this dandy. Now what, Box?

Some sixth sense must have caused Parker to look back toward the stern. That's when he saw me, and his eyebrows rose.

Baring his teeth, he shot his arm forward, ramming the throttle right to its stop. With it the *Skylark* leaped ahead like a racehorse out of the gate, blasting across the waves. I gasped as my arms suddenly felt like they weighed a hundred pounds each and were about to be torn from their sockets.

The lightning flashed again. In that brief moment I saw Parker's face, looking oddly skull-like, staring down at me from his pilot's perch. He screamed something, but his words were ripped away by the wind.

My feet were inches above the prop wash. If I slipped now, those savage blades would chop me into fish chum before I'd even have a chance to holler. The G forces were making my limbs feel like they were being stretched to the length of a gibbon's, but too bad. It was get onboard or die. Groaning, ignoring the pain in my shoulder, I agonizingly began inching myself up over the railing, finally landing in a sodden heap on the back deck.

Getting shakily to my feet on the bucking craft, I didn't have time to enjoy my triumph of man over physics. Parker didn't let me. Suddenly he was right there, a foot from my face, a length of rusty chain clutched in his fist. I only had a moment to register that, and to consider he must have set the cruiser on autopilot, before he swung that fist directly at my head. I've mentioned before he wasn't a small man by any means, and he put every ounce of his nearly three hundred pounds into that killing blow.

I never had a chance. Parker's fist slammed against my temple, and lights and trumpets and loud huzzahs exploded in my skull like the end of the world.

Then everything turned black, and I went away for a while.

♦ ◊ ♦

The feeling of rocking roused me. But roused is a relative term. It doesn't begin to describe the utter physical degradation I was feeling, the insane cranial pounding and sick roiling turmoil in the gut a good blow to the head always produces. It didn't help that the *Skylark* was heaving up and down in the lake swells it was ripping over like it was hacking its way across the North Atlantic.

I realized I was sitting up, and tried moving. Big mistake. Searing heat lanced through my shoulder and sparks of acid-yellow light went off behind my eyes. That was all it took as I turned and violently said good-bye to my supper. It was as I went to wipe my mouth that I found my hands had been tied behind my back, to something that felt like metal.

Before I could think more on it, suddenly the deck was awash with light. Parker again. He'd flipped on the big spotlights I'd seen fore and aft in the photos of the boat he'd shown me, and now I saw he'd tied me to one of those silly black wrought-iron benches somebody had bolted to the stern.

He was back up on the flying bridge, grinning down at me. I bitterly noted he was safely tucked back under its canopy, while the wind continued to hurl cold rain in my face.

"Miserable night, ain't it?" he yelled.

I almost didn't reply, wondering if shouting back would make me sick again. But it didn't matter; puking my guts out was the least of my worries. I hoped I wasn't concussed.

As galling as it was to admit it, Parker had me, well and truly. Blood caked my face, and beyond the circle of light from the boat, all was mounting blackness. We might as well have been the only two men on the face of the earth tonight. The lunatic way he was staring at me chilled me worse than the rain. Here was a man with absolutely nothing to lose.

My hands chafing against the rope, I whispered a desperate prayer. If God didn't step in, I knew I wouldn't live to see the dawn.

"Why all the lights?" I hollered back, my head pounding like a potato in a washtub. "Aren't you afraid somebody will see them and wonder what you're doing out here?"

"In this?" Parker laughed. "Not hardly. Anybody with smarts'll be inside with a hot toddy in one hand and a hot woman in the other."

"Smarts? So what's that make us?" I yelled.

He didn't answer, instead putting his hand on the throttle and pulling it back a notch. Instantly the RPMs on the engines slackened to a dull mutter. Parker continued pulling the lever toward him, and now the craft began to plane down, slowing to a crawl. But why? There was nothing solid out here to run into. Unless … oh, no. Even he wasn't that insane.

But he was. My fears were confirmed as I saw, straight ahead and reflected in the *Skylark's* running lights, the looming limestone face of a cliff.

Now I knew he was certifiably crazy.

"What are you doing?" I gasped, though I knew full well. Parker's answer sounded too loud as he cut the motors completely.

"Droppin' anchor," he replied, hitting the switch that released them clattering, before coming down the ladder to the deck. "And you, when I get around to it." Behind the ladder, he pulled open the door that led below deck. "But first I need to get what's in that safe."

"Forget the safe. Get us away from the cliff. Now."

He stopped and turned, the rain sluicing off his face.

"Now why would I do that? You can see for yourself the water's calmer here. That's why I came over to this side, to get my business done without gettin' bounced all over hell's half acre."

"You've never been on this lake before, have you?" I was unconsciously pulling on the ropes that had me bound.

"Sure I have, last October with Kitty. That's how I know the layout. So what?"

I motioned with my chin at the promontory hanging over us. It must have been at least two hundred feet high. "So that cliff's a killer. That's what."

"A *killer?*" he laughed, glancing up, even though the top was lost somewhere in the low-hanging darkness. "Looks like a plain old cliff to me." He looked back at me. "Yeah, I'd say it's plenty tall enough to keep us away from some of that wave chop."

"Forget the wave chop! Have you ever seen what this much water can do to limestone?"

He shook his head and I went on, "Well, I have. I fished this lake a lot when I was a kid. Limestone is the most porous rock there is, ask any geologist. Give it this good of a soaking and it gets unstable."

He frowned. "And this is important because ..."

"Rock slides, Parker! Get it now? Big ones."

"Rock slides," he grinned. "On a lake. You intrigue me, son. What an imagination."

"Didn't you see the slides we passed on the highway down here? And those were recent, maybe from today."

He was still grinning at me, not buying it, and my tone

became desperate.

"Listen, this whole side of the lake is made up by cliffs like this. I've seen what they can do. Nobody ties up to one after a heavy rain. And for sure not *during* one!"

His grin grew. "You sound scared."

"You'd be too, if you had any brains."

Parker pursed his lips, still smirking, and I knew then he'd sealed my fate.

"You should be scared, son," he said. "Heck, I'd be too, if I knew I was gonna finish this night out as bass bait."

I swallowed. That was one way to put it.

He went on, "But that was pretty good, I gotta admit, you tryin' to buy yourself some more time. That's what I call thinkin' on your feet. Or in your case, your butt." His chuckle was rasping. "I always did admire a sharp mind. They're a rare thing these days."

Pulling the door open, Parker got in a last shot over his shoulder.

"Much as I'd love to keep chewin' the fat with you, Box, you got an appointment three hundred feet straight down, and you don't wanna be late. I'll see to it. First, though, I gotta get what's mine." With that he disappeared down the passageway. I waited until I was sure he was really gone, then I began yanking on the ropes even harder.

It was right about then my thumb discovered a sharp piece of metal jutting out just a couple of inches up. Maybe it was some flashing left over from whoever had welded this bench, flashing they'd missed sanding off in their haste to get the job done. However it happened, I was grateful. With sopping fingers I slid the rope up over it and began cutting.

Below deck I heard Parker burst out with a string of cursing.

He was obviously finding the safe a tougher nut to crack than he'd banked on; I hoped he wouldn't figure out the combination until I was free of the ropes. I'd settle accounts with him then. Thunder crashed again and the rain began coming down even harder, if such a thing was possible.

Then it hit me—that wasn't thunder; clouds couldn't make that harsh of a noise. My blood froze. The water cascading down on my lips now had a distinctive mineral taste.

Oh my God.

"Parker!" I yelled. "Get up here! The cliff's going!" Nothing. *"Parker!"*

Either he hadn't heard me, or he was so absorbed in trying to get into that safe he'd tuned everything else out. The ominous rumbling from above was growing louder, and I could almost picture the groundwater spraying like a fire hose through the cracks in the cliff face. I should be able to picture it; as I'd told Parker, I'd seen it as a kid.

We had only seconds left. Even now the incredible pressure from all that water was forcing the limestone away from its foundation. My fears were confirmed as I heard smaller rocks begin hitting the lake, and then, horrifyingly, striking the boat itself.

Frenzied, I began practically dislocating my shoulders in my haste to get free of my bonds, my hands behind me sawing away like a machine.

"Parker!" I hollered again. "Get this tub moving! We—"

Too late. With an immense *craa-aack* something huge broke free far above, and time stopped.

Dread blasting through me, I buried my chin in my chest and screamed out the name of Jesus.

What happened next remains a jumble in my remembrance. There was a rush of air and a tremendous explosion, and somewhere below deck Parker screamed like the damned. A giant's hand seemed to lift us.

And at the same instant the entire length of the *Skylark* stood on its nose.

My disbelieving mind flashed back to the scene in *Titanic*, the one where the ship went vertical. Like in that movie, my feet slid out from beneath me, my wrenched shoulder where I'd been shot howling in pain. The only thing that kept me from tumbling down the hatch where Parker had disappeared was the rope holding my hands.

That's when the deck lights went out.

For a seeming eternity the boat hung suspended there in the blackness, violently bobbing like a toy in a bathtub, the darkness pressing down like a suffocating shroud.

And then slowly, with a shudder that reminded me of an old man easing his arthritic bulk into a Barcalounger, the *Skylark* settled back on her keel.

But not quite.

It didn't take a genius to realize by her tilt she was down at least twenty degrees by the bow, with an equal list to port. I know nothing about boats, but it appeared to me that whatever had happened to her was fatal. So how much time did she have left?

Who cared? I had to get off. Now.

The binding rope must have been nearly in two, because it seemed I'd only just again begun violently yanking on it when it suddenly parted with a wet snap. With the two pieces of hemp dangling from my wrists, I stood and took stock of how things were.

The answer was, hopeless. I was aboard a sinking cabin cruiser, in the dark, in the middle of an insane storm, with an injured, possibly dying, crazy man below deck.

Every bit of common sense I possessed told me to grab the
first thing that would float and go over the side. Anybody else
would have done it in a heartbeat. But like I said, Parker was
hurt—from the way he'd shrieked, probably badly—and even as
a part of me marveled in disbelief, I found myself slip-sliding
toward the hatch that led below deck.

I was wondering how I was going to see down there, and
what possible good I was going to be when I did, when with a
sputter the emergency lights flickered on.

But they were "lights" in name only. In comparison to the
bright floods I'd seen before, these were puny, yellowish things,
hardly brighter than the brake lights on the family Buick or the
pocket flash you smuggled into your pup tent as a kid. Still, they
beat nothing.

My hands on either side of the doorway stopped my slide.
In that weak illumination, I saw I'd been right about the condition of the *Skylark*.

She was doomed.

Water was washing over the bow, which in this light
appeared badly damaged. I could feel a subtle, inexorable pulling
on my feet, a seductive tugging urging me forward as the tilt
grew.

Acting more bravely than I felt, I plunged through the hatch,
hollering his name. "Parker!"

His answering cry was a weak gasp. "Over here, son. Oh my
God ..."

Stumbling down the stairs, at the bottom I turned, and then
stopped in mute shock.

The cabin before me had once been a homey, cozy retreat for
Kitty and her guests, as little as two minutes ago. The stateroom

was paneled in what looked like oak, and was furnished with comfortable-looking furniture and built-in bookshelves. A stereo had been in the corner. That system would never again be played, or the furniture used, or the books read. All of it, every-thing in the room, was upended, tossed, tumbled toward the center.

Where Parker lay pinned under a boulder the size of my desk.

I saw the scene all of a piece. Above him the shattered wood of the foredeck hung downward, the hole where the boulder had torn through an obscenity. That rock had blasted on down, catching Parker as he had obviously been tampering with the safe. But where he'd failed in cracking it, the stone had suc-ceeded. Kitty's treasure repository now hung sprung open, the door swinging wildly.

Next to him, another hole gaped in the floor. If the size of this opening was any indication, the rock that had made it was even larger than the one that had nailed Parker. And if it had passed clear through the hull, we'd be sliding under in mere moments. The fact we hadn't yet made me think that maybe all it had done was crack the fiberglass hull. But that tilt couldn't be ignored, and I'd bet my life we were taking on water somewhere below. I hoped it wouldn't come to me betting my life. But that hole wasn't the worst sight in here.

What I couldn't tear my eyes from was Parker himself.

He lay sprawled on his back, the rectangular-shaped boulder across his lower half. I could tell at a glance his pelvis and legs had been pulped to jelly under that massive weight. My fears were confirmed as I saw a massive amount of blood leaking out around him, staining the ruined carpet and the splintered wood floor underneath it a dark red.

And even as I stared, I knew without a doubt I'd never be able to shift that rock.

Seeing me, Parker's eyes lit up in weak hope. He began waving both his arms feebly at me as I made my way across the devastated stateroom.

"Help me, Box," he whispered as I knelt down beside him. "Get it off." Pointing his chin up, he hissed, "Oh God, it hurts ..."

Kneeling there, I'd never felt so useless in my life. I was amazed he hadn't gone into shock. Even in combat I'd never seen such a sight. Get it off? Who was I, Samson?

Tentatively I touched him here and there with helpless hands. "Parker ..." I licked my lips and started over. "Parker, I can't. I don't have the strength."

Both his hands grasped my forearm, his tone imploring. "Try. You gotta try ..."

And the crazy thing was, he was right. Even though I owed him nothing, I had to try. Because hang me for a fool, whenever I come across someone in real trouble, trying to help them is what I do. It's what I always do. Not that I succeed much.

Settling back on my knees to think, once again I began feeling light-headed. That's all I needed, I thought, to black out now. *Keep it together, Box.* Drawing a couple of deep breaths, I felt Parker's eyes on me, eyes I absolutely refused to meet.

Anxiously I took in the room. What in here could lift a rock that size? A block and tackle might have done it, but I doubted a craft like this would carry one big enough, and besides, with the cabin roof gone, where would I have put it?

Then I thought, a lever. That was it. I needed a lever, something strong enough, and long enough, to move that monstrosity, with a fulcrum for a pivot. Surely something in here could work ... could work ... work, work, work ...

Again grayness began nibbling around the edges of my vision.... It could work for the Turk, but they say he's a jerk....

Cut it out. No time for that now. Parker needed me to be clever ... because if I was clever I could *make* a lever ... just like that ancient thinker who said that if he had a lever long enough, he could move the world.... Who was that again ...? Archimedes ...? Wait a minute. What did *he* have to do with it?

With a will I forced my throbbing head to address the problem. *Come on, Box, think, remember your college math.* Lift plus mass ... *jumpin' Jack Flash, it's a gas gas gas* ...

I leaned forward, resting my hands on the sodden carpet, trying to shut out Parker's whimpering and at the same time clear my head. As I did I frowned. Sodden was right. As Shakespeare had said in one of his plays, *who knew the old man had so much blood in him?*

And then I realized it wasn't just Parker's blood I was kneeling in.

It was water.

I blinked, making myself accept what I was seeing. The force of the stone's impact that had made the hole next to Parker had indeed sprung the hull, just as I'd feared, and cold lake water was pouring in.

That's when I knew for sure he was a dead man.

He didn't know it yet, though, and I met his eyes at last. Desperation still blazed there, and it would have taken a stronger man than me to quench it.

But I didn't have to. Parker's lower spine was shattered, true enough, but I knew from watching enough medical shows on TV that he still had sensation from his waist on up.

I must have been right. His eyes bulged as he had to have felt the cold lake water creeping up his back, because his next cry was one of shattering hopelessness. *"No!"*

No use trying to shunt reality aside now; we both knew the truth.

"Box!" Parker seized my hand like a vise. "Help me, son! Don't let me drown!"

Like you'd planned for me? I almost said. But there was no point in tormenting him; he'd be facing his Judge soon enough. And in my time on this planet I've helped enough dying animals, victims of bad traffic or careless hunters, pass over to the other side with as much ease as I could afford them. Could I do any less for a man?

"Here." I grabbed a couple of dripping sofa cushions from the floor, pulling Parker as upright as I could and jamming them underneath him. He was a little higher that way. Even so, the water now lapped around his shoulders.

My feet were unsteady as I rose. The *Skylark's* downward tilt was growing worse, the whirlies from my head injury making me feel like I'd been booted in the skull by Pelé.

"You need something to breathe through," I said. "A snorkel, maybe. I'll go look." Turning back toward the passageway, I heard Parker's strangled voice behind me.

"Don't leave me!" He was weeping now, blubbering like a child. "Oh God, don't leave me.... I don't wanna die alone...."

I stopped and looked at him. "I'm coming back. You won't be alone." I swallowed. "I'll be with you when it happens." Then I turned and was gone.

Pulling myself back through the doorway and onto the rear deck, I was faintly surprised to see the rain had finally stopped, the sky lighter with a milky moon. But the wind and waves were still vicious, and I knew the respite might be only temporary.

Reaching the back rail, I frantically began pawing through

the bolted-down chests found there. If Kitty had stored swimming equipment aboard, this should be where it was.

But it wasn't. Of the three chests, two were empty, and the third held life jackets.

I stood, running a shaky hand through my hair. Okay, so a snorkel was out. How about a hose of some sort? A hose, but where would I find a …

The engine compartment. There had to be something there that could do it. Quickly I undogged the hatch covering the big marine motors. There, under the hatch, held on by spring clamps, was exactly the thing.

A spare radiator hose.

I ripped it free and practically fell down the passageway steps in my haste to … well, not to save Parker's life, certainly. That was beyond my power. But I could give him the chance to clean the slate before he crossed. Anybody was due that much.

Reaching him and again kneeling by his side, I found I'd almost been too late. The water was now flooding in at an alarming rate. Only his face remained above it.

"I thought … I thought you'd left me …" Parker spluttered, his eyes as big as plates.

"Open your mouth!" I barked, not waiting for him to comply as I pulled on his chin and forced the hose between his teeth. He gagged on the foul rubber taste, but I took my other hand and mashed his lips around it.

And not a second too soon, as the water rushed over his head, swirling around my hand.

Parker again clamped his hands around my wrists, staring up at me, his fearful face ghostlike under the water. I could hear his gasping breath coming from the hose's open end. The thing was maybe eighteen inches long. We had less than a minute.

I put my face to the water's edge, above his. "Can you hear me?" I yelled. "Squeeze my wrists if you can hear me!"

Squeeze my wrists? What was I saying? That was no good. His grip was already deathlike. I tried another way. "Blink, Parker! Blink if you understand!"

His eyes squeezed shut once, then jerked open, still locked on mine.

There was no time to pretty up the words. "Listen to me. You're going to die. Here, tonight, on this boat." The water inexorably rose. "Your time is up."

The gasping coming from the open end of the hose next to my ear grew louder, and Parker shook his head violently in denial, nearly tearing the thing from his mouth.

I tightened my grip. The time to share my faith had arrived. Here. Now. "It comes to us all sooner or later," I hollered. "You, me, everybody. But you have the chance to make things right. Right with God. Understand? One last chance."

The *Skylark* shuddered again and the tilt increased a few more degrees. Something told me somebody didn't want this conversation to happen. I didn't care. Shoot the devil and the horse he rode in on.

I yelled louder. "Parker! Do you want that? Blink once if it's yes. I'll pray for you."

He ignored me. The water was now up to the hose's end, a fraction of an inch from going inside. Still the man's eyes were locked on mine, as if by the act of holding my gaze his life would never end. But it wasn't my gaze that would do it. There was only one who could, and he was here, waiting, like me, to see what Parker would do.

And suddenly I found myself idiotically, stupidly praying. "Oh God, God ..." Of all the strange things I've ever done, this was the weirdest. I was praying for the soul of this man who earlier tonight had planned to drown me without a second's hesitation.

Only I was still here, and now he was the one on the far side of the water.

"Listen to me!" My fingers dug into him. "We're out of time! Blink once and—"

Gone.

Parker's chance vanished like a dream, as with a nasty gurgle the water at last breached the edge of the hose's open end, pouring down the tube and right into his mouth. Reflexively he released my hands like he'd been burned, ripping the hose away in panic, opening his mouth wide for a breath that both of us knew would never come.

That's when he screamed.

Huge, floppy bubbles erupted from the water, along with a muffled bellowing. Parker's hands began scratching at my face, my eyes, tearing and ripping at my shirt in his agony. Ignoring his fingers furrowing my flesh, I tried pulling him higher, but to no avail.

His death throes seemed to last for hours, but of course they didn't. Still the bubbles rose, but now the sound was gone. Parker's motions began growing more aimless. Then, finally, stopped. His eyelids fluttered, but the eyes themselves, glazing in disbelief, still held mine. In them it seemed I read resentment for this alien creature of light and air, this one who could still breathe while he crossed over into another place.

To this day, with all my heart I hope he landed safely.

But I was out of time myself. The cabin ceiling was now only two feet above my head, and closing in fast. Parker was dead, and I'd be too if I didn't get off this thing. Time to abandon ship.

But wait. Not yet. Kitty had sent me down here for the express purpose of keeping Parker away from her "treasure." I'd done that, but not in the way I'd thought. And in another few seconds that treasure, whatever it was, would be forever out of her reach, heading toward a resting place of permanent night on the bottom of Lake Herrington.

If I didn't snag it first.

To my right, a few feet underwater, the squat safe gaped open. I pulled in a breath of rapidly vanishing air and dove. With aching strokes I swam over and peered inside. I don't know what it was exactly I'd expected. Jewels maybe, possibly rare figurines, perhaps even money.

But all that was in there was a thick manila envelope, like one you'd find at any office supply store, sheathed in bubble-wrap and sealed with packing tape. This was her treasure? Whatever it was, I pulled it out, jamming it down the front of my jeans. I tried to surface.

When I did, my head bumped solidly against the cabin roof.

What the—? Oh, no. Oh, Jesus help me. The whole room already was underwater. And this is the part I was getting to when I started relating this tale, all those pages back.

Okay, stay calm, I thought. *You've got time. You've been in worse spots than this.* Well, I hadn't really, but Granny always told me to think positive.

For just a second I considered going out the hole the boulder had made, but quickly discarded that idea. As I said, the opening was submerged, and I could just picture me trying to exit that way, only to get skewered on the sharp edges of the shattered foredeck. No, the way out was the way I'd come in. My lungs burning in earnest now, I began swimming like mad for the hatchway.

That's when, for the second time tonight, the boat's lights failed. I nearly panicked then.

Once, as a kid, my dad and granny and me had taken a trip to Mammoth Cave, and while there we'd gone on one of those daylong tours. The blind cave fish and cave crickets I'd seen were creepy enough just by themselves, but the real terror had come when, deep inside, the guide turned out the lights. The darkness seemed to have a weight of its own, and some of the men in the group tried laughing it off, making feeble jokes, telling their wives or girlfriends to keep their hands to themselves.

But the jokes fell flat.

Especially to a five-year-old like me. I was frozen in place, suddenly seized with the irrational fear that if I moved just one inch, I'd fall backwards into that underground river we'd passed earlier. There I'd be swept deep into the bowels of the earth, where I'd be endlessly trapped in a watery grave, with only dead miners and blind cave fish as company.

In hindsight, of course, that was stupid. The river was miles past our group, and the guide had kept the lights off for only a minute. When he finally flipped them back on, it was to relieved sighs from the women and embarrassed laughter from the men.

But I hadn't laughed. I just wanted out of there.

Same as now.

From dead reckoning I figured where the opening had to be, and frantically I started for it. That's when I felt a tap on my leg. I turned, and touched the skin of his cold hand.

Parker.

He was pulling me toward him, *toward him!* I nearly screamed, before I realized this wasn't some ghost story grown real, just the random movements of Parker's dead arms in the current. Had to be, right? Right. I pulled away and again lunged for the opening. Thankfully I was right on the first try. Somehow I found myself inside, and began going hand over hand up the black passageway that now seemed three miles long.

A seeming eternity later I popped up, gasping and coughing. I paused for a precious few seconds, pulling in what felt like eight cubic feet of sweet night air, then I started crawling up the sloping afterdeck to make my jump.

Reaching the back rail I saw the whole boat was nearly under, and I took in the wild water raging five feet down. Without a life jacket I'd never make it back to the dock.

Then I remembered the storage locker I'd seem them in, and I bent down and began fumbling with it, my fingers nerveless. For a moment the thing resisted, then its lid sprang open. Seizing the first jacket I grabbed, I leaped with it over the side.

My shoulder had grown ominously numb, and it wasn't until the waves were breaking over my head that I discovered what I was clutching wasn't a life jacket.

It was a small, self-inflating raft.

Even better. I yanked the lanyard, praying the CO_2 cylinder was still good. It was. With a satisfying hiss the thing inflated in seconds, and I flipped it over.

It was only after I'd hauled myself inside that I turned and watched the last of Kitty Clark's beloved *Skylark* finally slip beneath the waves, as it started its long fall into endless night. For a moment I considered the place where it had gone, pondering the fate of other lost ships in other lost waters, each with their own cargoes of secrets and death.

Then pulling the folding paddle free of its strap, I snapped it open and began rowing like the devil himself was a jet-black homing torpedo that had acquired my range, and was bearing down hard.

17

*E*very fiber of my battered frame screeching in protest, I managed to slide the key into the lock of my room at the Danville Breeze Motel. I turned the knob and shuffled inside, dully accepting the fact this place looked like any other of a hundred—a thousand—similar ratty rooms in which I'd passed out or come to back during my drinking days. The same peeling flowered wallpaper, the same threadbare gray carpet, the same dribbling, ineffectual window AC unit, the same tiny, mildewed bathroom. Only the zip code here was different.

I tossed the envelope onto the cigarette-scorched dresser and began the process of laboriously removing my still-sopping clothes. Unbidden, a wry smile came on my lips as I peeled off my torn tee shirt. Good thing I'd found a spare, almost-clean one in the trunk, where I'd thrown it after last fall's pickup touch football game at the church. Along with my swollen and scratched face, the state of my clothes had very nearly kept me from getting this room. The clerk had thought I was an escaped lunatic. An extra twenty calmed him down.

As I removed my sneakers, I recalled the way I'd hours earlier made my way across the storm-tossed lake, frantically fighting the flimsy paddle as much as using it, finally coming ashore nearly a mile down from the dock at Gwynn Island. I'd lugged the raft up onto the bank, and then, after a moment's reflection, I'd pulled out my pocketknife and slashed it. Then I rolled it up and stuffed it inside a hollow log.

I'd wondered at my actions as I worked. I was reasonably sure no one had seen me doing my death-defying Evel Knievel act getting aboard the *Skylark*, and I knew it would be a while before Dale would venture out from his place above the bait shop and wonder where she'd gone. When he did, he'd probably figure the craft had been torn free from her moorings, to be recovered later. He'd list her as missing, and missing she would stay, unless Kitty ponied up the salvage fee—and after telling her what happened, I knew she wouldn't. For good or ill, the *Skylark* would remain in her watery grave.

But then so would Parker, unless she reported *him* missing—equally unlikely.

The only thing I could hope for was that some sharp-eyed cabin dweller wouldn't have put Parker and me together. I knew legally I wasn't liable for his death, but I also didn't, really did *not*, want this whole thing to come out. Bank on the media vultures to have a field day with it, and for all our differences, Kitty had been through enough. She was counting on me to keep her name out of the press. I would do my best to do just that.

After stashing the little orange raft in the log, I'd climbed and squished my way uphill through what seemed like a mile of miserable muck before spying the roadway and starting down it. Ducking my battered head against the wind, I began trudging my way back to the place I'd parked my car. Regardless of the fact it was April, I shivered as I went, trying to ignore both the increasing numbness in my feet and the high clouds scudding across the gibbous moon. That just made it seem colder.

After eons I finally reached the lot, and my car. Wearily slipping the key in the door lock, I risked a glance up at Dale's place. Still dark. I opened the door and climbed inside. It seemed my luck was holding, provided the balky Yugo turned over at the first try. It did, and I released the clutch and put it in first, starting the long climb up the hill back toward the main road as I headed toward town, and hopefully a room for the night. I'd make my report to Kitty tomorrow; right now I needed to crash.

"Crash" possibly wasn't the term I was looking for, as tired as I was. A place to sleep; that was the ticket.

Woops, ticket. I was more tired than I thought as I overcorrected the car, trying to stay in my lane. *Wouldn't do to get a ticket tonight, no sir, it wouldn't.* A cop might mistake my fatigue for inebriation, and that wouldn't do at all. In my state I might let slip any number of inappropriate things as to what I was doing on the road this time of night.

It was with relief that I reached the outskirts of Danville, and I began searching for an open motel. The selection wasn't tops. I passed a Holiday Inn Express, then a little ways down from that a Super 8, and next to that a small Best Western, all with their "no vacancy" signs lit up. What was going on?

The mystery was solved by the tall sign blazing outside the last place: GREETINGS 4-H FAIRGOERS.

Yeah, the 4-H Club. I'd been a member as a teen, the year Granny had helped me raise and enter Buster, our curly-headed roan Hereford bull calf, in the competition. We couldn't have known then that Buster was the only good animal we would ever get from Regina, our family cow, who resolutely refused thereafter to come up with another. I'd done my best with the calf, feeding him only the best silage morning and night, daily combing and brushing his coat, hoping for the day I'd enter him in the Clay County spring trials. Maybe if I won, then folks would stop calling us Boxes no-account white trash.

But it wasn't to be. I hadn't even made runner-up. The blue ribbon that year went to someone whose father was a cattleman, and that was that.

Whatever happened to me? I thought as I drove. *To that scraggly country boy who rescued a woodchuck from a well with his hands, only later to take those same hands and mercilessly pummel the town bully for calling his father a useless drunk ... although he was?*

Gone forever, turned into this battle-scarred person behind the wheel, a man who'd held another in his arms tonight as he'd died. But still one who tried—I nearly laughed—who always tried.

That's how I found myself in the center of town, taking the last remaining room in a fallen-down flea-trap motel that had to have been Danville's original inn. Leaving my wet clothes in a pile on the floor, I managed to wedge myself in the room's tiny shower, pull the hideous green plastic curtain closed, and turn the taps to two degrees less than boiling. Then I sat down and turned my back to the scalding spray, not caring much if the metal shower floor appeared less than sanitary. At this heat, any germs that survived deserved to.

Sitting in the billowing steam, I mused. Had tonight's events really happened? Had I truly watched a man drown before my eyes? Had I in fact escaped a sinking mini-yacht in the middle of a storm that would have given Stephen King pause? And more, had I done it all to rescue a "treasure" for a woman whose grip on sanity appeared tenuous at best?

An uncomfortable thought was now trying to burrow its way

into my mind. I tried to quiet it, but it banged harder. The idea taunting me was that the envelope in fact contained nothing more valuable than Kitty's childhood paper doll collection. If true, what a joke that would be. Wouldn't it? I decided right then I wasn't going home until I knew.

I gave the shower fifteen full minutes, letting the seething water burn the last of the lake's coldness out of my bones. But nothing could burn out the memory of Parker's dead eyes. I was thankful that the motel's boiler had been up to at least part of the challenge.

Shutting off the taps, I strode back into the bedroom, the last of the steam's tendrils following, as if they wanted to pull me back from the chance that Parker and I both had been played for fools. But I resisted. A man had died tonight for what was inside that envelope. Whether Kitty liked it or not, I meant to see for myself just what it was.

I pulled it off the dresser and sat down with it on the bed. Turning it over, I saw that what I'd thought was regular packing tape on the envelope was, in fact, what looked to me like that waterproof stuff. Not that I needed an excuse to see what was inside—after the events tonight, I was owed that much, at least— but now I had a reason to. Even with that tape sealing it, the lake water might well have damaged the contents during my violent escape. A conscientious PI like me needed to make sure what was inside was still okay. Anyway, that was the rationale I used as I took my knife and slit it open. Mouth dry, I peered inside.

Then I frowned.

Son of a ...

I fought the urge to bray a bitter laugh. Joke was right. It seemed I hadn't been too far off the mark with my paper doll theory, after all. Dumping the contents next to me on the bed, I felt like the biggest loser since Judas.

It was paper, true enough. The manila envelope held at least a score of black and white photographs peeping out of a paper covering, all wrapped in a frayed rubber band. Alongside them were a handful of small, nonstamped envelopes tied up with string.

And lying in the middle of it all, a tarnished, silver-plated locket and chain. Grinning at my stupidity, I picked it up.

Then my grin vanished.

I couldn't explain it, but I suddenly found myself seized with an almost malarial trembling. The quaking grew worse, dread grabbing me hard.

Now what? Was the thing cursed, like some lousy grade-B Universal horror flick from the forties? I didn't believe in such stuff, not as a kid, not now. But still, the locket seemed to give off a type of cold heat, like it had spent countless ages in deep space.

Put it back, a part of me pleaded. *Don't look at it. You can still walk away whole.*

But I never was one for listening to patently good advice; ask anybody. With shaking, sweaty hands I popped the locket open, staring inside.

And then nearly dropped it in shock.

What the—? My mind began gibbering in stunned denial, reality twisting sideways.

Inside the object rested a tiny picture. But not so tiny I hadn't recognized a much-younger Granny, seated next to my dad, who couldn't have been more than twenty. He was holding a sleeping infant, an unreadable look on his face. The baby was me.

And behind the three of us, her left hand on Granny's

shoulder as her right caressed my dad's, stood a golden-locked teen. A shyly smiling, impossibly youthful Kitty Clark.

My heart raced, blood pounding inside my skull. I'd been right the first time. A joke. That's what this was, the biggest practical joke of the century. *Hey, let's give Joe a coronary; it's funny.* But I remembered Tom Parker, wafting in the nameless currents three hundred feet down at the bottom of the lake. I doubted he was laughing. I know I wasn't.

There was only one thing that made sense about this, and it was so off-the-wall, I wasn't prepared to go there, not yet.

My hand twitching like an old man's, I slid the locket aside and picked up the paper holding the snapshots. I pulled on the rubber band, and it broke listlessly. Unwrapping the pictures, I began examining them one by one.

Every blessed one of them was of me.

They were in no particular order, not that it mattered. The first was of me at maybe six months. I was sitting on Granny's lap as she fed me some tasteless gruel at a scarred kitchen table that must have been old when she was a girl. I remembered that table well; I'd eaten almost every meal there until I'd left for Vietnam. Dad was nowhere in sight, big surprise. I somehow knew he wasn't the one who'd taken the shot.

The next one was of me at Christmas when I was maybe a year old. Again Granny was holding me, pulling a sweater on me that she must have made. I was gazing into the camera with the wide-eyed surprised look most one-year-olds do when you take their picture. In the background, slightly out of focus, my dad leaned forward in his busted, dog-hair-infested easy chair, trusty beer can in hand as he turned the dial on our Philco radio, looking for music. Dad was always looking for music. It always seemed to elude him.

The next picture showed me at close to the same age as I was in the locket, being rocked by.... Oh, no. There she was again. Kitty Clark. Who *was* this woman? What in the name of sanity was she doing in *our* house? Rocking *me*?

The rest of the pictures I won't bore you with. It was just more of the same, me as a baby, sometimes with Granny, sometimes with Kitty, never with my dad. There were close to twenty of them, and the odd thing was—besides their very existence I mean—was that none of them showed me older than three. Had the camera broken, and Dad never bothered to buy another? I guess that was right; I never recalled him taking snapshots of anything.

Once, when I was twelve or so, I casually remarked to him that I'd seen one of those newfangled Polaroid jobs down at the mercantile, and I told him I thought how cool it'd be to take pictures of stuff and get to see them right away. My dad had snarled then, something to the effect that life wasn't worth remembering. That effectively closed the subject.

I gathered the pictures together, rewrapping them in their paper before sliding them back in the manila envelope. I'd finished viewing them, and I'd seen the locket.

That just left the letters.

Cotton mouthed, I pulled the packet of envelopes over to me and undid the string. They came apart soundlessly. My trembling was better now as I drew the first one toward me, although something told me that what I'd find inside would be worse than what I'd seen so far. The letters weren't mine, true enough, but I didn't have it in me to leave them be, any more than I'd left the rest of Kitty's "treasure" alone. Parker and I both had paid for that right. I picked the envelope up. And it nearly slipped from my nerveless fingers.

In a childish scrawl, the inscription on it read, simply, "Joe."

But then I'd known it would. In some eldritch way I think I'd known where all of this was leading from the start.

Although the flap had never been sealed, I put the letter down on the bed unopened and unread.

I pulled over the next. Same inscription. Same handwriting.

The next, same.

The next, same.

At that moment, I came closer to needing a drink since the eight months I'd been a Christian. It's a good thing Danville and Boyle County were dry; if a smoky bar had been within ten miles of me, I can't honestly say I wouldn't have given them my trade that night.

Wiping my mouth with my hand, I drew the next random letter from the pile.

Then I opened it and slowly began reading whatever words of wisdom my mother, Kitty Clark, had written to the son she'd abandoned.

18

My cell phone felt slick in my hand as I punched in the numbers. I'd spent the last half hour reading each of Kitty's letters twice, the worst half hour I believe I've ever spent in my life. Now I wanted answers. And woe betide anybody who got between me and them.

Six rings, seven, and she picked up. "Hello?" Kitty's voice sounded tentative, and not just because it was three a.m. I don't doubt my fury was being transported over the wires.

"Howdy, Miss Clark!" I shouted with false bluster. "Top of the freaking morning!"

"Who ... who is this?" she whispered.

Your son, you useless hag, I almost snarled, checking myself at the last instant.

"Joe Box, reporting as ordered, *ma'am!*"

"Reportin' ... do you know what time it is?"

"Why, bless me for a fool, it's oh-dark-thirty!" I said. "Time to get up, throw some bacon in the skillet, and get after it, as my platoon leader, poor old dead Sergeant Nickerson, used to say!"

I could almost picture her frowning in bafflement as she said the next. "Bacon in the ... Have you been drinkin'?"

"No, but that's not to say that the thought of shaking hands with John Barleycorn hasn't crossed my mind this evening."

"What ..." She swallowed and started again. "Is everything all right?"

"Never better, Kitty. The rain here has stopped, God's in his heaven, and all's right with the world." *And Tom Parker and your precious Skylark are at the bottom of Lake Herrington,* I nearly added, but I figured I'd spring that on her in person. I wanted to see her expression when I did. Right then, my Christian walk seemed as fragile as a Faberge egg.

"So what do—"

"We need to talk," I broke in.

"... now ...?" She sounded almost childlike. It would have really touched my heart, had I not wanted to kill her.

"A few hours. I'm leaving Danville as soon as I get dressed."

"You're comin' down *here?*" she squeaked. "To Nashville?"

"Unless you've relocated to the Outer Hebrides since we last spoke."

"But ... I have a rehearsal this mornin'..."

"Break it," I said. "You'll want to hear this."

"Is this about my treasure? About Tom? Where is he? Is he with you?"

"Everything's safe. Tom's close by." Well, several miles away and three hundred feet down counts as close, I guess.

"What's that rascal got to say for himself?" she demanded.

"Right now, not much."

"I'll bet," she snapped. "You tell him—"

"I'm not telling him anything, Kitty." I was suddenly feeling as weary as if I'd just climbed Mount Everest. I'd have to count on caffeine and rage to keep me awake on the hours-long drive to her place. "I'm leaving now. We'll talk when I get there."

"But—"

I hung up on her.

The exit to the parking lot was back through the lobby, and I passed the same night clerk who'd checked me in just an hour before.

"Problem with the room, mister?" He was small and balding, with crooked teeth.

I nearly smashed him in the mouth for that, only stopping myself at the last second. My agony wasn't his fault. I tried to put a civil tone in my reply.

"No, the room's fine. Business. Came up pretty suddenly."

He looked as if he was going to say something more, but wisely kept quiet. I imagine he was relieved to have this scratched-up, banged-up, wild-eyed individual gone. Just one more tale to tell the guys down at the barbershop tomorrow.

I tossed the room key on the counter and left.

The Yugo I'd left unlocked—as if any self-respecting thief would want it—and I pulled the door open, pitching the manila envelope over to the passenger side before I slid behind the wheel. Slamming the door, I thrust in the ignition key and turned it.

Nothing.

"Not tonight, you hunk of junk," I gritted, savagely twisting the key. "Start or I'll burn you."

The car must have realized I meant it, for it quit screwing around and fired right up, sounding as smooth as I've ever heard it.

"Better," I said, releasing the clutch and giving it some gas.

With a screech of tires I whipped right onto Main Street, heading toward the interstate, and Nashville, and Kitty's.

♦ ◊ ♦

The next few hours passed in a blur. I took US 27 out of Danville to the Louie B. Nunn Parkway and turned west, then from there I hopped on I-65 south. Once during the trip I flipped on the radio, running the dial with my right hand while I steered with my left. Nothing much was on at this time of night, here a fuzzy rock station, there a dull-as-dried-paint talk show about alien abductions and crop circles. For a few tricky moments I managed to pick up a nasally preacher, going on about sin and retribution. Hell on one side, heaven on the other and only a knife-edge separating the two. I spun past the show. What he was saying was true, but right now I simply didn't want to hear it.

The only thing that came through clear as a bell was some all-country, all-the-time program emanating from some nameless burg far back in the hills. And wouldn't you know it, the song they were playing was one of Kitty's. *Please Forgive Me,* King Records, 1959. The things you hear when you wish you wouldn't.

I stopped once for gas at a Union 76 before the Tennessee border. While there I also bought two large coffees and a bear claw from a bored, acne-scarred youth with an Adam's apple as big as a walnut. Unlike the desk clerk, the kid didn't even blink twice at my appearance; when you man the till at an all-night interstate gas station, I guess you have to get used to the occasional odd sight. The inevitable pit stop to get rid of some of the coffee came an hour after that, as I approached the Nashville city limits, and a harsh yellow dawn.

The last time I'd been down here was on Kitty's nickel, and

then I'd come into the airport, to a waiting limousine and a smiling chauffeur. My arrival now was going to be a bit more downscale than that. But I've always had a pretty good sense of direction, and figured I could find my way back to her mansion in Belle Meade with no problem. After all, I was one motivated individual, as Sergeant Pickens, my army drill instructor, used to say.

I stayed on I-65, getting on the 440 loop south of town. I was on that for fifteen miles or so, and from there I exited to the all-but-private country road where Kitty lived.

I drove maybe three miles more before spying it. Pulling up to the gate, I leaned on the horn. The guard came out of his shack up to my car door with a scowl. I figured Kitty had either cleared me for entrance or I'd shoot this guy; right then, it made little difference.

"You Box?" The guard, a different one this time, was in his late sixties, with gray hair above a drinker's nose, resting his clipboard on his gut as he checked it. I made him for a retired cop, and hoped the fact my name was posted meant he'd give me no trouble. I always try not to kill anybody before noon. Besides, he was one of the brotherhood.

"That's me," I answered.

"Heard you was comin'." His scowl deepened as he gave me the once-over. I could almost see the wheels turning in his head as he pegged me for trouble. If he only knew.

"Kinda scuffed up to be seein' a famous lady like Miss Kitty, aren't ya?" he said.

I tightened my grip on the wheel. "I had a rough night."

"You and me both, pal." It looked like the guard was going to say more, but didn't. He shook his head and pointed. "Through the gate, pull up the drive to the left. The big house is a quarter-mile back. Wait until I buzz you in."

"I was kind of hoping to do an *A-Team* and smash my way through."

He narrowed his eyes but didn't answer, instead turning and trudging his way back to his shack. Once inside, he pressed a button.

The big filigreed gates swung silently open.

Beginning the long drive up to Kitty's mansion, once again I reflected on the similarities between her place and the last rich home I'd visited, that of the late Senator Henrik Ten Eyck. The Senator's place outside of Columbus was done up in a French style, while Kitty's was pseudo-Tara, but they still both showed how nice it is to have money.

I pulled the Yugo into the circular drive and left it at the front, getting out to find the mansion's big main door already swinging open. The smiling, snowy-haired black fellow shuffling out to greet me was the same one I'd met before, Blake, the everything man.

"Mister Box!" he rasped, wide-eyed. "What in the world happened to you?"

"I went two for three with a bobcat. The bobcat won."

Ever the discrete gentleman, he dropped it. "Miss Kitty gives you her regards. Follow me, suh."

I did, trailing behind him as we both made our way inside the foyer. I recalled it from a few months earlier, but then it hadn't been so dim. The April morning sunshine was shining brightly outside, but for some reason the heavy drapes in here had been drawn.

"Miss Kitty, she's having one of her bad headache days," Blake said by way of explanation as we went deeper into the house. "The dark helps."

Pity. And here I was, about to ratchet her pain up a few notches. We kept going, at last coming to the parlor I remembered, only now with both its double doors closed.

Blake opened one of them and stuck his head inside. "Miss Kitty?" he said softly. "Mister Box is heah."

Her voice coming from inside wavered a weak reply. "Show him in, Blake."

He turned to me. "She's inside, waiting for you."

I went to push past, but suddenly he grasped my forearm, his grip surprisingly strong. "We all like Miss Kitty, as I've told you before, suh." His dark brown eyes seemed to bore through me. "She's good to us. We don't take kindly to folks upsetting her. At all."

My return gaze was even. "That's not my purpose today, Blake." Well, it was, but he didn't need to know it. "Like I said a couple of months back, I just want some answers."

The old man held up a warning finger. "Well then. Be kind."

Without another word he stepped aside, letting me pass. I was a few steps inside the gloomy room before I heard Blake softly pull the door shut behind me.

I stood there, letting my eyes adjust. Kitty still hadn't spoken to me directly. A moment later I heard her from the far corner of the room. "Over here, Joe."

In the near-darkness I could barely make her out, her ghostly figure sitting on a large chair. For once she didn't look like she was about to take center stage. The platinum wig and heavy makeup were gone, revealing only a gray-haired old lady with a careworn face. I made my way over and sat down in the chair's mate next to her.

Peeling a wet washcloth away from her eyes, her smile was fleeting.

"Sorry about this. The dark, I mean. Sometimes I get these headaches, like to tear the top of my skull off. Migraines, maybe." Then her mouth fell open. "Land sakes! Look at you! What happened?"

My reply was clipped. "Nothing. Don't worry about it."

All the way down here I'd rehearsed this moment, running various scenarios through my mind, wanting to slash and tear this person who'd effectively ruined my life. But now that I was here, all the words were gone. What I saw before me was a dried-up old woman locked in a hell of her own.

"You came a long way to talk," Kitty said after another moment. "So talk."

"Tom Parker is dead."

I was looking directly at her as I said that, my eyes finally adjusted. I'd spoken the words in a calculating way, going for maximum effect. I wasn't disappointed.

She pulled back. *"Dead?"*

"As Julius Caesar. Want to hear how it happened?"

She opened her mouth to answer, but I beat her to it.

"Sure, Kitty, glad to. He drowned last night. Right before my eyes. I was closer to him than I am to you, and I held him as he crossed over. It happened in the *Skylark's* lounge. Oh yeah, I guess I forgot to mention, your boat's gone. Sunk. But hey, it's only money, right? You can always buy another. Here's a tip, though. Next time, leave off the wrought-iron benches." I showed her my wrists. "Tacky, Kitty, and hard on the hands."

She was shaking her head in incomprehension and disbelief. "I don't ... what do you mean ... "

"I made sure your treasure was safe before the *Skylark* went down," I plowed on. "Pretty tricky business, that, but I managed to hook it a few seconds before she sank. I almost joined old

Tom in Davy Jones' locker, but I made it out in time. Good thing for me."

Her voice was very small. "I don't understand.... Why are you *talkin'* like this?"

"I guess I'm still caught up in the moment. Gosh, it was just like the movies, Kitty. Some rocks fell from a cliff and smashed us. You should have seen it. Matter of fact, I wish you could have been there to share it. Tom would have appreciated it, I know."

"Lord have mercy," she breathed. "You'd better start from the beginning."

"Sounds like a plan," I agreed, and then I told her every bit of it, from her phone call yesterday, the one sending me after Parker, right up to now.

I realized I was using choppy sentences and plenty of body language for emphasis, as if I was hacking her to pieces with my speech. The only thing I left out was the nasty surprise of the manila envelope's contents; I'd let her spring that one open herself.

I wasn't disappointed.

"Poor old Tom ..." she mused. "Dead as a hammer, you said. He played me false, and that's a fact, but I sure didn't plan on him dyin' ..."

"Neither did he."

"So that's why you look like that. If I was you, I'd get to a hospital for a checkup."

"But you're not me," I said. "It's nice how everybody here is so concerned for my welfare. The guard, Blake, you. Like I said, Kitty, I'm fine." Which I was anything but.

She cleared her throat. "Anyway, the main thing is, you did what I asked. You got my treasure back."

"Yep. And it was well worth a man's life. I found that out myself."

"You found ..." Kitty gulped. "You're not tellin' me you *opened* it ..."

"Absolutely." My grin was savage. "Why not? The thing had already been torn. I wanted to make sure the contents hadn't been ruined. I always give value for money, Kitty. You should know that by now. Heck, you know me better than anybody."

"What are you sayin'?" She appeared to be shriveling before my eyes. "You mean you know who I ..." Her gasp was one of horror. "Oh *Lordie,* Joe, I never meant—"

I jumped to my feet. "To hurt me, right? You always meant to come back for your little boy, the one who cried himself to sleep *every single night, right?*" I was screaming now. "You never meant for me to be raised by a superstitious old woman and a drunk who beat me nearly senseless every day, isn't that right, Kitty? *ISN'T THAT RIGHT??*"

About then Blake burst into the room, moving faster than a man of his age had any right to. He was followed closely by a blond woman I took to be Veronica, the maid.

"Good gravy!" he shouted. "What's happening in heah?" He cut his eyes at me, then back at my host. "You all right, Miss Kitty?"

Tears streamed down her face as she waved them away. "I'm ... fine, Blake. Please leave us. Just ... just go."

The old man glared at me as if he wanted to throw me out bodily, the blood in his eye making me wonder if in his youth he hadn't been wicked quick.

"All right," he said darkly. "You need me, I'll be right heah in the hall." Giving me one last hot look, he and the younger woman left, pulling the door closed behind them.

I turned back to Kitty. She was bent over, sobbing. The way she was carrying on it was tough to make out her words. What a performance.

"You're right, Joe," she blubbered, pulling her hands away. "I never meant to have left you forever. But your father, Jed…. He started drinkin' when I was carryin' you. It scared him terrible, the idea of him bein' a daddy. He told me one night, when I was nearly due. Said his own daddy had been awful, and he was sure he'd be awful too …"

"Son of a buck was right, wasn't he?" I snapped.

She went on as if she hadn't heard.

"It was bad then, but a few months after you was born, it got a whole lot worse." She sniffled. "Joe, you gotta believe me, I hung on for the longest time, I swear I did, tryin' to make it work, tryin' to do my best by you. Jed's mama, Cora—your granny—did what she could, but she saw her husband's drinkin' binges startin' all over again with her son."

Like it did with me after him, I thought. *The sins of the fathers.*

Kitty wiped her eyes with the heels of her hands before going on.

"By the time you was three it was as bad as a person could stand. Night after night, never any end…. I'd been doin' some singin' at the church, and the pastor and his wife said I might be good enough to make it for real." Her eyes grew wide. "And there it was, my chance. Just like a miracle! But I knew I couldn't take you with me. I had no idea what was waitin' out there, how things would be for me, but I knew it was no place for a little 'un."

"Sweet of you. So you left me with a crazy man."

"I always meant to come back for you!" she wailed. "It was just gonna be for a while, until I got things goin' for us. Cora said

Jed was her son, and she could control him."

"Like she did with her husband, right?" I began stalking around, coming nearer to her bit by bit. "It didn't quite work out like that, though, did it? You were gone God knows where, leaving me to face that nasty drunk alone. Some hand you dealt me."

"But Cora was right there!"

"She was an old woman, Kitty!" I yelled. I was leaning over her, my hands claws. "She was *useless* against him!"

Kitty hung her head, her sobs silent now as they racked her body.

"Ahhh ..." I shook my head. I'd gotten the confession I'd sought, only to find it was ashes in my mouth. Rage and adrenaline had taken me only so far. I needed to be out of here, now.

I started walking a few steps away, then I stopped and turned.

"Something just occurred to me. How come Dad never realized it was you on the radio that first night you played the Grand Ole Opry? You'd changed your name, but surely he would have recognized the voice of his own wife."

"That's easy," she replied softly. "I only ever sang when he weren't around. Maybe I thought he didn't deserve it. Maybe ..." She shook her head. "As for the rest, there was lotsa reasons he wouldn't have known it was me. I never wore makeup around your daddy, ever. He didn't hold with it. By the time my face was showin' up in the press, I was wearin' a ton of eyeliner and rouge and lipstick and such. Plus early on I'd had my nose carved back some, just a little, and I'd taken to wearin' that big platinum wig over my sandy hair."

I took over. "And on top of that, the idea that Dad's wife, whom he'd been told was dead, was now a famous country music star was too far out to be believed. Okay. I can buy that.

But there's something I need to know." I stared hard at her. "What's your name, anyway?"

She drew a shuddering breath, eyes red and puffy above a snotty lip. "… my name?"

"Did I stutter? Yeah, your name. Not your stage name, either. Your real one."

"Drummond," she said after a moment. "Ollie Mae Drummond."

"You're a liar," I said evenly. "There weren't any Drummonds in Clay County."

"Knox County. Twenty miles south. That's where I met him. Your daddy, I mean."

The bitterness in my words nearly made me gag. "A lucky day for all concerned."

"Don't say that." Kitty's tone was sharp. "Jed was a louse, true enough, but it's only 'cause of me and him gettin' together that you're here today."

"Yeah, ain't that grand? I'll be sure to thank you some other time." I looked around the room for a second before I realized what I was after. Another liquor cart, like Kitty had had in her Cincinnati hotel room. "Got anything to drink? One for the road?"

"Not for you," she said. "After our first meetin' back in December I hired a feller to do some further checkin' up on you. Found out you was a recoverin' alky. I was wrong to have offered you a drink that day. I'll not do it again. 'Specially with your head injury."

"Don't go getting maternal on me now, Kitty," I growled. "It's a bit late for that." Then what she'd said registered. "Wait, you found out I once had a drinking problem? But how—?" I felt a flush of heat on my face. "You had me *investigated*?"

"I just wanted to know more about you," she sniffed.

"Unbelievable. This day keeps getting better and better." I blew out a breath. "So who'd you get? Cincinnati isn't exactly awash with PIs. Local talent or out of town?"

"Local, I think. He told me he lives in Norwood. A guy named Billy Barnicke."

"Barnicke? That rummy?" My laugh was harsh. "Well, takes one to tail one, I guess. Next time I see him I'll be sure to give him my regards for a job well done."

I paced again for a moment, the room swaying, before stopping in front of her.

"All right," I said. "Everything's on the table now. No more secrets. I know you, and you know me. But before I leave, I also want to know how this whole thing got started in the first place. You've been out of my life for nearly fifty years, Kitty. Why now?"

Again her voice had grown small. "Can't you call me Mom?"

"No," I said. "I can't. But you didn't answer the question. *Why now?*"

She twisted her hands together, her fingers knotting and unknotting like arthritic worms, before replying. But her answer was weird. "How old do you think I am?"

I frowned, not getting it. "Who the devil cares? What's that got to do with it?"

"Take a guess."

"This isn't a carnival act, Kitty. Try to stay on track."

It was if she hadn't heard. "I'll tell you. I'm sixty-nine."

I'd pegged her for much older. Hard living, I guess. Look at me, for instance.

"So you're sixty-nine," I said. "Again, so what?"

Then she threw me for another loop. "Do you remember Sudie Fetters?"

It looked like I had no choice but to play along. "The midwife? She was ancient when I was still a kid. Folks said she delivered most of the babies born in Clay County."

"That's true. You're one of them. She did so many deliveries most people just called her Mama Sudie."

I shook my head. Was it senility causing Kitty to keep going off on these tangents?

She went on, "But there's somethin' you may not know about Mama Sudie." She paused. "Mama Sudie was a witch."

That stopped me cold. "A witch? Where'd you hear that?"

"I didn't just hear it, Joe. I know it." Kitty gulped. "I know, 'cause almost fifty years ago she put a curse on me." She swallowed again. "And on you."

My mouth came open, but it was several seconds before I spluttered: "A *curse?*"

She shuddered. "It was three days before Christmas, and Jed had come home worse than normal, drunk from 'shine I guess he'd got from Lem MacElroy. I tried bein' sweet, puttin' his supper and a piece a' fruitcake on a plate and all, but he just hurled it across the kitchen. It was as I went to clean it up, squattin' down with a soapy rag in my hand, that he come up behind me and nailed me in the back of the head with somethin' hard."

I felt the lake's chill again, even though I was dry. Almost like Angela and Mitch.

Kitty stared past my shoulder. "After she got me cleaned up and into clothes that weren't bloody and torn, Cora pressed a twenty dollar bill into my hand. 'He's my son, Ollie Mae, and I love him,' she hissed, 'but sure as God made the mornin' he's a-gonna kill you someday. So you take this money and you head on down the road to Mama Sudie's place, and then you give it to her. You tell her Cora said it's for her to make you a charm, somethin' to keep you safe.'"

Kitty's eyes grew wide. "Cora says to me, 'You run to her, Ollie Mae. You run there and get you that charm. And then you keep on a-runnin'. Don't stop until you're miles away from here. I'll protect Joe, don't worry. You come back for him when you can; he'll understand it when he's older. But, Ollie Mae, if you don't run, and run now, you're dead.'"

Well, I was older, and I still didn't understand.

"Some story, Kitty," I said then. "So where does this curse of yours come in? I thought Granny told you Mama Sudie was going to give you a charm."

She looked haunted. "So did I. Didn't work out that way." She stared at a place on the wall past me. "On foot it took me pert'near an hour goin' down Bent Tree Road before I come to the turn to Sudie's house. It was so *cold* that night. So terrible cold. No moon to speak of and me bein' so banged up didn't make it go any faster, neither.

"Anyway, I finally get there, and start hammerin' on her screen door. After a long time, Sudie opens it and thrusts her coal-oil lamp almost in my face. 'Who's a-botherin' me this time of night?' she says. Old woman looked like a witch even then. Like to have scared me to death the night she helped birth you. Hard beady old eyes and gray scraggly hair goin' every which a way ... awful. Then she sees it's me. 'Ollie Mae Box,' she says with a frown. 'What are you doin' here?' I busted out cryin' then, and she tells me to come in."

Kitty now turned her eyes my way. "I'd never been inside Sudie's house before, Joe, but it was as spooky as I'd heard. No 'lectricty to speak of, just a sputterin' old fireplace in the corner and her coal-oil lamp for light. 'Well, girl, sit down and let's hear it,' she says.

"So I told her the whole thing, about Jed's drinkin' and him beatin' me and all, and how Cora was helpin' me take it on the lam. Then I told her about the charm. I opened my fist and showed her the crinkled-up twenty I'd been holdin'. 'This is for you, Sudie,' I says. 'I need you to make me up the best charm you can. One that'll keep me safe in the hard places and bring me back someday to my baby Joe.'"

Again Kitty shook her head. "That tore it. Sudie gets this terrible look in her eye and says to me, 'What do you mean, bring you back for him someday?' Her voice got real loud then. 'You mean you ain't a-takin' your little 'un with you?' I started cryin' again. 'No, Sudie, I can't,' I says. 'He'll be safe with Cora. It's just till I can make things right for us.' 'You mean right for *you!*' she yells. Then she gets this real awful look on her face. 'When was you born, Ollie Mae?' she says. I told her 1935. I said I'd just turned fourteen the week after you was born.

"'You can't do this!' Sudie says. 'Not tonight, anyway. But lemme make sure I'm right before I say for sure.' Then she gets up and goes and pulls a really big book off the mantle. I couldn't see the title, she held it close so I couldn't, but I could see it was plenty old. She opens it up and starts turnin' pages, mutterin' under her breath all the while.

"Finally she must have seen what she was after 'cause she stops with her finger on one of the pages. She reads for a few seconds, nods, and looks up at me.

"'When was your last time of the month?' she asks. Well, I knew it weren't proper to speak of such things, even with a woman, but somethin' about the way Sudie was starin' at me made me tell her. 'Last week,' I says. 'Well sir, that tears it,' she says, and slams the book shut. 'Ollie Mae, they ain't no moon tonight, you just had your monthly cycle last week, and this mornin' a rain owl was sittin' on my gatepost. The signs is all there. You leave tonight, girl, and before it's over the devil will take you and your baby both.'

"Joe, I liked to have fainted!" Kitty's eyes were huge. "I started cryin' again. 'Oh, Mama Sudie, don't go on so!' I says. 'Just make me a charm, and it'll be all right!' 'No, it won't,' she says, 'and I can prove it. Hold out your hand.' I didn't want to, but I did. Quicker'n I could spit, Sudie pulls a knife out from somewhere and cuts my palm! It didn't really hurt, though; the knife was that sharp. Then she flips my hand over, palm down, and moves it in a circle over her tabletop, watchin' as the blood drippin' down on it makes a ring. Then she lets go of my hand and practically throws it back at me. 'Now wait,' she says. She gets back up again and goes into the kitchen. A minute later she comes out, her fist clenched tight in front of her. 'Flaxseed,' she says, and opens her fist right above the blood ring. Them little seeds rain down, and suddenly Sudie's hunched over, countin' 'em.

"'Seventy inside the ring,' she says then, lookin' up at me with sadness and hate almost mixed together on her face. 'Ollie Mae, I'll ask you only once more. Do you mean to go through with this tonight?' I don't answer for a second, then I say, 'Yeah, I do.'

"'All right then,' she says. 'Here's what I'm readin'. The signs tell me you'll do all right in this world, but not so for your boy. Your life will be fine, but his'll be one of hardship and loss and pain. Until y'all reconcile, neither of your spirits can ever be at rest.

"'You got until your seventieth birthday,' she says, and she points at the tabletop. 'Seventy seeds, seventy years. If'n it ain't done by then, when your time comes at last, you'll find yourself bound for a sinner's hell. And when your boy Joe dies, he'll find himself in hell too.'

"The old witch then shakes her head. 'The signs ain't ever wrong, girl. That's just how it is, and I can't help it.' Her eyeballs looked like steel to me, Joe, as she says, 'So if you're gonna do it, then do it, Ollie Mae.' She spits on the floor. 'Do it and be damned.'"

19

*T*he sun must have gone behind a cloud sometime while Kitty had been speaking, because the light level in her room was now less. It seemed too appropriate for the dark territory we were both negotiating.

I went and drew the curtains wide. We needed the light.

"I didn't listen to her that night," Kitty said. "Who would? I wasn't the most educated girl in the world, or even in Clay County, but I know hooey when I hear it."

"But you believed it all the same, didn't you?"

Kitty paused again before answering. "Not at first," she admitted. "Not even for most of my life. Not until I got older." She swallowed. "I always carried with me how you looked the night I left. Sleepin' so sound. I kissed your sweet little seashell ear good-bye …"

"I remember that." The words were hanging thick in my throat. "Christmastime, angels. I thought I was dreaming. I felt you kiss me, and I smelled lemons. You always smelled like lemons, Kitty."

For a moment she couldn't speak. Then she roused herself. "Now here I am, old, and I saw how close to seventy I was gettin'."

"So it was time to buy a little fire insurance for yourself, huh?" I said. "Smart."

"It's not that way at all!" she shot back.

"Looks like it from where I stand," I replied, and I shrugged. "Listen, it's too late for both of us for your scheme to have worked, but still, I'm glad you had a full life."

I hoped I was man enough to mean what I'd just said. It sounded noble, anyway.

"Not as full as I woulda liked," Kitty said. Then she folded her hands in her lap. "What did your granny ever say had happened to me?"

"Right after you'd left, not much, as I recall." Again my throat suddenly grew tight. "There's not a whole lot a person can say to a three-year-old boy about why his mama left him. Stuff like that tends to go over his head. All he knows is he's in pain, and plenty of it."

Bingo. Got her again. From her wince and the way she clenched her hands, I could tell another one of my verbal rockets had hit home. Not that I was keeping score.

"As I got older, she told me more," I went on. "All lies, of course. Granny said you'd left to get away from Dad's beatings. That much was true anyway. But then she said you'd only planned to be away a couple of days, and had gone to Chicago to stay with your cousin."

"I don't have a cousin in Chicago," Kitty said. "Why'd she pick Chicago?"

"Who knows? I guess it was the first big city that popped into her head. Anyway, by that time I was going on six, and some of the bigger kids had started talking, saying you'd left our family to go be a whore."

"A *whore?*"

Bam. Nailed her again. "Yeah. I didn't even know what one was, but it sounded bad. I went home crying, and that's when Granny broke the news to me that you'd been dead for years."

My smile was crooked and not one bit nice.

"She must have been working on that one for a while, against the day she needed to pull it out," I said. "She really embellished it too. Said you'd been getting ready to board a train back to Toad Lick when you slipped and went under it. Of course, it was several more years before I thought to ask her why she'd not told me this earlier. When I did she gave me the usual banana oil about me being 'too young.'" My laugh was abrasive. "Stupid me, I bought it."

I sat back down in the chair I'd taken before, suddenly bone tired.

"My life went one way, Kitty, and yours another, and that's that. You got rich, while the three of us stayed as poor as Job's turkey." I began lightly rapping my knuckles against my knee. "So how come you never sent any cash back home? I don't know about Dad, but Granny obviously knew you weren't dead. We sure could have used the help. Remember how cold it gets in the hills in winter?"

She hung her head.

"No answer for that, huh?" I said.

"Cora wouldn't hear of it," she said softly, and she nodded. "You're right, Jed didn't know I was still alive. The story your granny told you about me dyin', she told the same one to him. I kept in touch with her, for a while. Every now and then I'd send her a Sears catalog with a letter from me tucked in it so Jed wouldn't get wise that I was still around. Later on, when I was doin' good, I did offer to send some money along, but she told me she couldn't have explained it to your dad, and that I should just set up an account for you for when you got older."

"I'm older," I said, sticking out my hand. "Let's have it."

She opened and closed her mouth for a few seconds, like a stranded fish, and I knew she was lying.

"Forget it," I shot, the words surprisingly venomous, my hand now a fist.

With a will I pulled in a breath and calmed myself.

"Getting back to Billy Barnicke for a second ..." Opening my hand back up, slowly I started rubbing it mindlessly back and forth on my jeans. "Did he tell you I married young? Not as young as you, but still, pretty young."

"It was part of what he called his"—Kitty said the next phrase carefully, the words unfamiliar in her mouth—"'preliminary background check.'"

Her smile was as faint as Orion's belt. "Your wife had a nice name. Linda." The smile flickered and faded. "Died young, Mr. Barnicke told me, years ago in a car crash on Christmas Eve. Only twenty-three."

"That's right. Did—" My voice caught and I started over. "Did he tell you she was carrying our unborn son at the time? And that my squad car was the first one on the scene?" I clenched my fist. "Did he tell you that I held her in my arms as she died?"

Kitty gasped, putting her hand to her mouth. Man, three for three. Somebody call Guinness, I was tearing her apart.

"Oh mercy, Joe," she said, wide-eyed. "I wish I'd—"

"Been there to help me through it?" My chuckle was bitter as gall. "At that point in my life, Kitty, you'd done a pretty good job of dying yourself. You weren't even on my mind. Granny and

Dad were both long gone, and only my partner on the Cincinnati police force, Sergeant Tim Mulrooney, was there for me. Did Billy happen to mention Sarge?"

"No ..."

"Pity. He's the best friend a guy could have. Well, next to his mom, of course."

Kitty stared at the floor, shaking her head, breathing hard.

"'The time has come, the Walrus said, to speak of many things,'" I quoted. "Lewis Carroll. I read him a lot as a kid. For escapism as much as anything else. Wonderland always sounded pretty good to me. Did Billy tell you I read a lot?" She still said nothing.

"No more games, Kitty." My inflection was even. "Time to lay it all out, all right? We're both too old to dance around. You hatched this whole meet-my-son caper when you saw the sand in your hourglass getting low. You'd believed some idiot curse, and you panicked. That bit of grand theater back in your Cincinnati hotel room was for the sole purpose of 'reconciling' with me, to save your skinny butt from hell."

"And yours too, Joe!" she spat, looking at me now.

"Ain't you the virtuous one." I began picking at my thumbnail. "You also told me Parker was in on it too. His performance wasn't on par with yours, but still, not bad. I hope you paid him a nice bonus. No wonder you freaked out when he left last night to steal your treasure from the *Skylark*. You told me that if he got his hands on it, it would ruin you. But you meant something other than money, didn't you?"

She nodded and I said, "So it looks like we're talking about plain old garden-variety blackmail here. Parker could have bled you dry over what he found, once he'd opened it and looked inside. If he'd let it get out you'd abandoned your baby son, exchanging me for your music career, it wouldn't have sat well with your legion of fans, would it?"

She didn't answer, and I said, "But what about Maria, your secretary? Was she in on it too? I'm only asking because of the hard way she was looking at me that day."

Kitty slowly bobbed her head. "Yeah, she was. But it wasn't just you. Maria don't like people. Especially men. Don't matter to me, though. She does good work."

My grin was toxic. "Glad to hear it."

Once again gazing down at the floor, Kitty muttered, "I musta been crazy stupid to think this was ever gonna work out right...." She seemed to be aging right in front me, if such a thing was possible.

Then she looked back up and said, "All right, Joe, I admit it. You're right. Right about it all. I confess it, okay? At the start, I brought Tom and Maria into it to make it more real, but it was my idea. Is that good enough for you?" Her voice rose. *"Is it?"*

I cocked my head, my smile cold.

"There, see, don't you feel better?" I said. "My pastor says it's good to confess your sins. Makes your heart soar like a bird, he says. Or in your case, a skylark."

My smile now was beyond cold. It had entered the realm of ice. "I'll bet your old heart is soaring now, isn't it, Kitty?"

She stared back down again, her lower lip trembling like a child's.

And like a light flipping on, suddenly I was supremely disgusted with myself.

Maybe it was my mentioning my pastor that had caused me to remember I was supposed to be a Christian, supposed being the operative word here. Right now, I was a fairly crummy one. What was it on those bracelets all the kids were wearing? What would Jesus do? Not act like I was, that's for sure.

I knew I could verbally whip up on this woman from now until the end of time, and it wouldn't change a thing. She was my mother, God help me, and I was killing her.

Inch by inch.

Okay, enough. I stood. It really was time to leave. I had a ton of things to sort out about all this, and I could do it better on the road toward home.

"Listen, Kitty, I ..." My hands moved aimlessly as again the words stalled. "I have to go. I'll call you later. We ... I have to go."

I took a step, but she stopped me with the next.

"It wasn't all fake, you know."

I turned around. "What?"

Her look was rock steady. "The calls and such I told you that's goin' on now. They really are. They were fake at Christmas time, that's true, but not now." I didn't answer and she went on, "I tried to tell you that last night, but what with the phones actin' up with the bad weather and all, I couldn't."

I sighed. "Right now, Kitty, you simply can't imagine how little I care."

"Well, you *oughtta* care!" Her cheeks were flushed, the brightness of her eyes letting me know her tears were barely being held in check. "I was so proud of you when Mr. Barnicke told me the whole town says you're a man of honor! So proud!"

She jumped to her feet. "Now I'm tellin' you my stunt has somehow turned real, and you're sayin' you don't *care?*"

The scarlet blush mottling her face was now spreading down her neck.

"Why won't you help?" she yelled. "What kind of son are you? Why won't you be the investigator everybody says you are, Joseph Jebstuart Box, and *solve this case for me?*"

"Solve it?" I yelled back. "Why should your problems become mine? I've already got more than my share. Especially now that I know who you really are."

I realized my hands were waving. And I couldn't stop them.

"I should just forget what you did to me all those years ago, like it never happened?" I shouted. "Tuck it away, shove it all back under the bed, where it's nice and dark and away from prying eyes? I'd be as crazy as you if I did that!" I barked a jeering laugh at her. "Solve your case, Kitty? For what? Another notch on my gun, another 'attaboy, Joe'?"

My derision toward her was boiling over like acid.

"Forget it," I said. "I only have your word for it that any of this is real. Maybe you're as in need of psychiatric help as I think. And that gives me cold comfort. What if—"

And then I stopped my raving. My spine was tingling like a million ants had just started a hoedown on my vertebrae. *Cold ... like cold water ... lake water ...*

It was almost like an epiphany. Like the silent opening of a long-locked door, I'd just felt the last piece of this insane puzzle slip effortlessly into place. That's happened to me every now and then in my career, but rarely. Each time it does, I'm amazed.

I tried to calm myself, to get my hammering heart under control.

"Wait a minute, Kitty," I panted. "I think I just nailed it."

"Huh?"

"I believe I know who's doing this to you."

She looked at me in puzzlement, and without realizing I was doing so, I took a step toward her. "Or maybe I should say, who *was* doing it. There's only one person that fits the bill, and I'll bet you know who."

She spread her hands. "I've been tellin' you, I ain't got no idea. Who is it?"

My grin was vinegar-sour even as my tone turned expansive. "Why, your friend and mine." I almost spit his name. "The ever-lovely, always devious, now-quite-dead Tom Parker."

Kitty's eyebrows climbed. *"Tom Parker?"*

"That's the guy." I nodded, finding myself growing unexpectedly cranked, like a dog on the hunt. "He played us both for fools. Like I said, think about it. As your manager it was Parker's job to know everything about you. Every part of your life, down to the finest detail. The crazy thing is, it was right before me all the time, and I didn't see it either."

My almost-grin grew as I went on. "Nothing about this scheme has tallied ever since you called me back in February and told me the calls had recommenced. Take it from a former cop, stalkers don't operate that way. They don't do their thing for a while, stop, and then start up again. It goes against their pattern."

My eyes grew narrow. "No, the way I see it, Parker saw what you pulled on me back at Christmas, and then for his own reasons he took over where you left off. I guess you were too close to it to figure it out."

The expression on my mug now had to have been a self-effacing grimace. "And stupid me, for the last couple of months I've been stumbling around like a moron, checking every lead I could think of, while missing the most obvious one." My chuckle was dry, and carried no humor. "Miss Clark, I believe I owe you a refund."

Kitty frowned, her tears forgotten. "But why did Tom do it? What the heck *for?*"

I started pacing again; a tiger in a cage had nothing on me. "That's the question, all right. The *sine qui non* of this whole mess."

Unconsciously, even unwillingly, I found myself slipping back into PI mode as I moved.

"Okay, let's start with this," I said. "Something changed for you and Parker between Christmas and now. Something big. What is it? Think hard, Kitty."

Her look grew pensive. "Nothin' that I recall." Then she said, "'Cept, of course, my will ..."

That stopped me in mid-stride, and I turned to her. "Your will?"

She nodded. "Yeah, it was a few months back. Tom said he'd been noticin' my health weren't lookin' any too good these days, and he talked me into changin' both my will and my durable power of attorney for health care."

I said the next slowly. "Changing them how?"

"Tom said that since he'd been my personal manager for so long, it just made good sense to be my manager for all my other stuff as well. You know, in case anything was to happen to me. It makes perfect sense, now that I know what he was up to."

I stared flat-footed at her, incredulous. "Why did you hold this back? It could have made all the difference in the world in the investigation, Kitty. Especially for giving Parker a motive. And on top of that, you're telling me you didn't have an executor for your will or a durable power of attorney in place when those documents were drawn up? That's bad."

She furrowed her brow, like I wasn't quite right in the head. "Sure I did. Ol' Albert Fussnagel, manager of the bank I use downtown. I've known him for years and years. But Albert ain't doin' a whole lot better'n me these days, so right after New Year's Tom said it'd be best if I switched 'em to himself. I did. But then a couple of weeks later I started gettin' a bad feelin' about Tom, that he might be plannin' somethin' bad for me, so without tellin' him, I changed 'em both over to a lawyer feller named Trikonis."

Trikonis? Yet another player. Any more and I'd start needing nametags.

"All right, this is the end of April, as near as makes never mind," I said. "When *exactly* did Parker have you make the initial changes?"

"I dunno." Again she frowned. "Like I said, last of January. Maybe the first part of February. I'd have to get the things out of my strongbox upstairs and take a look."

I nodded slowly. "Son of a gun. It all fits. That's about when you called me and said you'd started getting more harassing phone calls. But only you knew they were real ones this time."

"But again, Joe, why?" she said. "Why would Tom do such a terrible thing?"

"Only one reason I can think of. The oldest one in the world." My voice went flat. "Cold, hard cash. I'll bet when you gave Parker your durable power of attorney, you did it because he suggested it himself. He told you that in the event of your illness or incapacitation, that as far as your affairs were concerned, he'd take over everything until you got better. Made it sound real soothing for you, right?"

"He did," Kitty agreed. "He said that with my age and all, if I was to have a stroke or somethin', and couldn't talk, that by me doin' like he said, my businesses wouldn't be … how did he call it? … adversely affected. They could all still keep goin' until I got better." She shook her head. "What a joke. Lord have mercy, I see it clear now."

"And those businesses … I'll bet he held a seat on their boards, right?" I ventured.

"Yeah," she admitted grudgingly. "Like you said, Tom told me he had it all fixed so that if anything happened to me, he could still run everything, smooth as glass." Kitty's face and voice grew hard. "Stinkin' rotten thief …"

"Yeah, Tom fixed it, all right," I agreed, my smile anthracite. "Fixed it so he could run things like a bandit." I pressed her further, staring hard. "And it didn't have to be a physical problem, did it? It could be anything. Up to and including a mental breakdown."

A sick light flooded Kitty's eyes as she realized the depth of Parker's betrayal. "Are …" She gulped and started over. "Are you sayin' Tom planned it all along …?"

"No, Kitty," I said. "You did that. You started it when you first plotted your charade. Parker simply took your idea and boomeranged it right back at you."

She sounded like a little girl. "I still don't get it."

Obviously Kitty wasn't wanting to get it, and I made my reply as painless as I could, using small words. "If Parker drove you insane, then he could take everything you had, your house, your land, your businesses, your stocks, *everything*, and you couldn't lift a finger to stop it. You'd already given him your okay."

Her back stiffened as the penny finally dropped. "Why that … that lousy, rotten skunk! That dirty, no-good—" Words failed her, then she said, "If you hadn't told me he was already dead, I'd wish he was. I'd wanna find him a tall tree, and a short rope."

That made two of us.

She went on, "But what made him panic last night and try to steal what I had on the *Skylark*? What set him off then?"

"We may never know. Maybe he thought I was better at my job than I really am. Maybe he thought I was getting too close to uncovering his primary plan to seize your assets, and so he thought the time had come to activate his secondary plan, and he'd better grab what he could off your boat now, writing the rest off to bad luck. He couldn't have known your 'treasure' was only family heirlooms."

I rolled my shoulders.

"Anyway, Kitty, in a weird sort of way, your scheme worked after all. We've met now, and the masks are off. We'll just have to see where we take it from here."

The words stopped then, and she and I just stared at each other.

And I don't think I've had a more uncomfortable moment in my life, ever.

Down at her sides, Kitty's fingers twitched. I could tell she wanted to touch me before I left her. Ached for it. I was just as certain I didn't want her to.

Her mouth trembled as she tried to put together a smile. "Well, at least now, Joe, we got plenty of time to get to know each other. Looks like I dodged Sudie's curse after all."

"For the love of—" I shook my head. "You still don't get it, do you? There wasn't any curse. There was never a curse. It was just the ravings of some crackpot old lady who started believing her own press." *Like you, Kitty,* I almost said, checking myself at the last second.

I tried softening my tone. "You need to be certain of one thing, and it's this. A curse can't send you to hell. Only rejecting God's free gift of salvation through Jesus can do that. If there was any curse on you at all, Jesus took that on himself at the cross."

Her smile at me now was tender ... and a little wry. "Huh. Guess what Mr. Barnicke told me was right. He said you'd gone and become a Christian."

And then she said, "Me, too."

Kitty couldn't have shocked me more if she'd suddenly sprouted wings and circled the room. "*You?* When?"

Her knees creaking audibly in protest, she settled herself back down in her chair. "Oh, that's better," she said, before going on, "It was a week ago. Last Tuesday night, to be exact."

Her voice tightened. "Joe, I'd done come to the end of myself. Those calls and letters and death threats I'd been gettin' was about to send me around the bend. It was like some *Twilight Zone* show leapin' outta the box and becomin' real."

Her strained face was painted a stark, pasty white. It was plain the terror was threatening her again as her voice dropped. "That night I couldn't sleep because of it all, I was that scared. Things started gettin' terrible around here."

She swallowed. "Then they got a whole lot worse. The air grew close, then it got real cold and clammy, like an icebox, and I started shakin' like I had the plague." Her eyes widened. "Death was all around this house that night, Joe, scratchin' at the windows and rattlin' the knobs, wantin' in, wantin' *me*."

She gulped again, making a visible effort to toss the horror off. "Then I remembered a Bible some fan had sent me a while back. Usually I just have Blake toss out most of the stuff like that my fans send when it comes; where would I put it otherwise? But for some reason I'd saved that Bible and stuck it in my nightstand drawer. Without even plannin' to, I pulled it out and opened it and started readin'."

I was hooked now. "What part did you read?"

She shrugged. "You got me. Psalms, I think. Maybe Proverbs. Who knows? All I know was I was readin' it out loud, real loud, hopin' that thing outside could hear me."

"Did it work?"

"Must have. I'm still here, ain't I?"

I almost laughed. Much as I was trying to dislike the old bat, I had to admit she had grit.

"Anyway," she went on, "it was as I was readin' it that I found somethin' I guess the fan had taped inside the back cover."

Her small fingers made a shape.

"It was this little book, more like a pamphlet maybe, real butt-ugly yellow, called the *Four Spiritual Laws*. Ever hear of it?"

I did chuckle then. "Sure I have. It's pretty famous. They've been printing those things for decades. They're found all over the world, in all kinds of languages."

"Huh." She dropped her hands back in her lap. "It had what they called a plan of salvation at the end. More of a prayer, like. I prayed it." A look of wonderment crossed her face. "And don-cha know sometime durin' that prayer, Mister Death left my door."

That was as neat a way of putting it as I'd ever heard.

Kitty said slowly, "You know, I ain't real sure where all of this is goin', Joe. How things are gonna work between you and me. Now that we're both Christians, I mean. You're my son and I'm your mother, and there's no changin' that. But still, we got this … distance." Again her eyes glittered with unshed tears. "How do we get past that?"

"I don't know," I said, as truthfully as I knew how. "We have a ton of history between us. Most of it lousy. We might try, and still not have it work. But maybe … maybe we do it this way." I drew a breath, blew it out. "Maybe we start as friends."

That did it.

"Joe. My sweet Joe." Kitty's tears flowed unchecked now. "We got so much—"

That was as far as she got.

Her speech had been interrupted by two short, harsh

sounds. Sharp, high-pitched but muffled metallic zips, half-whistle and half-buzz, followed a second later by two heavy thuds.

Kitty and I looked at each other, and I stood.

The sounds had come from the hall, on the other side of the door.

My mouth went as dry as toast. Unconsciously I found myself reaching for my .38, before remembering I'd left it in the car. I knew those sounds, had heard them before when I was a cop on the street, decades ago.

With that, the door burst open.

I'd been right, but there was no joy in it.

The harsh zips had indeed come from a silencer, more properly called by those in the know a sound suppressor. The thing was screwed into the stubby barrel of a jet-black gun, a piece I readily recognized as a nine-millimeter Beretta.

A gloved hand, steady as granite, clutched the pistol, and that hand was attached to the one person I'd stupidly missed in my calculations.

Out in the hall, past the shooter and sprawled at odd angles in pools of shiny blood, lay the extraordinarily still bodies of Blake and the young maid.

Maria the secretary was smiling at me.

And her gun was pointed straight at my heart.

20

*T*his is usually the part where the villain says 'well, isn't this cozy.'" Maria grinned. "But I'll spare you that, at least."

At first neither Kitty nor I could speak, but she found her voice before I did.

"Maria Conchita Velez!" Kitty screamed. "What's goin' on?" Then she saw the bodies in the hall, and what little color she had fled. "Oh God! What have you *done*, girl?"

Maria Velez. Now I knew the last name of this person who intended to kill me. Kill us.

Maria's grin was as steady as her gun hand. "That's an easy one. I've just shot to death both of your toadying servants. Using this. Much in the same way as I plan to shoot the two of you."

There was a heartless intellect in her eyes, without a doubt, but also in those depths I glimpsed something else, something worse.

"Why, for pity's sake, *why*?" Kitty wailed in horror and grief.

I suppose the enormity of what was bearing down on her was hitting her hard. I know it was me, even though I was suddenly pretty sure of the reason "why."

Maria turned her grin my way.

"You're a smart man, Joe," she said. "You tell her. Earn your money."

I didn't plan on telling Kitty anything just yet. Frantically my mind was warping into light speed, trying to figure a way she and I could still walk out of this room alive. Feigning a nonchalance I didn't feel, I said, "There's only one thing I know for sure at this point, Maria. Somewhere along the line you bugged Kitty's house. You heard it all."

"Bugged my *house*?" Kitty cried out again, as if that was a worse indignity than getting perforated by a bullet. Without meaning to, she took a half step toward Maria. The other woman raised the gun's barrel a millimeter.

"Uh-uh," she admonished. "Don't want to die too fast, do we?"

Kitty stopped, turning anguished eyes my way. "Joe, *do* somethin'!"

"Anything you want, Kitty." I was keeping my eyes on the other woman. "Except charge an armed killer. Especially when the deadliest thing I'm packing right now is last night's bad breath."

Maria chuckled. "Commendable. As I said before, you're a smart man. You've just bought you and the old biddy here another couple of minutes."

Kitty's voice cracked. "Joe, what does she mean 'you tell me'? Tell me what?"

I was still looking at Maria, keeping my tone even. "She means, tell you the biggest thing I missed." I nodded at the woman. "You were Tom's partner. Am I right?"

Maria's sassy grin widened. "Give that man a cheroot. You're as right as rain, Joe."

I said nothing. This was her play; better to let her have her say, get it done, and grab my chance when I could. If I could.

"Yeah, Tom was my partner," Maria said. "True, not the one I would have chosen. But you know the old saying about ports and storms." As she spoke, the gun didn't move an inch. This woman had had training somewhere. Good training.

"I met him while we were both in the army," she went on. "Intelligence."

Wow. Better training than I'd thought.

Maria continued, "It was an unlikely pairing, all things considered. Tom was a sedentary desk jockey, while I did my best work in the field. Still, the man was good at what he did. We both were. PsyOps."

Kitty looked at me, her voice quivering. "What's PsyOps?"

My reply hung gummy in my throat. "It's military shorthand for psychological warfare operations. Mindbenders. Your head was played with by the best, Kitty."

Maria ducked her own head at me. "Compliment accepted." She looked back at the older woman. "Want to hear it? It's fascinating stuff. Really, it is."

"Oh Lord, why don't you just shoot us and be done with it?" Kitty choked out.

"Because I don't wish to," Maria answered. "Not yet, anyway." She was speaking in what I'm sure she thought was a civilized tone, but I was picking up an unmistakable bizarre edge. Having grown up the way I did, I knew exactly what it was I was hearing.

Howl-at-the-moon madness.

"No, what I wish, Kitty," Maria continued, "what I'm wishing for the most right at this second, is for you and Joe to hear me speak, because I like speaking, and also because no one besides the three of us—and poor dead Tom, of course—will ever appreciate the unalloyed brilliance of what I nearly achieved here."

Her seeming reasonableness left as she addressed me. "A lovely plan that would have doubtless succeeded, if not for your idiot talent of turning garbage into gold."

"Thanks," I smiled, my heart not in it. "I'll take compliments anywhere I can. Even from you."

I was hoping Maria was watching my eyes, and not my feet. I was gradually setting them, surreptitiously shifting my weight, awaiting my chance.

"But I interrupted your speech," I said, and I went for a mocking tone. "And it was a real dandy one too."

I wanted to see how much pushing this woman could take. Without her yanking the trigger, that is.

"You said you wanted to talk, Maria," I smiled. "So talk. You know you're dying to boast to Kitty and me of your superior intellect, and your sly plan. About to flat bust a gut over it. That's what this whole speech is about. So let's hear it all, then. Every twist and turn. You'll never have a more appreciative audience than us."

Maria returned the smile. "Sure, Joe, sounds great. Although I wouldn't be bandying terms like 'dying' too loosely, if I were you. Given your present predicament, I mean." Her smile slipped a bit. "And please stop that slow dance with your feet. Another inch and I'll be forced to end this now, and drill your sweet mother right through the pump."

Kitty gasped, and I did as Maria said, instantly freezing. She wasn't the only one who'd had good training. Sit, Joe. Stay.

"I suppose I'll start things off by confessing my name isn't Maria Velez," she said.

"That's a lie!" Kitty yelled, standing up, heedless of the gun pointed at us. It seemed she was royally ticked at having played the fool. "If it ain't Maria, then what is it?"

"It doesn't matter," the other woman replied. "Not to you, at any rate. Just like it doesn't matter that my partner's real name was something other than Tom Parker."

"What?" Kitty burst out again. "Sure it was! I saw his name and Social Security number on the paperwork when I hired him! Yours too!"

Maria turned my way. Her chuckle was conspiratorial, as if she and I were in it together, this jolly joke on Kitty Clark. "She really is a child, isn't she?"

Ignoring the jibe, I turned to the old woman, determined to keep my words soft. Kitty and I may have had our problems, but no way was I going to let our final moments be spent with her being made sport of.

"Maria and Tom worked in Army Intelligence, Kitty," I said. "I knew guys like them when I was in the service. Slickness and subterfuge were their daily stock in trade. Fake names and phony IDs came as easily to them as ..." I fumbled a moment with the analogy before it came to me. "Writing song lyrics does to you."

Maria nodded. "Thank you, Joe, neatly put."

She turned her attention back to Kitty. "Through a fluke, Tom—let's call him Tom, to keep it simple—and I joined the army on the same day. In different parts of the country, of course; we didn't know each other prior to our enlistment. While in AIT we—"

"What's AIT?" Kitty interrupted.

"Advanced Infantry Training," I answered. "It's what comes after boot camp is over. It's where the army finds out what you're good at."

Maria nodded and continued on, without missing a beat.

"We both scored quite high in languages, ciphers, land naviga-
tion, marksmanship ... well, suffice it to say, Tom and I found a
home in Army Intelligence. After a stint for a while at Fort Bragg,
we were assigned to Langley—"

"Wait a minute, that's CIA," I broke in, my head spinning at
the new direction of the tale. "How in the Sam Hill did two Intel
weenies like you and Parker end up working for the spooks?"

"I see you know your Tom Clancy," Maria said. "It wasn't as
difficult as you'd think. Tom and I were simply traded in an inter-
branch swap. By the late eighties budget cutbacks had forced the
CIA into laying off some of its force, so when the first Persian
Gulf War started, and the need quickly arose for some surreptitious fact-gathering, the army loaned us to them."

Wow. Let's hear it for Uncle Sam.

Maria went on, "It worked out well. Especially for us. The
Firm got a couple of top operatives for less than they'd been paying for their own spies, and Tom and I got access to scads of
secure data that would make most people afraid to ever leave
their homes."

"So where the heck do I come into all a' this James Bond
hooey?" Kitty demanded.

The other woman ignored her. "By the time the war ended—
which wasn't that long, remember?—Tom and I had dug ourselves a nice little nest at Langley. A nice little home. All the
information we'd squirreled away on worldwide politicians' pec-
cadilloes, who did what to whom and for how much, we'd managed to hide on one single, cutting-edge, but highly illegal flash
drive we'd stolen from the development lab during a fire drill we
rigged. That drive was going to be our meal ticket, Tom's and
mine, as we started applying the squeeze."

Kitty spoke up again, sounding dumbfounded. "Why, you

two-faced hussy! You black-hearted, mousy crook. All that work for just some cheap blackmail."

"Blackmail, yes." Maria nodded. "But not cheap. Not for those whose feet we planned to hold against the fire. No, for them, not cheap at all. And it would have worked." Her face hardened.

"Until the day came when we were told 'thanks, folks, but your services are no longer required.' The Cold War was over, they told us. 'No hard feelings, guys,' they said, 'but every intelligence department in the country has to cut back some. That includes you two.'"

Maria's eyes now blazed. "That's how the final indignity came about of Tom and me finding ourselves getting squeezed out. Our careers destroyed, before we'd had the chance to make full use of our plan."

"I love America," I grinned.

Now I realized where this woman's madness had originated. The seeds had been planted, and planted deep, when she'd lost her job. For an intellectual bully like her, being tossed into the street with the masses must have been intolerable.

"The day Tom and I left, we destroyed the flash drive," Maria said. "Stomped it to bits, and flushed the pieces."

"Temper tantrum," I said.

"Not at all," she said, still cool. "We'd been told the building security team was doing random body cavity searches on the discharged employees, looking for anyone walking out with classified data. After a quick conference in our office, we decided the risk of spending the rest of our days making little rocks out of big ones in Leavenworth was too great.

"All we managed to leave Langley with that day"—she tapped her forehead—"was what we'd stored in here. It wasn't what we'd planned, but it was enough. Enough for us to live reasonably rich lives for the next few years, offering our services to the highest bidder."

"Equal opportunity blackmail," I said. "What a concept."

Maria shrugged. "Foreign, domestic, it didn't matter. We were quite catholic in our generosity."

"Tell me where I come into this," Kitty demanded again.

"Anxious to die, are you?" the other woman murmured.

"So Tom was the computer guy, the head," I broke in, trying to buy us more time. Surely something would save us. The idea of croaking at the pleasure of this self-satisfied rat-girl was too awful to contemplate. I went on, "But you were the problem fixer. The hands."

Maria's dark eyes flashed.

"I was both," she flung back at me. "The head *and* the hands. Tom was the hacker, true, but he wouldn't have had the slightest sense of where to utilize his talents if it hadn't been for me. *I* guided him. *I* directed him. He answered to *me*."

Man, I stepped on her tail with that one. Maybe I could find a way to use that sore spot against her. If I had the time.

"If you were as smart a woman as you think you are," I said, "you'd know you're wasting an awful lot of energy slapping your jaws here. Aren't you even the least little bit concerned you've left two bodies cooling out there in the hall? What if the cops come?"

"Who's going to call them?" Maria smirked. "You? Her?" She wagged the gun a centimeter. "Do you know what's on the end of this?"

"Sure," I said. "A sound suppressor. I also know they're not foolproof, Hollywood movies notwithstanding. A suppressor is only good for a few rounds before the baffles inside are shot, then what have you got? Just a loud funnel."

"And how many shots did you hear?" Maria asked. "I counted two. As you said, those resulted in two bodies. This suppressor is good for at least two more." Her smile widened. "I always treat the rounds I expend like they cost me a hundred dollars apiece."

"This ain't gonna last forever," Kitty piped up. "Pretty soon people will miss me."

"No, they won't," Maria said patiently. "Last night you left a note on my desk upstairs telling me to cancel your rehearsal this morning. Although that wasn't necessary. You couldn't have known I record every call here, coming in or going out."

She turned her eyes on me. "And you can thank Joe here for the fact you won't be missed this morning. He told you to cancel your rehearsal when he called, and, using me, cancel it you did."

Maria's laugh was light. "The things a mother will do for her child, when he asks. Oh, by the way, I guess you should know I've taken all your jewelry from your armoire in the bedroom. Don't worry, though, it's safe in my briefcase in the hall. You'll no longer have need of it. But I will, especially where I'm going. It'll be as good as money there. Better." Her mad eyes twinkled merrily. "Call it a question of the greater good."

The killer cocked her head, drawing in a raspy breath. "*Anyway*, Miss Kitty Oh-so-fine Clark, the next thing you're expected for is a date you'll not be able to keep. Dinner tonight with the mayor. It was supposed to have been at your usual spot. The Palm at 140 Fifth Avenue. I know. I booked it. Eight o'clock sharp. And as always when you'd dine with her, you'd have the grilled swordfish, and Her Honor the steak Diane."

Maria grinned again, showing tiny, crooked teeth. "But you

won't be there to eat it. By that time you'll have been dead a while."

She tilted her head to the other side now, her grin fading.

"You were always so predictable, Kitty. So … staid. Didn't it ever grow tiresome? The same thing, day after day after day, never really taking a chance, never grabbing life by the throat and making it cough up a destiny for you. What a waste. I really believe I'm doing you a favor, helping you shuffle off this mortal coil."

The killer's smile was back now, and disarmingly sunny. "But even better than that, no more guilt over your past. Isn't that great? No more lies about your son. No more shame. You leave here clean as a new penny."

It was blazing, that smile.

"You really should be thanking me for this," Maria said. "I've completely cleared your calendar today. The only appointment you need to keep now is the one you have with the reaper. I've booked you and Joe for a one-way ticket to hell." Her titter was as crazed as I knew she was. "Truth be told, it turned out I was pretty good at this secretarial stuff. Not that it was ever going to be my life's work, you understand."

"You should have played to your strengths," I said, but she ignored me.

"Eight o'clock will come and go," Maria said, as breezy as May, "and then eight-thirty. But no one will be too awfully concerned at first, because the rich and powerful are different, and allowances must be made. But by nine, hands will be wringing, and calls will go out."

She nodded at the old woman. "And an hour or so later, Kitty, the lovely old front door to this lovely old house will be smashed to bits by Nashville's finest, and from then on it'll be a press carnival."

Maria lightly bit her lower lip, in some weird way trying for sexy, before going on, "By then I'll have been in Venezuela for twelve hours or better, sipping Mai Tais on the beach in Caracas in my new red bikini, gazing at the golden sunlight dancing on the waves." She turned her attention fully to me, her flirty tone gone as she became matter-of-fact. "I picked Venezuela because it doesn't have an extradition treaty with us, you know."

I nodded back. "I know." Slice it any way you will, Maria Conchita Velez was as nutty as a Clark bar. There *had* to be a way I could use that.

"After a lot of consideration, I know how my plan failed," she said. "It really wasn't a mystery. Once I factored in all the choices, only one answer came clear."

I couldn't tell if Maria was talking to me or to Kitty or to the air or to the spirit of James K. Polk. At that point, I don't think it mattered.

"Tom Parker," she said, bobbing her head once as she agreed with herself. "It was his fault. I see that now."

With an effort, she seemed to come back into the room. "Tom and I were between jobs, at a singularly bad spot when we came here, and we knew it. Our ready cash was nearly depleted. Steps needed to be taken. I directed him to use his computer skills to find some rich old person to relieve of their wealth. That he did."

Maria's intonation went flat. "He located you, Kitty. He found a lonely old woman badly in need of caring, experienced people. It seemed your previous manager had died unexpectedly, and your personal assistant had quit to get married. So the day Tom and I came here in response to your ad for both positions, showing up on your doorstep and offering you our services, you accepted us eagerly."

Her sneer was better than Oil-Can Harry's.

"Your eagerness to accept us was pathetic," she said. "Really, it was. The two of us had dummied up some excellent references, but we could have saved ourselves the effort. You took them at face value, without even checking. Big mistake on your part."

"I'd always thought I was a good judge of character," Kitty muttered. "Y'all both seemed so polite and competent. Tom bein' from the South is what really clinched it." Her look darkened. "What a fool I was. It seems I missed the mark pretty bad with you two."

"It's pointless to fret over that," Maria said evenly. "Especially now. Anyway, the days passed, and Tom and I settled in here, going about our duties, waiting patiently for the solution to our problem to present itself. But it soon became apparent that Tom's vision was too small. He'd thought that by us ingratiating ourselves into your life, we could find a way of making off with a small stash, possibly the family silver, or maybe lay our hands on enough loose cash to tide us over until the big one came along. But he didn't recognize something only a true visionary can."

Her expression turned thoughtful. "Tom couldn't see that *you* were the big one, Kitty. Little as you are. Not your cash, or your art, or your jewels. Plain. Old. You. That's what he missed. Perhaps he *couldn't* see it. Perhaps it was beyond his ability. But I know opportunity when I encounter it, however it's wrapped."

Maria smiled again, the epitome of friendliness. "Good fate usually disguises itself as something else. When I pointed that out to Tom, he was thunderstruck at having missed it. After that it was just a matter of finding the right scheme with you, and the right time to pull it off. Your plan with the fake letters coming here last Christmas was perfect." She grinned. "Letter perfect, to coin a pun. All we did was tweak that a bit, and make it real. The phone calls too." Her grin faded. "The only thing I couldn't have foreseen was your doggedness, Joe."

So that's what had driven Maria truly nuts. Me. She blamed me for wrecking their scheme to bilk Kitty out of her fortune. Lord alone knew where this was all going to end up.

"Last night, Tom panicked when you fired him, Kitty," Maria said. She spread her fingers an inch apart. "Joe, he told me you were *this* close to uncovering it all. I tried reasoning with him, but he was long past reason. I went into the bathroom to get him a sedative. When I returned, I found him gone. He'd taken off without my permission. Or my direction. Checking the room bug in here, I learned he was on his way to the *Skylark*, determined to grab what he could, cutting me out."

Her smile gave a new definition to the term smug. "Of course, he couldn't have known that would never have worked. Because I still had you, Kitty. And your trust in me. I tried calling Tom on his cell, to caution him that trying to remove me from the picture, to strip from me what I was rightfully due, was a highly stupid move, but he didn't answer."

"He probably couldn't," I said. "The weather last night up there had really messed up the phones."

"No matter. I knew eventually Tom would have to come back to me for guidance. Alone, he was helpless. All he saw was greed. And in the end, that greed cost him his life." Maria shook her head at Parker's apparent stupidity. "Some partner, huh? And in the end, he died for what? An envelope full of an old woman's dreams."

With a will she seemed to shrug off the memories.

"Oh well. No matter. The next time I try this on some other

rich, elderly bat, I go solo. A partner is redundant." She nodded at me. "Don't you agree, Joe? You've been solo for years. Don't you think a partner would have just hindered you?"

"Depends on the partner, I suppose," I said, but she wasn't listening.

"Anyway ..." Her eyes were fever-bright. "Thank you for letting me say my piece."

I could tell from Maria's body language that something had changed. Something bad. The air in the room suddenly seemed much colder.

"Your listening to me means more than you'll ever know," she went on. "Really. Now I can see more clearly the ways to avoid future mistakes, when I try this again."

"Girl, you're *crazy!*" Kitty yelled, eyes bulging. "Plumb *crazy!*"

Maria shrugged again. "Maybe." She moved her feet apart an inch. "But of the three of us, I'll be the one leaving this room alive."

That sounded like the death knell. For Kitty and me. I couldn't believe this was happening. *Come on, Box! Are you just going to stand there and take it?* Yeah, looks like.

Maria widened her stance just a bit more, now bringing her left hand around to join the right one in squeezing the Beretta's grip. She lined it up on my sternum.

"I was just showing off out in the hall," she grinned. "Sometimes I'm silly that way." She pulled her elbows in tight against her body. "It's always best to use two hands."

I was staring eternity right in the face. Cognitive thought fled, leaving only terror. Inside, I was praying. Hard.

My words were thick. "What about the guard at the gate?"

"Him?" Maria raised one eyebrow, her grin crooked and her words seemingly weightless and light and shimmering as air. "Him, I'll do last."

I saw her trigger finger growing white as it tightened down, taking up the last half-ounce of slack, and with a dull sense of finality I waited for the shot to blow through my heart.

And then something incredible happened, something I'll take with me to the grave.

Inexplicably, Kitty screamed out, *"My baby!"* ... and jumped in front of me.

With an evil, short hiss, like a steel snake, Maria's silenced Beretta bucked once, the round meant for me catching Kitty high in the chest. She fell heavily to the floor at my feet.

"No!" My yell was one of horror as I leaped over her toward the other woman.

Kitty's act of heroism had thrown off Maria's concentration. Before she could swing the gun around to fire again, I unthinkingly slammed my left fist into the bridge of her nose. When I did, I heard something snap and let go in my hand. But I didn't even feel it.

Maria crashed backward, ramming something hard before she hit the floor, her gun skittering free. She was either dead or unconscious, I didn't know and didn't care.

I dropped to my knees, gathering Kitty in my arms. Dread pooled like dark ice in my heart as I began rocking her. Just like I'd done with Linda. Not again. I couldn't go through this again. "Please, God, no, no ..."

Kitty's skin felt cool in my hands, and she smelled of lemons and of blood. The lemons, I remembered. The blood was new.

She reached up, wiping a tear from my cheek. I hadn't realized I was crying.

"Shhh, Joe, don't weep, darlin' ..." she whispered. "It's best this way ..."

I gulped. "Don't talk." Wildly I looked around the room. Where was the stinking *phone?* "I need to call an ambulance. I—"

"Don't matter ..." She gently shook her head. "I'll be gone by then ..."

"Don't say that!" I could hardly see her for my tears.

"At the ... end ..." Kitty murmured, gazing straight into my eyes, "I was good, wasn't I ... a good mom to you ... at the end ..."

"Please ..." I choked. It was all I could think to say. "Please ..." No. There was something else I could say, and the words burned raw in my throat.

"Don't go, Mama!"

I was sobbing now, still rocking her like she was a little child, rocking her as she so often did me, in my dim remembrance. "Mama, please don't go. Don't leave me again, please ..."

Her life's blood pouring like hot wax over my hands, I rocked her and rocked her.

"Shhh ..." My mother's eyes were filming over, even as she smiled up at me. She licked her lips, her tongue papery and dry. "I'll be ... waitin' ... but ... before I go ..." Trembling, she held up her left hand. "Help me ... get this off ..."

"Your ... your ring?" Why did she want me to do that? But I did as she asked, tugging it free from her finger and laying it down by my leg.

She pulled my head close now, holding my face in her wrinkled hands.

"Barnicke ... told me about ... Angela ..." Suddenly Mama arched her back with a shuddering gasp as a red-hot rocket of pain speared her. Her trembling body felt so small in my hands, like a bird's. A skylark's.

Then it passed, and again she looked straight in my eyes. "I

... I want you ... to take that ring ... give it to her ... and you ... marry that gal ..." Again Mama pulled in a sharp intake of air. But not in pain this time. This was ... different. It was as if she was seeing something over my shoulder, something just past me.

Something wonderful.

"Oh, Joe, look." Mama's face was beaming, shining like molten gold. "All this *light* ... "

"NO!" I screamed, and gathered her closer, even as I felt her slipping away.

"Just one thing more ..." Mama whispered, and I knew she wasn't speaking to me now, but to someone else. The one calling her home. "Just ... one thing ... more ..."

Then for the last time Mama pulled me close, murmuring her love.

And as she did, I was three again, and dreaming of Christmas, smiling in my sleep as her angel lips fluttered as softly as a butterfly on my ear.

21

As funerals go, my mother's was one for the books. Everyone who was anyone in country music showed up, as did, surprisingly, some from the worlds of rock, pop, and rap. From my scan of the sea of faces at the First Baptist Church of Belle Meade, Kitty Clark's music seemed to have cut across all ethnicities and genres.

Respecting her final wishes of no bad publicity or scandal, I remained just another anonymous fan who'd managed to snag one of the last open seats on the back row of the church balcony. Also, I hadn't told Angela or Sarge or Helen that I was going to be here. They had no idea Kitty was my mom, and I'd leave them to puzzle for themselves why I wasn't answering my phone. All I'd done was to call Dempsey Miller and ask him to look in on and feed Noodles, telling him something had come up and I'd be gone for a while.

I harked back to three days earlier, when I'd called the police out to the mansion, telling them there'd been a shooting. As a former cop I can truthfully say there's not a phrase in police jargon that'll get a whole bunch of squad cars in motion quicker than to mention gunfire.

Hanging up the phone, I quickly concocted the story I'd tell when they arrived. It had to be stark, simple, and most of all, believable. In the end, what I came up with was more fact than fiction.

I said that Kitty Clark had been thinking of upgrading her security system, as she'd been having doubts about the loyalty and honesty of her two employees, Maria Velez and Tom Parker. Kitty and I had been talking in her parlor when Maria, who'd been upstairs eavesdropping, broke in on us. Knowing her plan to rip off Kitty was destroyed, she sought to cut her losses and kill us all, Blake and the young maid included, and steal what she could, before heading down to her hidey-hole in Venezuela.

Like I said, mostly true. All I had to do to make sure my story hung together before the cops came was to burn in the fireplace the letters I'd been shown, and retrieve and stash in my car's trunk the disks from the recording equipment Maria had hidden upstairs. They weren't as hard to find as I'd thought; she'd simply secreted the gear under a false bottom in her lower desk drawer. Overconfidence. It gets them every time. The last thing I did was to take Kitty's "treasure" off the front seat and place that in the Yugo's tiny trunk as well.

The only really hairy part had come when the Nashville Metro lead detective, a sad-faced man with the unlikely name of Hec Bibbs, asked me what had happened to Parker.

"Sank out of sight, I guess," was my extremely honest answer.

He nodded. "Guy like him, he can't have gone far. We'll find him."

Not freaking likely, I thought, but kept my trap shut.

I also found out earlier the day of Mama's service that Maria Velez wasn't dead. She wasn't exactly alive, either.

That hard bang I'd heard just before she crashed to the floor was the sound of the back of her head slamming into the corner of the large antique occasional table behind her, crushing her skull and pulping the occipital lobe of her brain.

Maria was now in a deep coma, completely uncommunicative the doctors were saying, and by all signs she'd remain that way until the end of her days. I was glad I hadn't killed her; Maria's fate now was a thousand times worse. The irony was stark. Her vaunted intelligence gone, she was fated to live out her life as a vegetable. So now with Parker dead and Maria as good as, no one would ever know of Kitty's relationship with me.

Mama's memorial was about like you'd think, with eulogies coming hard and fast from one giant after another in the Country Music Association. My plaster-encased left hand—it turned out I'd broken three bones in it when I'd slugged Maria—wasn't hurting too badly, thanks to a couple of Demerol I'd been given at the hospital emergency room, and which I'd saved for this occasion. There were speeches as well from civic and charity leaders, each one telling of some deed, large or small, Kitty Clark had done to advance their cause.

That last one struck me. I can't say for sure why, but the idea of my mother willingly supporting charities seemed strange at first—maybe because of what she'd done to me as a child. But I guess she'd been as capable of sending the odd dollar or two to the Red Cross or the Kidney Foundation as the next person. More so, considering she'd been a whole lot wealthier than the next person.

In addition to the aforementioned speakers, the service was

laced with what I supposed were Mama's favorite hymns, sung by folks both well known and obscure. As I said before, it was obvious I'd underestimated my mother's ability to run the spectrum of the human condition.

The nearly ninety-minute closed-casket memorial seemed to go twice that, maybe owing to the astoundingly hard seats we in the balcony had to endure. Surreptitiously looking around, I noticed I wasn't the only one gritching my rear end back and forth, seeking comfort. At last the thing ended, and it was time to head to the graveyard.

I nearly balked then. Call me overly sensitive, but I wasn't sure if I was ready to share my loss with the media vultures, and maybe thousands of other people who'd be there. Only my grief would outshine theirs. They'd lost a great entertainer, musician, and friend. I'd lost my mother. Again.

But in the end I found myself joining the massive car and pickup truck caravan making its way the five miles down to the Belle Meade Cemetery. And oddly enough, for each and every one of those miles, at each intersection we crossed, people were waiting. Solemn and silent they were, the women wiping away tears, the men removing their hats and caps, their bewildered children holding to their parents' hands tightly as Death sauntered by.

Mine was one of the last cars to arrive, so I had to park quite a distance away from the gravesite. By the time I'd hiked across countless older plots to get there (and I've always hated that; it seems like the worst sort of sacrilege), the service was nearly over.

It sounds harsh, but I felt no great loss over that. In my heart, I'd already said good-bye. And after planting too many bodies in the ground, both in wartime and peace, including those of my wife and unborn son, I knew the drill far too intimately.

Finally, mercifully, it was done. First by ones and twos, then by groups, the crowd began to disperse, on their way back to their vehicles.

But I stayed right where I was.

Most of the mourners, those that saw me at all, must have figured I was some kind of hard-core Kitty Clark fan, unwilling to sever this final tie. That was fine with me. I'd asked Bibbs to try his best to keep my name and face out of the press, as a favor to an ex-cop from a current one. The excuse I used was an already too-heavy client load. Hah.

Amazingly, he'd agreed, and so the people going by me had no idea I'd been there to see the passing of the legend. I ignored them as I kept my distance, standing back nearly two hundred feet from the yawning opening of the grave.

Deep inside, my emotions were running rampant. Part of it was the knowledge that my time to join the sod-dwellers was coming, probably sooner than I wanted. Another part was my simply not knowing what I was supposed to do next.

It isn't every day a boy buries his mom.

Two of the last people to leave were Mama's new pastor, a large, florid-faced man named Navarro, and his wife. Climbing back inside the car that had brought them, he took her arm and guided her inside, his nod at me noncommittal. And why not? Again, he had no idea who I was.

Atop his backhoe, the gravedigger regarded me placidly, drawing deep on his cigarette. He had to have known it was bad form to start filling in the hole while even one mourner remained, or so I'm sure it says somewhere in the Big Golden Book of Funerals. He was getting paid the same to wait me out as he was to drop dirt.

Inside, I was as dry as desert air. I'd cried all my tears holding my mama as she died, and hadn't shed another one since. Right then, it seemed as natural as breathing just to stand there doing nothing, feeling nothing, comfortably numb, as Pink Floyd put it.

That's when I saw the other man.

He was about thirty feet to my left, in his late sixties, tall, gray-haired, and whipcord lean, standing nearly as far back from the grave as I was. But he wasn't looking at Mama's final resting place.

He was staring at me.

"Mr. Box?" he called over to me after a moment.

I nodded, saying nothing.

"Mister Joseph Box?" he pressed, now coming my way.

I figured I'd let him get closer before I answered. He was only fifteen feet away when I said, "That's right. Do I know you?"

He reached me at last. "Your picture I'd been given described you. My card." Taking it, I noticed for the first time that his eyes were large, coffee brown, and compassionate.

I glanced down at the card, then back up at the man. "Mister … Huckaby, is it? What do you want?" I wasn't purposefully trying to be boorish, but in light of my turmoil, it seemed the proper day for it.

"It's not what I want, sir," he smiled, his Southern accent soft and rich. "It's what I can do for you."

I scowled. "You've picked the world's worst time to be selling burial insurance."

He laughed lightly, and pointed down. "Hardly that. Look closer at my card."

I did. It was plain white linen stock with raised lettering, worthy of Mr. Yee/Lee's best efforts. The wording on it consisted of only two lines. "Wallace T. Huckaby, Esq.," with a phone number underneath. The tag on the end of his name I'd missed the first time.

"I know that 'Esq' stands for 'esquire,' so that must mean you're an attorney." I began to hand it back. "Sorry, but I'm not in the market right now."

"I'm afraid I've not made myself clear, Mr. Box," Huckaby said, "and for that I apologize. Let me start again. You see, I was your mother's attorney."

What he said took a second to register. When it did, I felt like I'd been booted in the guts. "My ... how do you know who my mother is? *Who* are you again?"

"Good, you're not denying it. That will make things a great deal easier."

My thoughts swirling, I absently motioned to a concrete bench a few feet away. "Maybe we'd both better sit down."

"Excellent idea."

After we were seated, Huckaby turned to me.

"I'll make this as simple as I can. Back at the beginning of February, your mother, Ollie Mae Box, whose stage name was Kitty Clark, was referred to me by her friend and banker, Albert Fussnagel. It seemed Miss Clark was being pressured by her manager, one Thomas Parker, to change both her will's executorship, and her durable power of attorney for health care, over to him. The lawyer that drew up those documents had died of natural causes last year. That's how she came to me, through Mr. Fussnagel's recommendation."

Huckaby shifted his weight on the bench. And for good reason; the April sunshine arcing down through the bright blue sky onto our faces was warm, but the coldness of the concrete under our haunches had to have been sapping the heat from him. I know it was me.

"I've been around the block enough to know what I was being asked," the attorney went on, "and sadly, I've seen this too many times before. An old person, usually a woman in failing health, is forced into changing her executor or durable power of attorney to suit the whims of either a grasping relative, or possibly an investor. It happens all the time."

"And you didn't try to dissuade her?"

"Of course I did. But to no avail." Huckaby shook his head at the apparent hopelessness of it. "Miss Clark was quite adamant."

"I think I know where you're going, so let me jump ahead here, and cut to the chase," I said. "Of the two documents you changed, the durable power of attorney was the one Parker really pushed for."

Huckaby nodded. "Exactly so. Her will's contents were immaterial to him, as if he knew he'd never need it. He never even asked who the heirs were. No, what Thomas Parker strove for, what he made Miss Clark strive for, was the effective placement of himself in full control over her affairs, should her health fail."

"And you did that." It wasn't an accusation, but merely a stating of fact.

"Yes. As I said, Miss Clark was resolute. If I hadn't done it, she just would have gone to someone else. And I know the quality of my work. For all concerned."

Something in the way he'd said that made me sit up straighter. "Mr. Huckaby, why are you telling me this?"

His reply was even. "Because it didn't end there. Two weeks after I'd changed those documents, she interrupted my dinner when she called me at home."

My spine started to tingle. Uh-oh.

"Thomas Parker and Maria Velez were both out of town that night," Huckaby went on, "and Miss Clark asked me to come over right away."

"What did she want?"

"She told me that after a lot of thought, she wanted me to make one last modification. She said she now wanted to change her will's executorship and durable power of attorney over to myself. I told her that would be viewed by any judge worth his salt as a conflict of interest, and recommended James Trikonis, a senior partner in the firm, for that task."

So that's who Trikonis was.

"Reluctantly, she agreed," Huckaby went on. "But she also wanted me to confirm that with all the shuffling around we'd done, the heir to her estate remained as is."

"Which would be who?" I knew what his answer was going to be, even before he spoke it.

Huckaby leaned forward, clasping his hands before him as he turned to me full on. "She left it all to her son. One Joseph Jebstuart Box. An estate whose valuation at last measure, counting her businesses, investments, belongings, ready cash, house and land, totals roughly six hundred and eight million dollars." He paused. "She left it all to you."

I couldn't answer, the import of his words robbing me of speech.

Huckaby nodded, realizing that I finally got it. "It always had been you, Mr. Box. Right from the start. It's all in here."

For the first time, I noticed he was carrying a thick nine-by-eleven manila envelope in his left hand, exactly the kind that had contained Mama's "treasure" from the *Skylark*. Only this was a treasure of an entirely different kind.

"In the event of her death," he went on, "I was also instructed to give you this."

Reaching into his suit pocket, the attorney withdrew a number ten plain white envelope, and he handed it to me. It was sealed, edge to edge, and only then did I notice it carried a handwritten inscription. The inscription read, "to my dearest Joe."

My throat closed. My mother's handwriting. I remembered it from Blake's sign he'd held at the airport.

Huckaby stood, his expression kind. "I have no idea what it says, Mr. Box. I'll leave you to peruse it in privacy. I'll be over there, when you're ready." Placing the larger envelope on the bench beside me, he began walking away toward Mama's grave.

I stared after him, my mind racing, my heart flying, not really sure if I was ready to see this final message from my mother. But in the end, I owed her that much. Slipping my finger under the flap, I pulled it open.

Then sliding the single piece of yellowed foolscap out, I unfolded it, and began to read.

22

My mother's handwriting was atrocious, and her spelling worse. But I understood it just the same.

Joe, it began, *if yoor reading this, Im already dead. Youll fine the date on this letter is June 27, 1970. I done made me a potful of money, more than I can spend, so I figurd it was time to make me a will. Albert Fusnagel, my banker, told me this lawyer he knows can do it rite, and keep mum. His name, the lawyers I mean, is Robert Dinwoody. I think thats how he spels it. I aint sure. Anyway, I told this Dinwoody about you, but only after making real sur he can keep his yapper shut. Albert says Dinwoody is OK for that. I did this caus I wanted to make sur you get my stuff when I die. Nobody els deserves it, and you might not beleev this, but I done all this for you, only now I wish I never had. I shud have stayed but I didnt. I was too scared. I hope someday I can meet you, and hold you one last time, but I dont know if thatll ever happen. If it dont, thisll be the way I can tell you that I love you. Dont think bad of me please. Caus I would have give every penny to kiss you onece more.*

Your mama, Ollie Mae

The paper nearly slipped from my fingers, to be snatched away by the capricious April breeze, but at the last moment I gripped it tightly. For the longest time I sat like that, staring at nothing at all.

When I did at last look up, I met the eyes of the gravedigger. He was still calmly smoking, as if he had all the patience in the world. He nodded at me as he flipped the butt away, then he pulled the pack out of his shirt pocket and slid out another.

Huckaby must have realized I was done with Mama's letter, and he started back over my way. He didn't speak until he was again seated next to me.

"Lovely day." He tilted his face toward the sun. "Two more like this and my crocuses at home should be blooming."

I looked at him. "Aren't you going to ask me what it said?"

The attorney returned the look, his smile kind. "Why no, Mr. Box. That's none of my affair. Knowing Miss Clark as I did, I'm sure that whatever it was, it was heartfelt."

I slipped Mama's words back into their envelope, my throat closing again. "That's the word, all right." My eyes were stinging, even though I'd been sure I had no more tears left to shed. "Final words are precious words. My pastor said that."

Huckaby nodded. "A wise man, I'm sure. And speaking of wisdom ..." He again reached into his suit pocket, now pulling out a second envelope.

"I already know the contents of this one," he said, handing it over. "Your mother instructed me to give you this as well, but only after you'd read the first."

I took it from him. "You say you know what's in it?"

"Yes."

I steeled myself for whatever it might be. "What?"

Huckaby patted my knee like a kindly grandfather. "Why don't you open it and see for yourself?"

I paused for a moment, then I did as he said.

Cautiously peering inside the envelope, what I found was anticlimactic, only what looked like a long, folded, mint-green rectangular piece of paper. Puzzled, I slid it out and unfolded it.

Then I nearly dropped the thing. Done up in fancy script, bordered by curlicues and flourishes, I saw it was a bearer bond, drawn on Albert Fussnagel's bank in Nashville.

The amount on it was ten million dollars.

Again words failed me, and I looked up at the attorney in stone bafflement.

"What—what's this for?" I finally managed to croak.

"An estate the size of your mother's will doubtless take some time to go through probate court. It could take a year, probably longer." He tapped the bond with his finger. "That cash should tide you over until the job is accomplished."

My look at him was beyond shell-shocked, I'm sure. "It … It'll do."

Huckaby glanced down at the larger envelope containing Mama's will. "Counting what you have in your hand, and what's inside that package, you're a very wealthy man now, Mr. Box." He pursed his lips. "May I ask a question?" I nodded, and he said, "Perhaps it's none of my business, but what in heaven's name do you plan to do with it all?"

I again struggled a moment before finally answering. "That's going to take some thought. Somehow—" I shook my head and started over. "None of this seems real."

He nodded again. "Indeed. I would suppose not."

I turned fully toward him. "Have you ever done this before,

Mr. Huckaby? Being the bearer of news like this, I mean?"

"Yes. Twice before. But never regarding such a … princely sum."

"That makes you the reigning expert, then. What in the world do I do next?"

"Are you asking me for legal advice?"

"I guess I am. Obviously Mama trusted you, sir, and you seem like a right-enough guy. I'm going to need help with … all of this. Will you require some sort of retainer?"

Huckaby's smile in return seemed warm and friendly, and right now I needed that. To say this was uncharted territory for me would beggar the term "uncharted."

He held out his right hand. "For now, this is the only retainer I'll need."

We shook then, and so my life entered a new phase.

♦ ◊ ♦

"I feel like the detective in a Victorian drawing-room novel," I said to the others gathered around. "Like my next line should be, 'I suppose you're all wondering why I've brought you here today.'"

"Good question," Sarge said. "So I'll ask it. Why *are* we all here?"

I started to answer, when outside my apartment window a robin trilled shrilly. As it did, Noodles jumped from Angela's lap up onto the windowsill, where he began frantically trying to claw the glass with his paws. Then he started howling like his heart would break with unmet longing.

Helen laughed. "Good heavens. Would you listen to that? The way that feline is carrying on makes me wonder if you've been feeding him enough, Joe."

"Yeah, I have," I scowled. "He eats like a teenager. The only problem is the store doesn't carry robin-flavored cat food. Every spring the silly critter acts the same way. One of these days I'll let him out after one just to see what'll happen."

Sarge took a pull of his coffee. "If those robins are anything like the ones down in Florida, they'll probably peck him on the head a good lick just to show him who's boss."

A few seconds more of caterwauling, and Noodles jumped back off the sill to the floor with a defeated sigh, his twisted tail hanging dejectedly. He was such a comically sorrowful sight that we laughed, and my heart swelled with feeling for them all.

The time was the first week of June, a full month and more after Mama's funeral. Still nothing new from Cullen. Just give him time.

For the past five weeks I'd been down in Nashville, telling whoever cared I was staying there while I tied up some loose ends on a case.

Which was true, in a way. What I in fact was doing was toiling away with Huckaby on the beginning details of the daunting task of settling Mama's estate. That is, he worked the details; I just said "Yep" every now and then and signed things.

My time there didn't arouse too much suspicion, I don't think. Angela knew I was working Kitty's case, and had heard of her death. Who hadn't? Someone said it had even made the third page of the *New York Times*. It wasn't a challenge for my sweetie to put two and two together. She realized I was finalizing things for Kitty and so didn't begrudge me the time I spent. But now I was home, and it was well past the point to bring my "family" into the real picture.

"Enough about Noodles and his diet," I said. "I'm going to need everybody's full attention here, because what I'm about to share with you all can't leave this room. I mean it." As I said that, I stood and began pacing like a caged wolverine.

Angela mock-shuddered, her grin a mile wide. "Good grief. You really know how to set the mood here. I feel like I'm about to hear a really scary ghost story."

Since I'd come back from Nashville, she and I had been doing better. It was as if we both knew in our hearts that, regardless of our differences, what we had was simply too good to die without a fight. Still, we remained cautious, like we were juggling Ming vases blindfolded.

"Not a ghost story, Ange," I said, "but a hair-raiser all the same."

"Are you gonna keep walking back and forth like that while you talk?" Sarge broke in. "It's like I'm watching a tennis match. And you know how much I hate tennis." Helen shushed him.

"Maybe. Sorry for the pacing around, but I feel like I've got enough nervous energy in my frame to light up Union Terminal, and three streets on either side."

"Yeah, tell me about it. You're making my watch run faster just being this close to you. It's like you're about to pop a rivet or something." The look Sarge gave me was exasperated. "Will you stand still and *tell* it already?" The others nodded their agreement.

"Okay," I said, stopping at last. "But remember. Not a word leaves here ..."

And then, what the heck. I told them.

◆ ◊ ◆

Although the ordeal I'd gone through had consumed almost six months of my life, the telling of it took less than two hours. It's funny how it works like that sometimes. The fact I wasn't interrupted by any of them even once helped. What really got to them was when I came to the part about who Kitty Clark really was to me. And how much her loss hurt.

As one, they came over and encircled me with their arms, Angela and Helen weeping, Sarge patting me on the shoulder—manly stuff, don't you know.

And then nobody said anything for a time. They were just … there for me.

"That poor woman," Angela murmured at last, rubbing the tears from her face. "All that pain, for all those years. And then the day you both reconcile, she's taken from you." Her eyes were still wet. "At least you know you'll see her again one day."

"Yeah," I nodded. "One day."

Finally, the women sniffling and Sarge clearing his throat, they took their seats. I was still standing, and that's when I told them about the will.

And the fortune.

When they all went silent this time, it was probably because they were stunned to muteness by its enormity. I know I'd been.

It was Angela who spoke up first.

"My … goodness," she said, blinking. "To say that's a lot of money would be the understatement of the year. Your mother … mercy, she must have loved you a lot, Joe." She reached up from her chair and took my hand.

I squeezed hers back. "Yeah, in her stumbling, fumbling, overcomplicated way, I think she really did. She'd initially hatched that 'obsessed fan' plot to buy her way out of that cockamamie curse that crazy witch woman had tried to put on her. But at the end, it was Mama's love for me that overrode her fears."

"Love is like that," Helen said. She looked over at Sarge with shining eyes as she stroked his hand. "Many's the time when the two of you were on late-night patrol, fear would try to rise up in my chest, conjuring up terrible pictures in my mind of mayhem and slaughter. But then I'd just remember how much I loved this grouchy cuss—" At that Sarge pulled her hand to his lips and kissed it, and Helen smiled—"and I'd think no, no matter what happens to this stubborn old Mick of mine, love lasts."

It was amazing, that look she was giving him. "And as I'd consider that," she said, "why then that old fear would just slink away to go bother somebody else."

"I've heard tell that love trumps all," I said. "So does forgiveness, I think. Because when I forgave Mama as she lay dying ..." I choked for a moment before I could continue. "I felt a weight lift from my soul, a weight I didn't even know I'd been carrying all my life."

For a little while then the four of us again grew quiet, each lost in reflection of what counts in the final tally of the heart. Even Noodles came and sat respectfully by my feet.

It was Sarge who broke the spell at last, the clearing of his throat sounding like a rusty muffler. "Tell us again how much Kitty left you. I ain't sure I heard you right."

With a will I shook myself, coming back into the present.

"Mr. Huckaby told me the estate valued out at a shade over six hundred and eight million," I replied. "Of course, unless he's pretty sharp with his skills, the inheritance taxes and such will eat up a bunch of that. Still, there's going to be a lot of it left."

"Over six hundred million ..." Sarge muttered, then he grinned crookedly. "Well, I guess it goes without saying you'll be getting yourself a new car. I mean, a Yugo hardly fits a man of your newly substantial means."

I scowled at him. "Yeah, funny man, I'll get something else as my main ride, but I'm still planning on hanging onto the little beast. I've made a lot of memories with it these last few months."

"How long did you say it'll be until the estate is settled?" he asked.

"Mr. Huckaby said at least a year, probably longer," I said. "With all of Mama's holdings to factor in, the whole thing is bound to be pretty complex."

"That's a long time," my mentor said, and he reached around back for his wallet. "How you fixed for cash until then? Need some help?"

"Uh, no," I smiled. "I think I'm okay for a while."

Sarge took his hand off his hip and narrowed his eyes. "You look just like that fool cat of yours after he's had a good meal."

"I guess that's because Mama had the foresight to advance me some of it early," I said.

"Yeah? If I'm not being nosy, how much?" Sarge got a dirty look from Helen for his crassness, but he just picked up his coffee cup and took a long pull.

I smiled, feeling unaccountably sheepish. "Ten million."

At that, coffee shot out through Sarge's nose, and he went into a wild coughing fit. Helen leaned over and pounded his back.

Finally he looked at me, red-eyed and wheezing. "Criminey! Holy smokes! You're telling me you have ten million dollars? In *cash?*"

"Well, no, of course not, not on me. It was in a bearer bond, and now it's in a discretionary account I set up at Albert Fussnagel's bank down in Nashville."

"Lord. Have. Mercy," Sarge muttered, sitting back heavily in his chair. Helen and Angela just gaped at me.

Strangely enough, the news of that account had gotten a

bigger reaction from the group than when I'd told them the original amount of the fortune. It's weird. I guess six hundred-plus million dollars is just too abstract an amount for most of us, but an even ten million smackers is something we can all picture.

"When the estate is finally settled, the first thing I plan to do is write out the tithe," I said. "But I'll have to figure a way to do that anonymously. That way nobody'll know who it came from." I went on with a grin, "I'll bet the pastor will flat have a fit when he gets it."

"A fit?" Sarge's eyebrows climbed. "I hope it doesn't stop his heart." I laughed, then he said, "Okay, the tithe first. That's scriptural. I can see that." He shook his head. "But even then, Joe, that still leaves a monstrous big pile of it left. What in the world are you going to do with it all?"

"That's just what Wallace Huckaby asked. And I'll give you the same answer. I don't rightly know yet."

I stared in thought at the floor a moment before looking back up at them all. "Even back in my darkest days of alcoholism, I still liked helping people. Lots of times I'd gladly split my last bottle of Scotch with some old down-on-his-luck rummy, just because I could. I guess it goes back to when I was a kid. Helping people was a way I kept sane in that crazy house I grew up in."

Angela nodded at me, her eyes tender. She knew where I was headed with this.

"So whatever I end up doing with all that money, it'll be to help others," I said, and I shrugged. "Not that I'm a saint. Far from it. It's just how I'm wired."

My girlfriend again reached up and took my hand. "I think you're wonderful."

I kissed her hand before releasing it. "Anyway, it looks like I'll have enough time to think about it. A year or more, like Huckaby told me. But the ten million I'll need to make some decisions on right away."

"A year's a pretty long time," Sarge said, and he scowled. "Can't this Huckaby guy grease the skids, make it go faster?"

"I don't even plan on asking him," I replied. "I'm not going to let this stuff go to my head and make me act like the kind of guy I always hated. Because in my opinion, money ruined Mama."

Sarge started to speak, but I held up a hand, cutting him off. "And yeah, I know what the scripture says. It's not having money per se that ruins people, but the love of it. First or second Timothy, I think. I'm not sure."

I started moving around again. "Here's the thing. It was Mama's fear of Dad's beatings that drove her out of our house, and my life, for too many years. But it wasn't just her fear that kept her away all that time. It was her incessant, driving hunger to acquire money and goods that did that."

I stopped and stared at the others intently. "Now maybe that wouldn't happen to me. Or maybe, like Mama said, 'the acorn don't fall far from the tree.' It could be the seed of greed really does run true, and with all that wealth staring at me, I'd find myself changing into something unrecognizable."

"Are you sure about that, Joe?" Helen said. "I don't think you're giving yourself enough credit."

"Maybe. I've always said there's not many things that scare me. Monster movies don't, at least not since I was six. The Clay County bullies I fought almost every day as a kid didn't. The Vietcong ..." I shrugged. "Well, yeah, they came pretty close."

"How about the bad guys we collared when we were together on the force?" Sarge said.

I curled my lip. "Nah, most of them were just coke-heads or two-bit wannabe punks you could blow away with a harsh remark, and you know it."

Sarge grinned his agreement.

"No," I went on, "I figure that by using Mama's money to anonymously help out others, it'll be a blessing for them, and a good legacy for her."

"Yeah, well, that's all fine," Sarge said, "but I hope you can trust this guy Huckaby." Again he narrowed his eyes. "'Cause that is one *whale* of a lot of dough to handle."

"When I asked the attorney for advice, and what he needed for a retainer, his answer was simple." I held up my right hand. "He said this was the only retainer he needed." I lowered it. "Where I come from, Sarge, that's worth more than ten reams of fancy paper."

There wasn't much he could say to that, so he just nodded his agreement.

Angela spoke up then. "Joe, I think I know another reason why you're doing this. It isn't just to have a cool ten million dollars, or even six hundred million. Now that you're set, and the pressure is off, you have the freedom to take on only the cases you *wish* to take. Right?"

"That's it exactly." I nodded. "I believe if I watch what I'm doing and invest that money carefully, I can not only help folks with it, I can grow my business the way I've always wanted to. By taking on the down-and-out cases, the hopeless ones, the lost." I met her eyes. "Like the people you and I saw downtown that day on our way to see Mitch."

The look of love Angela gave me almost made me melt, and I gulped.

"Well," I said, my mouth suddenly dry, "there's something

else I need to address here, and I guess this is as good a time as any." I knelt down on one knee in front of her.

Angela's frown was as cute as a button. "*Now* what are you up to?"

"Ange ..." I gently took her hands in mine, drawing a deep breath before I could go on. "I've been a fool. I know that's not a shock to you, but there it is. For all my life I've thought my daddy's sins would be mine, forever. That I'd be doomed to continue his mistakes for as long as I lived. And up till now, I've done a pretty good job of just that." I licked my lips, which felt as desiccated as chalk. "At the end, it took Mama's death to finally drive home the point I'd been missing all this time."

"What point, Joe?" Angela whispered, her eyes huge.

"That I'm not my father's son," I said. "But that I am, forever and always, my Father's son."

I bent down and kissed her fingertips, then looked up. "Most of my life I've been out of God's will. But I've come to find out, I've never been out of his hand." I choked up a second before going on. "Mama showed me that. She also showed me that people can change. That it's only too late if we let it be. And I know if I know anything, it's this. If I were ever to lose you from my life, I'd lose the very best part of it."

Her eyes now brimmed, and I smiled up at her. "The deaths of Linda and my baby son all those years ago nearly killed me. Maybe it did kill me, at least the part that feels. Ange, it took God's love, and yours, to pull me out of that pit." Softly I began massaging her fingers. "They say a man's blessed if he has just one woman in his life he ever really loves, and who loves him unconditionally in return. But I think he's doubly blessed if he has two." I drew a breath.

"Angela Marie Swain," I said then. "Will you marry me?"

The moment hung, and she didn't answer. My heart fell.

Then she bent down, and tenderly cupped my battered face in her gentle hands. "You sweet man." Her tears began flowing at last. "Of course I'll marry you."

We kissed, and behind me I heard Helen and Sarge both burst out in joy. But they weren't as joyful as I was. I felt like a kid who had gotten everything he'd asked for on his birthday. All that was needed to complete this scene was the *Hallelujah Chorus* blasting skyward, with all the stops out.

Breaking our kiss at last I managed to say, "Wait, I'm not finished."

"With what?" she asked.

"Wait." Still holding Angela's left hand with my right, I reached my other hand into my pants pocket, pulling out the small red heart-shaped box I'd picked up earlier. I placed it in her open hand.

She opened it up. Gazing inside, her mouth fell open. "Good heavens ..." she whispered.

Inside the box nestled Mama's ring.

"This was my mother's," I said, taking it out and slipping it on her finger. "She ... she wanted my wife to have it."

It was a moment more before Angela could speak. The sunlight streaming through the slatted blinds was making the huge diamond sparkle like fire.

"Oh, Joe ..." she whispered then, her tears falling like rain. "It's exquisite ..." She kissed me again.

Helen crossed over to her, Sarge in her wake.

"Oh, honey, congratulations," the older woman said, bending down and embracing Angela. "May I see it?"

As the two women began admiring the ring, Sarge glanced down at it. His eyes nearly popped out. "Good grief! What a rock!" He looked at me. "Just how big *is* that thing?"

I shrugged. "The Nashville jeweler where I took it for a cleaning appraised it out at a little over six carats. I guess he knows what he's talking about."

Helen's eyes glittered. "It's beautiful, dear. I'm ... so happy for the two of you...." Her own waterworks started flowing at last.

Then as we all stood, it was tearful embraces for Helen and Angela, and jarring back-thumps from Sarge for me, while Noodles stared around at it all, utterly bemused, but happy.

For a cat.

A few more minutes passed like that before my three friends—check that, my three friends, one of whom was now my fiancée—found their chairs once again, while I remained standing.

"Son of a gun, I guess that's it, then." Sarge's grin was enormous. "All's well that ends well, as some old dead poet once put it. In the end, good came from bad, just like the Word says, and one tragedy made room for a whole lot of miracles. Including this one!"

His grin grew as he slapped his thighs. "As the Aussies say, good onya, son. Real good. I guess that wraps everything up in one neat package."

"Well ..." I drew out the word, and Angela looked at me strangely.

"*Now* what?" she frowned, her happiness temporarily muted.

Instead of answering I went over and flopped down in my easy chair.

Noodles looked up at me, startled. This was going to be the hardest part of all to tell them, the most baffling element ... and, besides my impending marriage, the thing that just might change my life in ways that I couldn't yet imagine. But I was finding it hard to get the words out.

"Joe?" Angela sat next to me, again taking my hand. "What is it? What's wrong?"

I worked my jaws for a moment before they felt right. Then I said, "When I was holding Mama as she was dying ..." I started over. "Remember I said that she told the angel or whatever that had come for her, 'just one thing more,' and then she kissed my ear?"

"Yes," Angela said. Sarge and Helen had scooted right to the edge of their seats.

"It wasn't just a kiss," I said. The words seemed to be forcing themselves out. "It was ... in that last, dark, painful second, right before she kissed me, Mama whispered something in that ear. Something incredible."

The entire room was electric with anticipation.

"It seems—" I blew out a breath and said it. "Well, it seems I have a brother."

Nobody said anything for a second. Too shocked for words, I guess.

Sarge broke it.

"A *brother*?" he exclaimed then, while at the same time Helen burst out, "You have a brother? Why, that's wonderful, Joe!"

Angela said nothing, her expression unreadable. I think somehow she could intuit what I was going to say next.

"Is it?" My smile seemed a strange mix of sourness and black humor. "Is it really a wonderful thing, even if my brother's name is famous?"

"Famous?" Sarge said. "Who the heck is he? Somebody we know?"

I leaned forward, pulling my hands free from Ange's and

311

folding them. "It appears my Mama was a busy lady in her younger years, and not as discreet with her charms as one would hope." I paused, and then said, "My long-lost brother just happens to be one Vincent Scarpetti. The next Mafia don of our fair city."

I shook my head, grinning at the absurdity of it. "Now ain't that a kick in the teeth?"

READERS'
GUIDE

*For Personal Reflection
or Group Discussion*

Readers' Guide

Over the course of this novel, Joe Box is trying to reconcile the failures and hurts of his past with a newfound faith in Christ. Through relationships with friends, clients, and family, God is creating situations that will challenge, frustrate, and ultimately help Joe grow in his ability to deal with the past. In addition, many characters in *When Skylarks Fall* are involved in situations revolving around forgiveness. Some are striving to forgive themselves for past mistakes while others wrestle with their ability to forgive others. As you answer the following questions, think about areas in your own life that could be healed through the power of forgiveness.

In chapter 4 the reader learns that Angela has kept part of her past life a secret. What was she trying to keep hidden? When the truth came out, how did you react? Have you concealed portions of your past because you think others will think less of you if they know? How can revealing the truth about ourselves free us to embrace life?

Tim and Helen Mulrooney are with Joe and Angela when Angela's past is revealed. Do you think it was just a coincidence that they were there? Why or why not? What could they bring to this discussion? In what ways are friends important in dealing with life? How has God provided the support you needed during a difficult time in your life?

God's forgiveness changes people's lives. The day Angela accepted Christ, what resolution did she make? How do you think she felt when she read John 8:3–11? God gave her the strength to make a new life for herself. What specific changes did she make in order to keep her resolve? How has your life changed because you accepted God's forgiveness?

What was Joe's initial reaction when he learned about Angela's past? Upon further reflection, he came to two conclusions (in chapter 5) about one's past. What were they? How do you react when you learn that someone you put on a spiritual pedestal has feet of clay? How does God help you cope with the disappointment?

Joe gives a graphic description of Noodles in chapter 6. What does the cat look like? He concludes by saying he and Noodles have been together so long that he no longer sees the cat's scars. How can you look at your friends and family in the same way—seeing the true person rather than their scars or imperfections?

Joe's unlikely friendship with Quint is the subject of chapter 7. What do these men have in common? What differences do they have? What subject does Joe want to discuss with Quint? Are you in the same situation with a friend? How are you handling it?

In chapter 8 the reader is introduced to Bucky, a member of the mafia who has only four months to live. Before leaving this encounter, Joe feels compelled to talk to Bucky about eternity and tells him to do three things. What are they? What do you say to people in terminal situations? How do you try to minister to their spiritual needs?

In spite of Mitch's abusive treatment of her, Angela wants to try again to reach him with the love of Christ. How did Mitch mistreat her? List at least four ways. How is she an illustration of Jesus' advice in Luke 6:27–28? Have you forgiven and reached out to someone who has mistreated you? What condition is your relationship in today?

Joe has absolutely no love in his heart for or desire to forgive Mitch. Do you think it is harder to forgive someone who has hurt a person dear to you than to forgive someone who has hurt you personally? Should Joe change his attitude toward Mitch? Why or why not?

Angela's response to Mitch's offer to work for him in chapter 11 reveals her decision-making criteria. What guides her? What does she list as the benefits of following this plan? Do you follow this practice? How does Proverbs 16:1–3 work out in your everyday life?

As Joe and Angela struggle to get through their disagreement over how the Mitch confrontation was handled in chapter 12, what challenge does Joe issue? How actively are you trying to help a fellow believer on the road toward spiritual maturity? Which of your friends are you trying to mentor? Who is mentoring you?

In chapter 14 Kitty is upset because she doesn't have Joe's approval. What does he want to tell her? When the moment comes for you to share your faith, how ready are you? How does 1 Peter 3:15 apply to this situation?

Kitty learns in chapter 16 what a disaster it is to store up treasure "where thieves break in and steal" (Matt. 6:19). In what way did she do this? Who were the thieves? Have you ever put your trust in things or people who failed you? What happened when your misplaced trust was revealed?

How does Joe feel toward Kitty when he first learns about his past? What emotional stages does he experience as he confronts her? Have you ever gotten so focused on yourself and your situation that you cannot see the pain and suffering of others? How did God reconcile your situation?

What is the theme of chapter 19? How do you think this affected Joe's response to Kitty? When you learn someone is a believer, how does it change your attitude toward that person?

How do you think Joe and Kitty's relationship would have developed if she had lived? Do you believe in the healing power of forgiveness? How have you experienced it in your life?

What did Joe experience in chapter 21 when he forgave his mama? Have you ever felt the release of a burden you didn't even know you carried? What caused it? Have you extended forgiveness to those who have hurt you?

Read Romans 12:17–21. How was this demonstrated in Joe's dealings with Parker? With Maria? How can you apply this passage to your own life? Give a specific example.

At the end of the book, Sarge talks about what biblical principle? Think about specific times of trial in your own life and how you have changed because of them. Does believing this principle have an impact on how you now deal with troubling situations?

Joe says, "Most of my life I've been out of God's will. But I've come to find out, I've never been out of his hand." What does this mean to you? How does it make you feel about God's love for you? What changes do you need to make to be in God's will as well as in his hand?

The Word at Work Around the World

A vital part of Cook Communications Ministries is our international outreach, Cook Communications Ministries International (CCMI). Your purchase of this book, and of other books and Christian-growth products from Cook, enables CCMI to provide Bibles and Christian literature to people in more than 150 languages in 65 countries.

Cook Communications Ministries is a not-for-profit, self-supporting organization. Revenues from sales of our books, Bible curricula, and other church and home products not only fund our U.S. ministry, but also fund our CCMI ministry around the world. One hundred percent of donations to CCMI go to our international literature programs.

CCMI reaches out internationally in three ways:

· Our premier International Christian Publishing Institute (ICPI) trains leaders from nationally led publishing houses around the world.

· We provide literature for pastors, evangelists, and Christian workers in their national language.

· We reach people at risk—refugees, AIDS victims, street children, and famine victims—with God's Word.

Word Power, God's Power

Faith Kidz, RiverOak, Honor, Life Journey, Victor, NexGen — every time you purchase a book produced by Cook Communications Ministries, you not only meet a vital personal need in your life or in the life of someone you love, but you're also a part of ministering to José in Colombia, Humberto in Chile, Gousa in India, or Lidiane in Brazil. You help make it possible for a pastor in China, a child in Peru, or a mother in West Africa to enjoy a life-changing book. And because you helped, children and adults around the world are learning God's Word and walking in his ways.

Thank you for your partnership in helping to disciple the world. May God bless you with the power of his Word in your life.

For more information about our international ministries, visit www.ccmi.org.

Additional copies of *When Skylarks Fall*
and other RiverOak titles are available
from your local bookseller.

♦ ◊ ♦

If you have enjoyed this book,
or if it has had an impact on your life,
we would like to hear from you.

Please contact us at:

RIVEROAK BOOKS
Cook Communications Ministries, Dept. 201
4050 Lee Vance View
Colorado Springs, CO 80918
Or visit our Web site: www.cookministries.com